Damned If You Do
Damned If You Don't

THE EXONERATED

A Thriller

Book 2

By JC Ryan

This is the second book in The Exonerated Thriller Series.

Want to hear about special offers and new releases?

Sign up for my confidential mailing list www.jcryanbooks.com

Copyright 2016 by J C Ryan

This book is protected under the copyright laws of the United States of America. Any reproduction or other unauthorized use of the material or artwork herein is prohibited.

This book is a work of fiction. Names, characters, places, brands, media, and incidents are either the product of the author's imagination or are used fictitiously.

All rights reserved.

ISBN-13: 978-1533582843

ISBN-10: 153358284X

Contents

Prologue 6
Chapter 1 - Better players than you will ever be 15
Chapter 2 - Why? 23
Chapter 3 - Because you're my friend 31
Chapter 4 - Everyone is guilty of something 37
Chapter 5 - A woman's intuition 49
Chapter 6 - Go talk to your father 54
Chapter 7 - In college 67
Chapter 8 - Let's stick this to the wall 74
Chapter 9 - This crime scene's trace 81
Chapter 10 - The THEM Three 88
Chapter 11 - On it 101
Chapter 12 - Why did I even bother to talk to you? 111
Chapter 13 - Like the cat who drank the cream 119
Chapter 14 - Three witnesses 135
Chapter 15 - The lady doth protest too much 147
Chapter 16 - Regan's fox 157
Chapter 17 - Just drop it 168
Chapter 18 - When did we join the Organization? 171
Chapter 19 - What brought the two of you together? 182
Chapter 20 - Why did you do it? 203
Chapter 21 - All of us make mistakes 216
Chapter 22 - Limits to what I can do 224
Chapter 23 - No benefit for yourself 232
Chapter 24 - The world is a strange place 237

Chapter 25 - The bastard had robbed me again 246

Chapter 26 - Shall we tell her? 254

Chapter 27 - The scary thing 265

Chapter 28 - She jumped 267

Chapter 29 - She heard him curse softly 273

Chapter 30 - Just like old times 279

Chapter 31 - The other case 286

Chapter 32 - A puzzle waiting to be solved 293

Chapter 33 - Damned if you do 299

Chapter 34 - Spider webs 308

Chapter 35 - The private investigator or the detective? 313

Chapter 36 - Kill two birds with one stone 323

Chapter 37 - Either would do 328

Chapter 38 - Damned if you don't 337

Chapter 39 - Lady Luck 343

Chapter 40 - Rather stayed on death row 347

Chapter 41 - I'm ready 352

Chapter 42 - What it's like to pass out 355

Chapter 43 - What good does that do us? 364

Chapter 44 - Not an easy task 370

Chapter 45 - The family album 373

Chapter 46 - Touché! 384

Chapter 47 - A dead end 389

Chapter 48 - It was time to begin 395

Chapter 49 - It was a hook 403

Chapter 50 - Why don't you find out? 411

Chapter 51 - Stay with me 415
Chapter 52 - Epilogue.. 422
Other books by JC Ryan 430

Prologue

It wasn't the kind of letter she wanted to write on a computer and entrust to a hard drive, let alone send as an email.

Kristin lifted her fingers off the keyboard and let them hover in midair. Her hands were shaking... her fingers felt like ice. She'd bitten her nails and her cuticles down to the quick, trying to decide whether she really wanted to do this or not. It was *stupid*. And yet she didn't know if she really had a choice.

Dear Conrad, the letter started—and then stopped.

She chewed the inside of her cheeks until they too were ragged, then forced herself to stop.

She got up and started pacing around the second bedroom in her apartment, one of the many in the 1940's apartment building. She was setting it up as her first real office. She had used barrister bookcases along one wall. Okay, most of them were filled with paperback novels at this point, but she did have a few case law books in a stack on the floor that she was going to shelve as soon as she could figure out how she wanted to organize everything. Her computer desk was still the same cheap pressboard desk she'd had since she was in eighth grade, and had two worn spots in front of the keyboard where her wrists had been resting all those years. A framed picture of her parents hung on one side of her monitor, the notorious RBG on the other.

In other words, it was starting to feel like a real home. Even the overly shaggy green rug underfoot was something that she had chosen for herself. It was a pain to vacuum—she was always eating at her computer and getting morsels of food into it but it was hers, and she loved it.

It was one of those cool, damp early May evenings that made her want to open the windows and let in the fresh air. But she knew if she did, she would start shivering and end up slamming her windows shut while wrapping herself in the duvet off her bed. She compromised by pulling at the sticky old window in her office until it opened an inch and a half and putting on a giant black buttonless sweater that flipped over her shoulder like a scarf.

After a few more circuits of the room, she found her fleece slippers and put them on, scuffing through the overly shaggy rug. The cold, damp air coming from the bottom of the old double hung window smelled fresh and clean... like the fresh fog in the morning on the way to work.

She shouldn't write the letter. She knew that. But she'd already slept with the guy. So really, what harm could it do... other than completely destroy her self- respect? God, it was so... sordid. She'd slept with a married man, and now she needed to know whether he'd leave his wife for her.

She wanted the answer to be *no.* But in her dreams the answer was *yes*. She would wake up from a dream of a wedding out on the coast, a big grin stretching her face... and then she would shiver in terror. Having a secret affair was one thing. Spending the rest of her life trying to live down a status as *the other woman was* another. She was one hundred percent guaranteed to get fired from her paralegal job, for one thing. Her uptight, holier than thou boss would find some excuse to fire her. And then there was trying to explain things to her parents.

Was she in love with him? She knew that she couldn't seem to say no to him. Everything he wanted, she wanted too. She'd been in love before, or thought she had. It hadn't felt like this.

If only he wasn't already taken. She should just tell him she never wanted to see him again. Boom. Problem solved.

Her computer beeped through her headphones, which were sitting off to the side of the desk. One of the browser tabs flashed—she'd just received a message. She flipped over to the tab. It was her best friend, Nancy, saying she had seen Conrad's car at his wife's parents' house.

Nancy was just a *little* bit of a stalker. She should have never become a paralegal like Kristin. She should have gone with detective work. Blonde, tall, gorgeous, coordinated enough to play volleyball for a local league; she was everything that Kristin wasn't. She was also about ten times more unethical.

Want me to wait around for him to leave?

Kristin rolled her eyes. *Thanks, but no thanks!*

What are you doing, sitting around and moping again? If you want him, go get him.

At his wife's parents' house? Nancy, you are the classiest woman I have ever met.

You know it.

I'm actually trying to write a breakup letter. There. She'd typed it and hit *enter* without even thinking about it. It must be true.

Mmm-hmmm. Believe it when I see it. BCC me when you send it.

I'm going to write it by hand and send it snail mail.

Pffft. Why bother? Just tell him that the cow's not passing out free milk anymore, buh-bye.

So I'm a cow now. Thaaaaanks.

A grinning emoticon appeared.

You know I love you and just want you to be happy. Conrad gives me the creeps.

Why?

No reason. He doesn't like me. You know that.

He's only met you once.

Once was enough.

Rather than get bogged down in a conversation for the rest of the night, she forced herself to say goodnight. Then she closed all her apps and shut down the computer. It was much easier to pretend she had willpower when the blinking power light on her computer wasn't winking at her.

Then she pulled out a piece of paper from her printer, took out the nice pen that she'd received at her college graduation, and started writing a letter to Conrad.

She stared at the words *Dear Conrad* for half an hour before she realized that she had to write out the other letter first—the one saying all the things she would never allow herself to say. Then she would light it on fire on the stove and dump it in the sink to smolder before it set off the fire alarm.

Then she'd be able to write the real letter.

She took a deep breath and wrote….

Dear Conrad,

I realize that our affair probably doesn't mean as much to you as it does to me. We've only been together, what —five times? But I spend every day wondering when I'll see you again. You know all you have to do is ask, and I'll be waiting for you.

I love talking to you, spending time with you. I hate that we have to keep this a secret. I want to be with you all the time, be the person you come home to. You know that I'd never be a bitch about your job the way Penny is. I understand, truly I do.

I would do anything for you, anything you asked. I would stay like this forever, in secret—even though I hate it.

Just give me some hope that you'll stay with me, one way or another.

Forever yours, Kristin

If that wasn't about the most disgusting letter she'd ever seen, let alone written. Ugh. She disgusted herself. She folded it in half and tossed it in the trash—didn't burn it and didn't wash it down the sink.

Who was Conrad anyway? Some guy she'd slept with twice. *Twice!* And that she was crushing on so hard she was ready to throw her life away over it.

This wasn't love. Conrad always made her feel on top of the world. But the second she wanted something from him, the good feelings were replaced by guilt. The only way she could be with Conrad would be if she gave up her brains completely, as well as ditched Nancy and the rest of her friends...and her parents... and her job...and worst of all, somehow, her apartment.

She could choose Conrad, or she could choose her apartment.

She kicked off her slippers and ran her bare feet through the overly shaggy green rug.

"I love you, rug," she said. And then in a higher-pitched voice, "I love you too, Kristin."

There. Now that that was out of her system, she could write the real letter.

She bent over to pull another piece of paper out of the printer tray when she heard the knock at the door. She swore, put her slippers back on, stood up, and flipped the end of her sweater over her shoulder.

It was probably Nancy, who would sit on Kristin's couch and watch CSI reruns until Kristin finished her real letter, and who would then personally drop the letter into Conrad's hands at his wife's parents' house, pretending to be from Western Union or something.

She walked through the living room to the front door. She didn't keep the chain on—come on—Portsmouth was not a center of criminal activity. She only kept her door locked at night out of habit from the days of living in college dorms.

She opened it a crack.

It wasn't Nancy.

"Hey," he said. "Can I come in?"

Her heart fluttered.

"I need to talk to someone. I'm freaking out. And you're the only one I know who will listen and not judge me."

She thought about telling him no, but she couldn't. Talk about mistakes.

Instead she sighed and opened the door for him. Because really, he was right—she *would* listen to the problems he'd gotten himself into, and she *wouldn't* judge. She was just as bad. If not worse. He stomped his feet on the welcome mat, then came in.

"What's up?"

"I haven't been doing so hot," he said. "It's a long story."

She led him over to the couch and made him sit down. Her phone buzzed, but she ignored it. Instead she went into the kitchenette and put the kettle on a burner. If nothing else, a scream from the kettle would make a good excuse to interrupt the conversation.

***

Nancy tossed the phone into the passenger's seat. If she didn't want to answer, fine. But the text would show up on the screen of her phone regardless.

Heads up: Conrad may be headed to your place. Looks like he's ditching the party here.

On second glance, she wasn't sure it was Conrad. The guy looked a lot like Conrad—same height, same general size—but there was something upright about the guy that she didn't think she would have picked up on from Conrad himself.

Whoever the guy was coming out of Conrad's wife's parents' house was, he was being careful to make sure nobody could make out his face. Okay, it was a little foggy, a little misty, and the streetlights turned the evening into an eerie, slippery kind of place. *A good ambiance for a horror movie, no prob.*

Better safe than sorry. Forewarned is forearmed, and all that.

She added, *if it is him and I'm not sure, he's not taking his own car. He's taking someone else's. He wants some on the sly...what a jerk. Don't even open the door.*

She followed the guy for a couple of miles until she lost him after getting cut off at a stoplight. It was pitch black and foggy out, and all the taillights ahead of her looked the same.

She decided to head the bastard off at the pass.

She turned off the road and headed straight for Kristin's house.

If nothing else, she could let herself into the apartment with her key, watch CSI reruns off Kristin's DVR, and make absolutely positively certain she wrote that breakup letter.

She'd hand deliver it to him if she had to.

***

Panting, he let the fire extinguisher slide to the floor. His heart was thudding deep in his throat. He should have listened to his doctor about changing his diet and getting more exercise. That was all he needed right now, to have some heart attack and drop dead here on Kristin's floor.

The teakettle was still shrieking. He checked to make sure he hadn't stepped in any of the blood, and then circled around her to go back into the kitchen and turn off the burner. *Hopefully it had covered up most of the noise.*

Two cups sat out on the counter beside the stove. Pulling his shirtsleeve over his hand, he put one cup back on the shelf.

It wasn't as if Kristin belonged to him. He didn't think that...but jealousy was a green-eyed monster.

Everyone knew that.

He looked around the living room to see if he'd left anything behind. The condom was already in his pocket, tied off at the end. He might have left, he didn't know, hairs or skin flakes or something behind, but he doubted it. And if he had, he'd just say that it was from when they had actually been dating.

Shit, the fire extinguisher handle.

He edged around the room and walked up to the fire

extinguisher from behind where he would have been standing, to keep from tracking blood all over the room. Using his sleeve, he wiped the handle, then the cleaner parts of red paint in case he'd touched the thing with his other hand while he was swinging it around. He already knew his clothes had to go; her blood was all over them. His gym bag was in his trunk—not a problem.

Steam was still puffing out of the teakettle. It had all happened so fast that his zipper was still down.

He zipped it up and left, pulling the door closed with his other hand, wrapped in the cleaner of his two sleeves.

He'd parked a couple of blocks away.

People were nosy in this town.

Chapter 1 -Better players than you will ever be

The crabapple trees in the neighbors' back yard had gone nuts, big pink explosions of flowers that fell in drifts on the grass on either side of her father's white picket fence. A squirrel ran through the branches, knocking the petals down as it went. They fell lazily, like fat flakes of snow, and tumbled across the grass every time a puff of wind came along. The smell was incredible.

    Regan leaned on the rail of her father's deck, one hand wrapped around a cup of coffee. It was one of those rare days that she missed her cigarette habit from college, to soften the edges of the world when they got too hard.

    The neighbor's patio door slid open a crack, and a small white Pomeranian ran out, charged into the fallen petals, and plowed through them with its mouth open, yapping incessantly and spinning around in circles. The squirrel froze for a moment, then started cursing at the dog: *pwok pwok pwok, a pwoka pwok!*

    The dog froze in complete shock, then started attacking the base of the tree, scratching the bark with his claws. The squirrel continued to curse at the dog.

    Regan clenched her teeth together and laughed through her nose, trying to keep quiet as the dog began to circle the base of the tree, growling and trying to figure out a way to get at that squirrel. Neither one of them was going to win—it was obvious. It was all just a bunch of noise—empty threats.

    Jake came out onto the patio and put his arm around her waist. She leaned her head against his shoulder. One of the branches shook. Then a stick flew out of the branches and landed next to the dog. A second stick followed it. The squirrel was throwing things at the dog.

The dog went insane, all four legs rigid, barking so hard that it pushed itself a fraction of an inch backward every time it yapped. It was like watching a windup toy.

Regan stood at the rail and held back her laughter until the neighbor's back patio door slammed open and the owner, still dressed in a blue and white striped bathrobe at ten thirty in the morning, shouted at the dog to shut up.

The dog growled a question—*grrooo?*—and the owner said, "Shut up or it's a bath for you, bub."

The dog put its paws over its face and shivered.

Then she lost it, whooping with laughter and slamming the heel of her hand against the rail. Coffee sloshed over the rim and onto the back of her fingers.

"Can it, St. Clair!" the neighbor shouted. The patio door slammed shut, the dog made half a bark—*whuff!*—and the squirrel climbed to the top of the tree and made a flying leap over the fence to a tree in her father's back yard.

The patio door opened again, and the neighbor said, "You're not St. Clair."

"I'm his daughter."

The neighbor, balding, weak-chinned, and with dirty slippers, snorted and went back inside.

"They're done shouting at each other," Jake said. "You can come back in."

***

Her father stood in the kitchen next to the patio door with coffee mug in one hand, the other arm crossed over his chest, and his jaw jutting. Tall, handsome, not the least bit balding, and seventy years old, he was as vain as a Dalmatian and would have died before he appeared outside in a bathrobe after six am. He wore an unwrinkled red polo shirt, khaki pants, and a steel Rolex—her grandfather's watch. But his eyebrows were out of control, long gray hairs jutting in every direction. Uncle Paul must have really gotten to him.

She went to the sink and dried off the outside of her coffee mug with a paper towel, then topped it off. She didn't say anything, either about the dog or about Uncle Paul.

"When are you going to give me grandchildren?" her father spat out.

"As soon as they stock them at the supermarket," she said blandly. She'd prepared half a dozen responses to the question, and had already burned through the first two, the serious ones. "And then I'll bring you home half a dozen."

He grunted at her and took a drink of his coffee, but his eyes had a twinkle to them.

What was supposed to be a good day had been derailed by two old friends at each other's throats. But it would be all right eventually, i.e., only after one of them was dead.

"Now that the air is clear, let's get started." Jake said. When her father and Uncle Paul had started fighting, Jake had slipped into Delta Force mode, stripping all expression from his face and taking every bend out of his posture. When he used it against her, she wanted to shake him—but it would have been like shaking a statue.

She caught her father giving Jake a foul look over her shoulder.

On second thought, it was almost pleasant seeing Jake use Delta Force mode against someone else. She glanced back at Jake and smiled.

His armored-steel exterior loosened up enough for him to throw a wink at her. They walked into the dining room where Uncle Paul was still sitting at the table, his hands folded in front of him on the table. He had taken his hat and suit coat off and laid them on the table. Regan put her coffee at her seat then picked up his jacket, shook it out, and hung it on the coat tree by the front door. Her father sat across from Uncle Paul. Together they looked like chalk and cheese — the handsome, charming Charlton Heston lookalike, and the gray suited, gaunt cheeked strategist.

"Our next case is the Craig Moreau case," Jake said. "He's been in the longest, and his case looks fairly straightforward. He finds his parents murdered, is blamed for their deaths, and the murderer gets free."

Uncle Paul frowned. "So everything is already neatly tied up."

Regan's father grimaced.

Jake shrugged. "If you could tell us how the Organization got involved in this one, that would be great. I don't want to spend too much time spinning our wheels here. If he's guilty and you know it, just say so."

"I don't entirely remember the case."

Jake flipped the manila folder open. "Near Watertown in Upstate New York. Two parents, both in their early fifties, and their son Craig, aged twenty-nine, running a small dairy farm. The son comes home one night from his day job as a bank teller to find his parents dead in their RV, which was out of gas. He tries to perform first aid and gets covered with their blood.

"The cops proceed to arrest him for the murder of his parents, question him for eighteen hours straight, no food, no water, no phone call, and no lawyer present. They tell him that they've found the murder weapon in his room in the house, along with a missing gas can filled with gas in the back of his Jeep. They're lying. They *convince* the guy that he must have murdered his parents in some kind of blackout fugue state, and he confesses—then retracts his confession after his lawyer arrives. The prosecution *never* comes up with any kind of signed or recorded statement from the victim, whether a confession or otherwise. They just claim they got one.

"They give him a polygraph test but won't let anyone see the results. His DNA is all over the place. They lock him in jail with a snitch who says that he heard him confess to the crime—like we haven't heard that one before. A couple of character witnesses show up saying that he was a drunk and a cocaine addict and was desperate for money. An ex-girlfriend claims he always hated working for his parents, and threatened to kill her several times, both while they were dating and afterwards.

"The jury decides he's guilty beyond a reasonable doubt and gives him life in prison. He's been there since 1982. He's been in prison thirty-four years and is sixty-three years old now."

"At that age it might be more merciful to leave him there. He has become institutionalized. After that much time in jail he cannot survive outside. He can't even take a piss without asking someone's permission first," Uncle Paul said. "People past their fifties are rarely able to adapt to significant change."

Regan raised her hand toward him. "*Stop.* Uncle Paul, if your best excuse for leaving innocent people in prison is that it might inconvenience them to let them out, then you have officially conceded the argument."

He raised his eyebrows, which had been neatly trimmed and probably combed with a miniature eyebrow brush. "As you know, I never concede. I play to the bitter end."

"Do you know anything about the case or not?"

"I might remember a few details...if I were offered some coffee."

"Would you like some coffee, Uncle Paul?"

He smiled. "Yes, my dear, I would like some coffee."

Her father snarled, "Get it yourself. My daughter doesn't need to—"

But she had already stood up. She kissed her father on top of his head. "It's fine."

"When am I getting my grandchildren?" he snapped.

"When the stork brings them." She went into the kitchen and heard muttering and hissing behind her back, too low to make out. Her father's voice, mostly.

Jake said, "Let's keep this civil, gentlemen." By then she was returning with the cup of coffee and putting it on the table in front of Uncle Paul.

"Thank you, my dear. At least someone in this house still has manners. You remind me more of your mother every day."

"Her mother had at least given me a daughter by this age," said her father.

"By this age—" Uncle Paul cut himself off. He looked from her father to Regan. "How old are you my dear?"

"A lady never tells, and gentlemen should know never to ask."

His nostrils fluttered, his neck straightened, and he looked up at the ceiling. A web of winkles circled his eyes. "Don't be impertinent. I was there when you were born. You are...thirty-six years old."

"Close enough."

"I see." His shoulders slumped. "My apologies, I'm wasting time while I spar with your father. We can argue later. Let me tell you what I remember, without further ado. It's not much, I'm afraid."

"We'll take whatever you've got."

"It was out of my district, of course. Upstate New York was assigned to a woman who is no longer with us, and of whom I was never fond. There are members of the Organization, and then there are members." He tapped the fingers of one hand on the table while covering them with the other hand. "I believe the murder was looked into, and it was discovered that the man in question had been smuggling cocaine without the auspices of the Organization. He may have had connections to the Russian mob — I'm not entirely sure. Nevertheless, it was decided that the Organization would be better served without his presence in the area."

Regan said, "Did the Organization do anything to put him in prison?"

"No. We merely allowed it to happen."

"Then why did Marando have the file in his collection?" Earlier that year, Jake had broken into the apartment of a corrupt

21

Brooklyn detective in search of information on another case and found fifteen files of men in prison who were presumably innocent, put there by the criminal organization that her father used to work for—and part of which her father's best friend, "Uncle" Paul, now ran.

"Perhaps the reports I received were not entirely accurate. I was not the head of the district at that time. And, as you well know, it is often the case that when members of the Organization act in such a way as to cast doubts on their ability to handle their assigned tasks or territory, their first action is to conceal the situation from members further up in the Organization's food chain."

"A cover-up."

Uncle Paul waved a hand toward the folder in front of Jake. "The case is yours to research. Do as you will."

"You're not worried about us exposing the Organization or getting in the way of their plans?"

"As I said, it's out of my district." Uncle Paul sipped his coffee. "One of the traits of the Organization is that it encourages competition as much as cooperation. It's a game called 'survival of the fittest.' Feel free to play it...as long as you realize there are other people out there who are better players than you will ever be."

Jake just grinned.

Chapter 2 -Why?

The offices of Westley PI, LLC, had two things on the wall: a bamboo Chinese New Year Calendar from the nearest place that delivered decent sweet and sour chicken; and Jake's New York State private investigator's license. With the white vertical blinds, the cheap flat-pack desks, used office chairs and filing cabinets, the whole place had the feel of a cheap movie set.

So far, though, so good. He'd almost broken even last month, month three of the Great Detective Office Space Experiment. He'd been losing a lot fewer clients after his first meeting with them. Hey, that was fair. Asking someone to trust a guy to track down your cheating wife when you had to meet him at Starbucks didn't instill any confidence.

He preceded Doug into his main office and closed the door behind them, more for the look of it than the belief that the cheap hollow core door would keep their discussion confidential.

"What's up?" Jake asked.

"So you said you were looking at a new case to pursue," Doug said. Doug was a retired SEAL—one of those guys who looked like they could lift a fishing trawler in each arm and whose neck was wider than their chins. He stayed quiet and kept his eyes open, and if Jake needed to send in a guy who looked like he was built for violence but could be trusted to let someone knock him around without losing his cool, Doug was his man. *Look dumb, think smart*—Doug's motto.

He had a thick manila folder in his hands. Something was up.

Jake waved him over to the stackable office chair opposite his desk. Carefully Doug settled into the chair—a guy who's used to: a) breaking chairs or b) getting stuck in them. He wasn't overweight at all, even after five years of retirement. But three hundred and ten pounds of muscle still required a little care if you wanted to move it around without breaking things.

"We have one—the Craig Moreau case. One of the files we picked up from Marando's apartment."

"Yeah, I remember that one. But about that..." Doug ducked his head, looking down at the backs of his hands. "I have another case for you."

"Another case?"

"You know the guy that's about to be sent to the chair in New Hampshire? Conrad Wilson?"

"Yeah?"

"He's innocent. The execution is scheduled for June 1st, and uh, he's my stepfather's second cousin."

"Huh," Jake said.

"So I was thinking that you and Regan might want to take a look at the case, what with it being such a short turnaround and everything. I mean, win or lose, at least you wouldn't have wasted much time on it in the end."

Jake squinted but remained quiet. Doug still wasn't meeting his eyes.

"Look, I asked," Doug said as he stood. "I'm going to head back out to the Miller place, see if I can find anything in those boxes."

Doug was sorting through the paperwork of a retired woman who'd just been moved into a nursing home, trying to find property titles, wills, pictures of her kids—the important stuff —

and throwing out fifty years of receipts. Her son had actually given Jake an awkward hug when Jake agreed to send someone out to deal with the paperwork for them. Good thing he'd specified hourly—the woman was a hoarder.

"Wait," Jake said.

Doug stopped and hunched his shoulders in tighter.

"There's something you're not telling me. Is this some kind of mess we don't want to get into? Because if so, let me know and we can just pretend you asked me, and I said no. No hard feelings between you and your mom."

"It's not that. The whole thing stinks from beginning to end—a cop framed by the justice system. And if we get him out, I'll keep an eye on him, make sure he's legit. But..."

"But what?"

"But I feel bad bringing this to you. Like I'm taking advantage of you."

"Your mom is taking advantage of me, you mean."

They both chuckled. Jake waved a hand at him. "Don't worry about it, all right? We'll take a look at it and see if we can do anything about it. Are you guys close?"

"I've never met him. It's just that, you know. Mom heard about the Gibbons case, and she thinks that because I work for you, I can work miracles too. But then she also believes that everything she sees on CSI is real too."

**

After Doug left for the Miller place, Jake locked the front door, put up the "Out on assignment, please call the following number" sign, pulled the blinds across the glass, and turned off the monitor on the desk in the reception area. He considered running down to the hallway cafe on the first floor for a cup of coffee but dismissed the idea. June 1st was less than a month away. The least he could do was hustle to find out whether the case was worth bothering Regan about.

Instead he grabbed a bottled water out of the mini fridge in the reception area and sealed himself in his office.

Five minutes later, he had the gist of the case. It did look fishy. Detective Conrad Wilson had been at a party at his wife's parents' house in Portsmouth, New Hampshire. The attendees at the party included his brother, his wife, and three detectives, two who were from Wilson's hometown of Manchester and the other from Portsmouth. The shindig had been some kind of wedding anniversary/fundraiser for a local charity that all four cops were involved in, and the guests consisted of about forty people over the course of the evening, with all kinds of people in and out of the party.

During the party, which Wilson swore that he had never left, a woman named Kristin Walker was murdered in her apartment miles away, beaten to death with a kitchen fire extinguisher. In her office was a handwritten note addressed to Wilson, saying that she wanted to continue their affair and hoped that he would leave his wife for her—but would understand if he didn't.

The prosecution had bent over backward to make sure Detective Wilson looked like he *really* didn't want to leave his wife for her. Ever.

When Wilson was first brought in, he lied about his contact with Walker. Who could blame him? If everything had just blown over, it would have saved his marriage. That story didn't last long, however, and he soon confessed that he'd had two sexual encounters with Walker. It didn't negate the fact he hadn't left the party. Right?

Then one of Walker's girlfriends, Nancy Rossier, came forward. She had been stalking Wilson at the party, afraid he might break away to spend some time with her friend, Kristin Walker. She was convinced Wilson was Bad News. She saw someone who looked like Detective Wilson sneak out of the party and take a car—not Wilson's SUV, but a dark blue Chrysler. She followed him partway toward Kristin's apartment.

She lost track of the car in some fog at a stoplight—she wasn't a cop, just a paralegal who worked in the same law office as Kristin. When she lost the car at the stoplight, she drove straight over to Walker's residence. But, she had a flat tire and arrived forty-five minutes later. She unlocked the apartment with a key Kristin gave her a long time ago so she could come and go whenever she wanted to, and found Kristin in the front room—dead.

Questioning other residents in the small apartment building produced nothing. Some remembered a teakettle whistle going off for a couple of minutes about thirty minutes before Rossier had arrived, but that was it. The noise of the teakettle whistle matched the probable time of death.

The autopsy produced traces of semen in Walker's vagina, and DNA testing showed it to belong to Wilson. Further questioning showed he had been away from the party earlier in the day, about two to three-thirty in the afternoon. Wilson claimed he had been running errands for the party and had the receipts to prove it. But, the party supply store he'd visited was only a few minutes away from Kristin's apartment building, and he could have conceivably had time to visit her and go back to the party with his SUV full of balloons.

Even though it might have explained the semen, Wilson refused to change his story. He hadn't seen the woman at all that day, let alone had sex with her. And she had definitely been alive until about half an hour before the teakettle – she'd texted Rossier.

Because of signs of damage to Walker's vagina as well as some defensive bruising along her forearms, the jury concluded that Detective Wilson had indulged in a preplanned rape and murder and had given him the death penalty. The prosecutor, who was herself a rape survivor, seemed to take the case personally.

On the surface, it all seemed straightforward. A murderer caught by a plucky woman who'd been looking out for her friend's best interests, and had only by chance arrived a few minutes too late.

Nonetheless, further nosing around on the Internet led to a few elements that didn't hold up.

The main one was that nobody had actually seen Wilson leave the party.

One of the detectives at the party made a statement saying he had loaned Wilson his keys earlier in the day, but they were returned by the time of the party. Wilson denied ever borrowing or even asking to borrow the keys, but a second detective backed up the first one's story. It seemed like nonsense, unless you were looking at the story trying to find out whether Wilson had been framed for a crime he didn't commit. And then it looked like two detectives trying to create doubt as to whether Wilson had access to a second vehicle or not—a blue Chrysler, as it happened.

Other details also didn't match up. For example, an abnormally high amount of the semen had been found damaged. Wilson's defense argued that semen had been injected into the woman's vagina by the actual perpetrator, although they had zero suggestions for who that might have been. And no strange vehicles had been reported near Walker's house at the time the teakettle had been going off—blue Chryslers or otherwise. A polygraph test showed Wilson's conviction in his own innocence. Procedural issues were rife, too. Jurors had heard of the case before being seated—and hadn't been thrown out. Some hairs belonging to Wilson were found in the apartment, but the chain of evidence had been broken; someone could have swapped samples easily.

As Doug said, the case stank.

It looked bad, but it was clearly not enough to put someone in the chair or whatever they used in New Hampshire—not beyond a shadow of a doubt.

Half an hour of research on the Internet, and the case was already starting to fall apart. At least, it was worth bugging Regan about.

Jake sent himself a message on his secure phone—a nice little security feature that his hacker friend Alex Carr had set up for the "inner circle" of their little group of warriors for peace, justice, and the American way. It signaled to Alex and Regan that he needed to chat.

Alex called in first—no surprise, he always did. The guy basically lived online. Regan followed a few minutes later.

"What's wrong? Are you all right?" she asked.

He'd already answered the same questions from Alex. "Yeah, I'm fine. It's about the case...we might have to put it on hold for a month or two."

"Why?"

Chapter 3 -Because you're my friend

The Visitors' Center echoed with the shouts of two toddlers competing for their mother's attention on the other side of the room. Regan wanted to put her hands over her ears or at least move to a separate room. But Jessie always liked to meet her here where she could see the kids.

Big wire baskets, that unfortunately looked like cages, sat around the room holding grimy children's toys. Bright pictures the kids had colored, hung on the walls. Construction paper flowers with the kids' names on them had been taped around the doors. Board books sat on shelves next to the uniformed guards, in case someone wanted to read to her child.

It was homey, all right. As homey as a prison visitors' center could be until the kids had to leave and the wailing started.

The bigger of the two girls ripped the red telephone toy out of the other girl's hands and kicked it across the floor, the bells inside the toy chiming crazily, and a pair of eyeballs in the front rolling up and down. It smacked into a chair leg and stopped, the red handset flopping off the phone and onto the floor. Probably neither one of the girls had ever seen an old fashioned phone before.

The smaller of the two girls pushed her sister backward so she fell onto her butt and started crying.

The two parents, the mother in a prison uniform and the father in a cheap gunmetal gray suit, bent over to pull the two little girls away from each other. The prison guards all turned to look at them, to make sure the father didn't pass anything to the mother under the table.

They straightened up. The mother wrapped her arms around

the girl in her arms, whispering in her ear as the little girl shook her head violently, pigtails whipping back and forth, while her sister shoved her head onto her father's shoulder and sobbed.

Eventually the father stood up, holding his hand out for the other girl. The mother let her slide down to the floor and pushed her toward her father, but made no move to get any closer. Whether it was because they weren't that close anymore or because the guards were watching, Regan had never really figured out. Maybe it was better if she never did—the situation was sad enough already.

Jessie stared at the children with naked longing. She and Mark hadn't had any kids, thank God. Regan had trouble thinking of her friend as a mother. Her best memories of her on the outside were from college, the two of them hustling pool and drinking beer.

She and Jessie had been roommates. Regan, the statuesque blonde Hudson Valley girl, her tuition, room and board, books, and pocket money all paid for by her Uncle Paul, aka Pavo, and Jessie, the New Jersey scholarship black girl, scraping by on a cafeteria work study job. Regan had gone on to become a judge, just like her father. Baby faced Jessie had gone on to an abusive marriage, a paralegal job, a second degree murder charge, and prison. She was smarter and worked harder—not that Regan was a slouch—but she had still ended up here. Gravity always seemed twice as strong when it came to Jessie's shots toward success.

Finally, the two toddlers were dragged out of the room by their father, tears streaking down his face.

Jessie turned back to Regan, pushing her heavy black glasses up on her nose. "A real pair of angels, huh? You know the best way to smuggle drugs into Taconic? Stuff them into a baby's diaper. You make a deal with the janitor on duty. They get half the drugs, you get half, more or less. You think I'm joking, don't you?"

"Of course not."

"I have seen far, far worse during my time here." A third of her maximum sentence was over. Her first parole board meeting was coming up in June, less than a month away.

Regan grabbed her hand. It felt ice cold and clammy. "You'll be out soon."

Jessie raised an eyebrow. "Do you honestly think that?"

"Of course. You've had nothing but good time. Why would they keep you? They have too many newcomers to keep you around."

"There is nothing good ever going to happen to me, Regan. Just never."

Regan ignored her pessimism. "What are you going to do when you get out?" It worked.

"I'm going to have an entire chocolate cake to myself, get completely smashed on cheap red wine, and then I'm going to win the lottery and spend the rest of my life hip deep in naked men. What do you think?"

"Jessie..."

"I stopped being a threat to society when Mark stopped breaking my ribs. There was never any need to put me in here in the first place. They could have just believed me the first time I called in a domestic disturbance. Or the second. Or the tenth."

"You can't just...kill people."

Jessie looked away from her to where the door was closing behind the man with the two girls. "It was him or me by that point.

You know that."

"You could have stayed with me."

It was an old argument that she thought they'd put to rest a long time ago. But with the parole hearing coming up, Jessie was on edge.

"And put you at risk? What kind of monster puts her best friend at risk just to save her own skin? I know you're all 'oh pick me, pick me,' but the thought turns my stomach."

"The problem is that you have killed someone while there was no immediate..."

"Is that what you really think? That I shouldn't have gotten my hands dirty? That I should have let Mark kill me first? What if I did get free of him? You think he wouldn't have moved on to someone else?"

Regan looked around the room at the other women who were visiting friends and families. "I think you should have let the law handle it."

"I would be dead."

Regan shook her head. "I know you believe that. And you know that I disagree."

"I know you are in a position where you can afford to disagree."

"Please, Jessie. Can't we talk about something else?"

"What else do I have to talk about?" The cold hand gripped hers. "Regan, you have to help me. You're a judge and the daughter of a judge. Throw your weight behind this...make sure they know that you're behind me. Petition people. I am being held here unjustly. And I will continue to be held here unjustly until I die."

Regan's eyes turned hot. "You intentionally, deliberately killed someone, Jessie. You planned and executed a killing. An *ugly* killing. You didn't just hit him over the head. You tortured him. I'm not judging or condemning you, I'm just pointing out how the courts see it."

"Compared to the way he hurt me? It was nothing. And I have paid for it for eight and a half years. It's time I was done with this." She spread her hands and turned to look at the rest of the room, still full of parents, kids, broken families. "If you aren't going to help me, why do you come here? Why are you still coming to see me? It can't be because you enjoy the surroundings."

"I come here because you're my friend."

Jessie stood up. "You don't have a lot of friends, Regan. Neither do I. But if you're not going to help me, then don't come back. It's not so much that if you're not with me, you're against me. It's that every time I see you, I spend the rest of the week in a funk, knowing you're only showing up because you're loyal." She dug her fingers against the side of her nose, clawing away a tear. Her fingernails were bitten short, the cuticles stripped and bloody.

The guards were watching both of them now, openly staring with expressionless faces. It was like being watched by a mountain lion trying to decide whether she was prey or not.

"What am I saying?" Jessie said, already regretting her outburst. "Look at me, I'm a mess. You do you, Regan. Ignore me. If you come I'll see you, and I'll pretend that I'm going to get out of here, and that we're going to get back on the pool cue hustling circuit, and..."

"And cake and wine," Regan said, smiling.

Jessie let out a huge sniff and grabbed Regan in a hug. If they'd had the attention of every guard in the place before, it was like being surrounded by grenades now, waiting to go off. *Every second of every day was like this for Jessie.* Regan hugged her.

"Take care of that big hunk of man-flesh," Jessie said with a wry smile. "And if he ever does you wrong—if *anyone* ever does you wrong, let me know."

Regan blinked back tears. "Okay."

"You think I'm joking, from here in prison. But you remember what I said."

Chapter 4 -Everyone is guilty of something

For a high-rise penthouse in Manhattan decorated post-something-or-other Norwegian style with clean lines, bland colors, and cushions that looked like wooden butcher's blocks, it was pretty comfortable. Jake didn't exactly try to put his feet up on Pavo's desk or anything, but he did let himself lean back in the chair a little. The view was great. From up here the city looked almost clean and well run. It was one of those screaming blue spring days that seemed like it could erase poverty, delete heroin addiction, and fix your bike chain. You couldn't see all the broken lives, which was nice.

The manila folder—Regan had a million of 'em, as far as he could tell—sitting on Pavo's desk was full of information from the Wilson case.

After talking to the other two, Jake was all for switching to the new case. Alex was non-committal, almost... sort of disinterested... maybe distracted. Regan was more than slightly against it, but couldn't identify a reason why. It was weird. For a woman who hated the idea that women's intuition was a *thing*—give her a mountain of data and she was as happy as a clam—she was suffering badly from it now. The Wilson case, she said *"gives me the heebie-jeebies."*

When the woman who has no woman's intuition gets a case of the heebie-jeebies, you get a second opinion—especially if you are serious about her.

If anyone could find the fly in the ointment, it was Pavo, Regan's Uncle Paul, although he was not really her uncle.

So Jake had driven into the city while Regan was at work hearing a drunk driving manslaughter case. Nothing too demanding—but plenty depressing. If Jake could get enough information from Pavo to set her mind at ease, all the better.

However, Pavo must have been picking up on the same thing Regan was. At any rate, he kept looking up at Jake with pinched eyebrows as he read Conrad Wilson's case files. Jake couldn't tell whether he was disapproving of him or trying to read the *I Ching* in his laugh lines.

Finally, Pavo closed the manila folder and steepled his fingers in front of him. The sun shone over his shoulder and put down a shadow almost like prison bars on top of his blonde wood desk and crisp white leather desk pad.

"So, what do you think?" Jake asked. "Know anything about it? Regan says she has a bad feeling about it."

"I see," Pavo said. "You said to yourself, 'Who is the most cynical bastard that I know?' and came up with the idea of having me take a look at the case and poke some holes in it."

"Pretty much, yeah."

Pavo looked up at his ceiling, which was strips of pine that had been bent and molded to follow the curve of the outer wall. This whole building looked like a giant had grabbed it in his fist and stretched and twisted it a little, like taffy.

After studying the wood grain overhead for a couple of moments, Pavo snapped back to reality. "First of all, let me state that the Organization is not involved in every case of what you might consider to be misapplied justice in the nation. I struggle to maintain order in Brooklyn, personally, and I feel I am more successful than most of the other local members of the

Organization."

"Yeah, okay, granted."

"Second. I heard of the case, of course, when Detective Wilson was first arrested. And even if I had not, the media would have already done me the kindness of informing me. I followed the case with some interest for a time—it seemed to be one of those cases that might produce some detail of human nature I hadn't encountered recently—an intelligent criminal.

"However, my theory was once again proven correct, and Detective Wilson allowed himself to be sentenced to death row. In none of his appeals has he or his lawyers identified the important point, that one may sometimes commit a smaller crime in order to conceal a larger one."

Jake rubbed a spot on his chin that always seemed to make him think better. It was kind of like tying a string on your finger to remember something. As long as he was rubbing that spot on his chin, he wasn't getting distracted by every other thing that Pavo was saying. "Your theory?"

"I have a theory that everyone is guilty of something...and no one is intelligent enough to conceal everything."

"Not a bad theory. You think he should have told the cops that he'd ditched the party to pick up balloons, stopped off at Walker's house for a quickie, and come back to the party, which would explain the semen?"

"Exactly—whether it occurred or not."

"So why didn't he?"

"I don't know," he said. Abruptly he clenched his teeth and hissed inward, as if he was trying to cool his brain off or something.

"In order to conceal actions that could have worse consequences? In order to conceal someone else's actions, to prevent dragging more than one person down? Because he feels a sense of guilt in some matter and wishes for death? Because he craves the security of a prison? Because he feels that he can accomplish more from inside the prison than from the outside? In order to fulfill an agreement of some sort—blackmail, bribery, the payment of large sums of money to a loved one? To thwart someone else's plans who wishes to use him in a scheme not of his own design?"

"None of those sound very reasonable."

Pavo let out the rest of the air he'd been holding in. "They don't."

"But he's not part of the Organization, right?"

"I don't know. New Hampshire is not under my jurisdiction, and I no longer know who is in charge there."

"Secrets, huh."

"Indeed. As to whether Regan's intuition of the man has any basis in fact..." He shrugged. "In some cases, it is impossible to trust one's intuition. The water has become so muddied, that any guesses as to what lies on the bottom are useless without further cleaning and sifting. If she is trying to open herself up to the possibility that there might be tools, other than logic, with which to regard the universe and the study of human minds, that is well chosen. But I would like to note that all such tools must come back to logic and reason. To be human is to be guilty of *something*—almost always something worthy of punishment by death. None of us are clean."

Jake bit his tongue. Calling the guy out on his hypocrisy wasn't going to get them anywhere.

Pavo's eyebrows rose at the look on Jake's face. "Do you doubt me?"

Jake let his amusement show. "Not a word, sir, not a word. Buy me a drink sometime and I'll show you some of the blood on my hands. But you know Regan. This is probably the first time she's bothered to pay attention to it. She hasn't built up her resistance yet."

"That is true."

Jake couldn't help himself, "So, what are you guilty of?"

Pavo snorted and stood without honoring Jake's question with a reply. Jake stood with him. They shook hands. Normally Jake was a firm handshake kind of guy, unless the person tried to one up him, and then he'd unleash whatever Delta Force grip it took to intimidate the other person into yielding the floor.

Pavo's hand looked fine and delicate, almost like a piano player's, but the grip was like iron.

Jake decided not to fight back and returned a firm, but noncompetitive, grip. "I gotta say...I'm glad she isn't as cynical as you are, Paul. If anybody's going to figure out how to reach some kind of a genuine sense of justice in this world, and not just political expediency, it's Regan."

"That, also, is true," Pavo said. "It is one of the reasons I have supported her through her career... nurtured her as a tactician... protected her from the whims of the Organization."

"And yet, you seem to be pushing her toward it now."

Pavo tilted his head, as if surprised that anyone could have possibly interpreted his actions in such a way. There was a reason the old bastard had allowed himself to be drawn back into their lives, and it obviously wasn't that he wanted to mend bridges with the Honorable John St. Clair. "Perhaps it is time that her innocence be tested..." he paused for a moment, "mmmm, maybe not her innocence. Innocence is nothing more than a veil."

"Plastic wrap," Jake added.

"Just so. Her sense of justice, then. It is time that her sense of justice be tested."

"And you're the one who's going to decide whether she's worthy or not? Or is that the prerogative of one of your higher-ups?"

"No, not at all. When I was younger, I supposed myself an expert on jurisprudence, although I find myself less secure in my opinions of late. But it is my hope that Regan will judge herself. Although I would not be surprised if the Organization attempts to judge her as well."

***

The windows of the Thumbprint Cafe were filled with paper flyers advertising local musicians, tiny theater productions, and gaming groups. A few leftover Cinco de Mayo posters showed big-headed cartoons of men with mustaches wearing sombreros and grinning evilly as they played guitars or shook maracas. *We know something you don't*, they seemed to say. *You'll never clean up this town.*

Jake pulled the door open and ducked quickly inside. The smell in Greenpoint today was eye watering—something about the wind coming from the river. Supposedly Pavo, in addition to running the local Organization, was supposed to be running the sanitation district as well, and was trying to clean up Newton Creek.

Today was one of those bright, cheerful spring days in May

where the sky was blue, the trees had put on green leaves, flowers in flowerboxes were blooming...but it smelled as if the streets were covered in sewage. He kept wanting to look down at his feet to make sure he wasn't stepping in something. He let the door close after him, sealing him off from the street and some of the stink.

The inside of the cafe smelled extra strongly of ground coffee today. It was heavenly.

Jake walked up to the front counter. He'd seen the blue haired barista before. The blue hair was hard to miss, as were the tattoos, lip, nose and earrings.

"Coffee," he said.

Her eyes narrowed. She too was trying to remember his face. He held out his hand, and she took it. "It's Jake, Jake Westley, a friend of Alex's. I called ahead and told him I was going to meet him in a few minutes."

"He didn't say anything," she said in a petulant voice. "I'm Krista."

Jake tilted his head down and pointed at his cap. "Brooklyn Dodgers. That's me."

"Oh, yeah..." she said. "I do remember you. You a sports geek?"

"Nah. Just a reactionary."

"What kind of geek are you?"

In this kid's world—she looked like she was sixteen but was probably twenty-one or so—everybody was defined by what kind of pop culture they swooned over. Kind of a petty way to define people, in Jake's book, but probably better than going by politics or religion.

"Ah, I guess I am a sports geek. Basketball."

Krista looked up at his hat and raised an eyebrow. Then she turned around, pulled a mug off the shelf, and started filling it. He pulled a couple of bucks out of his wallet and tapped them on the counter.

"No charge," she said, her back still turned.

"I still get to leave a tip."

She turned around, watching the level of the coffee, which she'd filled to the brim without asking if he wanted cream. "If you dressed just slightly dorkier I'd think you were with the FBI," she said, her eyes slightly squinted.

Alex didn't hire dummies, which shouldn't have surprised him. This girl woman was Alex's first line of in-person security.

"Private detective, used to be Delta Force."

"Cool," she said. "I'm a serial killer geek."

"Serial killer geek?" Jake emphasized each word slowly.

"Abnormal psychology. I got stalked so often I decided to make it my major."

"It'd be easier if you didn't have blue hair."

"You'd think so...but trying to be invisible is just hoping the stalker follows someone else. Besides, I always have a wig in my bag if I need to erase myself on short notice. Mostly it's because I look like I'd be easy to push around."

"Huh," he said. "And are you?"

She batted her eyes at him. He was pretty sure the answer was *no*.

"I'll let Alex know you're here." She pressed a button under the counter.

"Thanks."

She glanced down. "He says to send you down. Nice to meet you, Jake."

"You too, Krista. Good luck with your degree."

"Thanks."

He slurped his coffee down to a level he wouldn't spill, then pushed through the *Employees Only* door and went down the stairs, making sure to duck his head under the low ridge of cement above him.

The reinforced steel door at the bottom of the stairs was shut and the two cameras in either corner above the door seemed to stare at him. As he approached the door the locks pulled back loudly, one after another—three different locks at least.

He pulled on the handle and opened the door. On the other side was a room full of computer geeks sitting at a long, two-sided bench stretching across an open, windowless basement room. Various posters covered the walls, declaring various fanboy allegiances. He wondered if Krista, studying abnormal psychology, could make anything of them.

The center of the bench was a row of huge monitors, some of them flashing with movies or games. The room was eerily quiet. Every single one of the geeks had on a pair of noise canceling headphones, and the loudest sound was the clicking of keyboards. The second loudest was computer fans. The air temperature was cool and dry—perfect computer weather.

Alex stood up from his place on the bench and walked toward

Jake with one hand out. "Hey."

Today he was wearing black pants, a teal shirt with gray suspenders, plus a black bow tie. His hair had been pulled back in a ponytail and the ends of his mustache hadn't been waxed to make them curl. Jake took the less dapper than usual outfit, along with the room packed full of hackers, as a sign that Alex was busier than usual.

As they shook hands, he noticed Alex's hand was warm and his face a little red, almost as if he'd been running. Alex led him past the row of hackers and through a door in the wall to the quiet room.

The room had eggshell foam on the walls and on the back of the door, the same kind that was used in radio station recording booths. There was no power in the room. The lights were battery powered, and the room was regularly swept for bugs. After Alex closed the door, he pulled a handheld scanner out of his pants pocket and ran it along the corners of the room, the doorframe, the overhead dome light, and along the edges of the white plastic-topped foldup table.

"Problems?" Jake asked.

"Working on a heavy assignment for the Feebs," Alex said. "They keep trying to get people in. I swear they have some kind of miniature drone technology, all the bugs that keep making it in here. If you don't mind?"

He waved the scanner at Jake. Jake stripped off his bomber jacket and hat, then raised his arms. Alex took a sweep over him, then his jacket.

The scanner's lights went off near the back of Jake's jacket. Alex ran an expert hand under the collar and came back with a small chip about half the size of his fingernail. From his other pocket, he pulled out a pair of pliers and crushed the chip, then left the quiet room to dispose of it.

He returned a moment later, then went over the entire room, Jake, and his jacket again.

"The Chinese?" Jake asked.

Alex gave him a look. "No, the FBI. They always keep an eye on me. And it's always worse when I'm actually working on something for them. What's up?"

Jake told him about his visit with Pavo. "I thought he'd be able to tell me something right off, you know. Something that would set Regan's mind at ease. But he couldn't, which now makes me wonder if we shouldn't leave this case alone."

"Which would mean either Wilson is executed or pardoned by the governor, depending on the current mood."

"Exactly. We might be leaving an innocent man to fry."

"I think they use lethal injection, but I see your point. When you mentioned the case yesterday, I did some digging, of course."

"And?"

"And I didn't find anything."

The last time Alex said something like that, it had been a big deal. "Someone's been erasing his records?"

"My apologies," Alex said. "I mean that his records look perfectly normal. Nothing's been obviously erased or altered. If something is being hidden, it's being hidden on a level below his online records."

"What level is that?" Jake asked. He was thinking of Pavo's

words: *'everyone is guilty of something.'* A police detective definitely wasn't someone who could keep his hands completely clean. At bare minimum, his innocence was long gone.

Alex lifted his eyebrows. "What level is below online records? Reality, Jake. Reality."

Chapter 5 - A woman's intuition

The front of Regan's house looked like an old-fashioned stone church, no steeple but a nice sharp peak in front with a small octagonal window in the attic that looked solemn. The garage door, much more modern, rolled upward with a satisfied hum, as if it was as glad to see her home for the evening as she was to be there.

Regan dropped everything just inside the kitchen door and disengaged the alarm system. Then she scuffed her shoes against the mat and looked around. The place was spotless as usual, thanks to her maid Ellen. But there were a couple of changes. For one thing, even though she couldn't see it, she could feel the presence of the gun safe in the cupboard just by the garage door, which she now kept locked at all times—even though you had to have a code to get into the garage.

She didn't feel like she was living in fear. And yet...

She picked the mail up off the floor and started sorting through it. Junk mail went into the shredder bin, real mail went onto the end of the kitchen counter, and papers from work went into the library, with its floor to ceiling shelves of books and repurposed dining room table in the center, covered with books. Her dress shoes went into the closet in the bedroom, and her work clothes went into the hamper. Gone were the days when she had come home and stayed in her work clothes all night; Jake had taken her shopping for soft, floppy sweatpants one day and she'd never looked back.

A few minutes later, she was in the shower. The drunk driver manslaughter trial was going exactly as expected—a thoughtless young woman who had considered it too much effort to catch a ride home, a college kid on a bike riding home from a frat party. They were both drunk, over the legal limit, but there was nothing in New York law that made riding a bike while drunk illegal. The fact that the thoughtless young woman was a single mother with a toddler and no close family nearby didn't simplify things either. The lawyers were having fun playing tug of war between them; she was bored with it already. She felt like telling everyone involved—even the lawyers—that she was going to take away all their licenses and throw them in jail for six months to make them think about the error of their ways.

She took a deep breath, tried to pack all the frustration she felt into it, and breathed it out toward the tile wall.

Outside the shower, she heard the door click. Jake called, "Regan, it's me."

"Shower," she yelled.

In a flash—in situations like this Jake could almost teleport—he had joined her in the shower and was soaping up her back. An hour later, she was calm, relaxed, well-loved, and thinking less about the frustrations of the day and more about: a) how well Jake knew her; and b) the Wilson case.

She'd been avoiding thinking about it all day. Jake just laughed at her whenever she tried to explain what she thought about the case. She stuttered, paced, twisted her hands, chewed on the ends of her long, blonde, normally non-chewed hair, even bit her fingernails, a habit she'd killed off years ago.

Now she lay tucked up under Jake's arm with her eyes closed and tried to work out just why it was so hard to think about the case.

Conrad Wilson had less than a month to live. It should be an easy decision to work on the case for a *few weeks*. Craig Moreau had been in jail for over thirty years and was in reasonably good health; another month's delay literally wouldn't kill him.

And yet.

It wasn't Wilson's looks. She'd stared at his face and thought he looked charming. He was open faced with blond hair and blue eyes, one of those guys who didn't just look like a cop, but looked like the kind of cop that you'd go running to immediately in an emergency—like in a hurricane. He looked like he'd be a hundred percent, straight-up, competent during a natural disaster.

Threatening? Not in the slightest.

Maybe he reminded her of someone from her past, someone who had struck her wrong, or someone she'd seen in a trial. She sifted through her memory, looking for some kind of twinge that would lead her to something definite—there wasn't even a twinge.

"Whatcha thinking?" Jake asked.

"About the Wilson case. Trying to sort out why I feel so ambivalent about him. He doesn't personally give me the creeps or anything; he looks completely trustworthy. And, as far as I can tell, he doesn't remind me of anyone...nobody from a case, not a lawyer or another judge, nothing out of a bad movie, not even anyone from college."

When she said *from college*, she wondered. Maybe? But if there was anything, it slipped away from her.

"The guy has less than a month left," Jake said.

"I know... I know... I just..."

"Just what?" She could feel his neck muscles tightening, hear the sound of his stubble scratching up against her hair. He was grinning at her.

She thumped a hand onto his chest. "Stop teasing. If I could put it into words, I would."

"Do you want to meet the guy?"

They'd talked about this with regards to the Moreau case—whether or not to meet with Moreau in person to get his side of the story before they went any further—and had decided not to. It had been her meetings with Andy Gibbons, the man they'd freed in their first case together, that had alerted not only the Organization that Uncle Paul worked for, but also the psycho Morrison Gray who'd stalked her for *'interfering'* in one of his cases.

Therefore, they agreed to visit Moreau only if it was truly necessary.

She squinted, trying to imagine visiting someone on death row. Because public executions were so rare these days, the spotlight was truly shining brightly on Conrad Wilson and his case. And she *hated* the media with a passion. If she came within ten miles of where Wilson was being held, she'd be on cable news for months.

She tried to weigh that rationally against the feeling she had against taking the case. If she could meet the guy, she might be able to put into words that horrible, vague, unfair, and unfamiliar feeling. If she truly wanted to pursue justice in this case—if she truly wanted to pursue justice at all—she had to meet with him before she turned the case down.

Or, just go through with the case and hope they could stay under cover, and her name would never be associated with his—stay under the radar.

The easy choice, the one that ninety-nine out of a hundred

people would make, would be to tell Jake to drop the case. Most of those people would barely feel a twinge of conscience sending the guy to his death. It wasn't their problem.

That would be them—not her.

She'd had nightmares all last night, and notwithstanding how relaxed she felt now, she knew she was going to have nightmares all night tonight too, Jake being with her or not.

Unless she agreed to take the case.

She closed her eyes. It would be easier to bust ass and get Wilson's case resolved over the next few weeks than it would be to fight her conscience. But if she tried to explain it like that to Jake, he'd just laugh at her.

She said, "No, I don't want to meet him. That would be practically begging CNN to bang on my door at three in the morning. We should take the case and work as hard as we can on it. Moreau doesn't know we're looking at his case—he won't even notice the delay."

"So, what you're saying is that it's easier for you to avoid the media than it is to avoid your conscience."

She could feel the amusement welling up through his belly. She sighed. No matter how she tried to hide, he always seems to know her true motives.

"Yes, yes," she admitted. "The little blue angry conscience fairy will visit me with nightmares if I don't do the right thing. Happy?"

He twisted around and kissed her on the side of her head. "Yes, actually," he said. "Very."

Chapter 6 -Go talk to your father

The manslaughter case had wrapped up earlier that morning with a conviction of first degree vehicular manslaughter for the defendant. The defense's argument that the victim being drunk and therefore had only himself to blame for his own death, had been dismissed by the jury after only two hours of deliberations.

Regan sat at her desk in the private area of her office and waited for Gary, her administrative assistant, to tell her when the sentencing hearing would be scheduled. She had a plastic pen in her hands, bending it with both thumbs as if she were trying to snap it in half.

She hadn't expected the jury to finish deliberations today. She'd expected it to go on, and on, and on. Strangely, she felt worse having the extra time on her hands.

The trees outside her window had filled out, lining the streets with green and softening the deadly dull gray cement buildings that made up ninety-five percent of downtown White Plains. Blue skies, puffy clouds, and a jet contrail across the sky formed into a code that read *get out of the office, Regan... you know you want to...*

She was restless.

The pen, one of those cheap white flimsy plastic-barreled pens that she kept in a bottom drawer, more for the purpose of destroying it rather than writing with it, abruptly bent in the center. She was tempted to bend it completely in half like a superhero with a bar of iron, but instead she dropped it in the garbage can beside her desk. Two other pens lay in the bottom of the can already. There was a bin outside the door for recycling, so this one just held three broken pens and a tissue. One of the pens was leaking blue ink all over the plastic liner.

"Regan," Gary called.

She jumped up, turned off her computer monitor, then grabbed her jacket before she realized she was acting like an idiot. She took a deep breath, then went through the nice wood door between their two offices, folding her jacket over her arm. "Yes?"

Gary raised his eyebrows. He'd finally stopped bothering about the bald spot on top of his head and had shaved it completely, while leaving his carefully styled goatee in place. "Out of here? I thought so."

Regan leaned against his reception style desk. "What makes you say that?"

"Spring fever," he said. "It's been hitting everyone lately."

"It's May. Shouldn't it be over by now?"

"Only among those enlightened souls who actually take a spring break vacation."

"I took some time off."

"That doesn't count. You were in the hospital."

Recovering from the last case they'd handled had wiped out six weeks of her life all together. It wasn't her fault that she didn't have any vacation time left for frolicking amongst the tulips. "What did you want me for?"

"Just to tell you they've scheduled the sentencing hearing on that manslaughter that wrapped up this morning. It's not until..." He glanced at a tiny calendar stuck to the inside edge of the high part of the desk. "...June 6th."

That was the same day Conrad Wilson was scheduled to be

executed. But that would be at six thirty in the morning—plenty of time to attend an execution in New Hampshire, then be back in White Plains...

"What time?"

He blinked rapidly at her. "Whatever time I tell you to go. Don't worry, I'll send your schedule. Like always."

"Morning or afternoon, smartass?"

"In the morning. Ten o'clock."

All right, so *not* enough time to make it back. She'd have to pick one or the other. But she'd always known that she would.

Regan shook her head, berating herself. What the hell was she thinking? She was already starting to assume they would fail to get Wilson exonerated. As if she wanted to fail? Wanted to see how a person dies? *Have you lost your mind, Regan St. Clair?*

"Tell your dentist I said hi," Gary said.

"What?"

"Isn't that where you're going that day, to the dentist? As long as you're after noon you should be fine."

"My dentist is on the 9th," she said. "I forget what time. No, this is a different appointment—it's with the executioner."

That got Gary's attention. "The what?" He closed his eyes and tilted his head back. "Oh. Ohhhhhh. The Conrad Wilson case. You and Jake are taking that on?"

She shrugged. She should have known she wouldn't be able to hide it from Gary, but she really hadn't expected him to get it out of her this soon though.

"Thinking about it," she said, even though she'd agreed to it the night before.

Gary's brown eyes popped open. "You know what you should do? Take the rest of the day off and go talk to your father about it."

"I can make decisions all by myself," she said tartly. In fact, it was exactly what she was thinking of doing.

Gary reached over the top of the desk and patted her on the shoulder. "Sure you can, Regan. You don't need, or at least don't plan to take, anyone else's advice at all."

She laughed. "All right, so why my father? Other than the obvious."

"Because he keeps calling me to ask if you're pregnant yet, and I have better things to do with the rest of my day than come up with witty responses."

She coughed and pulled away from the desk. "You, too? He won't leave me alone about it."

"The last time, I told him that your birth control pill packs are being automatically refilled by your housekeeper, and that you aren't the type of girl to surprise a guy with a pregnancy in an effort to make him propose."

"Gary!"

"Wait..." he paused and stared at her. "You're not, are you?"

"No!"

He spread out his hands in a *whatever* gesture. "Then don't sound so offended. He's an old man, Regan. He's anticipating the pleasure of undermining whatever disciplinary efforts you try to lay down on his grandchildren. I've seen it a thousand times."

"You *don't* have any grandchildren."

He pressed his lips together for a second and looked sour. "Mmmm, but my family's stuffed with them."

Gary's brother, Lawrence, was the bastard who had almost gotten her killed during the last case. "It's probably a good thing discipline's getting undermined in your family's case," she said.

"It is one of the few remaining joys of my days, seeing Mom turn my brother into a screaming ball of rage by sneaking her grandchildren cookies."

***

By the time she reached her father's house, it was early afternoon. She'd stopped at her favorite French place in White Plains, *La Ruche* (actually the only French place in White Plains), and had an early lunch with a copy of the *American Criminal Law Review* balanced against a drinks menu. Then she'd gone for a brief walk in Delfino Park past two groups of retirees playing softball at the diamonds and along the walking trail.

By then she was sure that her father had finished eating lunch and wouldn't be put out if she showed up, and it was time to go.

When she actually reached the front door, she hesitated. Her father was standing on the other side of the door. She could see his shape through the gauzy white curtain covering the slim window framing the door. At the bottom of the curtain were the toes of his red house slippers. Regan took a deep breath and pushed the doorbell.

A count of three, and then the inner door opened.

Her father said, "When…"

"When hell freezes over."

His face fell. She must have said it with too much confidence.

She leaned forward and kissed him on his grizzled cheek, then slipped past him into the house.

It wasn't like they didn't know each other. He knew if he kept hitting the same button over and over, she would dig in her heels and get stubborn. The joke was getting old. He needed to just let it drop.

She dumped her purse on the floor, hung up her spring jacket on the coat tree. and slipped out of her shoes.

"Have you already had lunch?"

"I ate."

"Coffee?"

"Yes, please."

Her father had put on khaki pants and a polo shirt; they smelled faintly of laundry soap. She would bet dollars to doughnuts that he'd only changed out of his pajamas because she was coming over.

He'd only retired as a district judge four years ago, and she missed being able to hop over to his office and talk to him. But more than that, she was starting to worry about him. What was he doing with his retirement? He wasn't traveling the way he said he would. As far as she could tell, he didn't have a girlfriend or even many friends.

He led her into the kitchen and waved her toward the small breakfast table by the patio door. In the mornings, it was almost too sunny to sit at the south facing window, and trying to read a newspaper was useless. But now in the afternoon the table was perfect, facing the neighbor's back yard. Most of the petals had fallen off his flowering crabapple tree and lay as a disintegrating brown mess on the ground.

He had coffee ready, poured a couple of mugs, and put them on the table.

"So what is it?" he asked.

"I'm questioning things," she said. "Myself."

"Yes?"

"It's about a case that's come up. Logically, Jake and I should take it. But... but... I keep having bad feelings about it. I keep trying to set myself up to fail."

"It's your intuition talking. You should listen to it."

"Daddy, sometimes intuition is wrong. If intuition could point the way to justice, then we wouldn't have so many young black men in prison who needed our help." The dossiers of people waiting to be exonerated had been particularly telling as to how easy it was to play on people's prejudices.

"I didn't say your intuition was *right*. I said it was *talking*." He cleared his throat and stared out the window for a moment. "This is about the Conrad Wilson case, isn't it?"

She gulped the too hot, too strong coffee and was grateful for it. However, it probably wasn't that hard to guess what she was talking about. Her father would be following the story as closely as a journalist. That was one thing she knew he did a lot of—watch the news.

"Yes."

"You and Jake are talking about whether to work on it."

"I've already agreed to work on it. And I still keep finding myself trying to undermine myself – and that's just wrong. If I didn't want to work on it, I shouldn't have told Jake yes."

"Could you still back out?"

"Of course. I don't think Jake would even argue with me about it. He'd be disappointed, though."

"Mmm," her father said.

"Mmm what?"

"Are you sure you aren't just telling Jake that you'll work on the case because you're worried about whether he'll be proud of you?"

"I'd like to think I have the bigger issues of justice in mind, too."

Her father went back to staring out the window. "It's always more complicated than it looks at first glance. Justice. You start out thinking all you have to do is make sure the lawyers play fair, and the laws are followed. Simple. Straightforward. Then you start noticing the laws aren't as fair as you thought they were, and that the lawyers can always find a way around playing fair, and that *you* aren't as fair as you thought you were. And you find yourself becoming a little softer, a little easier to push around for a while, because you can see where Lady Justice, being blind, has to have a little wiggle room.

"And then you start to wonder—what are the laws for, anyway? Why those laws, put into place in such a way? And why lawyers? Why judges? Why juries? Why do we think those things put together equal some ideal known as Justice? Does Justice, that elegant woman with her scales, really exist? Grind up a court full of lawyers and officers, suspects and victims — how many atoms of Justice will be in the mix? And you start to see..." He slurped at his coffee.

She slowly nodded. He was hitting the nail on the head—as he usually did.

"What you and I think of as the law is like an iceberg. The codified law and court cases, as intricate as they are, are just the tip of the iceberg, the part that floats on the surface. Underneath is the real mass of what we draw from, all the rules that nobody bothers to put a law to but that have to be obeyed, or else."

He waved at his clothes. "Like getting dressed for visitors."

"I know you were wearing pajamas until ten minutes ago."

"Half an hour, but you see my point."

"I don't know, Daddy. I think I'm still at the point where I spend most of my time making sure the lawyers play fair."

"You're starting to open up a little," he said. "Thinking about how injustice affects black people more heavily. Asking questions. Noticing patterns in the data."

"Being jerked around by intuition." She grinned wryly.

"Your mother found intuition easy. But then I think she had a better moral compass than either of us."

Regan's eyebrows rose. "Mom?"

He grimaced and stared down into his coffee, letting the steam surround his face. "She tried to explain it to me a few times, but I never understood it. Frankly, it sounded like something a hippie would say, something about not being mean to people. I could throw a thousand examples her way about how it was cruel to be kind, but it never threw her."

Regan smiled. Her memories of her mother were solidly the memories of a child or teenager; she'd died just before Regan turned sixteen, and Regan had never known her as an adult.

"I can just imagine you staying up late at night finding things to quiz her on. 'Should serial killers get a life sentence or the death penalty?' Things like that."

"Death penalty. Your mother said she wasn't sure about it at first, but then the Jeffrey Dahmer case happened..." His jaw clenched for a few moments as he thought about the famous serial killer and cannibal, beaten to death in prison.

Regan had remembered hearing about the case as a kid. The Wisconsin man had been a serial killer and cannibal, beaten to death in prison by a convicted murderer who claimed he'd been told to do so by God.

"I'm sorry... He was arrested the summer before she passed. One of the last... of all the... sorry, I just can't think about that case without remembering her in the hospital. All the life draining out of her, calmly explaining that they should put Dahmer to sleep so he wouldn't be abused in prison, that if anyone had to have the responsibility for killing Dahmer, it should be society as a whole, not some poor man already in prison who would get punished for it. I told her not to be silly, that Wisconsin had abolished the death sentence in eighteen-something, and that if anyone should be against the death sentence, it was her. But she said no, we'd stopped being able to differentiate between revenge and a merciful death, and it was a shame we couldn't do what needed to be done."

Regan blinked back the delicate little pricks that could grow into tears. She remembered her mother on her deathbed too, but they'd talked about other things. Friendships. Boys. How to tell when a friendship was worth keeping and when it wasn't. Whether Regan should think about becoming a judge, and whether that would stop her from being able to date boys. Whether she had to learn to cook or not. It had all seemed so vital at the time.

"I miss Mom," she said.

"I do too, honey. But we were talking about you, and about justice."

"You went off on a tangent."

"Did I?"

She sorted back through the conversation. "What do you think Mom would say about the case? And about me trying to sabotage myself?"

Her father chewed on part of his cheek. "It's hard to say. She seemed to pull her decisions out of thin air sometimes. I'd think I knew what kind of principles she had, and then—she'd say something that would knock me back. I never knew with that woman, and then she was strange about you."

"How so?"

"She'd be so protective of you...and then she'd boot you out into the deep end of the lake, as it were. Sometimes she seemed like she just wanted to watch you fail and take your pride down a peg or two."

Regan smiled wider. The tears were just a little bit closer. "I remember that. I remember learning how to ride a bike and her laughing hysterically while I kept falling over. She kept telling me if I didn't learn how to ride a bicycle by the time you got home that evening, you were going to be so disappointed in me you would take away the bicycle."

He chuckled. "Oh, that wasn't me you were worried about. It was Uncle Paul."

64

She snorted and stared at the table. The tears were welling up and she had to blink rapidly to keep them in check. "That's right. The bicycle was from Uncle Paul."

Her father chuckled. She glanced up. He, too, was staring down into his mug of coffee like a fortuneteller trying to read the future in a swirl of steam, but also probably hiding his incipient tears. "He was always scarier than I was. I had to fight for your respect. But Uncle Paul, well... They call him 'Fear' in the Organization. Did you know that?"

"Pavo. Uncle Fear." She paused. "Daddy, tell me about...how the two of you got involved in the Organization. I mean, *why*? Was it part of looking for Justice? Did you just get so frustrated with the law you turned somewhere else to look for it? Did it start out—like Jake and I?"

"You're worried that going off the beaten path is going to lead you astray, is that it?" her father asked. They were both staring at each other now, blue eyes piercing each other and asking each other to look away.

Regan swallowed. "I think I am. I don't think it has anything to do with Conrad Wilson. I think I'm terrified I'm turning..."

"Into Uncle Fear."

She nodded.

Now he leaned back, coffee abandoned on the table, until the front legs of the chair left the floor. He crossed one arm over his chest and put the other on his freshly shaved chin. He'd missed a spot along the side of his neck; the white hairs made him look even older.

Someday he'd be gone. The thought made her feel sick.

"It started in college..."

Chapter 7 -In college

The room had a high ceiling and a bay window with an excellent view into another brick and granite building full of dorm rooms not too far away. A quick glance out the window showed John that unfortunately the residents directly across from them weren't co-eds.

In his room, two desks lined one wall. Two narrow closets made the narrow entrance to the room even narrower. The beds had been arranged as bunks, leaving open only a small space at the end of the room near the bay window.

In the little alcove was a pair of lounge chairs covered in green corduroy. One of them held a guy he presumed was his roommate. He had a narrow wedge of a head with hair that already looked gray and thinning, and he was staring out the window across the green to the other dorm room, watching the others unpack.

John dropped his black steamer trunk on the floor and the powder blue, hard sided suitcase beside it, his mother's.

The guy had been holding his hands in front of him with his elbows resting on the hardwood arms of the chair, tapping his fingers together.

"Welcome," the guy said. "I am your roommate, Paul Travers."

They'd written back and forth a couple of times over the summer, just to make sure they wouldn't have too many problems with each other when the time came. Paul had seemed like a stand-up kind of guy, very reliable. Maybe not so big on sports or girls, but big on ambition—a trait John shared. He was going all the way to the Supreme Court. Just watch.

"John St. Clair," he said, wiping his hand on his pants and

walking forward. Paul twisted around in his seat and extended a hand. They shook. The hand was slender but had a grip of iron. When John tried to resist—he had tennis hands—the guy simply crushed him for a moment before letting up.

"Hey," John said. "No need to do that."

"What?"

"Shake hands so hard you're going to rip a guy's arm out of his socket."

Paul turned his hand over and looked at his palm. "I thought that was the accepted practice among men. To establish dominance." Paul grinned.

"You have to ask yourself, do I really want to establish dominance beyond a shadow of a doubt? In most cases, no. What you want to do is establish mutual respect. Strength through mutual back-scratching."

John had the gift of gab, inherited from his Irish Catholic grandmother. He often found himself spouting random nonsense that later turned out to be true. Not fortune telling so much as words of wisdom that weren't too difficult to live by.

"Hmm," Paul said. He extended his hand again.

John took it in a hearty grip. When he tightened a little, Paul tightened back. "Good," he said, letting go of the guy's hand. "Do that. If someone tries to gain the lead over you, you can go just a little harder on them. Let them know that you're stronger. Or at least more, uh, whatever. More willing to go the extra mile, let's say. But if they don't push it, you don't need to. Get it?"

"Got it."

"Good." He grinned at Paul. The guy was a chess wizard, had

straight A's, and read German philosophers for fun. From what John had put together, it sounded like his mother was a widow. It somehow was not even remotely surprising the guy didn't have a clue about how to shake hands—or that he would accept instruction.

Paul had gone back to staring out the window.

"What are you looking at?" John asked.

"I am watching the young men in the building opposite ours."

"Doing anything interesting?"

"Not especially."

"Then why are you watching them?"

"I have placed a bet with myself they will be kicked out of school before the end of the year and am gathering evidence to support or disprove my theory."

John had been bending over to unlock the suitcase, but paused. He looked out the window again. The two guys across the hall from them were standing on top of their desks, checking the plaster of their ceilings around the lights.

He chuckled. "Hiding places. They're trying to find hiding places."

"Just so."

John shoved the suitcase under the bottom bunk, then shoved the steamer trunk beside it, just to get it out of the way. Then he walked over to the other seat and sat down next to Paul. Their opposite numbers continued to investigate the room in the most suspicious way possible, pulling apart the two halves of their bunk beds, stripping off the linen, running a screwdriver over the floor tiles to see if any of them were loose.

"They have no idea they're being watched," John said.

Paul flicked his fingers toward the window. One of the side windows was cracked open. "I doubt they'll think to look outside their window until after they've done a bit more investigating. Eventually they'll realize that the outside of the building can be used for hiding places as well."

John tried steepling his fingers together like Paul, but it just wasn't his thing. He crossed his legs at the knee and leaned back in the chair. It felt like watching a movie.

"Here's the deal," John said. "I don't want in on your bet with yourself. Either way it goes, you're going to win."

Paul flicked his fingers again.

"But what I think you should stipulate is, except in case of possible death or dismemberment, you're not going to interfere. Just watch it as it plays out naturally. Don't put your finger in the pie."

Paul turned toward him, eyebrows raised.

"You're like a villain in a spy movie," John said smiling, although he was serious, his mouth running away with him again. "All the brains in the world, but no sense of when to quit. When things don't go your way, you start digging the hole you then fall into before the credits roll."

"And who are you, the hero?"

"Maybe. They don't usually let judges be the hero, though."

"You're going to sentence me to death someday."

"Not if you take my advice."

"Hmmm," Paul said. "Then I agree. No matter what happens in the room across from ours, I'll refrain from influencing it."

"Unless lives are at stake."

Paul shrugged. "If I'm not allowed to control how the pieces play themselves, then they have to take responsibility for *all* their actions."

A weird conversation had just taken a turn for the weirder, but John strangely found himself all right with that. "I disagree, but I can live with it."

"You think people should be saved from themselves?"

"I think they're a couple of kids who are going to get in trouble, try to get out of it, make things worse, and generally make their parents ashamed of them. The problem with guys like that, though, is they generally don't keep their damage contained. You keep an eye on them, hoping you can stop them before they go too far and screw something up permanently."

"You are a good man," Paul said.

"Aren't you?"

"My instincts are against it. But I'm willing to reconsider, given sufficient evidence to the contrary."

* * *

Regan's father finished his story still leaning back in his chair, staring out through the patio doors rather than at her. He'd crossed his legs at the knee and had one finger on his chin. Outside, the neighbor had let the little white Pomeranian out. The neighbor looked younger than her father, but still somewhere around retirement age—maybe early retirement age. He stood on his back porch for a moment, looking their way in a manner that struck

Regan as almost hostile. Then he went back inside as the dog ran around the yard and barked at everything that might conceivably hide a squirrel.

"We made it through college together. Sometimes I called him my best friend. Sometimes I didn't speak to him for weeks... usually when a girlfriend was involved. You might not believe it, but your father was something of a womanizer."

"Why am I not surprised?"

John smiled. "After college, I went to law school and he started working as an accountant. That didn't last long, though. He went straight into management after a year. By the time I passed the bar he was already making six figures. And this was the late Sixties."

"Was he already in the Organization then?"

"Oh, no. That was just natural talent. They weren't helping him at that point."

"But how did you get involved..."

He shook his head and dropped the front legs of the chair back down. "Not now. It's too much to talk about now."

Regan took a breath and finished the last dregs of her coffee. "I need to know, Daddy."

"I know. But I've spent years not thinking about this. Do you know what it feels like, knowing that you had some influence on a man, who then went on to do horrible things? Sometimes it feels like you're responsible for his actions. And don't tell me that everyone is responsible for their own actions. That sounds suspiciously like something Uncle Paul would say—like one of his favorites, *'everyone is guilty of something'*."

She turned the coffee cup around and around in her hands,

then pushed it away and claimed her father's, which he appeared to have forgotten. It was still warm. "This doesn't really help me with the question of why I keep trying to undermine myself on the Wilson case."

"I know. I guess what I'm trying to say is that it's a slippery slope, trying to take justice into your own hands. Even when you're trying to point out to someone else that it's a slippery slope, trying to take justice into your own hands."

"But that would mean doing nothing."

He spread his hands out. "I did my best. But then again, I learned to live with compromise too. And I handled some of the more obvious cases away from the court."

"Like Jake and Alex."

"Like Jake and Alex and others."

She finished her father's coffee, staring down at the last few swirls in the bottom. "Daddy, tell me. What happened with the college students who lived in the dorm room across from yours?"

When he didn't answer, she looked up. He was staring in her direction, but more through her than at her, eyebrows pinched together.

"Daddy?"

"Car accident," he said. And that was all she could get out of him.

Chapter 8 -Let's stick this to the wall

What with one thing and another, like having his apartment in Brooklyn and his office in White Plains, Jake had pulled up stakes and moved. It was too soon to move in with Regan who was going to kick and scream if and when it ever happened—she'd had every single detail of her place exactly the way she wanted it for so long. But it was not too soon for Jake to cut down on his daily commute to and from work.

It was weird, though. Setting up the apartment, he found himself wondering whether Regan would like this or that or the other thing all the time. Moving from a studio in Brooklyn to a one bedroom in White Plains also meant he had to pick out some actual furniture. And his full-size bed grew a size during the trip over—nothing less than a queen for Regan. It cracked him up every time he thought about it.

A third floor walkup in White Plains in the least generic building he could find, it had a varnished hardwood floor, electric radiators, a tiny pocket kitchen that was its own separate room, multiple closets, and enough room on either side of the bed that he could make it in the mornings without giving himself a full yoga workout. He bought curtains—one set of sheers and one set of light blockers—for all the windows, a coffee table—he bought a goddamn coffee table—and a rug for the bathroom. He was becoming positively domestic.

Not that Regan noticed, although he did catch her staring at his coffee table right after he bought it. She was probably trying to decide whether it was new or if it had been there the whole time and she just hadn't noticed. He decided to lie about it if she asked. Fortunately, she didn't.

She'd come over without calling. He'd only had a couple of seconds between recognizing her footsteps in the hallway and her knock at the door. "Jake?"

"Sec." He closed the lid on the pizza box, checked the living room for anything too man-cave-ish, and tossed his stack of files on the bottom shelf of the coffee table.

He opened the door and gave her a quick onceover, not just to make sure she was still a knockout gorgeous blonde almost six feet tall in her socks (she was), but to make sure she wasn't wounded, panicked, or otherwise distressed. She had this annoying habit of yelling at him for doing stupid things—then turning around and doing something twice as idiotic as anything he could come up with. But she looked fine, if a little strained around the corners of her eyes. She was doing too much again, he could tell.

"Come in." He held the door for her.

She did that civilian thing where she completely failed to see anything in the room except the part she directly interacted with. She took off her coat and laid it across the back of the chair he had placed just inside the door, then slid her arms around him and kissed him. Maybe she'd just missed him.

When she pulled back, she looked troubled. "Jake, I talked to my father today."

"How many times?"

She dimpled. "Only once."

"You think he's settling down a little?"

"Never. Laying down a plan to sneak up on me. I went to talk to him about the Wilson case. Jake, the more I research this case, the more I catch myself sabotaging myself. Trying to make myself fail."

He led her into the living room and seated her at the couch and made her put up her feet on the coffee table while he put on some coffee. Another thing he'd had to buy with the move—a coffee pot. He was so used to stopping at Alex's or one of a couple of other coffee shops he liked. He wasn't used to living in a town where you had to figure out how to *drive* in the morning before you could go out for a cup of joe.

When he came back, he said, "Are you digging up something that strikes you as being off, maybe?"

Despite sitting on his comfy couch and having her feet up, she had missed the point of relaxing entirely and was sitting stiffly upright with her arms crossed over her chest. "I feel like we're being used," she said.

"By a guy who doesn't know we exist."

She sighed. "I've told you I hate *'feelings'*. They reach up out of the darkness and try to strangle you every time you do something reasonable."

He sat next to her on the couch and pulled her over alongside him, tipping her over so that she had to lean against him. "So you talked to your dad about it. What did he say?"

"We got off topic. He started telling me about Uncle Paul, how the two of them met in college. He says he feels guilty that he had a chance to change Uncle Paul somehow, to a more humane and less ruthless person, and failed miserably."

"Eh," Jake said. "He can't blame himself for Pavo's actions."

"He does."

"I'm pretty sure Pavo doesn't blame *him*. What else did he say?"

She shook her head against his side. "He told me to listen to my instincts. Not necessarily to follow their advice, but to listen."

He kissed the top of her head; it smelled faintly of shampoo. "If we need to drop this case, we drop it."

"And let a man die."

"I didn't say it was a good idea. I'm just leaving the door open. Maybe he'll be pardoned. You never know. It's not our fault he's there, and I sincerely doubt it's only our responsibility. What's more, we don't even know if he is guilty or not. We've got nothing substantial yet."

"I don't like it. I feel like our good intentions are going to get used against us here—like with Jessie."

He'd talked to her about her visit with Jessie earlier; now *there* was a person that he had a bad feeling about. Jessie struck him as being a little bit too easily justified in murdering an abusive spouse. Who really knew what he'd done to her? She hadn't even tried to go to the cops first or document how she was being abused. If she'd waited a couple of weeks to gather evidence, she wouldn't be in prison now. Neither would she be complaining to her one remaining friend on the outside that life was hard and getting out on probation even harder.

Besides, poison was nasty. She should have just shot him. It would have looked a lot better at the trial.

Comparing Jessie with Conrad Wilson was difficult. Wilson hadn't asked for their help and wasn't trying to pressure them into illegal activities, which was part of the reason they weren't meeting with the guy. They were taking on the case because it was the right thing to do.

But, he could see how it might feel that way. The deadline of the execution was coming up too quickly. The pressure was on and making important decisions under duress—never a good idea.

"I think I kinda get it," he said. "You feel like you're being hustled into doing something. A high pressure sales pitch."

"Yes."

"Then we let it go. Or Alex and I look into it as much as we have time for, and we take whatever information we come up with and decide what to do with it. You stay out of it. Work on the Moreau case. Wilson will still have a Delta Force Detective and a computer genius on his side. It's not like we're incompetents."

She twisted up her face and smiled at him—one of those sweet, sexy smiles that practically screamed she wanted to be kissed. He leaned over and obliged her—not that he needed any encouragement.

"Thank you," she said. "You have no idea how much it eases my mind to hear you say that. I'll talk to Uncle Paul about the other case, and find out if he knows anything."

"I'll talk to Alex," Jake said, "which honestly should cover most of the work that needs to be done."

"My hero," she said.

If she felt like passing out rewards, he had no problem collecting them. He touched his forehead with his fingers. "Knight in shining armor at your service, ma'am."

She scooted up and wrapped her arms around his neck.

Problem solved.

***

The next morning was one of the good ones. Sunrise came early outside the sheer curtains. Early enough he didn't have to set an alarm, and Regan didn't have to go home. Instead he woke up enough to slide his arm underneath her neck and roll her toward him, pressing her against him. Her arm flopped over his chest and she wriggled in closer.

He savored the experience until his arm hurt and his bladder screamed at him to get up. Then he slid out from under the covers while feasting his eyes on her beautiful face. How anybody could take that for granted, he didn't know. Aside from waking up a couple of times when Regan rolled over, he'd slept like a rock.

After a few minutes of general wakeup routine, he started the coffee pot and turned on the TV so he could have the sound of the news playing in the background.

"... the governor has declined to review the Conrad Wilson case, and word has it that the president himself has stated that he will also decline..."

The coffee pot burbled. He shut it off.

"... concerns about biased treatment in favor of the police in New York are probably helping to fuel the controversy in New Hampshire. The current governor has said before, multiple times, he believes the people of New Hampshire have the right and the responsibility to put to death those people who are a danger to society. The polls show that the majority of people in New Hampshire..."

Jake reached the coffee table, picked up the remote, and shut off the TV.

A sigh came from the door behind him.

Regan stood in the doorway in one of his t-shirts, hair tousled, eyes fixed on the television screen. "I'm putting the Moreau case on hold," she said. "If we're going to handle this case, we're going to treat it with the respect it deserves. No half-assed efforts. If we're going to do something, then we're going to do it now and do it right."

She crossed the living room, half-hypnotizing him with her long legs, and disappeared into the kitchenette. A second later he heard the coffeepot being pulled out of the brewer, and the sound of liquid being poured into a mug. She reappeared, sucking the steam off the top, then taking a sip and wincing.

"And don't ask if I'm going to change my mind again. Justice isn't something that should be based on personal bias—or *'feelings.'*"

Jake wasn't about to argue with her. She was saying out loud what he'd been thinking all along. He didn't want to treat her like everything she did was a kind of test. But in a way it was—and apparently she'd decided to pass.

She sighed again and stared at the blank TV screen. "You think I would have learned that as a judge. But no."

He slipped an arm around her waist. "We're in this together, Judge St. Clair. Let's call Alex and set up a phone conference. We have less than a month. Let's stick this to the wall."

Chapter 9 -This crime scene's trace

The screens in front of Alex were a window to a world that stretched far deeper and was more complex than anything that could be shown on a two-dimensional screen. Yet they were the only way that world could be experienced. The various levels of data that could be extrapolated could seem mind boggling in their complexity, and yet were almost always an oversimplification.

A video clip was a simple image from which a human being might extract all kinds of useful information. The video clip was shown via a piece of software that had to be compiled into a language that a human could understand from a dizzying array of on/off switches—zero for off and one for on. Then it had to be retrieved from where it had been stored—more software, more programming, more zeroes and ones. Then it had to be moved from where the image had been recorded to where it was needed—the networks across which it moved were the underwater portion of a gigantic iceberg of software.

Then the image could be manipulated, turned from a two-dimensional image into a three-dimensional one, then projected onto a two-dimensional screen in such a way that it tricked Alex's brain into being able to more accurately visualize the space than when he had been watching the video. With sufficient concentration, it almost felt to Alex as if he had been physically ripped away from the geek cave and dropped into the simulation.

Alex squinted at his screen for a moment, then pulled off his headphones. The techno music vanished and was replaced by the sound of fingers hitting keyboards. He glanced over at his team. They looked intent, about eighty percent intent on their work and twenty percent intent on screwing around on underground game sites. Unlike his bosses at the FBI, he was able to grasp that actual productivity was tied to the relative interest of the task at hand—and he made sure he only handed out interesting stuff. This naturally curbed the amount of screwing around that occurred.

But it also meant that at moments like this, the rest of his team wasn't paying attention to his moment of stunned realization and didn't come running to look over his shoulders at his monitor screens.

He had liberated a video of the Walker apartment, the scene of the crime, from the archives of a local TV station. A few seconds of it had aired on television during the news, but the full footage covered the entire apartment with satisfying thoroughness. Now it was a three-dimensional space that delineated furniture, lighting, heating and a/c vents, and even posters outlined on the wall.

He remembered reading somewhere *'every contact between a perpetrator and a crime scene leaves a trace.'* Where was this crime scene's trace?

As well as the body, blood splatters, and other DNA evidence, of course, he had them set to separate filters and grouped together, so he could see the apartment both with and without the evidence of murder.

He could turn the filter on and see the blood covering the wall and posters on the wall behind the couch. It had sprayed in multiple directions and showed signs of arterial spray, blood that had splashed off of the body, and blood that had flung off the fire extinguisher as it collected on the surface. He had separated the different types of blood splatter; it all looked pretty legit. The murderer had started by beating Walker up on the couch, getting increasingly violent as he went. The blood splatters all traced their origins back to a position in front of the couch, leaving a cone relatively free of blood splatter directly behind that position, roughly pointed toward the front door of the apartment.

From the arc of the fire extinguisher he estimated the height of the murderer matched that of Conrad Wilson, as did the length of his arms. As he worked, he put together an animation of the murderer and how he had moved through the apartment. Through the front door—obviously—then into the living room and onto the couch. Presumably (although he didn't actually presume it), the murderer had sex with the victim on the couch. Then he had gone into the kitchen, picked up the fire extinguisher, and come back to the couch to beat Ms. Walker to death with it.

He had been very careful not to track through the blood and had circled around it as much as possible to re-enter the kitchen, where he had turned off the teakettle, picked up a towel and returned to wipe his prints off the fire extinguisher. He had then left the apartment, using the towel to wipe off both sides of the door handle, and dropped the towel back inside the door before closing it and letting the automatic lock engage.

After he left, Ms. Rossier, Ms. Walker's friend, let herself into the apartment. She said she walked directly to the body to see if her friend was alive, kneeling beside the couch and smearing almost the entire front of her body with blood. She pulled herself more or less together, then called emergency services and waited in place until the police and ambulance arrived. The police escorted her from the apartment. Her feet were a hefty size eleven women's, or a men's nine and a half.

The police had done a nearly textbook job securing the scene, and the forensics team had done really, really well staying out of the blood. The area near the couch had multiple footprints, of course, but the blood had been there almost half an hour by then, and the footprints had clearly been tracking through tacky rather than fresh blood.

So why were there footprints, size women's seven or men's five and a half, in the office area, showing evidence of fresh-tracked blood on the almost ridiculously shaggy green carpet? The footprints had entered through the front door, gone to the body, then back to the front door, then to the office area where they circled the room several times (searching for something perhaps), then exited?

No unexpected fingerprints were found in the room—just Ms. Walker's. Signs of Conrad Wilson had been found in the living room, bathroom, kitchen, and bedroom—the forensics team really was very good—but not in the office. Not even signs of Ms. Rossier's DNA or fingerprints had been found in the office. Ms. Walker was a woman who liked to keep her office private, a personal sanctuary.

Someone with small feet had searched that office, tracking Ms. Walker's blood around the room without leaving fingerprints or DNA.

And really, come to think of it, there was a suspicious absence of evidence in the living room as well. If the murderer and Ms. Walker had unprotected sex, as evidenced by the semen found in her vagina, shouldn't it have been on the couch and her clothing as well?

Alex was no ladies' man, but he'd always stayed in contact with the attractive, witty, charming FBI agent who had both caught him hacking their computers; and pled his case to Judge John St. Clair when he'd come up for trial. And she had always been *very* concerned about getting anything on the couch in her office, birth control pills or not.

Three of his on-and-off freelance employees had responded when he'd put out the call to see if any of them had any information about the Walker case. The THEM Three, as he called them, were conspiracy nuts who kept track of the Illuminati, all possible JFK shooters (including Oliver Stone, because why not?), the bloodline of Christ and Mary Magdalene, aliens, Elvis's current location, and Area 51. If there was a conspiracy, they had researched it.

Normally, he would have dismissed them as fruitcakes. But their ability to find correlations between any completely independent events actually made them excellent hackers and researchers—as long as someone stopped to comb through their results and weed out the noise, of which there was a lot. They'd told him that they, too, had been looking into the Conrad Wilson case, for fear Wilson had been framed by the Illuminati...or worse, *THEM*.

There was some sort of acronym for it. T-H-E-M. But he couldn't remember what it was, and he hadn't bothered to look through his files before he'd opened up a chatroom this morning. They hadn't been especially forthcoming about what their suspicions were. It was too dangerous to go into detail even in a secure chatroom on one of the secure servers in Alex's basement. But each of them assured him, *it would not be a waste of his time to look deeper into the case, especially with regard to the office.* Maybe he would finally start taking them seriously.

He sighed and dropped back into the chatroom.

back. interesting, he typed.

Immediately, a response flowed back at him from user

codenamebosco:

yes, very interesting, very interesting. THEY are WATCHING U.

He typed, *other info?*

yes. but not here.

k, he typed. *geekcave?*

UR BEING WATCHED. alt location.

?

cola

Codenamebosco logged out. The THEM Three were all apt enough hackers that they knew that it was a useless gesture, logging out as if the fate of the city depended on it. It wasn't like Bosco had erased the session files or any of the dozen other telltales they'd communicated. But asking them to act like normal people would have been hypocritical as well as counterproductive.

He looked up the name in his files in case it came up in conversation.

T.H.E.M.—*The Hegemony of Evil Maniacs*—the organization that controlled the world, a group of evil geniuses so hyper intelligent they made Einstein look like a zombie, had supposedly given themselves a name cheesier than the villains in a James Bond novel.

Right.

Alex reviewed the project reports his staff had dropped in his command folder, approved most of them and sent the projects off to the clients for review, sent one back to a freelancer with instructions to try again—she was fourteen and had a tendency to get sloppy when she had a bad day at school, and it had been dodge ball day in P.E. class—then logged out and left Krista in charge of the madhouse.

Cola, or in fact, any type of beverage name, meant nothing more secretive than "Pick up snacks and drinks and meet us at our apartment in an hour," all part of Bosco's clever plan to get free pizza and soda and to monopolize Alex's time for the night.

They'd probably found a new board game to try out on him. He hit the autodial on his regular phone and called in his order.

If the Organization knew about these guys, they clearly weren't too worried.

Chapter 10 - The THEM Three

Like other geeks of Alex's acquaintance, the THEM Three had more money than they knew what to do with, even the ones that stayed on the technically legal side of the law. They made their money with the Bitcoin boom. Each of them bought $100 worth of Bitcoins when it was launched at one cent per coin, under the overwhelming criticism and ridicule of their fellow geeks. In 2014, they cashed in when Bitcoins reached $900 per coin—walking away with a nifty $9 million profit—each—and of course the envy of all their geek friends. The three had moved out of their parents' basements and into an ugly blue clapboard townhouse in Bed-Stuy, a place that had to have cost over a million and was decorated in Silver Age Comics Posters and Ikea furniture that could almost pass as normal. Alex had sent Krista's best friend Kelly over to decorate the place; she'd done the three above-grade floors but absolutely refused to touch the basement.

He hit the bell a couple of times. When nobody answered, he punched the first digits of *pi* into the keypad until the door clicked, and let himself in, balancing the hot, fragrant pizza boxes across one arm. He set the plastic bag full of soda on the floor and kicked the door shut.

"Hello? It's Alex."

No answer. He carried the pizza boxes into the kitchen.

The floor was clean white tile with a rubber mat in front of the stove and the sink. The counters had been cleared and the smudges wiped off the front of the steel fridge, oven, dishwasher, and microwave doors.

He bit the inside of his cheek for a moment, then set the pizza boxes on the counter. Casually, he opened the fridge, surreptitiously, first sliding his hand along the handle.

Which was *clean*.

The inside of the fridge contained a gallon of milk, a gallon of OJ, a shelf full of assorted bottles of beer, and a plastic bag with broccoli in it. He touched the broccoli with the tip of a finger.

It was fresh.

Two options here: either the Organization had come in, killed all three of the THEM Three, then stopped out of some kind of horrified disgust to clean the kitchen afterwards...or one of them had a new girlfriend or... nah, that was not possible... but broccoli in their fridge...

He shouted, "Guys?"

Still no response. Alex knew he wasn't the kind of guy who could handle violence. It upset his stomach, completely fried his nerves. A hero he was not. But that didn't mean he was craven.

He swallowed and slowly approached the door to the basement at the back of the kitchen, an old wood door that had been painted steel gray to match the cabinets. He grabbed the brushed-silver handle—also suspiciously clean—and turned it.

The sound of laughter echoed up at him—a woman's laughter.

He took a deep breath and looked over his shoulder at the pizza boxes. If he was going to have to go through the ordeal of meeting the new girlfriend or killers or beast, he wanted to have some kind of propitiatory offering to bring with him.

He put his foot on the first step down, then pulled it back.

A situation this touchy called for napkins.

***

The THEM Three consisted of Bosco, Paddy, and TDB.

Bosco was from the Philippines and stood six feet, seven inches tall, and was of undisclosed weight that was never less than three hundred pounds. He had straight black hair, black eyebrows like two fat streaks of permanent marker across his brow, and a substantial collection of Grateful Dead t-shirts. He could quote the entire works of Monty Python and often would spend the entire day speaking in nothing but lyrics, quotes from obscure philosophers, and movie quotes. He had dropped out of law school to become a full time hacker.

Paddy was British and looked like the irate cannon ball that Bosco would juggle if he were a circus performer. He'd been a physicist and looked like the kind of guy you'd expect to be in the Special Forces, that's if you didn't know people like Jake. He claimed to have a sense of humor—but one did *not* simply ask him about how he got his nickname. That was forbidden territory.

TDB was the handsome one, the one most likely to have acquired a girlfriend. Tall, blond, handsome, broad through the shoulders, and could be trusted not to say anything too obviously off-putting if you took him out in public. He'd been meant for a football scholarship and a normal life... until he met Bosco and had too much fun in the college computer lab to turn back.

All of them showered on a regular basis. All of them occasionally dated. Not a problem.

But bringing a more permanent relationship into that mix—it had gone badly before. *Very* badly. Alex had almost called Jake for help once; fortunately, the young woman had stormed out, weeping copiously, while Bosco found TDB's tooth and put it in a glass of milk and Alex drove Paddy to the emergency room.

***

"Pizza!" he called down the stairs.

"Alex!" several voices shouted. "Come on down," TDB added. "There's someone we want you to meet."

Alex gritted his teeth and descended the gray carpeted stairs down into the basement. In a second the back of the big brown couch, L-shaped and big enough to hold a football team, came into view. The gigantic TV in front of it showed a video game, a first person shooter in which a woman aimed a sniper rifle across a crevasse at what looked like a dictator on the opposite side.

The view zoomed in, crosshairs aimed at the dictator's head.

"Wait," the woman on the couch said. She had short black hair and was sitting next to Paddy.

"I've got him in my sights," Paddy said.

"Yeah, but I built a cheat code in here. Aim for his ear, right in his ear hole."

Paddy's head tilted to the side. TDB was sitting beside Paddy facing the TV. Bosco sat on the side of the couch against the wall, his arms spread wide, grinning at Alex like an idiot.

Alex blinked.

The crosshairs centered themselves over the dictator's earhole and flickered orange for a second. Paddy adjusted them again, and they went solid orange. "Now?"

"Now."

The game zoomed out and traced the bullet from the barrel of the sniper rifle into the dictator's earhole. The dictator's head began to explode, then turned into a shimmering orange bordered portal. The soldiers around the dictator froze in place, just beginning to panic and aim their weapons toward the player.

"The hell," Paddy said.

"Now all you have to do is make it over to the other side in the next six minutes."

"What's through there?"

"Secret level."

"Nice." Paddy leaned forward. The woman on the couch beside him had effectively vanished from Paddy's world. He had six minutes to make it to his next checkpoint, and he wasn't going to waste it talking to some *female*. Even if she also happened to be the game creator.

TDB extended a hand over the back of the couch, waving between them. "Alex, Mary. Mary, Alex."

The woman on the couch beside Paddy turned around and waved. "Hi." She was black and hot as hell. Alex lifted his eyebrows at her. Great. He'd lost the ability to speak, or in fact to look like any kind of competent adult.

He forced his brain into overdrive, reminding it that he needed whatever information these three guys could cough up, as well as finding out whether he needed to keep a closer eye on them for a while. He shook his head to try to clear it, resumed breathing and said, "Meat, weird, or pepperoni and fish toes?"

She frowned. "What's the weird?"

It was tomato, blue cheese, artichoke, chicken, and bacon on white garlic sauce. He opened his mouth.

Bosco interjected, "It is forbidden to ask what the weird is. One must experience the weird. Fish toes are anchovies."

Which was true—that was the house rule. But Alex had never seen it enforced in front of an outsider before, let alone a girlfriend—not even one as hot as this Mary.

"Got it," she said. "Gimme pepperoni and fish toes."

"Ch... che... Check."

He carried the boxes over to the small table behind the couch that was reserved for food. TDB said, "Where's the soda?"

"In the entryway, you ungrateful jerk."

TDB jumped over the back of the couch and jogged up the stairs.

"So were you followed?" Bosco asked.

"No."

"Are you sure?"

"Of course not. No one is ever sure. But I doubt it."

Bosco nodded. On the screen, Paddy's character had crossed over the crevasse and was executing frozen soldiers as he worked his way over to the dictator.

"Weird, please," Bosco said.

The table contained a large stack of paper plates. Alex pulled out two slices of weird and handed them over the back of the couch to Bosco, sliding a napkin under the plate.

"Ah... mhh... one or two?" he asked Mary.

"One."

He gave her a slice of pepperoni with fish toes and a napkin. She folded the tip of the slice over on itself and started eating.

"Paddy?"

Paddy made a rude suggestion with his middle finger and continued playing. Right, later.

"So. You saw the footprints in the office," Bosco said.

Mary had turned back to the screen. Alex jerked his head toward her.

"She's cool."

"How cool? A hundred percent cool? Or like FBI cool?" Alex asked.

"A hundred percent," Bosco said.

"I'm right *here*," Mary said, mumbling around a mouthful of pizza.

Alex grabbed himself a slice of weird and a slice of meat and started eating the meat standing up. If Mary was dating Paddy, it didn't matter where he sat, but if she was dating *Bosco,* it could be a problem sitting between them. And if he took TDB's spot before TDB had a chance to defend it, he would get the cold shoulder all night. He *hated* social crap like this.

Bosco said, "Sit over here in the middle."

Alex made a face and carefully stepped over the back of the couch. In this company to cross in front of the screen was a bigger insult than sitting between a man and his girlfriend. He wedged himself into the corner of the L, sucking in his elbows and trying to take up as little space as possible.

"Who was it?" Alex asked.

"The footprints in the office? It was THEM, man," Bosco said.

"This doesn't help me in any kind of material way," Alex said.

"Does it tell me who actually murdered Ms. Walker? Does it tell me who directed attention away from the murderer and toward Mr. Wilson? No."

"I know you're not big on THEM, but try to keep an open mind here. When we're talking about THEM, it doesn't matter who does things. Members of THEM don't have individual wills, as far as acting in the service of their society goes. They just do what they're told."

Alex waved a hand, his mouth full of pizza. He'd heard this before. Paddy made it in through the glowing portal, which opened into a strange cartoon world full of unicorns, dolphins, high-powered guns, and cutout pictures of Hitler being forced to skip through the landscape, spewing statistics of the numbers of people killed. Alex shook his head and swallowed.

"Why Mr. Wilson?" he asked. "Did he make THEM mad or something?"

"He was a police detective. They're punishing him for looking into something he shouldn't have."

"If that was the case, wouldn't they have been better off killing him? Shutting him up permanently?"

"Maybe they didn't need to kill him."

"Or they don't believe in killing," Mary said.

Both Bosco and Alex snorted.

Paddy, firing off a pair of overpowered handguns in a frenzy to pick off all the Hitlers as fast as possible without hitting any unicorns, said, "Breeding program."

This was a new one to Alex. "Breeding program?"

"He's done something they don't want him to do, but he's too smart to kill. They need his genes." Paddy said it like it was gospel.

"Artificial insemination stores sperm for up to twelve years," TDB said, coming back downstairs with the bag of soda and a stack of glasses.

"Not a hundred percent of the time."

"What if someone else had a grudge?" Alex asked. "Not THEM. Someone not as powerful as THEM, who didn't have the stomach for killing? He was a detective. I would think that would tend to piss people off, digging around in the skeletons in other people's closets."

"Mmm," Bosco said, rubbing his chin. He was actually thinking now, not just fantasizing about a secret underground organization that controlled the whole world and, therefore, gave all the random crap that happened to him some kind of meaning. "Find out who has tiny feet among first degree contacts of the people he's put behind bars, like Cinderella. I like it."

Alex rolled his eyes.

Mary said, "And that's the portal back out. Congratulations, you have just survived the mind of Hitler."

Paddy sniggered. "Hitler's mind was wack." The character moved through a matching portal and came back out behind the dictator's head. Time started up again, and a mass of soldiers collapsed around Paddy's character as time started up again. He gave a fist pump, then held out his fist. Mary bumped it with hers. Paddy went back to playing, taking a flying leap over a damaged section of masonry to enter a Gothic castle, throwing grenades as he fell.

"Good play so far," Paddy said.

"Cha!" Bosco said. "Told you so."

Alex licked his fingers, remembered he had a napkin, and used it to wipe his face like a little kid.

TDB passed him a glass of cola. "So...do you have time to hang out?"

"Maybe."

"Cha!" Bosco said. "Victory number two."

"I'm right *here*," Mary said again.

Alex looked back and forth between them, Bosco grinning, Mary keeping a proprietary eye on the TV screen, and TDB leaning around Paddy and waggling his eyebrows.

"What?" Alex said.

"Girlfriend tests passed," TDB said. "Paddy likes her—"

"I didn't say I *liked* her," Paddy said.

"Do you like Alex?" TDB said.

"I never said I *like* him," Paddy said.

"But he's okay?"

"Yeah, I guess. And before you ask, yeah, I guess Mary's okay, too." The character did an aerial somersault, kicked two enemies in the head, and shot a third while still midair. Paddy glanced at Mary and nodded. *Respect.*

"And Alex didn't run screaming as soon as he saw her, *and* is willing to consider spending time around her. Therefore, she does not suck as much as the ones I, TDB, bring home."

Alex cleared his throat. He tried not to focus on the fact that he was probably flaming red in the face. "The ones you bring are..." His voice faded out. There was no point trying to lie. TDB's taste in women ran to hot women with no social skills in the geek world. "Never mind. They do suck."

"Any *other* tests I need to pass?" Mary asked, glaring past Alex at Bosco.

Alex pushed backward in his seat. In order to escape he'd have to hurl the glass and dive over the back of the couch. It could be done.

"Just one," Bosco said. "A test of checkers."

"Aw, you think you can beat me now?" she asked.

"No. But can you beat...him?" Bosco jabbed his finger toward Alex. "You can't. I promise you. It's not possible."

Alex closed his eyes, stomach lurching. He did *not* want to be part of the Girlfriend Trial. He leaned forward and put the glass on the table, then stumbled in front of the screen despite a grunt from Paddy. "I'm out."

"Aw," Bosco said.

"You pushed too hard," TDB said.

"What's the deal with you and checkers?" Mary asked.

"I was just shitting you," Bosco said. "It's like a samurai movie. Every hotshot kid who comes to town challenges the old samurai to a duel to make a name for himself. It's always the old guy who walks away, but that doesn't stop the kids from challenging him...and dying."

"That good, huh?"

"Better," Bosco said.

"Good thing I don't play, then."

"You were just talking smack to me."

"That's not the same thing as *playing*. That's just talking smack. Nice to meet you, Alex."

He was behind the couch now. She reached out her hand and he shook it. He stopped and shifted from foot to foot. "Look, I have a completely inappropriate question for you," he said. "Two, actually."

"Shoot."

"What's your shoe size?"

"Eight and a half."

He nodded. "And, uh, female question. The murder victim was murdered right after having sex...pretty rough...I'm assuming rape. There was semen in the vagina, but none on the clothes or the couch where it happened."

She stared at him for a minute. She had delicate eyebrows and a nose ring, which he'd missed earlier. He put a foot back toward the door. He hated being stared at, and he hated *staring* at people...period.

"Sounds fishy," she said finally. "Unless she was passed out at the time she was murdered, I'd assume she struggled or at least tensed up."

He nodded again. "I thought so, too."

"So you don't think Wilson did it."

He shook his head. She was still staring at him; he seemed to be completely unable to look away. It wasn't that he wanted to steal her away from Bosco. It was more like she was mind controlling him somehow. Although of course she wasn't.

"Why would you put a guy whose genetic material you're trying to save on death row?" She blinked.

Alex jumped like he'd just been freed from the mind control ray. "Exactly."

"Imagine you're THEM," Mary said. "The world's most intelligent evil geniuses ever. And all you really want to do is keep the stupidity of humanity from destroying the planet."

"Sucks to be THEM," Paddy said.

"Yeah," Alex said. He held up a hand and waved to the others. "Nice to meet you, Mary."

"Maybe next time Bosco won't be such a jerk," she said.

"Don't count on it," TDB said.

"Aw," Bosco said.

Alex grabbed a piece of the weird, waved again, and went upstairs and out.

Getting into the car, he wiped his hands on his pants and reached into his pocket for the keys.

His arms were still covered with goosebumps.

Chapter 11 - On it

Bright and early in the offices of the Honorable Regan St. Clair, it was time to get some serious record keeping done. While other offices struggled to handle pop-up audits, quarterly reports, and other requests, the office of Regan St. Clair was known for its eerie, almost preternatural efficiency.

A good secretary was at least fifty percent spy, and not the James Bond kind either. Their ilk was mainly to direct attention away from those people doing the real work from behind the scenes.

Gary slid his headphones on and cranked up some postmodern soul music on his computer— lots of bass guitar and samples from a dozen different Motown hits. White Plains in early May had its benefits, but being stuck inside working on the computer wasn't one of them. His part of the office didn't even have a window. He let his feet tap in time with the music.

It was quiet—too quiet. The best days were the ones where he was handling a dozen issues at the same time. Regan's current case was straightforward—no media, just a minor train wreck involving one of an endless string of automobile related manslaughter cases.

And yet Regan had suddenly stopped talking about legal cases. She almost always had a case or two she was chewing on—one from the books. Good judges studied case law. It was practically a commandment of her existence.

At the same time, she'd started opening up more about Jake and her relationship with him. In all the years he'd been working for her, he'd never heard her talk so much about the person she was seeing, or about a *person* at all. Her life was filled more with ideas than with people or gossip—until now.

He could buy that she was in love with Jake Westley. But he couldn't buy the way she brought him up whenever he asked how she was doing.

Smokescreen. Total smokescreen.

At first he'd tried to accept it. The last time Regan had let him into her life in any kind of significant way, he'd been forced to betray her to his brother, Lawrence at gunpoint. That kind of thing put a damper on a friendship, no matter how long ago it had been founded. But Gary had never been good with accepting unpleasant situations, or being left out of the loop for that matter.

She didn't tell him they were digging into a new case. She was telling him juicy relationship details to keep him distracted from the possibly even juicier case details. Apart from the Wilson case, which he had to extract from her, he couldn't even guess what they were working on.

The door of the office was open, and the music on his headphones had been set low enough he could hear anyone walking down the hallway. So when the sound of footsteps going up and down the hall started to change pace and direction, he tapped the foot pedal of the transcriptionist's rig, which he'd set up to pause the music, and slid the headphones off his head and backward over his shoulder as Regan walked into the office.

She passed through his side of the office looking worried. She barely saw him and certainly didn't greet him, just passed through to her office and closed the door behind her. Her chair creaked and the mouse thumped against the mouse pad as she woke up her computer.

After a few seconds he heard the sound of more mouse clicking, then spurts of typing—checking emails, then a sigh.

The chair creaked again. For a moment Gary had the hope that Regan would return to his side of the office, apologize for being so brusque, and confess that she needed his help. Then the typing and mouse clicking resumed.

He sighed, reeled in his headphones, and retreated into the safety of his tunes—a pipe dream.

Regan's schedule for today was to meet with the councils for the offense and defense—oops, sorry, the prosecution and the defense. Justice was *nothing* like a football game with the better paid ones winning most of the time—at least Regan would never hear him say so. Then there was a departmental meeting and finally a consultation with a group of high school students interested in going into the legal profession.

Gary's advice? *Make sure you have rich parents or at least a wealthy family friend.* Cynical? Yes, but true. It wasn't so much you needed money to get into a good school, but it was the rest of the advantages wealth gave you: connections, a solid childhood unplagued by poverty, education, and even more importantly, the sense that success was possible.

He'd come a long way from his childhood. Lawrence had come even farther. But it had twisted both of them, leaving Gary afraid of the spotlight and Lawrence with the attitude that his loyalty was available to the highest—or most ambitious—bidder.

He'd been dwelling on it lately. Was this what he wanted, being Regan's administrative assistant? Or was he second guessing himself because Regan had been holding back on him lately? He needed something to keep him out of trouble, or he'd start looking for some. Inter-office gossip was a rich well of possibility...but it was ultimately meaningless to both discover other people's secrets and to try to manipulate them.

Lawrence had the Organization to keep him busy and give meaning to his life. What did he, have? Zilch.

He sighed and leaned back in his chair, putting his hands behind his head. The ever recurring question: what did he want to do when he grew up? Assuming that happy event ever occurred. He was currently single, wasn't especially fond of pets, and had no real hobbies other than listening to music. He couldn't play, or rather wouldn't play his electric bass in front of other people; it was just too embarrassing.

Like countless other human beings spread across the face of the planet, the world had insufficient need of him personally. Any number of people could have done his job. Not as well, admittedly, but they could have done it well enough that Regan wouldn't have noticed any difference on a day like today.

He should go home for the day, or go out. Scratch the itch to get outside on a beautiful spring day. Indulging wanderlust for a few hours by getting in a car, pointing it in a direction, and driving away from here would probably see him right as rain.

His chest twanged; his throat tightened up.

Nevertheless, he turned off his system, packed a few things in his messenger bag, and turned off his desk light. He lay his jacket over his arm.

He was going. It felt as raw and final as if he were breaking up with someone. Incipient heartbreak. He was *definitely* being too melodramatic today.

He walked over to Regan's inner door and knocked.

"Come in," she said.

He opened the door gently, just enough to admit his face. He left his feet on one side of the threshold and leaned his face in.

She looked up from her computer screen. It was turned away from the door, and he couldn't see what she was working on, but from the look on her face it was something significant. She looked almost guilty or sickened. Her eyebrows pinched in the middle; her cheeks looked hollow.

"What's up?" she asked.

"Are you all right?"

Her lips pursed tighter together. She wasn't talking.

He said, "I've wrapped things up for the day."

"It's only nine thirty."

"Nevertheless, I'm done. It's a gorgeous day in May, and I have nothing better to do at the moment."

"Cabin fever," she said.

"Mmm."

She took a deep breath that sounded almost shaky, looking down at her hands which were still on the keyboard. "Have fun."

He wanted to say, *Don't you need me? Tell me you need me to do something for you...anything. Tell me not to go looking for trouble.*

But he somehow knew she wouldn't.

"You, too," he said.

The sound of typing resumed from her keyboard, more furiously than ever.

Regan's face was screwed up in a grimace, her eyes shining with tears. He let his messenger bag and jacket slide down to the floor and crossed through the doorway.

She looked up at him. "Regan, did something happen with you and Jake?"

She shook her head. "It's fine. Everything's fine with Jake. I'm fine."

"You're not fine. You're stressing."

"I'm *fine*." She raised a hand and shoved it across her cheek. It came away wet.

He crossed his arms over his stomach and leaned against the wall. He could stand there all day if need be. "Regan. You're stressing. I'm stressing. We need to talk."

"About what?"

"About whether you're going to include me in what you're doing...or not."

"I don't understand."

He snorted. "I realize I'm just a friend, but you suck at lying. You're working on a new case, aren't you? And Jake has asked you to keep me out of it because I might relay information to my brother. You don't trust me anymore."

Her lower jaw jutted out and she bit her lips. There it was. The truth of the matter.

"That's not true."

"Then tell me what you're working on."

She reached up to her monitor and turned it off.

He bent down and picked up his messenger bag and coat. He

needed a box. There were things at his desk he didn't want to leave behind.

"Goodbye, Regan."

He turned toward the hallway. He'd pick the stuff up later. Not what he'd imagined doing today when he'd come in to work this morning. But if Regan couldn't trust him, what was the point in working for her? If you couldn't trust the spy working for you, you needed a new spy.

"Where are you going?" she asked.

"I'm leaving."

"For the day."

"No, honey. I'm quitting. Resigning. I'll email you my letter from home."

"But...why?"

"Because you don't trust me."

"Of course I don't trust you. You're blackmailing me. You betrayed me to your brother."

He smiled, keeping his face carefully turned toward the hallway. He'd kept the threats and blackmail away from her so long that she didn't know what kind of awful pressure could be brought to bear. This was nothing.

"He had a gun to my head—literally."

She could have continued arguing with him. Instead she sighed. The wheels of the chair rolled a few inches. "I'm sorry, Gary. Please...have a seat."

He looked back again. She was standing behind her desk, one hand on the chair behind her. Her face was still screwed up in a grimace. The tendons on her neck stood out like cords.

He shook his head. "Regan. What's *wrong*?"

She shook her head and raised a hand in a *stop* gesture, then waved him toward the seat. He took his jacket and bag with him and sat. She sat across from him, folding her hands on top of her desk and leaned forward. She swallowed several times, saying nothing.

"Regan. Are you pregnant?"

Her jaw clenched. "No, of course not."

"Then what could possibly be worth all this drama?"

"We're working on another case."

"The Conrad Wilson case?"

She nodded.

He blinked. The Conrad Wilson case was in New Hampshire, not New York. And, as far as he knew, had nothing to do with the files that had been found in Marando's apartment. He would have put his money on Regan and Jake picking the Craig Moreau case next; he'd been sitting in prison the longest.

"Last time you told me you're thinking about it. You never told me you actually decided to take it on."

I'm sorry about that Gary… it's… it's just difficult to…"

"Trust me again?"

She nodded slowly.

"And you're upset because…?"

"It's all wrong."

"The case or me?"

She shook her head. "I'm trying to do this without you, without you even finding out about it. And it's impossible."

"Why? Because of Jake?"

Her face softened. She wiped her cheeks—with a tissue this time. "It's awful, isn't it? I get a new boyfriend, and now one of my closest friends is getting pushed out of my life."

His throat tightened again. Stupid high school drama—it never ended. At least he wasn't being beaten up behind the bleachers by the football team.

"Let me talk to him," Gary said. He hadn't seen the guy in months.

"No..." She shook her head. "I mean, yes, you can talk to him, of course. But I'm going to make the call here. You aren't your brother. I've known you for years. Even more important, we need you. If I can't trust you..." She shook her head again, then spread her hands out on top of her desk blotter and pushed backward, straightening up. "Jessie hates my guts; you know that? Because I won't magically get her out of prison. And now we have to work on this case that gives me the heebie jeebies for some reason, and I can't figure out why. And things are going well with Jake. He just moved to town a couple of weekends ago, and it's convenient, and it shouldn't mean that anything's different, but it does, and I'm fine when I see him and more than just slightly panicked when I'm not with him. This is the first time I've dated in what, two years?"

"Two years, three months and ..." he was counting the days on his fingers. "You conveniently broke up just before..."

She raised a hand. "Don't remind me. I'm ranting. I don't need facts."

A grin welled up out of his painfully tight throat.

"And I feel like everything is going so fast, and…and just keep worrying that I can't trust you to work on these cases with me, and I worry that I shouldn't ask you regardless, because of what happened last time, and what if someone gets hurt?" She turned her hands up. The fingers clasped and unclasped. She looked down at them like they belonged to someone else. "And my father—he keeps asking me if I'm going to give him grandbabies and talking about Uncle Paul like he's some kind of monster."

The hands clenched shut.

"I guess what I'm trying to say is that my head is a mess," she said. "And I need help."

He took a breath and held it. "You're letting me back in."

"Yes."

"Thank you. I thought I was going crazy. What do you need?"

"I need all the DNA in the apartment identified, and that means getting into physical evidence stored in New Hampshire and finding out who it belonged to. Alex did some digging. Someone came into the apartment and walked around—may have planted the Wilson DNA in the victim's vagina and may have altered or stolen something in the office."

He stood up, carrying his jacket and bag.

"Gary?"

"On it."

Chapter 12 -Why did I even bother to talk to you?

Downtown Portsmouth had more soul in one block than White Plains had in its entire city limits. It had the kind of downtown that other places had to hire architects to build. Brick buildings, brick sidewalks, a decided shortage of chain restaurants, one-way streets, dormer windows, awnings, parallel parking, and streetlights that looked like old oil lamps. All right, it was still designed to separate tourist chumps with as much of their cash as possible, but the shop owners seemed willing to let the pace slow down a little, be a little more enjoyable and individual—less corporate.

Jake sat outside the front of the coffee shop under some green striped awning in the late afternoon and watched tourists and college kids walking along the streets. There were lots of grandparents in t-shirts and jeans, wearing cross-body bags, and more than a few guys in their forties wearing khaki shorts and baseball caps. Even the hippies and hipsters weren't trying too hard—a lot of hoodies and headbands. A busker stood in the big brick area in front of the coffee shop, playing mostly Credence songs and doing all right with his thin, nasal voice.

He almost missed the woman he had come to meet.

Nancy Rossier had gone back to school and become a lawyer. The pictures of her from the case files showed her in baseball caps, windbreakers, and blue jeans. The woman he now saw wore a blue blouse, gunmetal gray jacket and skirt, and wore high heels—not sure if it was her. Fortunately, she glanced at him while she was pulling open the door of the coffee shop and froze for a minute.

"Mr. Westley?"

He nodded and stood up, wiping his hands on his jeans just to make sure.

"The Brooklyn Dodgers hat." She chuckled. "Dead giveaway."

He held out a hand and she shook it. In a few minutes they were walking the streets, drinking coffee and looking for an empty bench away from the busker.

"So you're looking into Kristin Walker's death," she said as they dodged around a jogger pushing a stroller down the sidewalk.

"Into Conrad Wilson's guilt," Jake corrected her.

"So you are not going to try and find her real murderer."

"Does that mean you don't think Wilson is guilty?"

She stopped walking and stared at him. He knew he had hit a nerve there, but her body language warned him to be careful if he wanted to get the information he had come for.

"At this point, it's not the priority. We have less than a month to investigate."

"We?"

"A group of people interested in justice." He spread his hands. "I know how it sounds. But it is what it is."

Her eyes narrowed, as if she had a few things to say about people who 'pursued justice' without bothering to bring in the real culprit. And she wouldn't have been wrong to say so. But she didn't dwell on it, not then. "And you're convinced Walker is innocent because…?"

"Several holes in the evidence, such as the lack of identification of anyone's DNA (except Conrad Wilson's, yours, and the victim's), some traces of blood that were tracked into the office area after the murder, and, uh..." He coughed into his hand.

"The way the semen didn't leak?" She glanced at his face and gave him half a smile. "Don't worry. You won't lose your man card over admitting that sex is messy."

"It's a delicate subject."

"Only if you're male."

"Maybe so, but to me it remains an uncomfortable topic to discuss with a lady." He shrugged. "I wanted to ask you some questions about what you saw that night. Is that all right?"

They turned the corner and the sound of 'Bad Moon Rising' faded. An open bench along the sidewalk opened up, an older couple standing up just as they approached. Jake stood beside the bench until Ms. Rossier seated herself, then sat beside her, close enough to keep anyone from sitting between them but far enough apart that it wouldn't look like he was trying to put the moves on her.

"I really don't give a damn about Conrad Wilson, Mr. Westley," she said, almost hissing like snake. "You can ask your questions. You never know when being polite to someone will pay off, and I live in the kind of profession that depends on favors. I always try to make time for good karma, but Wilson can go to hell for all I care."

Jake already knew she hated Wilson; he had to know why. "Any reason?"

She shrugged. "What did you want to ask?"

"In your original statement to the police, you mentioned something that never came up during the trial."

"The note," she said.

He gave her an admiring nod. "Exactly. The note. You said you were surprised to see it on the kitchen table."

"When I had been speaking to her on the phone, she mentioned she was writing a breakup letter, not one begging for him to run away from his wife with her."

"And yet the letter was in her handwriting."

"Yes. I saw it at the trial; the prosecution showed it to me. It was definitely her handwriting."

"So do you think the murderer forced her to write it?"

She made a strange face, almost comical, with her lips sticking out and to the side, and one cheek bitten between her teeth. She wasn't a courtroom lawyer, though—a tax lawyer if he remembered right.

"No," she said. "It sounded too much like something she would write—not *to* Wilson, but something she would write to herself, mocking herself. She was hard on herself. It didn't stop her from acting like a complete idiot. But at least she knew how bad it looked."

"Why do you think she would have written the letter?"

"Because she had to get it out of her system. Write the worst letter she could possibly think of, so when she wrote the real letter it didn't look anything like the other one."

"I'm not sure I follow."

Ms. Rossier stared out into the street as a string of slow moving cars edged their way down the narrow lane, searching for parking places and jerking to a stop every time one of the parallel spots opened up. Behind them, tourists walked past the shops. One of them shoved a fistful of garbage into a trash can. Another one locked a bicycle to a street sign. A white church steeple down the street turned almost pink in the light. Hip-hop played softly out of an upper-floor window.

"In order to write a properly scathing breakup letter, she had to write a completely humiliating run-away-with-me letter," Rossier said. "She had to really cut herself up in order to be even remotely unkind to Wilson. That's just how Kristin's mind operated."

"Ah."

"Wilson, he's charming. You've met him, I'm sure. But around women..."

"Actually I haven't met him... not yet."

She turned toward him—looked surprised, as if to say, *you want to get a man off death row but you haven't even met him*. Her eyebrows pinched together, and the odd twist of the lips happened again. She looked about two seconds from standing up and walking quickly away from him. "Why not?"

He wasn't about to go into the fact they were trying to stay under the Organization's radar. "Complications."

"Then you don't know how charming he is. It doesn't come across on the screen. You have to experience it to know what I'm talking about." Her face relaxed a little as she sank into memory. "Whatever he decides you're going to feel about him when he comes into the room, you feel that. Does that make sense?"

"No, sorry, not really."

"I struggled with it, too. I'm not easy to pull the wool over on. Being in the same room with him, it always felt like there was an itch in the back of my head—an incipient migraine, almost. There's something about me that fights people like that, and he knew it.

The looks he would give me... But Kristin would just sink under.

"When he was around, she did whatever he wanted. No questions asked. It wasn't until he was gone for a couple of hours that she seemed to come up out of his spell. His charisma always hit her particularly hard. But it worked on almost everyone. If he walked into a room—into a coffee shop or a restaurant or just down the street, whatever—it was as if everyone's conversation would get quieter and they would look at him, waiting to see what he was going to do."

"Sounds like he should have gone into politics."

"Yeah. A born politician or an actor. A young Dennis Hopper."

Jake leaned forward and put his elbows on his knees—time to bring the subject up again. "Are we barking up the wrong tree here? I mean, is he guilty?"

She ran her hands across her skirt, not suggestively, but to straighten out some invisible wrinkles. "I don't think he killed Kristin. Why would he? The second he walked into the room, she would have done whatever he wanted. I have no doubt that he could have talked Kristin into putting a gun to her own head and pulling the trigger. It might have taken a few months, but he could have destroyed her, just like that. He didn't need to brutally murder her. Where's the fun in that?"

Jake frowned at his hands. It sounded like the guy had some kind of super powers. On the other hand, maybe Ms. Rossier had dwelled on the guy for so long that her hate had taken on magical proportions.

"He should have started his own religious cult," she said bitterly. "Imagine how much fun he could have had with that."

Jake cleared his throat. He should probably wrap things up. "Who else might have had a reason to kill Ms. Walker?"

When she didn't answer right away, he looked up at her. One eyebrow was twitching; she was looking at him like he'd just spit on her. Clearly she wanted to keep ranting about Walker.

"A dozen different men," she said. "Exes. Kristin was one of those people that hypnotists love because they're so easy to put under. She would meet some loser, sleep with him until he got tired of the complete lack of challenge, and then get dumped for someone who wasn't a floor mat. She was sweet and essentially innocent and kind as hell. And she was easy. Exactly what most men claim they want in life, but when they find it they get tired of it fast enough and walk out."

Jake raised his hands. "Ms. Rossier. Anyone in particular?"

Her nostrils flared. "No."

He stood up. His coffee was empty. "Thank you for your time," he said, holding out his hand.

"Conrad Wilson can rot in hell," she said, staring with a deep hostility into his eyes, "along with every other man who ever used her."

He got the feeling he was not included in their number for some reason. Lucky him. All right. She wasn't going to shake on it, and he wasn't going to get anything else useful out of this. He nodded and let his hand fall. "Have a good evening."

She was shaking with rage when she spoke. "I'm going to get drunk, go home in a taxi, and spend the rest of the night remembering my dead friend's body on her couch, blood all over the place, and hearing one of the cops say, 'She left a suicide note' on the table. Good God, Mr. Westley. Why did I even bother to talk to you? You don't give a damn about justice for a woman splattered across her own living room. You just want to make sure that one more asshole goes free."

Chapter 13 -Like the cat who drank the cream

Jake spent the night in the cleanest Motel Six he'd ever seen in his life—as clean as a travel brochure. The floors were some kind of fake wood substitute with carpet runners over them that looked like they'd just come back from the dry cleaners. The paint on the walls was a bright blue and was, as far as he could tell, completely smudge free. The blankets on his full-sized bed looked like they'd been tucked in by obsessive compulsive sailors. The desk and chairs against the wall were cheap and vaguely Nordic, with a glass jar full of sand and seashells on top of it, with not a speck of dust or smudging on the glass. No paintings on the wall, and the window out into the parking lot was too short for the curtains; it was half the height of a normal window, chopping off just at Jake's eye level. He kept the drapes closed, ran his bug detector over the room, turned off the TV, unplugged the phone, and called Alex and Regan on the secure phone.

"Did she have anything?" Regan asked.

"Hard to tell. She hates men, that's for sure, especially men who had anything to do with her dead friend," Jake said.

"Okay."

He told them about the note and how Ms. Rossier didn't think it had been intended as anything other than a way for the victim to clear her head. He told them about the victim's other lovers, men who might have had a reason to want the girl dead, but he wasn't necessarily buying it. What reason would anyone have to kill her? She'd be an entry in a little black book, someone for a horn dog to call on a lonely night—not someone to get possessive over.

"She hated Wilson," he said. "Hated him. Said he was extremely charismatic and that he should have been a cult leader. He reminded her of a young Charles Manson—no, a young Dennis Hopper. She said something about Charles Manson but by then I was mentally checking out. She was ranting. She said he basically had the power to mind control everyone he met except her, and that's why he hated her...or something."

"Maybe he's just extremely irritating," Regan said. "The opposite of charismatic...if you're a woman, you take one look at him and decide he's pure evil."

Jake snorted. "That would be a hell of a thing to have working against you through life."

"Backpfeifengesicht," Alex said.

"Gezhundheit," Jake replied.

"It's a German word that means 'a face begging to be punched'." Alex explained to Regan.

Regan laughed. "Yes! That's it exactly. Wilson has a face begging to be punched."

Jake couldn't see it. He was just a *guy*. A guy who was sentenced to death for a crime he hadn't committed. "Let's focus here. Alex, did you come up with anything else on the case so far?"

"I spent most of my time looking at Conrad Wilson's brother, Cooper. Some unusual patterns come up in his financial records. I'm no financial wizard, but at first glance it looked as though he might be taking bribes. Expenses exceeding reported income, no new loans, that kind of thing. He's a building contractor, and a lot of money can pass under the table there, in both directions. It seems as if Cooper Wilson doesn't have a lot of impulse control.

When he suffers gains or losses on the contracting side, it's in big chunks that happen all at once. I'd say he'll be out of business in a couple of years when the IRS finally decides to audit him."

"So he's more or less clean," Jake said.

"No. Once I pulled out the data on the big chunks of money flowing under the table, which incidentally more or less evened out over time, there were still a number of smaller income inflows. I traced a few of those down more carefully and found they coincided with increased reporting of mileage on his business vehicles."

"Mmm," Regan said. "You know what that makes me think—someone delivering drugs."

"Or running some other kind of profitable errand," Alex said.

"What is the Organization like up in New Hampshire?" Jake asked.

"Uncle Paul says that it's none of his business," Regan said. "I believe him. I can just see him being that fastidious about butting into someone else's problems. Either they can handle the problems without him, or they can beg for help. In neither case would it behoove him to stick his nose in where it wasn't wanted."

"I disagree," Alex said. "I think it's much more likely that agents working for the Organization would be deeply interested in finding out everything they possibly could about other members so they could either stab them in the back or prevent themselves from being stabbed. There's no real benefit in a closed, competitive, secretive system like that in being loyal, as we saw from Gary's brother."

Regan had told Jake about having to pull Gary back into the

team, although not as a full member. Jake didn't like it, but he accepted it. As long as Lawrence, that murdering bastard, wasn't involved.

"Regardless," Jake said, "what we need to know is whether Cooper is involved in the Organization. We've seen the Organization isn't always perfect. They make mistakes. What if something went wrong here, and the real person who was supposed to be brought down was the brother, not Conrad?"

"Interesting," Alex said. "I hadn't considered that."

Regan made a dissatisfied noise in the back of her throat. "That feels wrong. Pardon my feelings. Ugh, just ignore me."

"No, what?"

"Nothing. Just... that feels like the wrong explanation. It's that whole face punching thing again. Conrad Wilson rubs me the wrong way. I just can't be rational about him."

"Noted." He flipped through a couple of channels until he found a show where a young couple was walking through a house, being led by a realtor in a suit. The scene cut to a group of workmen in white hazmat suits spraying a wall with thick white paint, then removing the entire wall. Lead paint removal, maybe. "I'm headed in to talk to Cooper Wilson in the morning as planned, unless something new comes up. Anything else I should know?"

"I'll call you if I find anything," Alex said.

"No," Regan said.

"Alex, get off the line. I need some lovey dovey time with my girlfriend."

"Roger dodger," Alex said. "Night, Regan."

"Have a good one."

The phone clicked. Jake smiled and let go of the tough guy act. Now it was time to talk to his sweetie while watching home improvement shows.

He was thinking of redecorating the apartment.

***

Portsmouth, New Hampshire, might have a lot of soul downtown, but it had some real cheap cracker boxes pretending to be million-dollar homes. The one that Cooper Wilson's company was working on looked like it had been assembled in a factory, with white siding, gray fake brickwork, a dozen different angles to the roof, and strips of sod laid out in rows in the front yard, turning brown at the edges. The windows still had stickers from the window company. Some people just had to have things that were brand new, no matter how awful they looked or how fast they fell apart.

The sidewalks were packed with tracks of mud, and the air smelled like sawdust. A few lots down, the just completed houses were replaced with bare frames and cement pads. A truck parked along the street advertised wood chips. Shrubs had been planted in front of the houses but only a layer of black plastic fluttered underneath them.

Jake parked his Corolla along the street behind the wood chip truck and walked toward the house. An argument was going on inside. It hadn't reached the let's-explore-our-breakability-options stage yet, but it had definitely passed the let's-just-calm-down-now stage.

He jogged up the sidewalk and pushed on the front door, which was slightly ajar.

The entryway contained a closet, new tile, and a side table still wrapped in plastic. A double-sided French door led into an office area with built-in bookshelves, but no other furniture. He bypassed the office and headed deeper into the house.

Two men stood toe-to-toe in the kitchen, or rather steel toed work boot to work boot. From the clean clothes and relatively unscuffed state of the boots, Jake took one of them to be management. The other one was probably the owner of the wood chip company, dressed in a dirty yellow jacket and boots that had seen better, less regulated centuries.

"You ordered bark mulch!"

"Cedar!"

"I have a signed order for bark mulch!"

"I called you on the phone and changed the order to *cedar* and you said you were going to send a new invoice because it was a quarter less per cubic foot."

"You never called me!"

"I called your office, whoever the hell I talked to, some kid!"

"You ordered bark mulch!"

"The rest of the goddamned neighborhood is cedar! What's so hard about it?"

A couple of other guys were standing around in the kitchen. When Jake walked in, they twitched and one of them raised his gristled hands. *Don't interrupt, it's not safe.*

But Jake hadn't been put on this earth to stay out of fistfights. He said, "Hello, gentlemen."

Neither one of them appeared to hear him. Jake snapped his

fingers. The managerial type glanced his way, then back toward his opponent. The volume of the shouting increased, but it sounded as though the argument was just circling around again, going nowhere.

Jake took a step closer, and the guy in the yellow jacket clenched his fist and started to raise it. Jake put his hand on the guy's fist.

The guy made eye contact. He had light blue eyes and deep crevasses in the skin around his sunburned cheeks. He smelled off, like he hadn't showered in a while, and he'd definitely been drinking.

He tried to jerk his fist out of Jake's grip, but Jake held it steady.

The guy bared his teeth, and the managerial type took a step backward.

Jake glanced back at him. "Cooper? Stay put."

Back to the guy in the yellow jacket. "Sir, now is not the time for a fistfight. Now is the time to have someone else drive you home. You're not sober."

"Don't tell *me* what to do. It was bark chips, not cedar."

"And you know, I find bark chips *very* attractive. But some people just don't get the appeal. I'd give it up as a lost cause, aesthetically."

"Stop screwing with me, kid. I can knock your block off."

"I have no doubt that I would not want you behind me in a dark alley. But right now...here...in broad daylight...while I'm ready for you? I think you might have a little bit of a problem."

"*He* called you."

"Actually, I called him. I need to talk to him about something, and he kindly agreed to meet me."

"You're on his side."

"I'm on the side of nobody taking a swing at each other. And bark chips, if it comes to that—but I think we're fighting a losing battle. Neighborhood like this, they have more money than sense. You know that."

"Cedar chips," the guy snarled with disgust. "Didn't tell *me* he wanted cedar chips."

Jake let go of the guy's fist; he lowered it. Jake patted him on the shoulder. "How about you and I take that truck of yours back to your office? I can tell it's already been a rough day."

"I'm fine." He stomped toward the door, scuffing his boots along the floor like he hoped to scratch it. But it was the same kind of flooring as had been in the hotel; the stuff must be made of diamond or something.

The managerial type put his hand on Jake's arm as he went by. "Back here in an hour, all right?"

"Sure thing."

A few minutes later, he'd convinced the guy to hand over his keys and was driving the truck full of bark chips through the streets of Portsmouth. The guy's name was Sam Olney, owner of Olney Fencing, LLC, and as fine and upstanding a man as ever lived and breathed in Portsmouth. He'd been drinking this morning, yes, but that was because, well, never you mind, turn right up ahead.

Jake followed directions and listened to the man ramble on about what a bastard Cooper Wilson was. As he wound down and started to sound like he was going to change the subject to local politics and the building codes depending thereupon, Jake said, "Wilson...isn't his brother up for the chair?"

Olney cackled. "Ayup, he is. Murdered a girl when she tried to get him to leave his wife for her. Beat her to death with a fire extinguisher for being presumptuous."

"Maybe that's why he's not being rational today."

"Mebbe so, mebbe so. But as far as I ever could tell, they weren't that close. One's a murderer, the other's a money grubbing bastard. A woman ever tried to have an affair with *him*, he'd be the one expecting the flowers and steak dinners."

***

Jake made it back to the house via a ride from Sam Olney's admin assistant, a twenty-year-old college kid who admitted that Cooper Wilson might have called to change his order and he might have missed it, although he didn't remember. The computer had been down for a week, and the slips of paper he'd been sticking all over the office in a feeble attempt to remember what was going on had a tendency to get whipped around by gusts of wind every time someone opened the door. The kid looked nervous and sad.

As Jake got out in front of the house, the kid said, "We're out of cedar chips. And I don't know if I'll have a job when I get back to the office."

"You probably have more to worry about when he wakes up from his drunk. He had the look of a man who was going to kill the rest of the day drinking and passing out."

"What am I going to do?"

"You're going to have to make up your own mind on that. You related?"

"Me? No. I just wanted a job to cover rent while I went to school."

Jake stopped with his hand on the door handle and gave the kid a serious look. "What you want to do is ask yourself, *Does Olney want help?* If the answer is no, then you don't need to help him. Give him two weeks and move on. But if the answer is yes, then you have to ask yourself whether you're the helping type, and how far you're willing to go."

The kid's dark eyebrows pinched together in the middle.

"What you *don't* want to do is hang around in the hopes that it'll all get better on its own, or that Olney will be okay until the end of the summer. He's an alcoholic who gets louder and more violent the drunker he gets. It's unfortunate and it's probably genetic. But that doesn't mean you're not putting yourself in danger."

The kid shook his head. He didn't believe it. "In danger? From Olney?"

"You better believe it." Jake opened the door and slid out of the truck. "Thanks for the ride. Remember this, though. if Olney doesn't want help, don't give it to him. You try to give an alcoholic help when he doesn't want it, you're asking for trouble. He's got no reason not to blame you for the next thing that goes wrong...for everything that goes wrong."

"Uh, okay."

Jake slammed the door. He knew he hadn't got through to the kid, but hopefully some of what he'd said would stick in his head the next time Olney got out of control. Situations like that, it was better not to get involved. Unless you had to.

Unless you were blood.

***

The air felt colder than when Jake had first arrived. It almost had a bite to it. The wind had picked up, and the air smelled fresh, coming in from the open water of the Gulf of Maine. The sky was bright blue with thin white clouds off in the distance. The leaves on the trees, where there were trees along the strip of new street, were thin and pale green, the leaves of cautious trees that had been bitten by frost later in the season than this.

The house was quiet. When Jake tried the handle of the front door, it was locked. He looked through the front windows and didn't see any movement. The street, not yet occupied by residents, had three white trucks with the Wilson name printed on the side parked along the street and his Corolla.

He stopped and listened and heard the sound of hushed conversation from off the street somewhere.

A trail of flat stones led around the side of the house. Fencing hadn't been put up yet, although the posts had been set in the ground. He followed the trail past an imaginary gate and into the back yard. The smell of fresh burning tobacco pulled him off the trail and around to the back of the house.

Cooper and his two men were on the back porch smoking. One of the two men gesticulated with his cigarette, snapping his wrist as he talked. If he didn't watch it, he was going to snap hot ash onto his boots.

Conrad Wilson was a handsome man with a broad smile; Jake couldn't get the image of Dennis Hopper out of his head now whenever he thought of the man, although he mentally removed all facial hair out of his mental picture. Cooper looked similar, although fuller in the face, with mouse brown hair, wide set eyes, a heavy brow, and a long straight nose.

Cooper's eyes locked on Jake's as he came around the corner. "Hey," he said.

Jake nodded and climbed up the steps onto the patio. There was already a wobble to the cheap wood.

"You get the old man back safe?" Cooper asked.

"And warned the kid off," Jake said. "Not that I think he'll listen. You in need of office help?"

"Not one who could lose a message like that."

Jake walked to an empty spot on the deck railing and leaned against it. The wood creaked.

"They bringing my chips?"

Jake shrugged. The guy who hadn't been gesticulating held out a package of cigarettes; Jake waved him off. "Not since high school," he said.

"Smart." The guy pulled a cancer stick out of the package with his lips, then lit it.

Cooper gave the guys a look, and they wandered off the deck and around the side of the building. "You wanted to talk to me about my brother's case?"

"A few things."

"Are you going to get him pardoned?"

"Exonerated. We're out to prove that he didn't kill the girl in the first place—in other words he is not guilty. Pardoned means you are guilty but you don't get punished. They just let you go."

Cooper's shoulders dropped an inch, and he let out a breath that Jake hadn't realized he was holding. His face broke into a deep grooved smile, and he held out a hand. Jake shook it. The resemblance between brothers was complete now. It was the same kind of devil-may-care grin.

"I thought I'd never hear it," Cooper said. "Someone looking out for my brother. I paid detectives, back in the day...but they all dried up."

Jake raised his eyebrows in question, but Cooper's eyes were looking up at the sky, past his shoulder. He shook his head. "You ask me whatever you want. Who's paying for this? Do I need to chip in?"

"It's covered."

"Must be a political thing." Cooper looked back down, a sunny expression on his face. "What do you need to know?"

"The party," Jake said. "I need to work out whether Conrad could have gotten away beforehand."

"During the party? He couldn't have. I could see him the whole time, unless he was in the bathroom, and that was maybe five minutes at a stretch. You know how it is. There's always some emergency at a party like that—just too much going on, too many people to talk to. I had crowd control, and he had everything else. If something had gone wrong—"

"Everything else?"

"He managed the caterers, the kids who were passing out drinks and appetizers, making sure the trash got picked up, the cleanup staff, and the kid who was parking cars. He was the guy who had to check the bathrooms and make sure they were holding up. You know."

"Seems odd that the positions weren't reversed."

"He wasn't as familiar with the area as I was. We were born here, of course, but he'd been away for a while. He knew most of the people there, but I know everybody. I get around."

Jake nodded. He wanted to ask the guy if he'd heard of Pavo and his crew, but it would have derailed things, regardless of the answer. Moving on. "You've covered that territory before during your statement and at the trial. What I want to know is whether he could have gotten away before the party."

"Before the party? What for?"

Jake winced a little. While Ms. Rossier had been able to discuss semen and vaginas without batting an eye, he wasn't too sure that Cooper Wilson was up for it. It might prove too distracting. "Let's just say that it might be relevant."

Cooper shrugged. Clearly the line of thought that Jake was following had never crossed his mind. "Of course he left the party. He went and picked up balloons at the party supply store."

"How long was he gone?"

"About an hour and a half."

Which, to Jake, seemed an unusually long time. How long could someone stand to wait in a party supply store without going completely insane? He said, "Did you know that your brother was having an affair with Ms. Walker, the victim?"

Cooper stuck his hands in his pockets and locked eyes on Jake. "Nope."

"Did you suspect he was having an affair, period? Remember,

your brother and his ex-wife are divorced now, and the only thing that's left to protect is your brother's life."

Cooper grinned. "You're on to me, huh? Yeah, now that it comes down to the wire... Yeah. I did think he was having an affair, but not with Walker. Or rather not *just* with Walker. Apparently he only slept with her a couple of times, but he'd been coming to Portsmouth to see Mom and Dad just a little too often for a while—nine months, maybe. Conrad...he was a ladies' man—not like me. I'm a one-woman man. Life's too short to make it that complicated. Frankly I can't be bothered. But to Conrad, it was his joy in life. Love 'em and leave 'em.

"You could tell who he was going to be sleeping with as soon as he walked into a room. He could turn on the charm like a flood lamp. All you had to do was glance over the women's faces. Some of them couldn't stand him at first sight. Some of them looked at him like he was an interesting work of art... You know, the same way some men look at women, like, 'I'd do that if the chance came up, but I'm not going out of my way for it.' But some of the women, married or not, their faces would light up when they saw him. God's gift to women...some women."

"So you think Ms. Walker was a target of opportunity?"

Cooper chuckled. "I like that. Yeah, a target of opportunity. A quick and easy piece of ass on the side of his piece of ass on the side. I don't know how Penny put up with it for as long as she did."

"Do you think he could have been seeing his main squeeze in the window of time he was picking up balloons?"

"Do I think he was? I know he was. He came back looking like the cat who drank the cream."

"Do you know who she was?"

"Not a clue."

"Is there any way you could find out?"

"Other than just asking him? No. He'd been doing this for years at this point. He was a complete professional at keeping his trail clean so Penny wouldn't find out. If he hadn't been arrested for murder, she never would have either."

Chapter 14 - Three witnesses

Two pm and the parking lot of the big white clapboard house that had been converted into a steak sandwich place was still full. Jake parked on the street a couple of blocks away. The wind was blowing toward him, and he caught a face full of tomatoes, oregano, French bread, and beef. Even the smell of open water coming in couldn't carry it away fast enough.

Two ancient Rolls Royces were parked at the far end of the parking lot, which butted up against an empty lot crowded with trees and bramble. Jake crossed the parking lot to the building, entering under a green plastic awning. Nobody was standing outside waiting in line, a good sign. He opened the door and went in.

The outer walls were covered with wood paneling, dartboards, and tiny holes. The interior walls had been torn out and replaced with black support beams. The floor had more green and white checked tile than any hundred people could play checkers on. The specials had been drawn in neon marker on a plastic blackboard—sangria and lobster rolls. The bar was separate from the food counter, attended by an enormous blonde with arms as big as most men's thighs. She had a big smile and hard blue eyes. At the bar in front of her were two cops in green uniform shirts and olive pants.

The last group of people Jake needed to meet were the three cops who had been at the party and testified so blatantly in Wilson's favor it had made the judge and jury so suspicious they had to look deeper to find the lie that must be hidden underneath.

Two of them—the ones he was meeting now—were still on the local force and were willing to talk to Jake before their shift started at three thirty. The third had left the force shortly after Wilson had been sentenced and was working as a private security guard. Interestingly, over the phone he'd refused to meet with Jake—flat out refused, either with or without the other two.

One of the cops, an older gentlemanly type, turned to look as Jake got closer. Jake held out a hand. "Jake Westley, private investigator." He didn't bother to show them his license; either they would trust him or they wouldn't.

"So it wasn't just your normal BS," the bartender said. "Huh."

"Clark Turnbull, at your service," said the first cop. He looked at least six feet tall and had silver hair along the sides of his head, with a light brown comb-over on top. He shook Jake's hand with a firm but essentially neutral grip.

The second introduced himself as Dan Stenberg. He was a foot shorter and had blond hair and a round face with narrow-set, ugly eyes. He'd tucked his pants into the tops of his shiny black boots and had hung his handcuffs prominently off a loop of his belt. Jake immediately labeled him as one of the top ten police officers he hoped never to be pulled over by after midnight.

The blonde bartender led them over to a vacant table in the middle of the room, Turnbull taking a beer with him to his chair. Jake had no doubt the man would be sober as a judge by the time his shift started.

The woman laid plastic menus in front of them, snapping the edges on the wood tabletop as she put each of them down. The two officers ordered without looking. Jake glanced past the appetizers and soup-n-salad sections, then ordered a super steak special.

"Excellent choice," the bartender said, then swept the menus off the table as professionally as an Atlantic City casino dealer. She walked over to the front counter and gave the order to a kid in a pink shirt at the counter.

"Conrad Wilson," Turnbull said. "Off to the chair, he is." His voice was a low rumble.

"Yeah," Stenberg added with an expression of satisfaction. "It's not electricity, though—lethal injection. And you lay on a stretcher—no chair. But yeah, essentially, he's headed for the chair."

Turnbull rolled his eyes in slow motion as he reached for his beer. He apparently had a literal sloth somewhere in his genetics. Every movement was slow and considered. Maybe he was already drunk.

"I thought he was a buddy of yours," Jake said.

Turnbull rumbled, "Just because a man is on the Force doesn't mean he's worth a damn."

"Yeah, and that's Turnbull talking." Stenberg sneered. "If guys like us can see that—"

Turnbull lifted the tips of his fingers, and Stenberg cut off. "I'm babbling," he said suddenly. "Fact is, Conrad Wilson and I didn't get along. Turnbull liked him better than I did."

"That is true."

"But I can't say that either one of us liked him a whole lot."

Turnbull didn't disagree with that statement. Jake said, "The party."

"What about it?"

"You said he didn't leave it."

"That's right, he didn't," Stenberg said, "as our statements reported at great length."

Jake said, "Yeah, that was what I wanted to talk to you about—the great length. The two of you went on in far, far greater length than was necessary."

"So?"

"So I think it was one of the reasons the judge and jury were so suspicious of Wilson—the lengths to which you went to support the guy, minute by minute, as well as where the other cars were."

"Never let it be said we don't support each other on the Force, whether or not we like the guy," Stenberg said.

"So if Wilson wasn't the guy who left the party to head out into the fog, the guy that Ms. Rossier followed for a few miles, who was it?"

Stenberg shrugged. His face had spread into a predator's grin. Jake got the feeling the guy had too many teeth.

"No idea."

Jake turned to the other man. "What about you, Officer Turnbull?"

"I'm afraid I have no conjectures at this time."

Jake squinted at him. He was too thin and narrow, and Jake had a hard time imagining that anyone could mistake Turnbull for Wilson unless both of them were wrapped in NASA space suits. As far as Jake had been able to tell from the few videos, Wilson walked and moved like a normal guy, not a sloth. But maybe.

"Aren't you about the same height and general build as Wilson?"

"He is much broader than I am," Turnbull said, "as well as

several inches shorter."

"Yeah, and Wilson walks and talks like a normal person," Stenberg added.

The enormous blond bartender brought them a pitcher of ice water, a stack of red plastic glasses, a pile of napkins, and some plastic utensils. "Back in a sec with your food, boys."

"Thanks, Marge," Stenberg said. She winked at him.

"Were you there the entire time the party went on?" Jake asked Turnbull.

"Yes," Turnbull said. "I was present and accounted for the entire length of the party. I arrived at six thirty and did not depart until the police arrived at approximately nine o'clock. When I did depart, I left with the police. I returned for my car at one am in the morning."

It was almost word for word from his official statement, as well as the trial transcripts.

"You?" he asked Stenberg.

"Me? I'm five foot four and I weigh a hundred and ninety pounds."

"Tell me anyway."

"I went out for a couple of smokes," Stenberg said, "outside where nobody could see me unless they also were smoking. I went twice. There was nobody else there."

"How long were you gone?"

"Fifteen minutes, tops. Not long enough to drive from the house to the victim's apartment, let alone bang her, beat her to death, and get back before someone else noticed I was missing."

***

The meal seemed to stretch on endlessly. The sandwich he'd ordered was good, but watching Turnbull work his way through his beer, moving and talking and *chewing* in slow motion started to get on his nerves. But finally it was over. He paid, and he fled the scene.

Neither one of the two cops struck him as a criminal mastermind, but they hadn't struck him as sharing any kind of *esprit de corps* with Wilson either, which in Jake's experience was rare. He got in his car and waited until he saw the two of them come out of the restaurant at a snail's pace. Stenberg's mouth moved without pause. He'd spent most of the meal talking about Wilson and what he'd been like on the force—a real stuck-up snob, if Stenberg was to be believed, which Jake didn't. He'd also had a few choice words to say about the third cop who'd been with them at the party, Jay Hatchell, who was apparently a real stick in the mud and an overachiever who lived by the book and sucked up to people because he actually respected them and not because he was trying to brownnose. In Stenberg's world, you could and should brownnose if you had to; that was just office politics. But respecting a guy like Wilson, who was just plain rude, didn't sit well with him. Jake rolled his eyes as the two of them got into the same marked local police car. He'd spent most of the meal restraining himself. At least Stenberg took the driver's seat.

He thought about following them but blew it off. They would be heading for the police station, just two old friends reporting in to work. The smell on Turnbull's breath would be dismissed—business as usual.

He checked his phones, both of which he'd turned off during the meeting. The secure phone seemed almost to accuse him of wasting time. What had he found out today? Not a whole hell of a lot. He checked his regular phone; someone had left a message.

The third cop. Jay Hatchell.

He wanted to meet with Jake at four at the same place Jake had met with Ms. Rossier.

Hey. Excellent choice.

***

The coffee shop was hopping, packed with students hunched over laptops, guarding tables from the tourists. The tourists were just as happy to drink their coffee outdoors today. It had really warmed up since the morning and the wind had died down. In fact, it had become one of those classic spring days that made you dig out the short pants and go on a picnic. He comforted himself with the knowledge that White Plains was just as ugly as always and he could take Regan out tomorrow if the weather held—if she'd let him. It would depend on whether he dug anything up.

Jake took a look around, trying to pick out Hatchell from the crowd. But there were a number of guys who would have fit the bill—square jawed and wary, handsome in a Charlie Sheen kind of way, except obviously more of a straight arrow and less of an asshole. No wonder he'd never gotten along with Turnbull and Stenberg. Ah, never mind. He didn't want to dwell on those guys anymore. He'd met lots of good cops. It was just that working on these exoneration cases naturally brought him into contact with more of the bad ones. It would be like assessing the character of a Special Forces unit based on the guys who had been court martialed.

One of the guys carefully kept his eyes off Jake as he walked through the coffee shop. He looked young, college age except for the lines around his eyes. He wore a UNH hoodie and typed furiously on his laptop. He had no headphones on, and the corners of his eyes kept tightening up. Jake would have put his money on this guy, no question.

Jake walked to the counter and ordered a cup of coffee. He'd never gotten into the latte craze. He appreciated it—it was what put a Starbucks or some local coffee shop on every corner—but the idea of spiking his coffee with milk and sugar syrup had never really appealed. He sometimes added some cream, that was it.

He paid up. The guy in the UNH hoodie had packed up his laptop and was standing up, slinging a messenger bag over his shoulder. Jake walked out of the coffee shop and waited outside the door.

UNH hoodie man came up beside him and stuck out a hand, which Jake shook and released quickly. The two of them walked along the sidewalk to the end of the block, turned, and passed the bench where Jake and Ms. Rossier had seated themselves the day before. At the end of *that* block Hatchell turned again, leading them alongside a main thoroughfare, loud with traffic and busy with eyes. But there was no parking along the road. Anyone pulling over to watch them would stick out like a sore thumb.

"Hi," Hatchell said finally. Even though he was three or four inches shorter than Jake, he was walking too quickly for Jake to drink any of his hot coffee without burning himself. Jake decided not to screw with the guy's pace. He didn't need coffee as much as he needed to ask questions anyway.

"Jake Westley."

"Jay Hatchell."

"Pleased to meet you."

Hatchell's gaze swung from side to side as they walked. "Look, I know they're not on patrol on this side of town—they're not supposed to be on patrol on this side of town. It's a pain, you know? So they manage to get assigned somewhere else most of the time. But that doesn't mean that someone couldn't casually mention that they've seen me walking around downtown. So let's keep this short."

"Is there somewhere else you'd like to meet?"

"Keep it short."

Feeling like he was back in the Delta Force talking to a local contact under the nose of some warlord, Jake said, "I want to know why the three of you went nuts testifying that Conrad Wilson didn't leave the party."

"You caught that. Good. I won't ask who you're involved with or why you're doing this. Let me state this clearly. Conrad Wilson did not leave that party once it had started. The three of us arrived at six thirty. I made it a point to keep an eye on him throughout the entire affair."

"Why?"

"Because I didn't care for the guy."

"Why?"

"It doesn't matter. He just rubs some people the wrong way. I suspected him of something—it turned out to be nothing. But I was in the mood to hold it against him, just enough to hope he was doing something stupid that I could report."

"Okay. You watched him all night."

"Until the cops arrived to arrest him."

"And he didn't leave."

"I watched him go into the toilet, I watched him come out. He never stepped off the property."

"Got it. What about before the party?"

"Couldn't say. I wasn't there. It sounds like I would have had more luck then; he was missing for about an hour and a half. I suspected he was having an affair with someone in Portsmouth—not Ms. Walker, but someone."

"Another question," Jake said. "Did either of your two associates leave the party?"

"I don't know. I wasn't keeping an eye on either of them. Stenberg smokes like a chimney. He was in and out all night anyway."

"Is Turnbull an alcoholic?"

"Looks that way. He wasn't as bad back then, just an after work happy hour kind of guy. I hear he's worse now, going downhill."

"Do you think that either of them are lying somehow?"

"Misdirecting. I think they wanted to bring attention to Wilson for some reason. They were careful not to make any accusations. They were careful to look like they were his best friends on God's green earth."

"Why?"

"No idea."

An unmarked van swerved in the lane opposite them, and Hatchell glanced at it, then resumed looking back and forth, trying to take in everything but really just swinging his head back and forth. If you wanted to see everything, you kept your head straight forward and let your peripheral vision do the work.

"What made you leave the force?" Jake asked.

Hatchell glanced toward him, then away again. His jaw clenched several times. "I don't like to talk about it, but I was strongly encouraged to leave. They found porn in my locker. Bad stuff. There was talk about having me charged with something."

"Not yours, I take it."

"No."

"Do you feel like you knew something you weren't supposed to know? That you had seen something someone didn't want you to see?"

Hatchell snorted. "I felt like I was being followed everywhere I went. Every phone call I made had some kind of clicking noise in the background. My lights flickered...I got stuck in elevators all the *time*. It was crazy. My girlfriend got a couple of threatening letters in the mail from a guy she used to know in high school but never dated, telling her that if she knew what was good with her, she'd break up with me. My dog was hit by a car.

"Everybody said I was going crazy, cracking under the strain. I wasn't mean to be a cop, you see. At least that's what they started to say. So I left."

"Why didn't you—"

"Apply for jobs in another town? I did. Jobs dried up. People who were less qualified got hired. My guess is that some rumors went around. In the end I took what I could get."

They crossed a street. Hatchell stopped in the middle of it to glare angrily at an unmarked white van parked along the side of the road. He waved at it. "See? See? They're still following me. I can't get away from them."

"From who?"

"No idea. Them, all right? Just *them*."

Hatchell did an about face and started walking the other way. Jake turned to join him. Hatchell looked over his shoulder, face stiff with anger. "Our interview is at an end, sir. I hope you have better luck than I do. God help you if they start following you around."

Jake walked back to the sidewalk and waited as Hatchell strode down the block. The unmarked van started up, pulled into the street, and signaled for a left turn to follow him.

The traffic kept it blocked for a long time, but eventually it was able to pull out onto the road. By then Hatchell had disappeared. Jake waited until it was out of sight, then returned to his car.

He wasn't followed.

Chapter 15 - The lady doth protest too much

Uncle Paul was a public servant, the guy who ran the sewers across the city. It was an important job but not one on a level with, say, the head of a major world corporation. And yet his office was a luxury penthouse on the top of a Manhattan skyscraper. Why nobody thought this was remarkable was beyond Regan. He had security guards. His secretary had a bigger office than hers and Gary's put together. The rent was probably astronomical.

It was all very cool and modern. The walls of the building were slightly curved and seemed to ripple. The wood flooring looked like it sucked up the sunlight and spat it out as a warm, golden, happy feeling. The air smelled as clean and pure as if it were a windy day in the dead of winter in northern Canada. The views? Incredible. The kind of views you got in movies—not real life.

Uncle Paul stood as she came in, his face as enigmatic as ever. Behind him was a view of Brooklyn, then open water. He came around the desk and led her to a small conversational grouping deeper within the room, uncomfortable looking, tan linen chairs. The coffee table looked like it had grown directly out of the floor, with the "feet" of the table bending out of the wood flooring.

"Hello, my dear," he said.

She gave him a hug, feeling the cool skin of his cheek against hers. "Uncle Paul."

He stepped back and smiled at her, the smile looking no warmer or friendlier than his normal face. It was like that saying, *'Keep making the same face and it'll get stuck that way.'* "Have you come to tell me that you're going to join the Organization?"

"Don't you start too," she said.

"Excuse me?"

"My father wanting to know if I'm going to give him grandchildren any time soon. And now you with the Organization. The answers are no and no."

He gestured toward a square chair with a stiff linen covered back. She sat; the chair was far more comfortable than it looked. When she leaned back, the chair gave slightly, inviting her to relax.

Uncle Paul said, "That is a shame on both counts. You should consider that primiparous over the age of forty generally tend to have more medical issues. It would be better to have a child sooner rather than later—when it's too late."

"My biological clock can tick all it wants."

He sat across from her, plucking at the knees of his trousers to keep the folds neat, and stayed leaning forward. "As you wish. If, however, you have decided not to personally bear any children, have you considered donating ova? Your genetics are excellent, really excellent."

She crossed her legs at the knee, straightened the knees of her pants, and fixed Uncle Paul with the *Look*.

He cleared his throat and looked away for a moment, then leaned back in his seat, as if to acknowledge that the pushy part of the conversation was over. "My apologies. We old men often get carried away with these things, you understand."

"I understand. But enough is enough. I'm almost ready to think that the two of you are in cahoots to make my life difficult."

"We merely want what is best for you."

She rolled her eyes. "You've stated your respective cases. Duly noted."

He nodded, then glanced out the window for a moment, looking both momentarily younger and more worried. "Part of the problem with successfully building an empire is that one is continuously looking for an heir who won't be a disgrace—who shares the same values."

"I'm not that heir," Regan said.

Uncle Paul waved his fingertips, then brought his gaze back to her. "I'm sorry. I've been distracted today. What have you come to see me about, if not childbirth or the Organization? The only other area of expertise that I have is on sewers, and I trust that you aren't in straits that requires knowledge of how *they* operate. No matter how noble the aims with regard to sewers, there is always the smell and other less savory elements."

She shook her head. "I said I didn't want to join the Organization, but it is about the Organization."

His eyebrows rose.

"We have decided to look into the Conrad Wilson case that's coming up in New Hampshire."

"Ah. And you wish to query whether the Organization is involved, while ensuring your father cannot hear what response I make."

"In essence, yes."

"That is a wise decision, and in fact, I anticipated there was a strong possibility you might make it sooner or later, and have gone to the trouble of doing some research on the subject."

"Thank you."

"Is there a reason for you to be wary of the Organization in this case?" Uncle Paul said.

"Not particularly. I just wanted to make sure we weren't stepping on your toes... give you a head's up." She took a deep breath. "Also, I keep trying to talk myself out of helping Wilson. I tell myself there's no rational reason to feel the way I do, and then... it's one of those 'the lady doth protest too much' situations, really."

"Shakespeare," Uncle Paul said. "Gertrude speaking to her son Hamlet, Act Three, upon the implication that her theatrical doppelganger makes herself suspicious by over protesting her fidelity. Yes, I see. Are you faithful to justice? That is *your* question."

He settled back into the chair, his eyelids sinking half-closed. Regan did the same, letting herself enjoy the chair, the feeling of wealth and power that filled the room. What would it be like, to control the resources that Uncle Paul had?

Besides being a devil's bargain?

"Would you like any refreshments?" Uncle Paul asked. "A game of chess later, perhaps?"

"Coffee and chess afterwards," she said.

"Excellent." He steepled his fingers in front of himself. "Have you ever heard how your father and I became friends?"

"At college."

"Yes, but more specifically, we happened to be college roommates. But, as you may know, often times one's college roommates are quickly forgotten or left behind."

Her lips tightened a fraction. He continued.

"Friendship is an entirely different matter. We were brought together by our neighbors across the quad. We quickly discovered that we could look out of our window in our dormitory at Columbia into the room of two young men who had apparently decided upon lives of petty crime. We bonded over their exploits."

"He did mention that, actually, the last time I saw him. He seemed upset about it."

"I think he was unhappy about how it all came out—both in what happened to the young men, and how I reacted to it. Did he tell you that?"

"No, he said it was a story to tell another day."

"Ah," Uncle Paul said, half of the world's smallest smile on his lips. "In short, he wanted me to take action in order to prevent tragic consequences, and I did nothing."

"How so?"

"The two young men had begun selling illicit substances from their dorm room. This was before the craze for marijuana had really begun, you understand, and before it had become an illegal drug under the Controlled Substances Act. It was, nevertheless, forbidden on the campus.

"The two young men sold marijuana, heroin, and a new drug that came to be known as LSD—perhaps other drugs as well. I'm not sure. Over the course of the year, it became increasingly obvious that one of them was skimming the profits from the other, who was becoming increasingly addicted to heroin. I refused to inform the authorities. Your father tried to guilt me into doing so multiple times but failed."

"Why didn't he rat on them, since you wouldn't?"

"Oh, he did. They were quite clever. The evidence always seemed to disappear before anyone in authority could investigate. I suspect they had a friend in the campus security department. Your father was eventually told to stop harassing them."

Regan frowned. "Then what made him think that you could do anything about it?"

"I have my ways," he said. "At any rate, the young man who was skimming profits was caught at it by the young man who was addicted to heroin. The two young men left their dorm room to continue their conversation in a more private location. One of them shot the other. The police gave chase and drove the other, who had stolen the car they were using, into the Hudson. He either died from a gunshot wound or from drowning, I can never remember which."

"Daddy said it was a car accident."

Uncle Paul's eyes tightened, pulling the wrinkles subtly across his face, deepening the hollows under his cheeks and the dark circles under his eyes. "A prevarication—almost, but not quite, a lie. One thinks of your father as a man of integrity, but there is a subtlety to it that one can't quite anticipate."

Regan shrugged.

Uncle Paul blinked twice, then cleared his throat. "Your father blamed me for their deaths. Rather, he blamed me for not attempting to prevent them."

One of his hands made a gesture in the air that reminded her of a man about to lift a burning cigarette to his lips. He caught himself, flicked his fingers, then steepled both hands together again. She'd never thought about the gesture before—but maybe he'd done it to help keep himself from smoking cigarettes.

"Our friendship continued until your mother died, and for a few years afterwards. It really only collapsed as it became clear that you had no need of our continued presence in each other's lives. But the seeds of the end came from that first year in college, perhaps even the first day. The end, as it often is, was contained within the beginning."

"That's sad," she said. She didn't really know what else to say.

"It is," he agreed. "But you haven't come here to mourn the death of an old friendship or to celebrate its awkward resurrection. You would like the information that I was able to obtain from my Organization sources about the Conrad Wilson situation."

She nodded. Uncle Paul had dragged her completely off the rails, and she hadn't even noticed. "Yes, please."

The fingertips tapped together; his eyelids fluttered. He would sometimes make the same face in the middle of a chess game, when he was trying to remember what games the moves he was about to use had been previously used in. He already knew how to win—he was merely retrieving the necessary information to coach Regan through her defense.

"The member of the Organization that I know in New Hampshire is a rather unpleasant woman," he said. "I feel that she has entirely the wrong philosophy about her stewardship, which she uses as a means of gaining power rather than caring for her constituents, as it were."

Regan raised her eyebrows and looked around the room.

"I have acquired power and reputation as a result of caring for those I oversee," Uncle Paul said, letting his eyes slide around the room. They fixed on nothing in particular, didn't reflect pride or even a real appreciation of possession. Then they returned to rest on her face. "They have never been my goal—merely a means to an end."

"If you say so."

"I do say it. If you chanced to meet her, it would make more sense. Regardless, what I have learned is that the Organization was not directly involved in the arrest and conviction of Conrad Wilson. In fact, the Organization would be pleased if I took a personal interest in the matter. They seem to think that Conrad Wilson would be a benefit to the Organization if he were able to be freed."

Regan felt her jaw clench and her hands stiffen at her sides. She forced herself not to cross them over her chest. "A benefit to the Organization? What kind of benefit? As a drug runner?"

"The Organization is involved in more than the drug trade."

"What, then? Prostitution?"

The Organization sounded great in theory, at least when Uncle Paul talked about it—a secret organization that added order to the chaos of the world. But in reality it was just one more group of scumbags out to make a buck off of someone else's misery and shift the consequences from the guilty to the innocent.

"You have created an erroneous picture of what the Organization does on a routine basis, I fear."

"Tell me the Organization is uninvolved in prostitution. Just tell me."

He flicked the fingers of one hand. It wasn't important for the conversation. "An intelligent man such as Conrad Wilson could be used in multiple capacities. As a detective, he would make an excellent influence in the legal system and with other police officers. As an intelligent human being, his understanding and assessment of difficult situations could be valuable in leading or advising others. As a father he might be..." Uncle Paul winced. "...an excellent provider and teacher to his children, generally improving the intelligence levels in the world."

"A sperm donor to breed a super race, you mean."

Uncle Paul rolled his eyes like a teenager, his chin tilting upward. "You are in the most irritating mood today, my dear. I wish you would learn to process unpleasant ideas in a more graceful and internalized manner, rather than lashing out at people who might be able to provide you some assistance. You're the dog that bites the hand of the master, I swear."

She smiled and bared her teeth. Unfortunately, he wasn't looking. "You said that the Organization wasn't directly involved in his arrest...does that mean the Organization was indirectly involved?"

Uncle Paul's head returned to an upright position, eyes fastened on her and eyebrows slightly lifted. "As a matter of fact, I'm not completely sure. My point of contact assured me that the Organization was uninvolved, even tangentially. However, from the way she stressed the issue, it sounded as though she wouldn't have allowed the Organization to touch the man with a ten-foot pole. That may mean that someone was involved to have him arrested and framed to cover someone else, or that the man is already involved in the Organization in some capacity but under the aegis of another manager, or even that my contact finds him personally repugnant for some reason. It did feel as though, as you say, the lady doth protest too much. Although I strongly suspect that the probability of her fidelity to the concept of justice is rather smaller than yours."

Chapter 16 - Regan's fox

Regan stared out her window and watched birds swooping in and out of trees along the streets. Tiny black specks swooped into the sky, out of sight along the road, then back up into view, at which point they looped and dove into the thick leaves on the trees, bringing insects back to their nests.

She couldn't hear them; the only sounds in her office were the soft hiss of the air vents, blowing out cool air rather than warm now, and the sound of Gary typing in the other room, his fingers buzzing along.

Outside, bees would be harvesting pollen from flowers. Insects would be laying eggs and chewing on leaves. Birds would be collecting insects and worms for their young. Spiders would be catching flies...

She sighed. She'd been thinking about justice again, and how uncomfortably close to a predator she had to be sometimes.

"Gary?"

"Yes, hon?"

"Dial up Laura Provost for me."

She could have done it herself, but she wanted Gary to know she trusted him with the information, and to give him the opportunity to record the call, if he wanted it.

Laura Provost worked for the District Attorney's office in Brooklyn, an Assistant D.A. She had proven both corrupt and useful in the Andy Gibbons case, a contradiction that sometimes made Regan's head hurt. Could you be both corrupt and genuinely part of the engines of justice? If so, what did that mean for the concept of justice—*was* justice, as a pure idea, corrupt?

She reached for her desk drawer and went as far as to put her hand on the smooth silver handle to open the drawer where her ibuprofen was kept, when Gary said, "I have her on line one."

She let go of the handle and picked up the handset. "Laura? It's Regan from White Plains."

"Regan," Laura said in her icy voice, a voice that made Uncle Paul sound warm and compassionate. "What a pleasure it is to hear from you."

The tone of her voice seemed like a threat—either make it profitable for Ms. Provost in the next five seconds, or face the consequences. Regan smiled. She had a hold on Provost, and they both knew it.

"An opportunity has come up, and I thought of you," Regan said.

"Oh?"

"The Conrad Wilson case."

There was a few seconds pause on the other end of the phone, long enough for Regan to lean forward and peek out the door of her office and look at Gary. Behind his high-sided reception desk, she could only see his close-trimmed head, upraised black eyebrows, and mischievous eyes.

"An opportunity," Provost said. "Of what sort?"

"Of the exoneration sort," Regan said. "Additional information may be available."

"For a price, I presume." Provost said.

"Don't be ridiculous," Regan said. "For a small favor down the road, perhaps. Are you interested? I'll buy lunch."

Provost made a thoughtful noise from the back of her throat. Regan thought she heard a soft click, not the kind of sound that the phone made when Gary started monitoring and recording the line, but as if a door had opened.

"Lunch," Provost said brightly. "Not today, of course. Too far a drive! But I'd be delighted to meet with you tomorrow, if you like, in White Plains. I've never been, you see. You'll have to recommend a good place for lunch."

"Excellent," Regan said. "Why don't you meet me at the Westchester County Court building at eleven, and I'll drive after that? And what kind of restaurant? Any allergies?"

"Oh, I'm not allergic to anything but calories, and I make a rule never to count them when out of town. I like French, if there is such a thing as a decent French restaurant in White Plains." Provost gave a bright, tinkling, and utterly artificial laugh. It sounded like smashed glass falling out of a window frame.

Regan forced a broad smile onto her face. "I know just the place."

***

Regan hadn't been to *La Ruche* for months. She'd gone there a little too often with Jake to discuss Andy Gibbons' case and had attracted a little too much attention. But the discussion with Provost had made it practically a mandate for her to go.

When the phone rang, telling her Provost was at the front desk waiting for her (ten minutes late), she gave Gary a look that wasn't quite an eye roll but was definitely a plea for sympathy.

"I don't see what the problem is," he said. "You're going to your favorite restaurant for lunch, the one that you've been holding yourself back from for months. Just because sweet lover boy isn't going with you doesn't mean you can't enjoy it."

"But Provost," she said.

"I wouldn't want to be lunching with her either," Gary admitted. "But we all have to put on our big-girl pants sometimes, don't we?"

She flashed him a smile, slung her black canvas briefcase over her shoulder, and took the elevator downstairs. Lately, she'd been doing more stairs—but probably coming down to meet Provost with a glow to her cheeks and a slight whiff of exertion would be a bad idea.

The inside of the elevator was paneled with brushed silver metal panels, not quite mirrors, that reflected the shapes of the passengers back to them. The panels weren't quite flat, and had a tendency to distort her shape like a funhouse mirror.

She saw herself first as an incredibly tall, thin woman—far taller than her already almost six feet in height, not counting her half-inch heeled shoes. Unfortunately, the wall panel distorted her head along with the rest of her, and she looked more like a gray-skinned alien with her stretched out head and dark blue eyes than a supermodel. Then the elevator stopped and let one of the clerks from the fourth floor on, a man she recognized but didn't know. She had to shift to the side to make room. Her shape wavered and became much shorter, bulging in the middle. She had become a pregnant dwarf, rotund and presumably happy. Not to mention how happy it would have made her dad if that image in the mirror was real.

She leaned from side to side as the elevator sank, trying to find some kind of happy medium, or at least her own natural reflection, but the elevator panels didn't cooperate.

Finally, it reached the ground level, and they both got off. Provost was waiting at the reception desk for her, toes turned outward and her leather briefcase flat on top of the desk as if she'd slammed it there. Her hair had been dyed dark brown and cut in a straight bob across her shoulders, with blunt, subtly under curled bangs to go with it. Her face was narrow, sharp and foxlike—a long nose that just barely turned up at the end. *All the better for sniffing out advantages with.*

On the one hand, Regan found the woman humorless and unpleasant.

On the other hand, it was probably better for society as a whole that she worked for the state and not as a private defense lawyer. Once again, justice was served. Maybe.

Sort of.

Regan walked over to her and held out a hand. Provost let go of her briefcase, narrowed her eyes at the security guard (as if she were about to snatch the case off the desk and make a run for it), and then turned to face Regan. A hand was extended slowly and almost rudely. The handshake was limp and cool, more of a brushing of Provost's fingertips—or a kissing of her ring that Regan had gotten completely wrong—than anything else.

"Laura," she said.

"Regan, so glad to see you."

"Shall we?"

"I've been looking forward to it all morning."

Provost had used Andy Gibbons' case to claw her way up the ladder in her office—not a full rung to taking the actual D.A. position, but a fractional rung, edging herself just slightly past one of her competitors for the post should the current D.A. ever step down. She'd had to be forced by Regan and Jake into pursuing justice for Andy—but it had profited her.

Of course she was looking forward to talking to a two-bit judge at a second rate French restaurant in White Plains. She knew she'd like the taste.

***

La Ruche was busy, and they had to wait a few moments in the lobby before they were seated. Provost looked around at the Art Nouveau ads on the walls, all green demons holding liquor bottles, women with long hair in chiffon robes presenting cups of coffee, and foul tempered black cats.

The maître-d' kept giving Regan nervous looks. First, one of the regulars, famous for coming to the restaurant alone and eating almost exactly the same meal, almost every day, starts coming *and bringing a complete dish of a man with her*, and smiling and chatting pleasantly. Then they both disappear. Then the regular reappears with a humorless woman carrying a briefcase. This, the maître-d' seemed to say with her nervous glance, could be trouble.

Regan smiled at her. The lobby smelled heavenly, buttery pastry and rich onion soup. Her stomach growled. She edged over to the woman and said, "If possible, could the two of us have a table...off to the side?"

Jake had bribed a waitress to move them away from the other tables once. She didn't quite have the nerve for that.

"It may take a few more minutes," the woman said.

Regan let her eyes slide back to Provost, who sneered at a Lautrec poster of a can-can woman kicking up her heels. "That's fine."

The woman pressed her lips together and nodded. *The regular requested a favor...the situation may prove troublesome, but the tips would be good for whomever was willing to deal with it...*

In a few minutes, the two of them were seated against the wall, with at least a single table between them and the occupied ones in all directions. The place was too busy for them to have anything further away—but subsequent tables were being filled on the other side of the room now. Regan made a mental note to make up for the tips at the other tables their waitress would be missing because of them.

Provost sneered at the menu, which—for lunch—was a double-sided laminated sheet of cardboard. Fortunately, she kept her opinions unvoiced, if not exactly hidden, and the waitress took their order without suffering from anything more than a slightly sarcastic lilt to Provost's voice.

Regan ordered her usual, French onion soup and a chicken salad on a croissant. *Oh, yes. It was going to be brilliant eating here. It was probably safe to come back on a regular basis.* She'd have to check with Jake, but...

She pulled herself back on track. She had unpleasant business to conduct.

"So," she said.

"The Conrad Wilson case," Provost said, eyeing the room. At one point the building had been a barn. The wood beams from the loft overhead still remained, although the room was open all the way up. The white plaster added to the rustic feel. "I'm assuming you have some solid evidence that he didn't do it. Otherwise, this meeting has already been a waste of my time."

Once again, Regan had to remind herself that she had adequate blackmail material on this woman to control her for the rest of their lives, and that the woman was confrontational and rude by nature. She picked up her cup of coffee and sipped it.

"Two points of interest," Regan said. "First, we've been able to use some new technology to establish the person who tracked the blood into the victim's office was not the murderer or one of the victim's friends—a third party heretofore unsuspected. Also, we should be able to prove that the semen found in the victim's vagina was placed there after her death."

Provost's eyelids fluttered, then tightened. She drummed her polished mauve fingertips on the tablecloth. "Those two facts, if true, might have helped us get him released—if we had more time. In order to make this a sure thing, we need more."

"I am aware of that," Regan said.

"Do you think you can get anything in time?"

"I don't know," Regan said. "I have a few good people working on it."

The end of Provost's foxlike nose twitched. "I know this is bad form...but you mean that you have people in the Organization working on it, right?"

Regan shrugged, trying to repress a smirk. She didn't need to confirm or deny. It wasn't like they were actually doing each other an exchange of favors. Provost would have to do what Regan told her to do, regardless. "It's not material. We're going to keep digging until either it's too late, or we have the information we need. The question is, will you be ready to bring the information to the courts in New Hampshire? Or are there additional contacts you need to make?"

"I could use another contact in the Organization," Provost said.

"And I could use a pony," Regan said disgustedly. "Is there anything you actually *need*, or are you just grubbing around for what you can get?"

Provost's lips thinned into a narrow mauve line, and unattractive wrinkles lined up between her eyebrows. "No."

"I have hard copies of the information we've put together," Regan said, "and a thumb drive with the overlays of the blood spatter information we used."

She reached into her briefcase, unzipped it, and pulled out the manila folder with the information, then unhooked the thumb drive off her keychain and laid it on top. Provost reached out with her narrow, long-nailed fingers, and pulled it across the table toward her. She leaned over and slipped it into her briefcase. The catches on the leather case were so quiet Regan could barely hear them over the low conversation coming from the tables around the room. *A stealthy briefcase, full of secrets and probably lies.*

The two of them stared at each other awkwardly. Provost still looked angry. Regan had nothing more to say to her, no interest in speaking to her at all.

She sighed. If she wanted to keep her hold on the woman, she had to make it easier to put up with potential blackmail than it was to angrily storm out of the room.

"I'm sorry," Regan said. "I didn't mean to come across so rudely."

Provost's nostrils flared slightly. Then she nodded, looked down at her plate, and unrolled the linen napkin from around her silverware. "This place is charming, in a rustic kind of way. No way to have it in the city, of course. It's practically a German beer tent in here. You'd have to close down the streets."

"You've been to Germany?"

And then the woman smiled, not one of those wide, brash, ugly smiles that she flared onto people like a flood light, but a stiff, thin little smile that turned down at the corners—and yet was unmistakably not a frown. "A boyfriend while I was in college. We went to Munich during Oktoberfest..."

And then she told Regan the story of how she had lost her boyfriend one evening—not breaking up with him but *losing* him. He'd gone to the toilet and had never come back, leaving her with a "friend" of his who had tried to molest her. This was before cell phones had been so widespread, so it wasn't as easy as dialing him and leaving him an irate message. Besides, he'd left his car keys with her, and so she was worried.

She'd tracked him down like Sherlock Holmes on a murder case, using her knowledge, not of soil types (a la Sherlock Holmes) but of his favorite beers. By the time the waitress had brought their food, Regan was smiling. Upon finding him, Provost returned his keys and dumped him—he'd ended up in the apartment of a blonde, large bosomed waitress, not of the beer tent that he'd left her in, but in a small pub thirty miles out of town. A bull, several dogs, a thorn bush, someone else's underwear, and a couple of Vietnamese drunks had been involved. It turned out that she'd been out drinking with the man who would become the D.A.—he'd been an assistant at the time—and had told him the story. Later, she'd been hired on the strength of it. He was always expecting her to come up with the solutions to every mystery she came across, whether she had enough clues to solve it or not—a real life murder mystery style detective.

They both rolled their eyes at that. The legal system was not as simple and straightforward to navigate as it was in a murder mystery. Most of the time, it was perfectly obvious who'd done it. It was just a matter of jumping through enough hoops to prove it.

By the end of the meal, Regan had to laugh. Provost wasn't as bad as she'd thought—no, Provost *was* as bad as she'd thought. She'd do anything to keep the D.A. impressed and herself on the narrow path to inheriting his job when he retired, no matter how corrupt or brown-nosing.

But Regan's attitude toward the woman had changed. She was a fox, all right. But now she was Regan's fox.

Chapter 17 -Just drop it

Jake leaned back in his chair with his feet up on the desk. Across from him on the wall was his enemy...the calendar from the Asian delivery place. The space between the current date and Conrad Wilson's execution was getting smaller, one square at a time.

He needed something in the office, but he wasn't sure what. Not flowers or anything. Maybe a dartboard. He needed to do something with his hands so that he could distract himself when he was trying to think. Some guys were drinkers. They needed to get drunk in order to come up with intuitive leaps. He was a motion guy. He couldn't think if he wasn't moving. And the office, especially now that he'd moved in a couple of semi-comfy chairs so that his clients could talk to him without sitting on cheap folding chairs, was too crowded to pace.

Conrad Wilson.

Why wasn't the guy defending himself? Whatever he'd been doing while he was supposedly picking up the balloons and stuff for the party, he wasn't talking about it, even with a lethal injection looming in front of him.

It would have been easier if he could have just gone to talk to the guy, but it would be a complete breach of their own strict security protocol put in place after Andy Gibbons' case. If he or Regan went to see him, the Organization would be all over it like a bad rash, especially now that Pavo had asked around about him. Everybody's antennae would be up in the air. Even though Provost would present the information to the New Hampshire cops, it wouldn't be enough. They would still be exposed.

And besides, if Wilson wouldn't tell his lawyer and every other person on the face of the planet what he'd been doing—it had to be bad. Worse for him if it came out than if he were executed? What could it be? Or did Wilson have something last minute up his sleeve? Had that been his plan all along? Or did he want this? Did he *want* to be dead?

Mentally, Jake was just going around in circles. He knew that. But he'd cleared his desk, metaphorically speaking, in order to work on the case. Unless he pulled one of his buddies off something, he had nothing better to do.

The phone rang. He leaned forward and answered with a sense of relief. At this point, almost anything had to be better than dwelling on the Wilson case. "Hello?"

"Westley," a hoarse voice said. "Oh God. Westley."

Jake jerked his feet off the desk and leaned forward. The groaning of the chair drowned out whatever the guy said next, sounded like a moan. "You okay? Who is this?"

"It's Jay Hatchell."

"Are you okay?" Jake asked, slowly and clearly. "Do I need to call nine-one-one?"

"No, I'm...fine," Hatchell said. "Not injured. But I had to call you."

"What happened?"

"I shouldn't have said anything to you," he said. "Oh, God."

"What's going on?"

"I shouldn't have said anything...I should have just stayed home that day. It's horrible."

"Is someone blackmailing you? Threatening you? Jay, I can help. You just have to tell me what's going on."

"I can't, I just can't. But I had to call you and tell you to drop the case. Just drop it—or else."

"Or else what?"

But Hatchell didn't answer. The call cut off and the line hummed. Jake tried to call the line back, but it was no use—nobody answered. The next morning, the operator's bland, computerized voice told him the line was no longer in service.

In the end, he had to go pace around the neighborhood for almost an hour before he finally decided not to tell Regan about it.

At least, not until he found out what happened to Hatchell.

Chapter 18 - When did we join the Organization?

Regan sat at the counter in her kitchen with her father beside her. The two of them stared at the pound cake loaf in front of them. A selection of ice cream in quart containers ranged beside it: fresh cherry, chocolate, peanut butter cup, and—of all things—green tea ice cream. A punnet of the world's tiniest, reddest strawberries had been set out on the counter, too.

Jake was helping one of his retired SEAL friends bust open a divorce case. It had suddenly gone really sour with the client's wife threatening to kill herself and her kids if she didn't get what she wanted, and Jake's friend had called him in to help spell him on shifts in a white van around the block—far enough not to get caught by the wife, but close enough to make a dash to the house.

The client had let them set up spy cams in the house, including the bathrooms. As Jake had said, he didn't care whether the wife killed herself or not—the world would probably be a better place without her—but she didn't need to drag the kids into it. When she made that threat, she lost her right to privacy as far as they were concerned.

Regan wasn't sure she agreed. Instead, she'd tried to argue him into taking the kids out of the house and dealing with the fallout later. But they didn't have enough evidence on the wife yet, and Jake, his friend and the client didn't want to risk letting the wife get any kind of custody access whatsoever.

It was a sad, ugly situation, and rather than tie Jake up for the night by arguing with him, she'd let him go with a clipped "Goodbye", and then she called her father. Something she was discovering was that he actually was a good listener, as long as she didn't let his crap about grandchildren get under her skin.

"Your housekeeper is evil," her father said.

"It does look pretty good."

"Except for that green stuff. What is that, anyway?"

"Powdered green tea."

"Who puts tea in their ice cream?"

"There's coffee ice cream."

"That's different."

"Come on. It's just like the stuff you get at a sushi bar."

"Ugh," her father said, making a childish face of repulsion. "Raw fish. What kind of psychopath eats raw fish? There are all kinds of mites and things crawling in that stuff."

"There are not. They check."

"Oh, sure. Because that makes it less disgusting, knowing that someone's had their hands all over my raw fish."

Neither one of them had moved since Regan finished setting out the ice cream from the freezer. For all that neither one of them could stand coffee with sugar in it, they both loved their sweets.

"Why couldn't she have just left you some vanilla?" her father asked. "You know where you are with vanilla. You can eat just a little bit of it. It's like a sauce. You use it to hold the rest of your dessert together. But with three different flavors like this, you pretty much just have to get out the big bowls because nobody's going to be able to scoop out a reasonable amount of ice cream at this point."

"*Four* different flavors."

"If you don't tell her that we dumped that green tea crap down the garbage disposal, I won't."

She laughed and pulled the pound cake over to her. It was already sliced—in great big slices that nobody could possibly claim were part of a sensible diet. Ellen didn't believe in restraint when it came to desserts. And honestly, neither did Regan.

She served up two slices of cake on little plates, then dug around in her drawers until she found a melon baller with its tiny scoop. She had no memory of buying it. It had probably been in the back of a drawer when she'd bought the house. She scooped out ice cream for herself and her father while he took a teaspoon and dug the tops out of the strawberries, complaining constantly about how small they were. Whenever her back was turned, he popped one in his mouth. She could tell because the strawberries kept staining parts of his teeth red.

Four scoops on her cake, and three on her father's. She started putting the ice cream lids back on.

He squawked at her. "I don't think so. You have more ice cream than I do."

"You didn't want any green tea. I do."

"You just put another scoop of chocolate on there, missy."

She smiled and added another scoop.

"More than that," he said. "What's that? Add all those tiny little scoops together, that's hardly a whole scoop of ice cream."

She added a few more scoops of chocolate to both their plates, then put the boxes away. When she turned back around, her father had portioned out the strawberries onto their plates, giving himself far more than he had her.

"Should we eat out there?" She pointed toward the door to her library, the room formerly known as the dining room when the previous resident had lived here. It still had a big table, but it was usually stacked with books pulled off her floor to ceiling bookshelves rather than china place settings.

He glanced toward the door, and she grabbed most of the strawberries off his plate and hid them in her fist.

"Out here's fine," he said.

"Want some coffee?"

He glanced down at his plate, then glared at her. He didn't say anything, though. She'd tricked him. And by his rules, whatever you could fool him with, even for a second, you could get away with...

For as long as you could defend it.

"Sure," he said.

She walked over to the coffee pot and poured two cups from the carafe. It was awkward doing it one handed. When she turned back, all the strawberries had been picked off her plate—except the ones touching the green tea ice cream.

She almost laughed but managed to turn it into a cough. She handed her father his mug, then went back for her own. When she'd settled herself at her stool on the other side of the counter, she held her hand over her cake and opened it—letting the captured strawberries fall out. They'd stained her palm splotchy red, but seeing her father's face—one cheek bulging—made it worth it.

Her father snorted, then chewed and swallowed. His spoon had already decimated his first scoop of ice cream and a good quarter of his cake.

"Too lonely to spend the night alone with no boyfriend already, eh?" he said. "Soon, you'll be thinking that it'll be time to get a cat or a dog to keep you company."

She could see where this was leading. She picked off one of the strawberries with the tip of her spoon, then added ice cream and cake, and ate it. Cherry ice cream with strawberries—an odd combination, but not bad.

"Or a grandchild," he added.

"I was thinking of becoming a crazy cat lady," she said. "Sixty cats or so. What do you think?"

"I think a grandchild would be better."

"Sixty cats would be quieter. And they wouldn't smell as bad."

"The first couple of years," her father said. "After that the kid would keep itself clean—mostly."

"Do they ever just shut up, though?" she asked.

He snorted again. For a while the only sound was the satisfied clinking of spoons against plates, and the slurping of coffee. The green tea ice cream was all right, too.

When Ellen's dessert had been paid its rightful respects, Regan covered the cake, loaded the dishes in the dishwasher, and wiped up the counter.

Her father said, "I've never known you to be especially tidy. When did that happen? For Jake?"

She rolled her eyes. "Having a maid makes you much more aware of the mess you're leaving behind. Every time I throw a tissue at a garbage can and miss, I think, 'Oh great, now Ellen has to clean that up.'"

"I'm pretty sure most people don't reason it out quite like that."

"It's only fair."

Her father snorted again, then took a deep breath and cleared his throat. "Well, spit it out."

"What?"

"When was the last time you invited me over to your house for any reason, let alone after supper for *cake*?"

She smiled ruefully. He was right; it had been a long time. She hadn't thought she had ulterior motives when she'd called her father earlier that evening—but now, looking at it like this, maybe she did. "No reason."

"Come on, Regan. Confess."

She leaned her head on her hand, putting her elbow on the black marble countertop and staring toward the kitchen window. The sun had just set, and the sky outside the window was dark blue streaked with red and orange clouds. She remembered looking out over Brooklyn from Uncle Paul's penthouse.

It wasn't really Jake's behavior that was troubling her. Whether or not it was ethical to put a camera inside a client's home to collect evidence of illegal and harmful behavior of the client's spouse was an argument that she mostly felt on an intellectual level.

No, she was still troubled about Uncle Paul. It was hard, shifting from a childish view of the man to realizing that there was a reason he'd become a stranger to her and her father, to understanding she might never be able to sort out what she felt about him—he was just too complex.

"I've been thinking about Uncle Paul," she admitted. "I went to see him again this morning to tell him we were working on the Wilson case and make sure the Organization wasn't involved."

"Where, to the penthouse?"

She nodded.

"What's it like?"

Her father hadn't ever been there—that's how long the two of them hadn't really seen each other, before their recent encounters, at least since Uncle Paul had taken the office, what, ten years ago, when the new building opened? Regan had gone to visit him the first week to say congratulations. He'd accepted her box of chocolates and kicked her butt at chess, just like he had earlier today.

She described it for him.

"Too much," her father said. "It's too much luxury for someone in his position. I'm surprised he doesn't have the IRS all over him."

"He might not be worried. The Organization might have his back there, too," Regan reminded him.

"Bah."

"He says the wealth isn't important in and of itself, only as a means to an end."

"The ends always turn out to justify the means where Paul's concerned," her father said disgustedly.

She shrugged. She didn't want to listen to him rant about Uncle Paul, really she didn't. She wasn't sure why she'd let him pry it out of her. She sipped her coffee and wondered how to steer him away from the conversation without him noticing.

"Did he have anything useful to say?" her father asked.

"I suppose. We talked about what happened to those kids you watched in college, and why you were so angry at him."

"Oh, so he figured it out finally, did he?"

Her father sounded bitter. She glanced over at him. He quickly picked up his coffee and slurped it. She looked back toward the setting sun outside the window.

"No, I don't think so," she said. "Not the way you want him to. He's still hurt and puzzled by your behavior. He still thinks you were wrong to ask him to intervene."

"He let two kids die."

She took in a breath that seemed to chill her from the inside out, then released it. "I don't know, Daddy. You can't force people to do the right thing."

"You can judge them if they don't."

"Pressuring someone falls in the same category as forcing them."

"It does not."

"Then why is blackmail illegal?"

He drank more coffee; she turned away from him and finished hers, then got up for a refill. Her father held out his cup, waggling it at her. She filled it from the other side of the counter, like a waitress at a diner.

"I shouldn't have said anything," she said. "It just makes things worse, to bring things up that can't be reconciled."

"Tell that to Andy Gibbons," said her father.

She sighed. The sky had turned murky and black, only a few purple glimmers on the bottoms of the clouds now. "So if you disapprove of him that much, tell me why he was your best friend until I got out of college. What made your friendship fall apart, if it wasn't that?"

"The Organization," her father said. "It pushed and pushed at him until he was forced to choose between loyalty to me and to it. He didn't choose me."

"What happened?"

Her father raised his hand in a *stop* gesture, then slurped his coffee. "How's your couch?" he asked.

"My couch?"

"I can't sit here on this stool for much longer. And the story you want to hear, it won't make sense unless I tell you some other things first. Specifically, what it was like in the Organization at first."

She was on her feet in a second. "It's not the best couch in the world—not as good as the chairs in Uncle Paul's office, that's for sure."

"The chairs?"

"They were *much* more comfortable than they looked."

Her father chuckled as he slid of his stool and put his hands to the small of his back, leaning left and right so far that it pulled the sides of his polo shirt almost completely out of his khaki pants. He rolled his shoulders and tilted his head from side to side, accompanied by a chorus of cracks and pops. "He's still using the old chair trick, is he?"

"The old chair trick?"

"He buys several sets of the same chairs, and has the guts torn out and rebuilt. Three sets, usually. One of the sets is damn uncomfortable—thin cushion over a board, the seat tilted so that you're always sliding off, one leg shorter than the others, that kind of thing. One is rebuilt to be the most comfortable chair you've ever been in—ergonomic support, leaning backs, gel cushions, soft fabric, even seat heaters like you put in a car, so you're always the perfect temperature. The other set is just normal—neutral. If he does anything to those, he adjusts the seat so you have to sit up straighter when you're talking to him. You got the good seats. Did he talk to you about grandchildren?"

She led the way into the living room, presenting the couch with an ironic wave. Her father picked one of the boring gray armchairs next to it and pulled open the drawer on the end table, pulling out a sandstone coaster and setting his coffee cup on it. Regan settled next to him at the end of the couch. A car drove by with its lights on and she winced. She still hadn't forgotten that a lunatic had driven up her driveway in a Jeep filled with explosives and practically blown the front of her house off, despite the stone facing on the front. She'd replaced the couch and all the rest of the damaged materials with stuff as close to the old materials and furniture as possible—but the fear still lingered.

She got up and closed the blinds, and the drapes on top of them. Memory: sometimes it wasn't the best of all possible healers.

"The subject of grandchildren did come up," Regan admitted.

"And?"

"And ova. He wants me to donate my eggs if I decide not to have any. For the betterment of the human race, I think."

Her father grunted; she couldn't interpret the look on his face. He sipped at his coffee. Concerned, he looked concerned about something. He stared toward the door to the kitchen and the hallway for so long she started to worry he was completely lost in thought.

"You were going to tell me the story of how your friendship with Uncle Paul fell apart," she reminded him.

He sighed, a sad breath in and a sad breath out, the sound of a faithful dog at the fireplace, beset by human children, being noble for the cause. "Do I have to?"

"Please."

He straightened for a moment, then puffed out his cheeks. "Where to begin."

"Joining the Organization."

"That's just it," he said. "When did we join the Organization? It was long before we realized there was one, what it was, or that we'd become part of their operating resources. When did we first encounter them? Hard to say. Even back then, it was pretty widespread. It could have been as children."

"Start where you first realized what was going on."

"That's no good. If I start there, it won't make any sense at all."

Chapter 19 - What brought the two of you together?

Their freshman year had come and gone. Summer break had seen John returning back home to White Plains and working all summer as a pool guard, the same job he had since early high school.

He'd been quieter than usual, of course, simultaneously simmering with anger and chilled by doubt. He'd gone to the inquest by himself. The medical examiner had sorted through the evidence: the two young men had fought, that much was clear, then had stolen a car and gone out for a drive, during which they had an accident.

John had been disgusted with the situation, with himself for not stepping forward, and with Paul.

Paul was the genius. Clearly it was his responsibility to come forward and present what he knew. If he presented it, the medical examiner would have to believe it. There was something about the way Paul laid out an argument that left no question as to whether or not it was true, false, or just speculation. You felt when he was done talking you could throw your arms around the facts and cling to them, no interpretation necessary. Instead, Paul had left the rest of them to muddle through with their doubts, questions, cover-ups and lies. Nothing was said of a gunshot wound, even though a couple of people had seen the body at the morgue. It was hard to mistake a hole in the center of a guy's chest as anything but.

John had sworn to himself as he'd climbed in his father's car, that he'd write to Paul and tell him to find another roommate. But he found himself putting it off, day by day. Tomorrow he'd write—the day after that—next weekend. He was too busy with all the high school girls throwing themselves his way. It was like shooting fish in a barrel, except it didn't burst open the barrel. Then it was August and too late to find a new roommate for either of them. He should have said something before he left. He'd say something when they returned. He'd sleep in someone else's room for a few nights until things got straightened out.

Then he was on his way back into the City, dragging his trunk and his suitcase up to their old room.

He got out his key, but the door was already open. He pushed open the door. The lights were off and the room was in shadow; it was past noon and the sun had shifted out of the room and was lighting up the windows across the quad so brightly that it was hard to see in them.

The two chairs were back, or else they had never left. You weren't supposed to leave anything in the dorm rooms over the summer. They had people coming in and out all summer for symposiums and things—summer classes. No rest for the wicked, what? He dragged his trunk into the room and dropped it on the floor.

Paul sat in his chair, facing the window. His hands gripped the arms of his chair.

John said, "Hey, Paul. How's it going?"

They hadn't written to each other all summer, not even to check each other's classes or find out when the other would be arriving.

"It goes well," Paul said. "How does it go with yourself?"

Awkward as always. But John found his shoulders releasing. They'd been tight and tense all summer, as if preparing for a blow that every day was more likely to come.

"Great, now that I'm back," John said. "The old hometown has its charms, but I'd rather be here." He surprised himself by actually meaning it. The world was a crazy place.

***

They met her on an expedition to the vicinity of Barnard College, the women's college associated with Columbia University and Millbank Hall, one of the several fine dorms available to the young women who attended there.

It was one of those fine early autumn days in which the heat suggested the oppressiveness of July, but carried a chill behind it, buried deep under the surface. The leaves hadn't started to turn yet, but they'd lost some of their fullness, and their leaves cast thinner, lighter shadows on the open grassy areas. The air smelled almost fresh, only just sprinkled with the smell of trucks and cars roaring past on the streets.

The two of them had been invited to a picnic in Riverside park by a couple of women from Barnard, women who were clearly in a competition to see who could scoop up the handsome law student from White Plains while not snubbing his less handsome friend too badly. Clearly Paul Travers was going places, he just needed a woman's touch to straighten him out a little.

The two of them had agreed to watch each other's backs: no promises, and nothing that could be construed as such; nothing past a chaste kiss on the cheek; and definitely no alcohol. Some of those college women were real predators.

They met the girls in front of Millbank Hall, two women whose names John couldn't remember—Helen and Mary, say. One was a redhead with curly hair and a button nose—Helen—with a green knee-length dress, interestingly low cut, flared from the waist, with enormous pink flowers on it. The flowers clashed with her hair. She had impressively long, full eyelashes that were probably fake, and looked like the kind of woman who could be relied upon to spend an hour in front of the mirror every morning.

The other one—Mary—had dark hair and a bob cut that flipped out at the bottom, and wore white plastic earrings that matched her straight, large-collared white dress. She looked as though she possessed slightly more intellect than her friend Helen, and therefore had been assigned as Paul's ostensible date on the picnic, although clearly it was understood that John was fair game to both.

John and Paul were in charge of the beverages—nothing but lemonade in a big plaid thermos, sorry girls—and the women were in charge of the lunch, which was contained in a red wicker basket with a wood top. Helen, who had won the toss for John, was stuck carrying the basket out of the building. She handed it to John, who looped it over one arm and held out his other for her. Helen wore ornate sandals with pink plastic jewels and narrow, tall heels—just the thing to be seen in. Mary had on black flats.

It looked like their tactics were split—Helen going for flash, Mary for endurance. John had learned to read women's clothes with a close eye. It was like Victorians sending messages with flowers—more intricate, perhaps, but just as clear for a man who knew what to look for. He gave Paul a significant look, one eyebrow up, to remind him that there would be a test of sorts later. Paul had accepted John's theories about women's clothing, but he had the worst time trying to sort them out for himself. The meaning of the depth of a neckline was as difficult for him to navigate as a boy from Iowa lost in a Norwegian fjord.

They walked the few blocks to the park and followed the paths down the hill toward the river. The parkway buzzed with cars. In a couple of weeks, the park was going to be ravishingly beautiful, full of color. But just now, it was perfect for a picnic. Windy, sure, but that was only going to make the girls' dresses more interesting.

They followed the walkway to a sunny spread of grass under a wide sycamore tree; Helen took a scratchy, brown and yellow plaid blanket out of the basket and spread it out on the grass.

The picnic basket seemed like something out of a magician's act; sandwiches, two types of pasta salad, a green salad, hard-boiled eggs, a wedge of cheese, and four perfect, ripe plums were all produced, along with plates, napkins, silverware, and small juice glasses.

Paul poured out the lemonade with all solemnity, watching the women's faces. Helen didn't react; she wasn't here for the booze. Mary showed slight signs of disappointment.

The four of them got lost in meaningless chit-chat. Well, three of them were lost. One of them was straining to keep from bringing up more interesting topics of conversation, like Greek philosophers and recent advances in the field of statistics. But, having been carefully coached otherwise, Paul limited himself to on-topic, mildly witty repartee. It was enjoyable, watching him thaw a little in front of the girls.

Then *she* walked by.

On her own, nose in a book—the cover was bright blue with a cartoon of a boy and dog with a stopwatch on its stomach—she followed the path in front of her feet, seeming to swerve by radar out of the path of a bicyclist. She wore a blue skirt, a button-up white shirt, and a plain tan cardigan sweater with the shirt's collar points pulled out over the top. She had on gold-rimmed eyeglasses and a little coral lipstick. Through her short, curled gold hair she had a ruler straight part and tiny gold stud earrings.

Mary and Helen giggled at her. The girl had walked off the edge of the sidewalk and stumbled, then glanced up, turned her page, and kept walking. In about a minute she had disappeared behind a tree and a cluster of male students. One of them twisted around to look at her, but she was out of sight.

"A particularly entertaining example of the female student?" Paul said.

"Oh, Linda," Helen giggled, refilling John's glass with lemonade. "She's not here for her MRS, that's for sure."

"Literature," Mary said. "She's supposed to be reading the *Iliad* and *Don Quixote*. You'd think she didn't have anything to do. But of course she's a teacher's pet—what do you expect?"

Paul looked at John with a pinched look between his eyebrows. John mouthed the word *later*. "What's she going to do with a degree in literature, if she's not looking to get hitched? Teach English?"

"She wants to be a writer," Helen said, "and write for women's magazines."

"Why shouldn't she?" Paul asked.

John hooked his thumb and made a cutting gesture over his throat with it. Part of the risk of taking Paul anywhere was that he'd ask the logical question—no matter how illogical it was to do the asking. Anything resembling politics had to be explained slowly and patiently. And in 1965, Women Writers meant Politics.

Paul nodded, but it was too late. They'd let loose the kraken.

"What's a woman like that going to contribute to society as a writer?" Helen said, picking up the cloth napkin in her lap, shaking it out, and laying it back down. "Especially in a women's magazine? What's she going to do, write about children and household cleaning tips? She'll be childless and living in a tiny apartment in Harlem. And then she'll be broke and out on the streets."

Mary snorted. "She's going to be married with six kids and living in Iowa in five years."

"Six kids in five years," Helen said. They both laughed.

Paul's face was starting to look ugly. John changed the subject and jollied the two women into talking about their future plans. Mary was taking mathematics and Helen was taking education. Their plans after graduation were about as flimsy and transparent as a negligee.

Finally, it was over. Nobody was drunk, going steady, or engaged. John thanked them profoundly as he escorted Helen back to their dorm. The two women were polite but not overly warm. John had warned Paul to downplay his future prospects. Interest in the two of them had been greatly reduced over the course of the lunch. A couple of stick in the muds going nowhere. Hopefully word would get around. John had his choice of women; he was tired of being hunted like prey.

Paul, though, he struggled with women. Linda might be a good pick for him. Someone intelligent enough to keep up.

***

John kept an eye on Riverside park, finding excuses to linger in front of Millbank Hall, then in the same basic area of the park. He brought popular novels along with him the way one would bring bread crumbs to feed the pigeons. Then he found the book Linda had been reading when they'd seen her—it was a strange one, all right. After reading it, he stopped carrying around novels and started carrying around editions of famous philosophers. The pages of Locke and Descartes passed under his thumb without his catching sight of her. Then he started Plato.

It was October, and the leaves had changed to gold and red and mostly fallen. The air hung with mist almost continuously. The grass was still green, and the bushes were still peppered with bright colored leaves. But for the most part, the trees were gray and heavy looking—almost ominous.

After the first couple of fishing expeditions, Paul had abandoned him. Women, he said, were not going to be a significant part of his life—neither were children. Paul claimed he would happily provide services as a godfather and so-called uncle if John should produce any, but his time would be better spent elsewhere—perhaps in the law library. Here he would give John a squint, as if trying to give him a hint.

John ignored him. Paul was spending his time preparing for a career running a business, and was studying history. John was preparing for a career in justice. Philosophy actually suited him better. Questions of what was good and evil, and whether it was possible to know the difference (or anything at all) seemed much more pragmatic to him than who had won the Battle of Agincourt and how. And if he had to listen to Paul go off about Machiavelli one more time, he'd go mad.

John sat on his usual bench in the park, wearing a sport coat, a sweater, and a cotton button-up shirt and read Plato for about an hour, until the damp air had him sneezing. Plato was a little bit more authoritarian than he liked, a bit too quick to get rid of democracy and replace the will of the people with his idealized philosopher kings, who in John's opinion didn't, and couldn't exist. The closest person he'd ever met to such a man was Paul—and

Paul couldn't be trusted when it came to right and wrong. Paul's attitude was to let everything work itself out, from questions of traffic right-of-way to a pair of drug addicts contemplating murder. He couldn't see that two people or two ideas could both be right. One of them would be more likely to win than the other—that was all. A kingdom run by Paul would be survival of the fittest.

He realized he'd been staring off into space for a few minutes and looked down at his book to make sure he'd marked the page. He reached down to dog-ear it, and a hand reached down out of nowhere and slapped it.

"Stop that," a woman's voice said, followed by a sharp tearing sound.

He glanced up. It hadn't been a gentle tap. A torn piece of lined white notebook paper filled his vision, fluttered, then stuffed itself into the spine of his book. The pages closed around his hand, still in the middle of the book, then the book was taken away from him and the impromptu bookmark checked to make sure it was secure.

Linda sat next to him on the bench, glaring at him from behind her wire-rimmed glasses. She wore a blood-red sweater over a blue skirt and a white cotton top, and a real furnace burned in her eyes.

"I can't stand people who dog-ear their pages," she said, then tossed the book back in his lap and stood up.

He grabbed the book and started following her as she strode down the cement pathway. "Wait. Linda?"

She slowed. "Yes?"

"I have a friend..."

"Oh, you do, do you? Would that be the friend that nobody else will go out with on a date? The smart one with the heart of gold, that you think would be a perfect pairing with bookish Linda? Like crackers and cheese?" Her black strapped Mary Janes snapped against the concrete, even through the layer of damp autumn leaves.

John cursed under his breath. "Yes."

"Tell him I'm busy...washing my hair...on whatever nights he's available. I'm not looking for a date or a husband."

"I know. You're a writer."

"Hmmm," she said, slowing down a fraction. Her voice was still angry and sarcastic. "Is your friend also a writer? Is that the logical connection there?"

"No, he's not a writer," John said. "He is, in my opinion, the smartest son of a bitch you could ever meet. But he has a missing ethics bone."

"And you were looking for me to provide it." She sped up.

He jogged after her, still clutching the book. "I've been hanging out in this park for over a month, trying to find you again. The two women I was with when I saw you first clammed up on me."

"Hyenas. But you're worse. You're a predator chasing down prey."

"I read that book you were reading, just to see what it was all about. *The Phantom Tollbooth.*"

She stopped in her tracks and he shot past her a few steps. When he looked back at her, her nostrils were flared. "You auditioned me as a date for your friend...using the book I was reading."

"I thought it was interesting. It made me pay attention in my philosophy class."

"Good for you." She started walking again. He fell in beside her. She was right—he was chasing her. But was it for Paul's sake, or just out of sheer amusement? Was she teasing him, walking away to hold his interest?

He decided it didn't matter. "Philosophy has a lot of questions that I can't answer. But it seems to me that it's more important to ask the question than find the answer."

"How trite."

He blinked. It had seemed like an original idea to him when he'd had it just then. "Trite?"

"An idea, overused and therefore of little import, can be described as trite. Lacking originality."

"I know what trite means."

"Then you must think that nobody has ever had that thought before. That you, in your first semester of studying philosophy, must have miraculously invented it."

It was a harsh statement—but essentially true. He'd been trying to impress her with it. He chuckled. "I'm going to be a judge," he said. "What with Paul's so-called pragmatism and my classes, I've been having trouble finding an answer to the question of what is right. The deeper I look, the more I realize there's no easy answer, or even a system of answers, even though that's what the law is supposed to be, a system of answers of what is right and wrong, and how to deal with that. Today I was reading Plato—"

"Plato," she said, with contempt. They were turning a corner, headed back up toward the street.

"—And I had to stop and wonder whether he ever second guessed himself. Replace a bad democracy with a good tyrant who, incidentally, happens to have the same traits and beliefs that Plato himself did. It seems pretty obvious. 'If only I were in charge...' But is it possible to have a good, fair government for all, if it's run by the educated and smug?"

She stopped and shook her head. "And you say your friend is the smart one?"

John grinned. He had her hooked—finally. "You should meet him sometime. Bring a friend, we'll do a lunch for four someplace—my treat."

***

John wasn't used to being the other date, the one who filled out a foursome. Linda's friend was a peach, though, a brunette with a wide red mouth and a boisterous laugh—Janine. She wore a yellow sweater and a plaid skirt with a matching scarf and looked like she'd be comfortable walking just about anywhere in it, from reading a book on the beachside to dining in Manhattan to ducking through trees in the wilderness. A thoroughly put together girl, all vim and vigor. He should do this fourth wheel thing more often.

They went to a cafe on the other side of Morningside, a place that must have been there for fifty years or more. The tin ceiling had dirt in the corners, and there were big, old-fashioned mirrors all along one wall. The others had oil paintings with fat gold frames. It looked like everything had been stolen out of a museum.

They had cappuccinos from a gigantic espresso machine that ran from the marble countertop almost all the way to the ceiling, with buttery pastries out of a glowing glass case. The place had an air of old Italian men meeting over cigars and brandy. He kept catching a man out of the corner of his eye that looked like the director Hitchcock, jovial and somber at the same time, the corners of his eyes pulled up and the corners of his mouth pulled down. But when he looked at him straight on, his face was too weather beaten to be the famous director's.

John leaned back against the velvet seat and let the chatter of the place wash over him. At the next table, Linda and Paul seemed to be hitting it off well enough, talking about a couple of chess matches and whether or not the Soviet Union was going to make it another decade or not.

Janine leaned forward. "What do you think? I think the Soviets are going to keep on going, just as long as the West does."

"I think it's been a long time since I've had such a good afternoon."

She nodded. "You don't think they'll be around too long, do you?" It almost sounded like an accusation.

"I think they're too dishonest," he said.

"So is the West."

"Nobody ever said the West was honest—especially not the Soviets."

"And you think that's going to make a difference?"

"People always discount the power of honest dishonesty."

"You're very cynical."

"I try not to be. But it's hard not to be, coming into contact with humanity all the time."

The corner of Janine's wide red mouth quirked. "You don't come into contact with humanity. You go to Columbia. You come into contact with ideas."

Even through his haze of satisfaction, he could tell the conversation had taken a stranger turn than he could have guessed. He felt like he was being pushed and prodded—a real turkey, checked to see whether he was done. "Some of my best friends are ideas," he protested, just to be ridiculous.

Janine rolled her eyes. She knew when she was being put on. "Your best friend is Paul."

"That's true," he said.

"What brought the two of you together?" she asked, just a little too intently.

"Nothing logical," he said, raising his voice a little. "We shouldn't be friends at all. We should be enemies."

Paul looked up at that and gave him a quick grin. A bead of sweat formed at one temple, then started rolling down his cheek. He took his handkerchief out of his pocket and dabbed at it.

The look on Linda's face told John he should have been watching things between the two of them more closely. Her eyebrows were pinched together, and she was leaning back in her chair. The front two legs were just off the floor.

Janine lifted an eyebrow. *See what happens when we don't watch the children?* "Linda," she said.

"Yes?"

"Why don't you switch tables with me for a while? John's not much for politics. He just keeps teasing me."

Linda pressed her lips together, then visibly swallowed back the emotion. "Of course."

She stood up stiffly, and Janine hopped over and took her spot without gentlemanly assistance. John stood up and went through the ritual with Linda, then seated himself against the wall again.

The crease hadn't eased up between her eyebrows, and she was visibly attempting not to frown.

"For what it's worth, he has all the social graces of a snapping turtle," John told her.

She swallowed, letting her head bob, and looked down at Janine's cappuccino, which she'd finished off already.

"Would you like another? Glass of ice water? Something else?"

"Ice water, please."

John did the errand for her, and came back with two glasses and two paper napkins to put them on. "Now, tell me. What did he say this time?"

Her eyes slid over to Paul, and the line between her brows relaxed a little. She seemed puzzled, as if she couldn't remember what had been upsetting her. "Nothing, I suppose. The more he talked, though, the more wrapped up I seemed to get in it. I wanted to agree with him, even when he said things I disagreed with— which is ridiculous."

John leaned against the back of the chair. "Happens all the time. You can't seem to argue logically with him. The best you can hope for is to stand your ground, no matter how reasonable he sounds."

"How do you argue with him?"

"Me? I don't."

Paul and Janine seemed to be going at it hammer and tongs over the Soviet Union now, whether they'd last it out or collapse.

Janine called them a "necessary balance," and Paul smirked. John studied the ceiling and let their voices fade into nonsense chatter. Paul already had a counterargument worked out for that one; John had already listened to it and played devil's advocate earlier. Arguing with Paul was all right as long as it wasn't over a position that one didn't personally hold. As long as the emotions weren't involved—it stayed clean and logical.

"What do you think about Janine?" he asked.

Linda stiffened, straightening her back and lifting her chin. "She's a friend."

"For how long?"

"Since the beginning of the year." She sounded defensive. That meant she was picking up on it too, whatever was off about Janine—the strange pushiness.

The bells over the door jingled. A woman came through the door and walked to the counter.

Just then, Paul and Janine raised their voices, and the woman looked over at them. It was Mary, the brunette from the date with the red headed Helen. Her eyes skimmed past John and Linda, and fastened on Janine.

The man at the counter said something to her, and her eyes snapped over to his. She shook her head, turned around, and walked back out.

"What was that all about?" John asked.

Linda shook her head. She looked as mystified as he was. The line was back between her brows.

Janine said, "All right, you've convinced me. The Soviet Union will collapse under the weight of its own inefficiency and corruption. The only way it can save itself is if it allows its people as much freedom to break its laws as its government has."

Paul blinked at her; John groaned. Paul was going to be insufferable for days. Janine didn't have the kind of look on her face that said she was just going along with what Paul said because she found him attractive, or because she wanted to pick him up like a prize at a fair. Her face was just as cold and logical as his.

Paul, on the other hand, was clearly smitten.

John looked back at Linda. Of the two of them—oh, who was he kidding? Of all the girls he'd met, he liked her the best. Felt most comfortable. Why fight the switch?

Because of that strange pressure he'd felt, that's why. Something was up.

It felt like a test.

***

Regan leaned back in her chair. Her father was staring off into the rows of legal cases over her shoulder, row after row of what should have been cut and dried—laws—but was really shaded with all kinds of gray areas, exceptions, and loopholes. His face had gone soft—thinking about her mother, probably.

She stood up and carried their coffee mugs back into the kitchen. She had a feeling that he'd be lost in thought for hours if she let him. He'd barely notice if she turned off the lights and went to bed.

She refilled their cups, then dumped out the rest of the pot down the sink. She'd imposed on him too long tonight as it was. She rinsed out the pot, then upended it to dry in the dish drainer.

She would have let him drift off without bothering him, but

there was something she needed to make sure of. Janine, the girl with the yellow sweater and the wide red mouth. Was she the Organization member who'd signed up Uncle Paul, and then her father? Or was her father distracted by his memories?

She brought the cups in and set them down on the coasters loudly enough to make her father start a little. His eyes focused on her, and he gave her half a smile before holding the hot cup of coffee in front of his face.

"Your mother," he said. "I always get lost when she comes up."

"That's why you don't like to talk about her."

"Part of it. But also because she wasn't the kind of woman you could just put into words."

Regan chuckled under her breath. He'd done all right so far. It was good to hear about what her mother had been like, before she had a family to take care of. And Regan knew all her memories of her mother were colored by her young age, and by the devastating grief she'd felt at her passing.

"So you both loved her, but it sounds like it was pretty clear who she was interested in."

Her father shrugged. "In retrospect it was clear. At the time it felt like she was torturing both of us, leaning toward one of us one day, then the other the next."

Regan shook her head. "It was always you, Daddy. From the second time she saw you until she passed away. I could tell."

"I wish I'd been able to."

"She probably thought you were being an idiot."

"She did mention that a time or two, yes."

Regan took the handle of her mug but didn't pick it up. Her father picked up on what she was about to ask and tensed up a little, holding his mug tighter between his hands and pulling in his elbows and shoulders.

"Daddy, I have to ask. Was Janine the member of the Organization who got you and Uncle Paul involved?"

His jaw shifted and the corners of his eyes tightened. "She was."

"And Mary, the dark haired girl from your double date, she was in the Organization, too?"

"She was."

The way he said it made it sound like there was more to the story. As if he wasn't willing to come out with it exactly, but he wouldn't lie about it if she managed to ask the right question.

"What about Helen?"

"She was in, too."

"Were they targeting the two of you especially? I mean, that sounds like a lot of people for it to be a coincidence."

"They...they targeted a number of people."

"At Columbia? Or all over the City?"

He put the mug back down and stared deep into her eyes. "All over Columbia," he said. "At the time, one of the board members was part of the Organization, and he strip-mined the place—the brightest and best, people sure to go far. Or to marry those sure to go far."

She hadn't remembered Columbia being a hotbed of corruption. "I never ran into anyone."

Her father shook his head. "No, you did. I promise you. The

200

board member is still there, even if he is a bit doddering. But you didn't come across as an especially susceptible target."

"No?"

"What would you have said if you were in the argument that Janine started about the Communists?"

Regan frowned. "I would have said that I didn't have enough information to go spouting off an opinion."

"What if she had insisted?"

"I would have told her she already had my opinion, and if she didn't like it, she could go drink cappuccino with someone else."

"Exactly," her father said. "And why do you think you would have said that?"

"Because it's true?"

"Because your mother and I coached you—over and over and over again. We taught you what to say to keep people from pressuring you into giving your opinion when you didn't want to. We taught you how to resist—"

Regan ticked them off on her fingers. "Boys, drinking, drugs, secrets from friends who were going to hurt themselves and others, do I need to go on?"

"No, I remember. We weren't training you to resist just the normal things, but to resist the Organization, your mother and I. We knew they'd come after you."

"Because of you and Uncle Paul."

"And your mother."

"Mother was in the Organization?"

Her father shook his head vigorously, the half-smile back on his face and his eyes lingering on the books over her shoulder. "Oh, no. Not a chance. They had their eye on you because they knew she'd been able to resist them, and there was a good chance you would too. They assumed because of me and Paul they'd be able to get to you—we'd want you in, they thought. One big happy family, except for Linda. But of course, both Paul and I had our reasons for wanting you out of it. Me, because I could see it for what it was. And your Uncle Paul, because he thought it would be better for the Organization if it stopped pressuring people into joining."

"Pressuring?"

"Blackmail," her father said. He raised a hand. "Don't ask. That's enough for tonight. Just know that the Organization doesn't just invite you to join. It finds the people it thinks it can use—not just because they're useful, but because they're *usable*, and then puts the screws to them. It's harder to say no when you have your heart's desire right in front of you.

"It's even harder when everything you think about yourself is at risk. They don't just blackmail you. They tear apart who you thought you were, show you how low you can sink, and then convince you they're the only ones who can appreciate you for who you really are. Thank God I had your mother, that's all I can say."

Chapter 20 -Why did you do it?

Her father had gone home hours ago at midnight—although it felt like it had only been minutes ago. Her alarm clock, a smooth silver box on her nightstand, read 3:47 am. Her body told her to go back to sleep.

She forced herself to sit up.

Her phone buzzed on the bedside table. Jake might be in trouble, something having to do with the case he was on. She grabbed the phone, unlocked it, and said, "Hello?"

A buzzing tone was her only answer.

She blinked to clear her eyes. The phone buzzed again—but not the phone she had in her hand.

The secure phone was in the nightstand's drawer. She jerked the drawer open and grabbed it. Yes, this one was the right one. She'd received a blank text from Alex—a signal to call him as soon as possible.

She swore and stood up, grabbing her robe and flipping on the overhead lights. Now she regretted dumping out the coffee pot last night. She'd take anything now, even if it was cold.

She shuffled into the kitchen and started a fresh pot. If she was going to have to go into emergency mode, she needed to be more awake than she was now. Then she leaned against her sink, took a deep breath, and dialed in—ready for the worst.

Alex picked up right away. "Regan?"

"Hey, Alex. Should I panic?"

"You should get ready to celebrate, I think."

She exhaled and let her shoulders drop. "At three in the

morning. You call me at three in the morning to celebrate. You're going to give me an ulcer. I was afraid it was bad news."

"Sorry. But I found what happened to Wilson's missing time."

Her skin prickled with goosebumps, and she shivered. "Say that again."

"Hang on a second."

A beep came over the line, and Jake said in a sarcastic drawl, "You know it's like three in the morning, right? Almost four? And that normal people aren't awake at this hour?"

Alex said, "I found what happened to Wilson's missing time."

"You're shitting me," Jake said. "Sorry, I mean, of course you found out. Where was he?"

"At his mistress'."

"Huh," Jake said. "How many women does that guy have on the side anyway? Who was it? Anyone we know?"

"No." Alex rattled off the information, Ashley something. Regan pounced for the grocery list stuck to the fridge and tried to write it down—and missed most of it. "Don't worry, Regan," Alex said. "I set up a second network for Gary and a few other people. I'll get him the details."

Regan's eyebrows rose and the corner of her mouth formed an involuntary smile. Alex never would have done such a thing without talking about it with Jake first. Gary's days of being blackballed were over apparently, although she wouldn't have been surprised if Alex didn't have a thousand security measures in place to monitor him and make sure he wasn't giving information to his brother Lawrence again—or anyone else.

"What about Jane?" she asked.

"We don't need her on this," Jake said.

"She's set up on the network," Alex said. "So if and when she does need to be part of something, she's available at short notice. But I believe Jake is correct in this case; she doesn't need to be brought in at this time." He cleared his throat. "If, that is, you are all right with the various hours being charged to you on the case. If you think someone is overcharging..."

Regan laughed. Alex was *so* scrupulously honest, it was hard to remember sometimes he'd been busted by the FBI for hacking and probably had access to every system of any significance in New York City. "No, no, it's fine. You're not going to break the bank any time soon."

Alex paused, then cleared his throat. "It's suspicious that the world's most honest judge is so rich."

"It's Jane's fault, mostly."

"I know," Alex said.

"But now you're wondering whether the world would see it that way, if a scandal ever broke," Jake said.

"Hmm," Alex said. "Yes. I'd like to talk to Gary about setting up some kind of damage control plan for that."

"Feel free," Regan said. "He's probably already got one. He's got that kind of suspicious mind...I think it's because he gossips so much."

"*Anyway*," Jake said. "This is such good news that I don't mind being dragged out of bed for it. Thanks, man."

"You're welcome, and goodnight." Alex clicked off. He hated to be dragged into small talk and any goodbye that lasted longer than a millisecond seemed to give him indigestion.

Jake said, "I'd stay on the line and tell you about the case, but I really just need some sleep."

"Goodnight, Jake. I want to know the second you find out something."

"Of course. I'll start in the morning. After coffee. After lots of coffee."

She smiled. "I'm going to carry around a warm fuzzy in my heart this morning through all my cases—sunshine and roses all around."

"Uh-huh," Jake said. "You'll be in such a good mood that everybody will get five extra years in the slammer—for their own good."

***

The narrow steps up to the door creaked and wobbled—not exactly in the best repair. The black mailbox on the side of the house by the steps was stuffed full of weekly ads, so full the top was standing partly open and the damp air was getting into the cheap paper, making it ripple and stick together.

The front yard was mowed, and the plants looked cared for. A car was parked beside the white clapboard house, a late model tan Cadillac that had been professionally cleaned recently enough that it still had that fresh waxed look.

Jake opened the white screen door, backing down a step to let the door pass. He couldn't see a doorbell anywhere. The house was in one of those neighborhoods that looked like it had been around for a while and might have predated electricity.

He stepped back up to the interior door, as bright red as a new barn, and knocked on the frame. Behind the glass and the lace curtains, he could see the lights were on, but he couldn't catch the flicker of a television or computer screen anywhere. He could almost make out a hallway ending at a yellow galley style kitchen, past the curtains.

He waited to a count of twenty, then knocked again.

If she didn't answer soon, he was going to try checking on Jay Hatchell again. The guy had practically disappeared—cleaned out his bank accounts and left town without letting anyone know where he'd gone. Even Alex was mystified.

And he still hadn't told Regan.

Inside the house, stairs creaked. Outside, a couple of cars drove past on the wet street, their tires hissing behind him, one after the other. It wasn't cold outside, but it was just the right kind of heaviness of misting rain that you couldn't stand to have your jacket on *or* off. With it on, you were steaming hot. With it off, you were shivering. Either way you were damp.

A shadow moved through the hallway toward him, crossing in front of the pale light in the kitchen, then coming down the hallway toward him—a Caucasian woman, plump, wearing a gray t-shirt with black printing on it, and a cardigan.

She came to the door and opened it. The air coming out of the house smelled like air freshener. Pine.

Ashley Gledhill had the kind of face that comes from watching too much Netflix by yourself in the evenings. She looked older than her birth certificate said.

"Can I help you?"

Jake held out his P.I. license. "Jake Westley, private investigator.

I'm looking into the Conrad Wilson case."

Her eyelids fluttered, and for a second Jake could see something attractive in her. Then it slipped away. "Conrad Wilson," she said. "Are you trying to get him pardoned?"

The technicalities between being pardoned and being exonerated could wait for later, if ever. "Yes, ma'am."

"Just let it go," she said. "That's my advice to you." There were dark circles beneath her eyes, and a deep set of grooves between her eyebrows. Her hair had been pulled back with a tight band, and her bangs had grown out in the most unflattering way possible—too long to be tucked back behind her ears, too long to leave down. She had them clipped back with a pair of plain brown barrettes.

"I'm sorry?" he asked.

She blinked at him again. The animation was draining out of her features, and she was shifting on her feet, getting ready to close the door on him. "Someone doesn't want Conrad out of jail," she said, "and they'll do anything to make sure he's put to sleep. Just like an unwanted dog."

"Wait," Jake said. "What makes you say that? Something specific?"

Ms. Gledhill took a long, thin breath through her nostrils. The corners of her mouth turned down; her eyes glistened with tears. She sniffed. "You're a bleeding heart, aren't you? Out to do some good, whether it causes trouble for anyone else or not."

"Not really, ma'am. But the people who hired me are."

She flashed him a quick smile. There it was again—not so much beauty or prettiness as handsomeness—good eyebrow and cheeks, a strong chin. But it had been crushed out of her over time. According to the information that Alex had sent over, she was a year younger than he was. She looked ten years older.

"Come in," she said. "I'll put some coffee on, the way our grandparents used to, when people came over to the house. Or maybe that was just my grandparents. They were constantly inviting vacuum cleaner salesmen over for supper...hobos...just about anyone who stopped by the front door. I thought it was nuts when I was younger. Now it's starting to make sense."

Jake smiled tightly at her, not sure whether he should thank her or protest that he didn't need a free meal.

She brought him into the living room, a nicely decorated room that seemed just a little out of style, with tan Ikea furniture, modernist wall clock, and teal wall sconces in a beige room. The flat-screen TV was covered with dust; a stack of books lay on one of the end tables next to the circle of a permanent coffee stain.

The woman needed a dog. Or at least a cat. A rabbit, maybe. Definitely something to keep her company.

He sat as directed on the couch, then took off his leather jacket and laid it across his knees. It was wet. The books looked like fiction destined one day to become Oscar winning dramas, the kind of thing you liked to read in coffee shops in the hope of starting a conversation.

A coffee pot rattled in the kitchen.

She came back in with a pair of cups. "You can put it down anywhere. I'm not exactly the world's most fastidious housekeeper."

This was the woman for whom Conrad Wilson had left his wife's party. He almost pitied her. "Thank you," he said. The coffee was bitter and burnt and in a blue cup marked SAVON'S CHEVROLET BUICK CADILLAC GMC. It had been sitting in a glass carafe too long. It was damn near truck stop coffee.

She sat in the teal chair next to the couch. "Getting paid hourly?"

He nodded.

"That's good. You should never work on a flat fee—either hourly or on commission, if that's your thing." She managed a local car dealership, according to Alex's research, and did well enough by it to bring home a shiny Cadillac. She slurped at her coffee mug. "So someone finally tracked me down."

"Yes, ma'am."

"Want to tell me what finally gave me away?"

Jake shrugged. Alex had compared various visits that Wilson had made to Portsmouth, established which chunks of time were missing, and compared them. Then he'd tracked down all prepaid cell phones in the area at the time, and found a few areas of overlap. But that wasn't something he needed her to focus on at the moment. "A combination of things. Not something the press is likely to dig up on their own."

"But you're going to tell them, aren't you?" she asked. "God. I hate them, reporters. They crawl over you like maggots."

"We'll do what it takes to prove that Conrad doesn't deserve to be executed. If that means telling them about you, then...yes. We'll try not to, but may have to tell them."

She shrugged. "I've been expecting it for years. I told myself I wouldn't come forward, but I wouldn't deny anything—for God's sake, it's Conrad's life we're talking about. But then he never named me, never. I have never understood why."

"Trying to protect you?"

She flashed a smile at him. "Conrad was never that protective."

"How long were the two of you lovers?"

"You don't know?" When Jake shrugged, she said, "About two years, off and on. He didn't love me; he was just impossible to resist. Very thrilling. I was in need of a little adventure. Making love to a married man seemed to be the answer. I felt like quite the siren."

She glanced around the room, giving it an ironic half smile. "My den of sin. Do you like it?"

"Ah..."

"Don't answer that." She put her cup of coffee down on the end table between them. "It's almost a relief to be able to finally talk to someone."

She didn't seem particularly relieved. In fact, the lines between her eyebrows tightened.

"What happened the day of the murder?"

Her jaw shifted. "He arrived at about, oh, I don't know, one thirty or whenever it was. He stayed with me about half an hour. We made love, then he left. The next I heard was on CNN."

Something in her statement struck him wrong. Not anything she'd said. All of that seemed pretty straightforward—something she'd left out.

"What did you do between the time he left and the time you heard about his arrest?"

The lips tightened.

"I straightened up and made myself a meal. I drank a couple of whiskeys and wandered the house for a while. It was so foggy outside I didn't want to go out, but I felt restless."

"And then?"

The jaw shifted again. The eyebrows drew together until they almost met in the middle. "You know, don't you?"

He suppressed a reaction, trying to let her see what she wanted to see in him. But it didn't work—he felt her slipping. Lie to her or don't, that was the question. He said, "I know that some suspicious sperm was found in the victim's vagina."

"Suspicious," she said.

"Not...as fluid as it should have been. As if it had been produced earlier, then inserted, uh, artificially."

As soon as he said it out loud—he knew what she was hiding. She'd had sex with Wilson...then done something with his sperm. He didn't think she was the type to show up at a murder scene. Someone must have bought it off her.

"You know," she repeated.

"I can guess."

She looked down at her legs, covered in gray sweatpants. It was like she was deliberately camouflaging herself, getting ready to fade into the background. Make a break for it, like she'd been waiting for a long time.

"I wasn't kidding when I said you should stay out of it," she said. "Someone paid good money for that used condom that I handed over that afternoon."

"Who?"

This time, instead of a shift in the jaw or a clench between the eyebrows, she leaned back in her chair and looked out of the front window. Another car drove by, wheels hissing on the wet street. A woman walking a small terrier of some kind, both of them in yellow rain jackets, passed along the sidewalk.

"It's been a long ten years," she said. "And I find myself filled with more regret every day. You don't know Conrad. I regret what I did to him. The closer he gets to his execution date, the more I think I should come forward. It will take so little from me, really, and yet here I am, waiting for someone like you to show up instead of doing what I should have done a long time ago."

The combination of depression and strangeness was really starting to get to him. Suddenly he sneezed into his elbow. His whole body was allergic to this woman's attitude or pine scented air freshener. He wasn't sure which.

"Who paid you for the condom?" he asked.

"I didn't know at the time," she said. "But I found out." She wrote something on a corner of printer paper that had been torn off and handed it to him. Jake unfolded it—a name, Shasta Leighton, and an address. It was written in pencil; he stuck it in his front pocket.

"Used car dealers," she said. "We probably know more about people than we really should. Give us a license plate number, and we can find out anything."

He couldn't help a quick smile. If she hadn't sounded so depressed, she might have reminded him of Gary for a minute.

"She's just an accountant," Ms. Gledhill said. "Just an

accountant. When I found that out, I thought to myself—Ashley, you have utterly no idea how the world works. There are mysteries moving under the surface of things you will never understand, and never hope to understand. Just stay out of it."

Jake frowned at her. It sounded like...it almost sounded like she'd had a run-in with the Organization. But supposedly they weren't involved.

She took a breath. "It went like this. A few days before the party, I got a phone call from someone. They told me they knew about Conrad and that I'd be meeting him on the day of the party—he'd already called to arrange it. They made an offer for a significant amount of money. It wasn't an offer I couldn't refuse, but I chose not to refuse it. Conrad and I had sex; I saved the condom. The woman arrived an hour after he left. I wrote down the license plate number on her car. She brought me cash in a plain envelope, took the condom in a freezer bag, and left."

Ms. Gledhill was still staring out the window, watching the traffic go by. Was she checking the license plates? The makes and models? Did she ever see cars she had personally sold?

Was she afraid someone would be coming to get her?

"Why did you do it?" Jake asked. "Did you need the money?"

"No," she said. "I don't know. It was just something I thought I had to do, at the time."

"I don't understand."

She gave him a half smile, once again almost handsome looking as the wryness passed over her features. "I don't know if a guy like you would ever understand. Wilson was starting to scare me. He was...rude. As if having sex with me was some kind of punishment.

I thought at the time he was getting ready to leave me. But it felt like he was planning something worse. It was like I wasn't a person.

"I was scared, all right? Scared. And I made a mistake. It was only later I realized I had made a mistake. I was watching the trial on the news, and they showed a clip of Conrad being led into the courtroom with handcuffs on. He looked up at the camera and I thought, 'My God. What have I done?'"

Chapter 21 -All of us make mistakes

Jake pulled up in front of the little blue cottage. It seemed cheery enough, considering how thickly the rain had started to fall. A pair of brown barn doors hung where the garage door used to be. The front yard was filled up with hosta plants and square cut bushes. A white Ford Taurus sat out front, parked along the street. The streetlight had turned on early, and the rain glistened on the windshield and slick surfaces of the plants.

He peered in through the front window, a big bay with white latticed panes. The curtains were open and one of the windows was cracked an inch at the bottom. Lights were on, but not in the front room—from deeper within the house.

Behind the house was a big gray building, three stories tall, paint peeling, boards warped, with roof shingles turned green, or askew, or missing entirely. Some of the windows were broken. Between the two buildings was a gray recycled plastic fence, very solid looking, and high enough it would block the line of sight from the back windows on the little blue cottage. It was like the cottage was pretending the old factory or whatever it was didn't exist.

A quick call to Alex had established the house still belonged to Shasta Leighton as a primary residence. It was one of those situations Jake could easily overthink—go up to the front door and knock, or call ahead and see if she was home or busy.

He'd established over the course of his career as a private investigator it was almost always better to go up to the front door and knock. He parked in front of the Taurus, watched the house for a second, then pulled his collar up.

The rain rattled on the roofs of both cars and along the street. The flat slap of raindrops hitting the hostas was the loudest, though. The leaves quivered as the downpour dragged at them.

He marched up a brick walkway to the front door and pressed the doorbell, a neutral *ding-dong* ringing through the house.

A second later, he sensed but didn't see a presence behind the inner door. A small arched window covered the top of the door. He lifted himself onto his tiptoes and saw the top of a head on the other side of the door, hesitating.

"Hello?" The voice echoed from the other side of the door.

"Ms. Leighton?"

"Yes? Who is it?"

"I'm Jake Westley, a private investigator. I'd like to speak with you."

"What's it about?"

"The Conrad Wilson case," he said.

"Oh God," the woman on the other side of the door said. "That. You've come from Ashley Gledhill, haven't you? She's trying to save him."

"I've come from her, but I don't work for her, ma'am."

"Who do you work for then?"

Jake stared down at his boots and the waterlogged welcome mat underneath them, a fancy blue and gold pattern that was sinking into a depression in the top step, and sloshing water over the soles of his boots. "I'd rather not have this conversation out here in the rain, ma'am."

The inner door opened, and a short, round faced black woman appeared, wearing oval glasses and a worn Florida A&M sweatshirt. "Let me see your license." She cracked open the screen door, and Jake passed her his license case.

"You're from New York."

"Yes, ma'am."

"Does that count?"

"As long as I abide by local regulations and requirements."

"Hmph." She passed the leather case back out, then opened the door. "Come in. And dry your shoes off. Normally I don't mind it when my top step gets someone's feet wet. About the most I get for visitors are people trying to sell me something. Let 'em stand out in the rain."

He followed her into the hallway and let his shoes dry off on the rug, then hung up his hat and coat on the brass hat stand. The floors were all hardwood; the woman was walking barefoot. He bent over, untied his boots, and slipped them off.

"I'm just screwing around on the Internet," she said.

The house had an old-fashioned feel to it, more in the layout of small, separated rooms than anything else. The walls were a light gray with white trim, and the pictures were all in silver frames. The front room featured modernist furniture and a bright red accent couch. One of the more stylish houses he'd been in lately.

She led him into the kitchen, humble white appliances that didn't quite fit against the laminate counters. Cast iron pans hung from hooks on the wall; a single painted shelf held all the dishes in stacks, with mugs hanging over the sink. The dinette table was covered with a plaid plastic tablecloth, and the chairs had been painted darker gray. A bright red commercial display shelf held bottles of liquor – scotch and tequila mixed among vodka, rum, and a cocktail shaker.

She sat him at the table and filled a silver kettle at the sink. "It's all collapsing like a house of cards, isn't it?"

"Ma'am?"

"You find Gledhill somehow, Gledhill points the finger at me, and now you expect me to be able to lead you to the next one in line."

"The next one in line?"

She put the kettle on the back burner and gave the knob a vicious twist. "You don't think I killed that girl, do you? Look at me. I'm an accountant, not a murderer."

"I didn't say you were, ma'am."

"But you're looking for whoever killed her, aren't you?"

"We're looking to clear Conrad Wilson of murdering Kristin Walker. There's a slight difference."

"Hmph. You think that fine bit of difference is going to keep me out of prison? No. So I wouldn't expect too much cooperation from me, personally."

"You could just pass the buck, ma'am."

"Oh, you think the judicial system will pass me over if they have bigger fish to fry? Somehow I find myself unconvinced."

She lifted a cup off its hook under the shelf, then left the room out of another door, down a dim hallway. Outside, the rain sloshed against the window in bursts, as if someone were bailing a bucket against the glass.

Ms. Leighton came back in, holding another, non-matching, much larger mug, brightly patterned porcelain with a silicon top. She set it on the counter next to the other mug, then sat next to him at the dinette.

"Let me tell you something. If the courts make it as far as me, they won't be able to go any further. I'm the last one in the chain they'll be able to track down. You see, I have a blackmailer—an anonymous one—and what they tell me to do, I do."

Jake's eyebrows lifted. *They?* "Is your blackmailer from some kind of an organization?"

She frowned at him, her eyebrows meeting behind her glasses. "Why would you ask that?"

"We've run into some suspicious characters, who didn't seem entirely motivated on their own accord. As if they were working for someone else," Jake said. *Yeah, that sounded about right—without being too right.*

"I wouldn't have the slightest idea about that," Ms. Leighton said. "Although I wouldn't actually be surprised. Some kind of organization running around and blackmailing people, just on the off chance they might end up useful? Sure, why not."

"How did the blackmailer contact you?"

"I have a phone," she said. "I check it once a day for a text message. If there is one, I have a number to call that can't be traced."

"I know how that works," Jake said.

"Well, I checked the phone; there was a message. I called and talked to someone who had his voice altered, so it sounded like I was talking to a computer. I got my instructions and I carried them out."

"What exactly were your instructions?"

She pressed her lips together. "You're not my lawyer. I've said as much as I'm going to say about that."

Jake mentally cursed himself. He should have guessed her limits better and not asked the question—at least not so directly. If he'd come at her a little less head-on, he might have gotten more. "I have a strange question for you. Not about your instructions. Just... were you paid afterwards?"

"What?"

"The people we've run into before. There was a pattern to it. The blackmailer would have some kind of hold over them, but wouldn't ask for money, just favors. And if these favors were carried out successfully, then some kind of legitimate-looking windfall would come their way—all above board. The kind of stuff that got reported to the IRS, and that you could spend without having to worry about getting caught. Does that sound familiar?"

He watched her face as he asked. Her eyebrows pinched together, meeting in the middle again. Then her eyes opened, and her right hand tightened on the tabletop, the neat short fingernails clenching. Her nostrils flared.

"Familiar," she said bitterly. "Who are they? What do they want? What are they *doing* to my life? If you know how to get rid of them—" She shook her head. "Never mind, it's never that easy, and you couldn't care less.

"But let me tell you something, though. I didn't deliver the goods. I just picked them up and drove them to a coffee shop downtown in a freezer baggie, inside one of those cloth shopping bags. I ordered a soy latte under the name 'Linda Blair' and left the bag and the latte at a table while I went to the toilet.

When I came back, the bag was gone and a sticky note with a

smiley face was under the latte. Those bastards...here, hang on. Take a look at it."

She got up again, disappearing down the dim hallway. She came back with a clear plastic freezer bag, sealed and then stapled shut past the seal, to show if anyone opened the thing.

Inside was a yellow sticky note marked with permanent marker. A quick smiley face, no border, two dots and a swash for the mouth. Below it—

Thank you. From one woman to another.

"Playing on my sympathy," Ms. Leighton said. "Can you believe it? And yes, right after that I did get a windfall, if you count having one of the best sales months in five years a windfall. I look back now, and I have to."

"Fingerprints?" Jake asked.

"Mine, for sure," Ms. Leighton said. "Which means you can't keep that."

Jake nodded and handed it back. "Have you been contacted since then?"

"A few times. Mostly telling me to pick up something here, and drop it off there, or to ask someone for money." She made a face. "I told them not to do that to me anymore after the first time. I couldn't make myself push for it. I was a single mother with two kids. Drugs... I can see driving drugs or something back and forth, but not that."

She went back into the hallway, then returned empty handed.

"Two questions," Jake said.

"Maybe I'll answer them, and maybe I won't."

"What's your shoe size?"

"Eight and a half." She stuck out one bare foot and wriggled the toes. It didn't look especially small; he'd take her word for it. "And?"

"Can I leave you a number to call if you find out anything? Or even if you get worried about your blackmailer."

She snorted. "I thought you were going to ask me what I did that I'm getting blackmailed for."

He shrugged. "All of us make mistakes."

"That's true."

He stood up, and she did, too. He held out a hand and she shook it. Then he dug a business card out of his pocket. "This is my agency. If you need something, call me."

She looked up at him coolly. "All right."

The kettle had begun to hiss; he could smell a little bit of char coming off the burner. A lot of little successes and failures could happen in between setting a kettle on to boil and the whistle going off.

Chapter 22 -Limits to what I can do

The elevator up to Uncle Paul's office seemed to move at a snail's pace, stopping every other floor to let someone on or off. A number of people saw the penthouse button lit up on the panel and got off quickly.

The last of the office workers departed the elevator with a dozen floors left between the current one and the penthouse. Regan rolled her head on her neck, letting it crack, then rolled her shoulders.

He'd *said* the Organization wasn't involved, but that's not what it sounded like when listening to what Jake discovered. And it wasn't really possible two such organizations existed. One of them would have cannibalized the other by now.

The elevator slowed and came to a stop. The light above the doors began blinking—a double dash on and off.

Regan rolled her eyes. "Really, Uncle Paul?"

The doors opened. The elevator had stopped short of the floor level outside—about a foot lower. A man waited for her—Lawrence, Gary's brother and traitor extraordinaire.

"You," she said.

"Mmm," he said, ducking through the doorway and hopping down into the elevator. He had a hat in one hand and a briefcase in the other. He punched the *STOP* button and the doors closed.

The elevator started upward again with a slight jerk. Lawrence put a hand on the railing.

"I thought I'd catch a ride with you since we're headed in the same direction," he said.

What was his name in the Organization? *Fiducioso*, that was it. *Faithfulness—a misnomer if ever there was one.* She didn't answer him, just shifted her weight a little away from the rail. If he was going to attack her, she wanted to be ready for it, to twist a gun out of his hands or kick him in the crotch.

Jake had been trying to coach her—and she'd been trying to take it seriously—but he kept telling her she'd never know how she'd react until she was actually in danger. Some people just couldn't fight back.

She didn't think she was one of them, even if she never did become an MMA fighter. She wished Jake were there just to remind this scumbag of the knockout punch he got from Jake a few months ago.

Lawrence coughed delicately into his elbow. "Regan... Ms. St. Claire. You need to get out of this case as soon as possible. Your hound dog has just stepped on some fairly big toes, or so the rumors coming out of New Hampshire goes, and they're beginning to wonder just how stable our little family is here in New York."

"Oh? So Shasta Leighton is involved in the Organization?"

"My warning was free, Ms. St. Claire. If you'd like more information about it, you're going to have to trade for it."

She snorted. Of course Lawrence hadn't gotten on the elevator by coincidence. He had something he wanted from her. Funny how a lifetime of being tall, blonde, and very attractive had prepared her for that kind of thing.

"What?"

"I want information on your friend Jessie Bell."

Gooseflesh sprang up along her arms. "Leave Jessie alone."

"What are you going to do to stop me?" he asked.

She raised a hand, palm out. "Get lost."

"In previous generations," Lawrence said, still leaning casually against the elevator wall, "the main focus of recruiting within the Organization was among the rich and powerful. But later on, some of us started to realize it was the less fortunate who made better members—the ones who had more potential than they were allowed to develop... the ones who would be grateful for a boost upward... the ones who would be most terrified of a fall.

"I play because I like playing the game." He gestured his hat toward himself. "But you'll notice that I'm the one of the two brothers who is wearing the suit and tie and hobnobbing with important men—not my brother. Although I will admit he's the smarter of the two of us. I can accept I'll never be the best player in the game or the top one. I'll never have ultimate control over the pieces.

"But the Organization at least allows me to participate to the extent of my abilities. They use me, Ms. St. Claire, but isn't that what all of us really want? To be used well... and rewarded commensurately?"

Regan refused to get drawn into his psychotic rambling.

The elevator stopped. They'd reached the penthouse. Regan pushed past Lawrence out of the elevator, storming past the admin's desk and into Uncle Paul's office.

Lawrence didn't follow.

***

The last rays of sun bounced off the skyscraper next to them and shone in the window. The tint had been shifted so it blocked the worst of the light. Otherwise Uncle Paul, with his back to the window, wouldn't have been able to see the screen of his open laptop.

He looked up, then closed the lid. "Hello, Regan my dear. Good to see you again."

"You said the Organization wasn't involved in the Conrad Wilson case."

His eyebrows rose. "You've found something."

"Jake—"

He raised a hand, and she cut herself off. His eyes rolled upward, and she saw a small dot on the ceiling. "I had an unfortunate encounter earlier that I had to record," he said. "Alas, I have not yet had the camera or the attendant microphones removed. I have no doubt that anything currently being recorded will be deleted by my administrator, but let us be rather safe than sorry."

They walked into the front reception area, and Uncle Paul stopped at the desk. "Have the cameras and microphones removed while I am out."

Uncle Paul's secretary didn't raise his gaze from his workstation. "Yes, sir."

"I shall return in a few minutes."

"Yes, sir."

Uncle Paul took Regan's elbow and led her back into the elevator.

"I was just in here with Lawrence."

"I would assume your conversation was being recorded then, if I were you—and now."

She nodded and leaned back against the wall. The double dashes above the doors were still flashing—the elevator had left its normal control systems. She wasn't sure how she felt about that.

It came to a stop not much later, and the doors opened on what looked like an ordinary elevator floor. But there was no floor number by the door. "Where are we?"

Uncle Paul led her out into a service corridor with a cheaply carpeted floor and a narrow beige hallway. The space overhead hadn't been finished. Tin air ducts crossed over a network of metal pipes, the fluorescent lights were cheap, and the heavy, metal doors were deeply set into the walls.

"A secret floor," Regan said.

"Hardly a secret. It's a maintenance area—power, water, sewer, heating and cooling, and the endless server farms. A place visited more often by computer technicians than a secret conspiracy that runs the world."

"The archives," Regan said.

"Oh, yes. Those too, most of which are stored on the servers... A few humble rooms are still filled with paper filing cabinets, however. The winds of change blow in gusts rather than a steady breeze."

They walked down the corridor, turning first one way, then another. Regan was quickly lost. Her only hope of getting out of here was following Uncle Paul back or laying down a trail of breadcrumbs.

They turned into a small break room with a refrigerator, a set of cupboards along one wall, a microwave, a plastic folding table and folding chairs. The table was the twin of the one in Alex's basement quiet room. Otherwise, the room didn't match.

"You're sure this is safe?"

"Relatively speaking," Uncle Paul said. "A great deal of secure information is stored on this level; the safeguards are relatively thorough."

Regan sat in the folding chair and laid her hands in front of her. "Jake found out where Conrad Wilson was during the missing time when he was supposed to be picking up supplies for a party."

"Yes?"

"He had a mistress."

"Quite the profligate, wasn't he?"

"The mistress was bribed into turning over the used condom."

"To a member of the Organization?"

Regan said, "To a woman who Jake didn't think knew she was a member of the Organization, but who was being run by the Organization nonetheless."

"Blackmail?"

"That's what he said. Someone got a hold on her, then used her to run errands and paid her for that."

"That sort of pattern suggests Organization involvement," Paul murmured.

She looked toward the ceiling which was covered in white acoustical tiles, speckled with gray and black holes. No way to tell whether they were being monitored.

"On the way up to your office, Lawrence got onto the elevator.

He told me Jake had been stepping on some pretty big toes, and that we should watch it."

Uncle Paul's eyelids fluttered, half open, half closed. "Why he would do that, I haven't the slightest idea."

"He asked me about my friend Jessie."

One eyebrow pricked upward.

"And then he gave me this speech about how the Organization used to be made up of rich white guys—I think that was what he was trying to get across—but that now it was making better use of less advantaged people because they'd be easier to manipulate. He was trying to exchange information about the middleman in the Wilson situation, not the mistress or the blackmailer, but the one who'd picked up the condom."

"What did you tell him?"

"Nothing."

"And he could not have expected you to... I wonder," Uncle Paul leaned forward, balancing his chin in his hand, "what his purpose could have been. It almost sounds as if he were challenging you—either take care of Jessie's problems, or he would. But what would he gain? Competition? I suspect another layer of manipulation embedded in the question."

"Sure," Regan said. "It's manipulation all the way down with him."

"Let me state again that I know nothing of any connection between the Organization and the Conrad Wilson case," Uncle Paul said. "This doesn't mean there couldn't be one. Only that I don't know about it. The one hand often hides things from the other. And Lawrence isn't the only one who has learned to play both sides against each other—or multiple sides, for that matter. It is a web of conspiracy and deception further clouded by good intentions. I cannot discount the possibility of bribery or corruption from within.

"However, I must caution you. If Lawrence is warning you about rumors involving Jake, then I would increase your security to the maximum, and honestly, you should consider removing yourself from the situation. You are being watched again. No doubt, I shall be called upon to answer for you and your associates' actions, and I shall defray suspicion as best I can. But you have called too much attention to yourselves again, and there are limits to what I can do."

Chapter 23 -No benefit for yourself

The Brooklyn District Attorney's office had the air of an old fashioned newsroom, all sturdy wood desks, filing cabinets, and shelves. The difference was that here, the newspaper morgue had been replaced with all kinds of boxes and evidence bags.

Regan had her soft-sided briefcase on a strap over her shoulder; she also rested her hand against the handle. The materials they had collected, had been carefully assembled. Read in order, they told the story of how Conrad Wilson had gone to a tryst with his mistress, Ashley Gledhill, who had been bribed by Shasta Leighton for a semen sample at the orders of her blackmailer.

Rather than send Jake back for the rest of the story, they let Alex dig it up. Shasta Leighton had an affair with a professor back at Florida A&M, a professor who had used a personal connection for her to obtain her current position, farther north and out of his hair. It wasn't much—Regan had become used to dealing with murderers as well as the various scumbag defendants she saw in her court—but having it come out would have been enough to cost Leighton her job. Any and every irregularity on the books would have become, retroactively, her fault. It was just like in the Organization—once you were guilty of something, people could blame you for anything.

Whoever was blackmailing her remained beyond even Alex's reach and the reach of Uncle Paul's other contacts in the New Hampshire Organization. At least that's what Uncle Paul told her.

She believed him, but she also wondered—was he being naive? Uncle Paul, naive—it didn't feel right. But he seemed overly trusting of his contacts too.

She passed through the main office and into Laura Provost's

hard walled office built into the side of the room.

Provost was waiting for her, standing up at her desk with her knuckles resting against the blotter. She smiled.

"Tell me you have everything we need," she said, extending a long fingered, cold hand for a shake.

"We have enough," Regan said. She closed the door behind her and sat, then pulled the manila file out of her briefcase. She pushed it across the blotter to Provost.

Provost flicked the folder open with the tips of her fingernails, which were painted a brighter red than normal—the claws were out. "Let's hope so."

She flipped past the cover page and started going over the information. It was mainly a combination of three things: the blood splatter map Alex had put together, printed on separate layers of acetone; a statement from Ashley Gledhill, taken by the police department in Portsmouth; and a security image file of Shasta Leighton at the coffee shop she'd visited in order to make the drop-off. The file was ten years old and had been stored on an old hard drive in the back of the office, supposedly erased. Alex had worked his hacking magic there too.

A representative still photo had been printed out and included in the manila folder, but the entire file was contained within an encrypted email sent to Provost. No doubt Provost had already reviewed the materials—her current flipping through the paperwork was a formality. A triumphant one, if Regan was reading her hawk-like expression correctly.

"We may not be able to get an exoneration out of this," Provost said. "But there's no way we'll miss getting his sentence commuted, maybe to life. The political situation is already out of control. Have you been watching it?"

Regan shook her head. She couldn't care less about the politics. Who would benefit by having an innocent man executed? Who would benefit by keeping him in prison for the rest of his life or setting him free? It turned her stomach.

"You should. There are certain people who now owe you an enormous favor."

Regan sighed. "Do you have what you need or not?"

"I still want that killer," Provost said. "And I want this weird conspiracy tracked back to its source."

"Be my guest," Regan said.

"Don't you care?"

"We've looked, but we didn't have enough time for that. Besides, that's a job for the detectives. Let's hope this time they'll do a better job."

Provost stopped with her fingernails resting on a picture of Shasta Leighton's face. "I thought you were all powerful, or at least placed very close to people who were."

"Power has blind spots, apparently, when it comes to out-of-state cases." Regan didn't want to get into a long drawn out conversation with Provost.

"Ah," Provost said, looking back down again, admiring the paperwork in the file. "How true. How very true. You know this is going to destroy Leighton, don't you?"

"I hope not."

"Oh, it will. Reporters aren't very good with abstract concepts like private property and not interfering with the scene of the crime, but they're very good at putting two and two together. They'll want to know who paid for the semen. Someone will get hold of Gledhill's statement and release it. Blood in the water. Do you think Gledhill's going to kill herself?"

"What?" Regan pushed back against the arms of her chair—taken aback.

"She has that look... complete and utter despair... the face of a woman who is checking out. I'll see if I can have someone up there do a suicide watch on her, at least until Wilson is pardoned. Having her kill herself would just be a distraction at this point."

Regan closed her eyes. It was a small, drab office for such a cynical deal to be going down.

"Do you have enough or not?" she asked.

"It's enough to at least stop his execution," Provost replied. She closed the folder and rubbed her hand across it. "But keep working on the murderer, all right? And the blackmailer."

Her relationship with Provost had gone all topsy-turvy. Regan was supposed to be the one giving orders. She stood, feeling drained.

It was out of her hands now. It had been out of her hands from the moment she had emailed the files to Provost. She just hadn't been able to realize it yet—that was until now.

No more worries about whether she was doing the right thing or not. No more struggles between right and wrong—other than to clean up any fallout that landed next to Ashley Gledhill or Shasta Leighton.

The cold hand was shoved toward her again. Regan took it automatically, even though touching it made her feel ill with herself.

"St. Claire... thanks," Provost said. "I mean that."

The room felt like it had started to spin around her. She grabbed the arms of her chair and lowered her head.

"Are you all right?"

"Dizzy," Regan said. She straightened up and forced the feeling away. The last thing she wanted was for this repulsive predator of a woman to have to try to take care of her, even just to bring her a glass of water. "I'll be fine."

"Thinking about all the fortune and fame you're bringing me and getting no benefit for yourself," Provost said. "You're sure you don't want your name on this?"

"I'm sure."

"Excellent. Well, I hope you feel better soon." Provost chuckled. "You're good, you know that? If you ever decide to quit being a judge, you can always hit me up for a job. I'd get some good legwork out of you."

Regan turned and fled, flinging open the door, then jerking it shut behind her. The walls were so thin she could hear Provost chuckling through them.

Chapter 24 - The world is a strange place

"It's done," Regan said, twisting her hands together in front of her on Jake's desk. "I've handed over the evidence to Provost. What happens now is out of our control."

Jake could see Regan looked distressed. Her face was paler than usual, her hair pulled back in a severe bun that seemed to stretch out a pair of hollows under her cheeks. Okay, so the lighting in his office wasn't the best—just some cheap fluorescent bars overhead. And maybe the flat white wall paint in the cramped little room wasn't the best thing to bring out Regan's natural beauty. But still.

Jake muted the phone headset for a second and said, "You okay, Regan?"

She shook her head, then muted her headset, too. "It's the same thing as always—my doubts about this case."

"What doubts?"

"Exactly. *What doubts.* I wish I knew."

Alex cleared his throat. "Guys, is there a problem? You both just went mute."

They smiled at each other across the desk and thumbed the sound back on. "Sorry," Jake said. "Regan says she's still having unnamable doubts; stuff she can't put a finger on. But, like she says, it's too late to do anything about it now. This isn't something Provost would let go of, not for a million bucks."

"I want you to keep researching to find who the actual murderer is," Regan said.

Alex cleared his throat again. "Do you remember the THEM three?"

Jake frowned at Regan, who shrugged. "No," he said.

"I don't think you mentioned them. Not as such."

"The three guys who subcontract for me..." His voice trailed off. "Okay. I have a number of subcontractors. Three of them live together in the same house. You haven't met them. They were the ones who had the suspicions about the footprints in the office."

"Good work," Jake said.

"Right, well, they do good work, but they're also a little nuts, and they think there's some kind of conspiracy against Wilson, some reason to keep him locked up and alive but away from the public. The consensus is he's being used for breeding material in some kind of project to make the human race more intelligent."

Across the desk, Regan rolled her eyes. No doubt about it, Alex had some weird acquaintances.

"Which just illustrates my point. At any rate, they came in yesterday to the coffee shop for an unscheduled meeting which, from them, is about as unlikely as snow in July."

"So?" Jake asked.

"So they wanted to talk about Conrad Wilson. Before you ask, yes, I asked them if they had any additional evidence for us, or if they had any guesses about who the actual murderer was. TDB said—"

"TDB?" Regan asked.

Alex cleared his throat. "It's a nickname. The Dumb Blond. He looks like a Brad Pitt copy."

"Ah."

"TDB said if he had to guess, it would be some random guy the

238

girl had dated before. He, TDB, is the one of the three who's done the most dating. So, he says we should be looking for someone who dated the girl before Wilson. He said it feels like one of those situations where something got out of control very quickly, and the guy panicked and killed her so she couldn't talk, or maybe the guy got jealous when he found out about Wilson."

"Ugh," Regan said.

"Something I noticed in the evidence on the case was they didn't dig very far back into Kristin Walker's prior dating history. I wasn't able to get anything online about who she dated—unfortunately, nobody kept her computer as evidence, and I have no idea what happened to it."

"The friend," Regan said. "Nancy something, Nancy Rossier. She would know."

"I'll get on that," Jake said. "Good suggestion. We should have picked up on that."

"Make sure you add a bonus to whatever I'm paying them," Regan said.

"Hang on," Alex said. "I'm not done yet. That wasn't the reason the three of them came to see me. It was something else. Two of them wanted to tell me they were having bad feelings about the case—the same kind of thing that Regan's having. The other one, Paddy, said he wasn't having bad feelings about the case, but that Conrad Wilson was definitely some kind of predator, and that had been his opinion all along."

Jake bit the inside of his cheek. Regan closed her eyes and slumped forward on her elbows. Her eyebrows were pinched together so tightly a red line appeared between them.

"Oh God," she said. "What have I done?"

"I asked them what they meant," Alex said. "I mean, bad feelings. It could have been bad anchovies on a pizza. They've never really been 'feelings' kind of people before. They couldn't tell me, but they'd been arguing about it all day. I asked them what had triggered it, and they said that there was a clip that had been playing on CNN about the case. A reporter had obtained permission to do an interview with Wilson, and they'd been watching it on and off ever since."

Jake leaned over to his monitor and flicked it on, then shook the mouse to wake up the computer. "I gotta see this," he said. A quick search pulled it up. He turned the monitor so Regan could also see. She shook her head and held a hand out in front of her to block the view.

The file was only a minute long. "Okay, I'm going to take a moment to watch this," he told Alex.

"Go for it."

Jake clicked on the file. The scene opened with the anchor, a blonde woman with side-parted hair and a hard, vulturish look in her eyes. She summarized the case, then said a press conference was planned to address new evidence tomorrow at two pm. Then she talked about how they had obtained an exclusive interview with Wilson before the new information had been obtained, and that they would play it now.

She turned her upper body slightly away from the camera, and her image was replaced with that of Conrad Wilson.

In his photographs, Wilson was a handsome looking man with light, almost white hair, a broad face, and a wide, thin mouth. He rarely smiled, at least not in photographs. The few videos Jake had seen of the man were of him being led past reporters, his hands handcuffed behind him, head lowered.

This was the first time Jake had seen him in motion.

At first he spoke animatedly, smiling and frowning, looking serious and focused as he talked—whatever the question demanded.

If Jake had been expecting the guy to have a flat, inhuman expression on his face... hey, he'd been wrong before. The guy came across as charming, almost eager to have someone to talk to, glad of the attention.

It was only when he reminded himself the guy was about to be executed—as far as he knew—that it seemed even a little strange. He was in a pretty happy mood for a guy about to be executed for a crime he didn't commit.

Then he noticed the man's eyes. They were deep, striking blue and really stood out from the rest of his pale complexion. It almost seemed like the pupil had swallowed up most of the eye in a black pit. Something else weird about them. They sparkled, almost like he was getting ready for a good cry—an attitude the rest of his face didn't reflect as he merrily answered the reporter's questions. But maybe that was due to the cameras. A full on media interview didn't just mean reporters and cameras. It meant bright lights, some of them behind white screens and some of them shining straight in your face.

Jake glanced over at Regan. She was hunched down into her shoulders, staring at the man as if he were a snake.

Jake grimaced. He still wasn't seeing it. The guy was a little bit off, but that was all.

Okay, he blinked a lot, and when he wasn't speaking, his lips rested in a thin straight line, almost as if he were partially sucking them into his mouth to make them even thinner. And every time he spoke, he almost always started by shaking his head. *No, no, no.* Even when the actual answer to the question he'd just been asked was a *yes*.

As the interview went on—it was mostly fluff, having been taken before Regan had delivered the information to Provost—his face turned redder and redder. One second he would be smirking; the next, he would be forcing his face into a frown.

Up and down the guy's lips went as he struggled to keep from bursting out in laughter.

After a while, it started to grate.

Wasn't the man worried? Wasn't he looking ahead to the end of Conrad Wilson, the police detective? See ya, no more, goodbye? Or could he just not repress whatever black humor was going on inside his head long enough to behave himself for an interview that might help persuade the governor to pardon him? Surely he knew that a lot weighed on this? It was as if the man was looking forward to his execution. Almost like those serial killers who left hints for the cops on the crime scenes, helping the cops to catch them—relieved when they were finally caught.

"Ugh," Regan said. "Just shut it off."

Jake leaned forward to click the mouse and was startled to notice the stiffness in his shoulders and neck. The front of his head felt like an oncoming headache, swollen and a little warm. His fingers had gone cold and forced themselves into a relaxed position, ready to grab for a weapon. His feet were flat on the ground, spread on either side of the chair in such a way he could jump in any direction at a moment's notice without losing his balance.

"I still don't see it," he said, "but I feel it. I'm tense—real tense."

Regan turned her head to face him. She looked terrible, hollow cheeks and eyes about to burst into tears—the picture of regret.

It shook him a little.

"What did your guys have to say about him again? Remind me," Jake said.

"One of them, Paddy, says he's always known the guy is guilty of something, although not the crime he was accused of. The other two are just now coming forward to say they have bad feelings about the case, even though they were both totally behind his being innocent before."

Jake walked around the desk and stood next to Regan. She slipped her hand into his and leaned against his side.

"Tell me he will never be able to find out about our involvement in this case," she said.

Jake squeezed her hand.

It didn't make sense. Normally Jake would be the first to pick up on a bad guy. His guts would have been screaming at him. This guy? He wasn't setting off the right alarms—just made Jake feel a little tense. The guy was innocent.

"The possibility exists," Alex said. "Jake didn't leave personal information with Ms. Gledhill, but he did leave Ms. Leighton his card."

"Not now," Jake said. Regan's fingernails were digging into his hand. "Did the... whatever their names are... did they have anything further to say?"

"About the case, or in general?"

Jake fought back a flash of anger. It sounded like Alex was trying to hide something using some kind of technicality. "Just spit it out, Alex."

"They, ah, said that they'd been contacted by someone about joining some kind of underground hacker group that believed some kind of international conspiracy was running the world. These are the guys who are obsessed with conspiracies, if you remember— The THEM Three."

"THEM," Jake said. "Do you think they're talking about the Organization?"

"I told them I would check it out and see if the hacker group was legit. I strongly suggested I would be using my contacts in the FBI, although that will not be the case. I did warn them," Alex cleared his throat again, "that any groups suggesting there was a conspiracy running the world would, logically, have been infiltrated by the group running the world, and therefore would be little more than a tool of the larger group, or a complete waste of time."

Regan chuckled under her breath—twisted logic.

After a polite pause Alex said, "I also warned them it might also be some kind of sting by the FBI, collecting blackmail material so they could be roped into working for the Feds. Unfortunately, an attractive young woman with considerable geek creds is involved."

"Which do you think it is?" Jake asked. "The FBI, some kind of crackpots, or the Organization?"

Alex waited a couple of moments before answering. The sound of the ends of his mustache being twisted mingled with the sound of computer fans running. "I've met the hot chick in question. She's sharp. I've already caught her playing games within games. If she's not part of the Organization, then there's another group out there, even bigger and worse than the Organization, waiting for us to discover it. Like peeling the layers of an onion and finding there's a pocket universe inside."

Jake shook his head. "A what?"

"A pocket universe is a…"

"Never mind the sci-fi stuff," Jake said. "I'll take your word for it. Conrad Wilson might be trouble once he gets out of prison. The Organization's on the move again, and a group of your friends are at risk from a hot nerd chick."

Regan started chuckling again. "For people who started out wanting nothing more than to save an innocent guy from a lethal injection, we're facing a lot of complications."

"When I was in high school, I thought I would be working for Google for the rest of my life," Alex said seriously. "The worst thing I could think of was being forced to wear a suit."

Jake frowned. "You wear suits all the time, even though you don't have to."

"Truly the world is a strange place, Jacob Westley."

Chapter 25 -The bastard had robbed me again

Conrad Wilson's interview must have gone around the world a million times before it reached Byron Parker. He wasn't a fan of horror flicks, or he might have run across it sooner. Horror fans were passing around the clip, comparing Wilson to Anders Breivik, the Norwegian terrorist who murdered almost seventy kids at a summer camp. The two men shared the same eerily grinning face, the same startling blue eyes.

Physically, they both looked a lot like Byron. Although to be honest, it had been a long time since he had grinned — eerily or otherwise.

It was radiation treatment day for Byron. He'd just spent an unending, almost unendurable, few minutes underneath the molded mesh mask that pinned his head down to the table while a machine aimed ionizing radiation into his brain. His cheeks always ended up looking like they had been left out on a park bench, covered with crisscrosses of pale and red marks from the mask digging into his face. No matter how hard he tried, he always spent the time during treatment straining against the mask. He couldn't relax. The staff had given up on trying to make him relax. As long as he stayed perfectly still while he was fighting against the mask, they turned on machines and aimed the death rays into his skull. The only question was whether their death rays were doing more harm than good. He was suffering from constant headaches, blurry vision, weird half blackouts where he'd be doing something like driving and have no idea where he was or how he'd gotten there, and a constant sense of vertigo. Every action seemed surrounded by déjà vu, as if he'd done it a thousand times already. His life felt both completely predictable and completely out of control. And if he'd had an easy way to kill himself, he'd have taken it. In fact, he'd tried: sleeping pills, a gun, and a hot bath with a razor, but always chickened out at the last moment, just before it was too late.

He was a coward; he'd always known that.

He was so wrapped up in himself he wasn't keeping track of current events—not that he was obsessed with the news or anything. He was more of a Boston Celtics fan. Not that he'd paid them much attention this year; he'd been too wrapped up in his own problems.

So when he did finally see the interview with Conrad Wilson, it was at his doctor's office, waiting for the mobility van to pick him up. The cops had finally taken away his driver's license after his latest accident, and he was down to public transportation. His girlfriend had left him months ago when it started to look like he was going to be more of a pain in the ass than he was literally worth. And the strange thing was, he couldn't even blame her for it. It was what he would have done.

He was sitting in a reception room full of gray-on-mauve patterned chairs, brown carpet tiles, and a couple of flat-screen TVs on the walls, flipping through an old issue of *Sports Illustrated*. The television volume had been turned down low and sounded like people whispering gossip to each other. Only a few of the other chairs held patients. A slow morning. It felt like every time he came in for treatment, which was every day of the week, the waiting room was emptier, the streets less packed with cars, fewer old women out walking their dogs or puttering in their gardens, and fewer young ones pushing strollers.

It was two weeks until his last day at work. It felt like the whole world was closing up shop, getting ready to flip the sign from *Open* to *Closed.* When he, Byron Parker, was gone—it was all over. The whole world felt like a giant con set up to fool one man—him.

These thoughts weren't unusual; he was always morbid after radiation treatment.

Something—fate, destiny, random chance, the devil—made him glance up.

A mirror image of himself, smiling instead of frowning, looked up at him from a cheap plastic table, wearing handcuffs and orange prison scrubs. The guy was fighting a complete breakdown, Byron could tell.

The nurse at the desk looked up too, and said, "Oh my Gosh, Mr. P! That guy looks just like you. Uh, no offense, I mean."

"None taken," he murmured. He'd missed the beginning of the interview. He knew who it had to be, but he told himself that he might be mistaken until he saw the name flash across the bottom of the screen. It was Wilson, all right. The detective who'd somehow been thrown in front of the bus that should have come barreling down the street after Byron Parker instead.

He'd never actually considered him, Conrad Wilson, as anything other than a gift from the gods. A happy accident. A voice in the back of his head had tried to tell him no accident had been involved—someone had deliberately set the guy up. He'd buried that voice. So what? As long as he, Byron Parker, had been kept from having to suffer the consequences of his actions that night, then it didn't matter. Probably the guy deserved what he got. Even if he wasn't guilty of murdering Kristin, then at least he was guilty of *something*. Otherwise, whoever had it in for him wouldn't have set him up. After all, the guy was a cop, he would've made many enemies. It was a twisted kind of logic, but it worked.

Now, though.

Conrad Wilson looked positively *happy* in the interview. Facing death, he had a big grin on his face. All was right in Conrad Wilson's world.

That bastard.

Wilson had stolen something from him. The green eyed monster, that ugly presence that had ruined his life time and time again, reared its ugly head.

The bastard robbed me again—first Kristin, now this. Byron rubbed the marks on his cheeks. Never mind it wasn't something he'd wanted at the time; it was something he wanted back now—desperately.

Fame.

Fame...

...and death.

***

The interview with Conrad Wilson was something you could've missed if you weren't paying attention. The news that the real murderer of Kristin Walker had come forward, you couldn't.

Alex sent Jake and Regan messages as soon as he heard—but they were already both glued to the TV, sitting on the edge of the bed in her bedroom. Regan put her fist in her mouth and bit her knuckles. She didn't want to miss anything. It was coming so fast. One second she'd been called by Provost who accused her of trying to ruin a good case with melodrama. The next, every channel on TV was showing clips of a man walking into the Dover District Court in New Hampshire, wearing a suit and looking sunburned. His name scrolled across the bottom of the screen: *Byron Parker, aged 43...*

Then the press conference with the District Attorney, William H. Gardner, flashbulbs going off, a dark gray curtain behind him, wearing a black suit and a green paisley tie, with eyebrows that came to little peaks and lively eyes—he looked like a devil the way he practically grinned at the reporters. She wouldn't have been surprised if he were completely drunk from celebrating. The problem of what to do with a man on death row when you didn't want to be personally involved, at any point, with executing him had been completely resolved.

Parker had a tumor in his brain the size of an egg—and not a quail egg, either. A big fat duck egg that was making him pass out at random times—a tumor that wasn't responding to treatment.

He'd decided he was done fighting for his life, and had decided to come forward to pay for his crimes and let an innocent man go free—finally. Gardner, reading carefully from a prepared statement, told the audience that Parker regretted letting Wilson take the fall for so long. His only regret was not being well enough to make a public statement apologizing for his actions.

He was an old flame of Kristen Walker's. He'd come over to her apartment for sympathy—his current girlfriend had just left him. Walker seemed willing enough. But when things turned sour between them during an argument, he beat her with the fire extinguisher in the kitchen, then fled.

He said he knew nothing about the evidence that had been found that implicated Conrad Wilson.

Gardner paused, and Regan filled in the gaps. Parker had no

doubt implied that *someone* in the chain of command using an overenthusiastic police officer or officers had been responsible, trying to get rid of Wilson based on some kind of personal conflict. But that wasn't something to be told to a room full of reporters.

He looked back down again and finished reading the statement. Conrad Wilson would be released from prison and helped to begin his life anew as soon as possible. A few pieces of paperwork still remained to be processed, but he would be out within twenty-four hours and had already received several offers of employment from various police departments in need of a good detective.

Gardner finished with a smile and started taking questions.

Regan muted the television and turned to Jake. He wore a button up shirt over an Iron Maiden t-shirt. The leather bomber jacket had disappeared with the warmer weather. His hands lay in his lap, folded together.

He turned to look at her. "So much for our date."

She grimaced and started to tell him that of course they could still go—to a game of some local baseball team that she'd never actually heard of before—but he raised a hand. "We're both going to be on the phone all night. Let's just order a pizza and do it some other time."

She laughed. "You already know me too well."

"That you put work before pleasure? Of course. I wouldn't change it for the world, either."

He leaned toward her, and she put her need to find out exactly what was going on on-hold long enough to run her hands through his hair and meet his lips for a series of long kisses. Finally, he gave her lips a resounding, comical sounding *smack* and leaned back.

"That's as much as I can take for now. Let's find out what we can, as fast as we can, and meet back on this bed in say, two hours."

"Two hours," she said. She laughed again. *Conrad Wilson is no longer my problem*. It was like a weight off her shoulders. She felt like flying. "Two hours is too long. Let's make it an hour and a half."

He leered at her, one eyebrow lifted, and she kissed him again. It was good to be free.

The first person she called was her father, not because she thought he had valuable information, but because she felt so far off the ground that she needed to tell someone who could understand the full import of the news. He was appropriately happy for her, with a cautious edge to his tone that helped bring her off the crazy high she was feeling. Conrad Wilson hadn't actually been freed yet. Something could still drive his exoneration off the rails, however improbable, the possibility was there.

He helped ground her without making her feel like a fool. She thanked him and got off the phone.

She had another call to make—to Uncle Paul. This one was a more practical call. She wanted to know if he'd been involved in the job offers Conrad Wilson had supposedly received. He admitted he might have spoken to someone in Brooklyn PD about the possibility. It would be good to keep the man within arm's reach for a time. In addition, the department had a vacancy that would be nicely filled by a man with experience, who wasn't involved in any departmental infighting. Interviews would still need to be done, paperwork to be completed, of course.

Then she called Provost back, then got on a conference call with Jake and Alex, then called in a few favors so that Provost's evidence wouldn't be wasted, then...

An hour and fifteen minutes later, she was in Jake's arms, still unable to wipe the grin off her face.

Chapter 26 -Shall we tell her?

An hour and fifteen minutes later, Paul arrived at John's house—a long, silent car pulling up in the driveway, and Paul stepping out with a tidy leather overnight bag in hand. It was one of the kind that folded at the top, and it made him look like a doctor performing a house call.

John let him in the front door, holding open the screen for him. Paul went inside and laid his case on the floor by the coat stand, then hung up his light coat. He still wore a suit and tie. He'd come straight from his office at the top of Manhattan, at John's request.

The lights in the entry hall were on, but most of the rest of the house was dark. The two of them looked stiffly at each other for a moment; then John opened his arms and embraced Paul.

The bridge had to be mended, whether they were comfortable with it or not. That was clear now. After a moment, they let go of each other, then John patted Paul on the shoulder. He locked the door and turned out the light as Paul picked up his overnight bag again. Then the two of them walked deeper into the house.

"You're sure they know," John said.

"If only the man, Parker, had come forth with his incredible revelation twenty-four hours earlier," Paul said. "They have been watching Provost."

"I thought you said you controlled her."

"I do. However, someone has been going behind my back, placing agents in my territory. They don't like the conflict of interest that my resuming ties with you and your daughter could present to them. I am, of course, less than completely trusted."

"Is Lawrence behind it? Fiducioso?" He opened the door to the basement and turned on the light.

Paul preceded him down the stairs. "That *boy*."

"He's passed even your boundaries for—"

Paul raised his empty hand. "We don't have time for those old arguments, John. I have made a bed, which I sleep in every night. That doesn't prevent me from classifying Fiducioso as a particularly bloodthirsty and noxious bedbug."

John grunted in reply. They'd been at each other's throats for so long, it was going to take him a while to change his habits.

They reached the basement and Paul headed to the spare room to put down his bag, then returned to the main room. John had come downstairs and run his gizmos around the room to check for bugs, then sealed the windows so that no one would be able to see inside, unless they pressed their faces against the glass. He might not have the technical prowess of the boys who worked for Jake, but he could still hold his own.

"What do you need me to do?" he asked.

"We need to obfuscate who has been working for Regan," Paul said. "Specifically, Jacob Westley. We need to arrange matters so that it is clear he has been working for you... and, through you, for the Organization."

John had known for the last several hours, since Paul had called him earlier, in fact, this was exactly how it had to be. Nevertheless, he said, "Damn you, Pavo. Pulling me back into this."

"I had no hand in this," Paul said. "And I take no pleasure in it."

"That's not true."

John checked the panels covering the narrow half-windows one last time, then turned on the lights.

Which didn't stop the damn dog next door from immediately starting to bark. John swore at it softly. "How can it tell? How?"

"One of the lights is going out," Paul said. "If you listen carefully, you can hear it hum."

John shook his head. He'd never been a man for small dogs. He took a deep breath. "I'm going to need a whiskey for this. Would you like anything?"

"A smoky Scotch, if you please."

"You hate smoky Scotches."

"It has been a nerve wracking evening, John. I feel a great temptation to try to keep up with your drinking—but we both know that that is a bad idea."

John chuckled and walked around the felted pool table to the small teak bar on the far side of the room. The basement was homey, several couches around the edges of the room, a large projection screen, shelves full of detective novels and mementos, both his and Linda's.

The room hadn't changed much over the years.

He poured two Lagavulins in a pair of old fashioned crystal glasses, a large cube of ice in each. Paul had seated himself on the ghastly orange and white couch that Linda had loved so much, one ankle balanced on his knee. He looked around the room with a blank expression, as if he didn't recognize most of it.

He handed one of the glasses to Paul, then sat beside him. The room always seemed haunted, which generally was fine with him— he could almost smell Linda's perfume as her memory moved through the room, wearing a yellow sundress and a headscarf bending over the table to line up a shot, or sitting across his lap, noodling against his neck. He took a sip of his Scotch.

"I'm assuming you have things for me to sign and date," he said.

"No," Paul said. "I have your signature on file and have for years. I've had a document specialist working on the papers for hours. They'll be ready in a day or two, and then I'll have them planted appropriately. All that I required was your consent—or rather, I wanted it."

John snorted. "If you didn't need me, then why did you come?"

"I needed a reminder of why we're doing this," Paul said. "Why I walk the paths of the less than righteous in the name of righteousness."

"Because you have no concept of mercy or forgiveness. Don't even mention righteousness," John said.

Paul turned to look at him. He'd always been thin. At that moment, he appeared positively skeletal—desiccated, like Boris Karloff in *The Mummy*.

"That is correct," he said. "Forgiveness... it is beyond me."

John raised a glass, and Paul raised his.

"To Linda," John said.

"To the goddess who happened to be your wife," Paul said.

They clinked the glasses together, then drank.

"Do you remember..." John said.

"The last time I was in this room? Of course I do," Paul said. "You had just left Brooklyn."

"With my tail between my legs."

"With your family intact," Paul said. "With your wife and daughter alive and with you, and a promise from the Organization that they would not hunt you for the rest of the days of your life. It was a victory."

"If so, it was a humiliating one."

They both drank again.

"It was the end of everything," Paul said. "You said you would never forgive me for what I had done to her, to make her cry."

"I have," John said. "I understand it better now. You pulled attention away from the three of us."

Paul pressed his lips together, sipped his whiskey, then grimaced. "I murdered a man. Not with my bare hands, but it was my acts that condemned him. An innocent man died because I did not have time to shift the blame onto a guilty one."

"Aren't you the one who always says that everyone's guilty of something?"

"I paid so little attention...he may have been. But I did not trouble to find out."

"It still bothers you," John said."

"Yes. It bothers me still. But worst of all..."

***

Linda sat on the ugly orange couch John had jokingly bought at a thrift store last week, knees and ankles pressed together, both hands clutching her knees through her flowered skirt. Her wide blue eyes watched Paul intently, following him as he walked back and forth over the ugly brown carpet on the floor. Paul pressed the tips of his fingers against the wood of the pool table as he walked.

A tiny hitch in his side screamed volumes—he'd been hurt.

So had John. The cast on his arm was just the most visible sign of the damage he and Paul had gone through in the last few days. *Thank God* they'd stopped the man at the sewer station before he had a chance to get at Linda and Regan. But the fallout was still uglier than either of them could have imagined.

"Your husband will never truly be free of the Organization," Paul said. "Between the two of us, we have done what we could to limit his involvement. If they call upon him, that is, if *I* call upon him, then he will be required to provide assistance."

"But you won't," she said.

"I will do my honorable best to ensure his assistance is not needed."

"How...how could you do this to him in the first place? How could you give away his future like this?"

Paul looked at John; John shrugged. He'd told his wife he'd joined the Organization of his own accord, but she managed to find out the truth anyway. He'd only joined to protect Paul from being used, as best he could, which turned out to be not very well at all.

John started to say, "I chose..."

But Paul lifted up a hand, and John let it go. Let his friend confront his wife. Let them face each other finally, instead of stepping between them all the time.

Paul's face looked much older than its actual years. The man was forty-five, not seventy, but John would have been hard pressed to prove it with anything other than a birth certificate. It looked as though he'd been starving himself, too. His thin frame looked diseased, as if the flesh had been eaten away from the inside.

The effect of having a bad conscience, maybe.

Paul watched the two of them, John and Linda, sitting together on the couch. When he glanced upstairs, John knew what he was thinking about—Regan. The girl who looked so much like her mother. The girl who wasn't exactly little anymore, and whose heart would be broken if her Uncle Paul went to prison.

"The man the mob killed should not have been the one to die," Paul said. "He was only in the wrong place at the wrong time. Someone else should have 'discovered' the body of the mob's hitman and reported it to the police. Someone else should have been made an example of, and it should have been me, not an innocent man. It is the responsibility of the Organization that it, and not the innocent, should bear the brunt of retribution for its acts, no matter how well intentioned.

"As you said earlier, Linda, intrinsically my life is not more valuable than other lives. I argued that my life was more valuable because I provided a greater service. You stated any service I provided was more than offset by my being..."

"Such a phenomenal asshole," she murmured.

"That is correct. I have looked at your assessment and come to the conclusion that I cannot know whether that is true. Am I doing more harm than good? Is my weighing of the situation so biased that I have become a truly evil man, rather than a pragmatic one? I allowed another man's death to save my life. What do I owe his family? What do I owe society, for all that he might have contributed to all of us? I cannot know."

Her jaw flexed. She glanced at John, not sharing the glance with him, but looking him over and thinking of the broken ribs and arm, bruises, and cuts all over his body.

"What do I owe you?" Paul asked. "That is another question I cannot answer."

He had stopped to watch her face, which had turned more and more from that of an old friend into a flat, hateful grimace.

They stared at each other. John waited for the fur to fly. All he knew was he was too tired and too hurt to keep throwing himself in between them.

"And in fact, it is relatively unimportant," Paul said. He crossed his arms over his chest and looked down at his trousers and polished shoes. "The important question is not what I owe anyone, but what I can do for Regan."

"I don't want you in her life," Linda growled.

"I accept that your desires are against it," Paul said. "However, there is the question of what she wants and what she needs. I have found myself in a position where I have to make judgements about the best way to influence the future in a positive direction. I, myself, will never have children. I see myself as the poisoned fruit from a poisoned tree, as it were. And I would not like to risk influencing her too directly any longer.

"However, it would be my privilege to ensure she has the finest education. The two of you on John's salary cannot afford to send her to Columbia. I will ensure the funds are available in a timely fashion. I will also ensure she has the funds necessary to set herself up in whatever profession she chooses. I will do these things regardless of whether you accept my next request."

His fingers dug into the arms of his suit jacket. "Please. This would mean a great deal to me. I would like to continue teaching Regan how to play chess—once a month, at a location of your choosing, by mail if necessary. I will not speak to her of the

Organization or of any other part of my life. I will listen to her troubles and give her advice on protecting her rooks."

Paul had already run the plan by him, but John had refused to agree to it without Linda's concurrence. He'd had enough of hiding things from his wife.

She glanced at him, this time to get his opinion.

"I'll go with whatever you decide," John said. "What he says is true... mostly true. We can scrimp and save and pay for Columbia."

"The couch," she said.

"It's an honest couch. Cost us all of twenty-three dollars."

Her eyes suddenly glistened with tears, and she reached over to him and took his hand. Her hand was so small, yet seemed strong enough to crush him in half. He stroked the skin on the back of it.

She turned her face toward Paul, looking at him with hard eyes—yet eyes half-filled with tears. They'd known each other as long as she and John had known each other—had been forced into a friendship with each other. Then Paul's affection for her had deepened into love.

Once upon a time, he would have done anything to make her happy, and she would have indulged him gently, knowing she had his heart in her fist. They'd never cheated on John—nor had he ever so much as suspected it of either of them. Linda didn't love Paul. That was all there was to it.

John knew in her head she was stripping away the money. She'd never cared much for it, other than that it was honestly obtained. When he'd decided not to take money from his parents when they got married, she supported his decision, even though she was the one who bore the brunt of any sacrifices.

So take away Paul's offer to support Regan through college and get her set up in her career, what was left?

An old friend who wanted to play chess with their daughter.

On the one hand was the danger that he would teach her to play dirty—to cheat. There was also the danger that the business of the Organization would rub off on her somehow, either to threaten her safety or to drag her into that whole mess.

On the other hand—he was an old friend who wanted to play chess with their daughter.

Linda's face softened.

But not too much.

"You may visit her once a month to play chess," Linda said. "I would prefer you don't return here. Whatever steps you need to take in order to never cross my threshold again, take them. But you may meet with her. As to any college or other funds, you can talk to her about that when the time comes. By then she'll be old enough to make up her own mind."

He nodded and unpicked his fingertips from the sides of his arms, one finger at a time, then straightened up slowly.

He nodded toward John, looked at Linda—a whole world of repentance went into that look, the same kind of thing that John had seen a hundred times in court, as a condemned man said goodbye to his family—and walked toward the guest room where he'd left his bag just inside the door.

His long thin frame darted down and came back up with the bag.

He unzipped the top, reached inside, and pulled out a cloth bound book. The gold letters on the cover glinted as he lay it on a small table by the stairs.

Then he walked upstairs, slowly and deliberately, still trying to hide the hitch in his walk.

His footsteps crossed the living room. Then the front door opened and closed.

Linda laid her head against his shoulder. He made no comment when it became wet.

The book was *To Kill a Mockingbird*.

***

"—Worst of all was knowing Linda had placed her trust in me, and I had failed it," he said. "I have been haunted by that ever since."

John nodded. He'd been haunted by a couple of things from back then, too. "And now we come together once again, for the sake of my daughter."

"Shall we tell her?"

"No. Never."

Chapter 27 - The scary thing

It was a bright and sunny June day, the skies wide open, the birds singing, the cameras rolling. Conrad Wilson stepped across the threshold of the prison, took two steps forward, spread his arms up to the blue dome of the atmosphere, then folded forward, got down on his knees, and kissed the sidewalk in front of the prison.

It was grimy and just slightly damp from a foggy morning that had burned off a couple of hours ago. One minute he'd been out in the exercise yard in a gray haze wearing orange prison scrubs. The next he was walking out of the building in a new suit under a blazing yellow sun. A miracle.

The sidewalk under his lips was pleasantly warm, even if it did smell like piss, dog shit, and cigarette butts. He sat up. His lawyer, Marco Ottaviano, handed him a white monogrammed handkerchief with which to wipe his lips.

Ten years in prison for a murder he didn't commit. And now he was free.

Man, oh man. A bunch of reporters were trying to ask him questions. Later on, maybe he'd talk to a couple of them, but not all of them. That would look like he was desperate for attention. But maybe CNN and a couple of the other big ones, a few exclusives. What was that show? *Sixty Minutes*. Was that even on the air? What channel did that run on?

One of the reporters was leaning in tight, shoving her microphone in his face. "What do you think about the news of Byron Parker's debility from brain cancer?"

Wilson grinned. The reporter couldn't help it. The corner of her mouth turned up as she looked at him, waiting for an answer.

"I think that question's going to have to wait until after my first hamburger," he said. Everyone laughed. Then a limo pulled up.

He straightened his shoulders, sinking deeper into his suit. It was fun toying with the press; he'd always enjoyed it. They were like greedy kids forcing their way into a shop, holding their hands out for free candy. But he needed to keep it under control—limit the amount of hamming it up that he did. Soon he'd be looking for a job, doing interviews. A good detective didn't stand out—not unless or until it was required.

And dear God, after everything had fallen apart on him, it would be good to get back on the job, doing something—he pleaded—hadn't changed too much during his time in the slammer.

At least he had something the other candidates wouldn't have: experience behind bars, up close and personal with hundreds of rapists, thieves, and murderers. He'd made it a point to listen to everybody's story—everybody who would talk. He'd been digging down deep into the minds of criminals.

The scary thing was, they weren't that far off from normal people.

Chapter 28 -She jumped

In the bright June sunshine in Portsmouth, New Hampshire, at a cute little Indie coffee shop downtown, Nancy Rossier leaned back against the plastic cafe chair's back and thought what a shame it was Conrad Wilson had turned out to be innocent. For the last ten years, she'd made it her duty to hate him. It was hard to come to terms with his innocence. Sure, she still hated him—not for killing Kristin anymore, but for how he used her and for the slime ball he still was.

The coffee spiked with a triple espresso was helping, though.

Baby strollers, bicycles, and bimbos drifted across the streets, backing up traffic. The sidewalks were full of tourists—it was Labor Day, and Portsmouth had changed in character from a pleasant college town near the ocean to a tourist trap, filled with pleasantly smiling sharks out to scam the unwary out of as much as they could get. The other tables and the brick sidewalks were all filled with people up from New York City, or Boston, or wherever the hell they came from, in their endless streams, as well as pickpockets, traveling salesmen, street performers, three-card monte players, small time cons, and every other rip-off artist in the area. Everyone who was able to leave town for the summer had done so and put up their houses for rent on the Internet.

In fact, she was planning to do the same—take off for two weeks to Paris and rent out her cottage while she was gone. The person renting her house would be arriving here to meet her in ten minutes. If all went well, she'd be on a plane across the ocean in a little under four hours. If they weren't here in twenty minutes, oh well, she was still leaving—even if it meant giving up over three grand in rent.

The coffee was all right. *But it would be better in Paris.*

She pulled out her phone and started scrolling through news articles with a stiff flick of her finger. There was Wilson again, arms in the air, then bending forward to literally kiss the sidewalk. Come on, that was just disgusting. When asked about the fate of the man who'd surrendered in order to save his life, all Wilson had to say about it was that he wanted a burger.

That guy. Cold as ice.

She made a pact with herself she would never force herself to *like* the guy, even if he ended up getting a detective job in the area and she, by some unfortunate circumstance, had to work with him on a case for one of her clients.

Five minutes passed, then ten. Nobody showed up. Nobody even looked her way twice.

Fifteen minutes, the coffee dregs in the bottom of the cup were cold and sour, truly unpleasant, and she was weighing three thousand dollars against waiting around another five minutes. The assholes who were renting her cottage had her cellphone number; if they were going to be late, they should have called.

She stood up, found a public trash can, and dropped the paper coffee cup through the circular hole with a thump.

She checked her phone again. No calls, and she had four minutes to kill before she would let herself walk out of here and off to her car.

She felt like a fool. The person she'd talked to on the phone had no intention of showing up. Every second she was standing here was a second wasted.

A couple of plump, sweatshirt and shorts tourists, seeing she had left her seat unattended for two seconds, took over her table, and looked up at her with wide eyes practically begging her not to shout at them for being assholes. It was pitiful. The bar and grill down the street invited her to step inside and grab a seat at the bar, get something to eat before she hit the airport, and the lines, and the delays, and the snacks... but it also invited her to drink a couple of gin and tonics too, and she didn't really want to get started on her vacation too soon.

Ah, screw it. She gave the tourists who had taken her table a look that said, *you can have it...you tacky bastards*, and stalked off down the brick sidewalk, dodging both dogs and little kids on leashes, dancing around benches, and doing a slide around grim-faced local joggers who really should have done their running earlier in the morning.

At the end of the block, she turned down a side street. It was still bad, but not as crazy with people. Cars parked nose to tail as far as the eye could see.

She followed along the street for another two blocks, then turned again, another two blocks, another turn.

Finally, she had reached her car. It was parked in its usual spot in a tiny parking lot next to a converted church/garden center. The fact she knew where it was, in Nancy's opinion, more than offset the distance she had to walk to get to it. She'd been parking here for over a decade, long since before Kristin's death, whenever she had to park downtown. Even in her most drunken state she could find it. And for some reason, the parking lot was both free and never quite full.

The house on the other side of the garden center was for rent with a big sign out front.

The weird thing was, she thought she could see a dim flash of light inside, as if someone were taking her picture.

She already had her keys in her hand, an old habit from college. She unlocked the driver side door and slid into her seat, then put the keys in the ignition.

A sound from behind her made her look back over her shoulder out the back window.

Behind her, someone was coming out of the vacant house and walking toward the car with a quick pace.

She pushed down the lock by her door, another old habit coming back into play.

The guy was probably just walking down the street, headed toward downtown, but... she didn't like it. She got a flash of his face, not long enough to recognize him, before he got too close to the car and the roof cut off the view of his head.

He walked up beside the car and knocked on her passenger window.

The rational, sane thing to do would be to ask him what he wanted—not rolling the window down, but not panicking until the guy showed signs of being an actual threat.

Instead she turned on the car and pulled backward out of her parking spot. The guy stood in place, then took a step backward and turned around, heading back toward the house marked FOR RENT.

The streets downtown were narrow and dangerous at this time of year, with a stupid tourist likely to jump out in front of her at any second. She kept her eyes peeled and congratulated herself on not giving in to the urge to be "nice." Staying safe meant being a little rude from time to time, to people who probably didn't deserve it.

She followed her usual route out of the area, which in order to avoid as many bridges as possible, was a bit of a circuitous route, first leading away from the airport, then circling around. Again, something of a routine.

She pulled up to a stop sign next to a blind intersection, slowly easing forward.

Suddenly, the engine cut out. She cursed, shifted into neutral, and tried to start it again.

The engine didn't even turn over.

A few more tries convinced her it was pointless. At least she had a decent amount of time before she had to make it to the airport— plenty of time to call a cab.

She dialed in the number on her cell phone as she got out of the car and popped the trunk.

Inside was her rolling bag and her carryon, two red bags that would stand out easily on a baggage turnstile. She hefted them out, then strapped them together for easier wheeling. The cab dispatcher assured her she would be sending a cab as soon as possible, and definitely they would be able to get her to the airport on time, but it might be a few minutes because of the season. Nancy told her that was fine and asked to be transferred to a towing company. The phone beeped, then started ringing again.

It was going to be a pain in the ass, but she would make it to Paris just fine.

She couldn't help feeling it was all the fault of the guy who was supposed to meet her to pick up the house keys.

Someone at the tow company picked up and said, "Hold

please," and put her on hold before she could protest. Distorted, off-key music, some pop song that sounded like it came out of someone's nightmares, now played over the phone.

Nancy sighed and slammed the trunk.

She jumped.

On the other side of the trunk was a man, standing in front of her with his hands in his pockets.

Grinning.

Chapter 29 -She heard him curse softly

Regan sat in her office chair. It had been impossible to focus this morning. She'd found herself up and down, talking to other judges about their cases, haunting the break room, bending pens and flipping pencils between her fingers, looking out the window with longing at the idyllic blue sky dotted with fluffy white sheep clouds. She was restless, restless enough to find herself shredding paper strips out of her desk calendar, restless enough to tap her head against the wall until Gary walked into her half of the office and glared at her. But every time she looked at the work she needed to do, whether printed or on the computer, the letters seemed to swim in front of her.

Gary said, "Regan. Go home."

"And do what?"

"Annoy someone else. You're worse than useless. You're distracting me from actual work."

"Remind me again what useful work you actually do."

"Don't even go there."

She swung herself back and forth on her chair. She had the ineradicable feeling she was missing something—that she should be doing something important. But the fact was, her caseload was light right now, and the hurry-up-get-it-done pressure of getting Conrad Wilson out of prison before his execution was over.

She needed to find a way to focus on the next case, the one they had started just before the Conrad Wilson case came up. Craig Moreau wasn't getting any younger in prison. Even if he wasn't on death row—thirty-four years in prison was almost as bad as death row.

She drummed her fingers on her desk, bounced a mechanical pencil on its eraser until most of the lead was shattered inside, and played with a couple of metal paperweights, flat heavy metal daisies. She felt like chucking one through a window.

Wrong. All wrong. What she was doing was wrong.

What the right thing to do was—she had no idea.

The phone rang. She pounced on it even before Gary could tell her who is was. "Hello?"

"It's me," a woman's voice said, taking a second to slide into place. "Laura Provost."

Regan mentally sorted herself out of her funk and tried to think professional thoughts. Her current, sadly flaky and distracted state had to be deeply hidden. The woman was a predator.

And a distraction, which was a relief.

"Have you heard the news?"

The way Provost said it sharpened Regan's attention—made it stop dancing around the room. She unhooked her feet from those of her chair and put them flat on the floor, then sat up straighter. She glanced back at Gary, who had his headset on and was standing up at his desk but staring downward at his computer monitor.

"No, what?" she asked, as Gary's eyes widened and his mouth dropped open.

"Nancy Rossier was found murdered."

Goosebumps sprang up on the skin of her arms under her blazer. "Murdered. Where was Conrad Wilson?"

"Here, in Brooklyn."

"You're sure? The whole time?"

"He was in the middle of a job interview, Regan."

Her head was stuffed with cotton. "I'm sorry. That guy. There's just something about his face that gets to me every time. I just automatically assume he's guilty."

"Of what?"

"Everything."

"Then why did you work so hard to collect evidence to get him out?" Provost snorted. "No, wait, let me guess. Because you knew you had it in for him, and you figured it was only fair to bend over backward to save him."

"Bingo."

"I'll never understand you."

"You just did."

"You know what I mean."

Regan began tapping her fingers on the desk again. As far as distractions went, the call had been distracting—but not for long. She was back to feeling restless again.

"You're *sure* he couldn't have pulled one of those stupid murder mystery tricks, where it seems like he was in one place while really he was somewhere else?"

"Really and truly. They found her body this morning downtown in a vacant house. The owner checks on the place every night before bed, then again in the morning because of all the tourists in the area."

"Sorry?"

"You live in White Plains; nobody ever wants to go there. But other, nicer parts of the world get afflicted with people from other places, called tourists, who have no business being in the area and who wander around and get underfoot all the time."

"I've heard of them," Regan said drily.

"They're like mice. You have to practice constant vigilance. So the owner checks the vacant house this morning, and it's been broken into. There's glass all over the sidewalk in the back of the house. He calls the police but doesn't go in himself. He's convinced a bunch of drug addicts is sleeping it off inside, and he doesn't want to deal with them."

"Drug addicts or tourists?"

"Shush. The officers go up to the house, open the door, and hear a scream. They find her stabbed in the chest but still alive, moaning on the floor. She dies on the way to the hospital with a heroic and frankly handsome EMT on the scene. You'll see him when you watch the news. Yummy."

"And how does this mean that Conrad Wilson couldn't have been involved, if he's at an interview now?"

"She'd been stabbed what seems to be seconds before the officers arrived, at approximately nine fifteen this morning. Wilson's interview started at nine."

It was a difficult admission, but she faced it. She was actually disappointed it couldn't have been Wilson. "What about her killer?"

"They didn't see him. They found evidence she'd been raped and are running tests to see if they can come up with any DNA matches. They found some fingerprints and are running those, but as far as signs of someone running out of the house or hiding in the basement—nothing."

"Did she say anything before she died?"

"No, she didn't. The EMT—if you would watch the news once in a while, you would know this already—said she seemed pretty out of it when they found her. I think she might have been drugged."

Regan took a deep breath. Provost laughed. "It's not him, St. Claire. You're just going to have to find another suspect for your evil genius fantasies."

"Fine," she said, disgusted that it was so easy for Provost to see through her. "What do you think about Wilson as a possibility for the detective squad? Is he any good?"

"Oh, he's good," Provost said confidently. "I watched his interview videos. It was very impressive."

"What was? And is there anything you don't stick your nose in?"

"Not if I can help it," Provost said, a pleased tone in her voice. "It's hard to put a finger on. He's such a... well, he smiles all the time. And he's such a brown-noser. He's very good at it—a real charmer. In fact, when you see him looking straight at the interviewer, Ralph Johnson, who has a reputation as being a bit of a bastard, Johnson kind of freezes. It's like he's being instantly hypnotized. Then Wilson looks over his shoulder at the camera, and Johnson comes back to life again. If anything, I would say that Wilson is downplaying his skills as a detective on his resume... he seemed to know almost everything about Johnson as soon as he saw him, from his family life to his temperament, to the fact he knew the man's grandmother's name was Margaret—almost supernatural."

"Probably just a conman's tricks," Regan said.

"As long as the conman is on our side, working to collect information for us and help us solve cases, I'm fine with that."

"So is he getting hired?"

"Confidentially, yes."

The chair in Gary's side of the office rattled, and Regan looked back through the door at him again. He had disappeared from view. In the background she heard him curse softly.

"Johnson tested him out to see if he would accept. Wilson laughed and said he wanted time to talk to a realtor. He still owns a house in Manchester, New Hampshire, he wants to go through and see if there's anything he wants to keep. He'd been hanging on to it, I gather, because he had this idea he'd be able to get his old job back when they realized how wrong they'd been to send him to prison."

"What did they do, by the way? Offer any restitution?"

"No. Get this. They still haven't contacted him, to offer a job or even just to apologize. Wilson's lawyer is practically drooling at the opportunity to strip their coffers. But I think really Wilson's ready to let bygones be bygones, and move on."

Chapter 30 -Just like old times

Cooper was driving a big white repair van from his company that echoed like a drum every time they hit a pothole in the gravel road. His hands were at ten and two, and his face turned toward the road. Shadows from the thick trees shading the road flickered over his stubborn, loyal face.

The radio played Eric Clapton's, "Lay Down Sally." The signal fuzzed in and out as they drove up into the mountains on the winding road.

Clean new clothes, blue jeans, and a button-up shirt over a t-shirt, a fresh shave with a new razor, aftershave splashed on his cheeks—it was a brand new day for Conrad Wilson.

The bad news was ten years had passed and the world had left him behind.

It could have been worse. It could have been twenty or thirty years; like some guys he knew who were still in prison. Imagine leaving prison and finding out about cell phones or the internet—going from the Eighties to now. The thieves would be the ones who had it the worst. The way technology was changing, spend more than a couple of years behind bars and you'd be lost, let alone the fact that most of the money was online now.

The good news was ten years had passed and a lot of Conrad Wilson's problems had left him behind, too.

His wife had left him, almost immediately, which meant he was single and carefree. And his mother had passed on.

His dad had passed before Conrad had been put away. He'd never had to go through the stress of his son's trial, et cetera. His mother, on the other hand, had seen everything, never letting the grim look of condemnation off her face. She'd never had his back. From day one she'd judged him. No matter what he accomplished in the world, she'd just shake her head and look away. In many ways they'd been complete opposites. The kind of mother you loved but weren't too shook up about when they passed on.

But she'd left the cabin to Conrad, not to his brother, Cooper—a nice gesture, but totally unnecessary. He'd been offered a job in Brooklyn. And, while it might be nice to get up to the mountains once in a while in the summer, he'd have to hire someone to take care of the place during winter.

He could hire Cooper to do it, but that could be considered just a mite bit insulting, hiring your brother to take care of the cabin he was supposed to inherit.

Maybe he would do it. Have to see the place first and how things had held up.

Even though there was nobody behind them, Cooper turned the blinker on to signal their turn up the steep, narrow driveway, then did the almost U-turn at a reckless twenty miles an hour. Conrad laughed and grabbed the dashboard as the van barreled up the drive, turned sharply, then skidded to a stop in front of the house.

"Still got it," Cooper said. "Please, officer, don't pull me over for reckless driving." He held his wrists out, two tanned thick bars covered with rough gold hair, sticking out of the sleeves of his jacket. "All right, officer. I'll go quietly."

On the other hand, some things never change. Like Cooper's bad jokes.

"I'll let you go this time," Conrad said. Cooper laughed. His voice had grown a little harsh from smoking for the last ten years, but it still had its charms.

They got out of the van, engine ticking, and stood in front of the house.

The front yard, such as it was, was overgrown, the big evergreen bush at the side of the house shot through with birch suckers. The roof looked all right—aside from the suckers growing in the gutters. The siding was a little dinged up, and one of the windows was cracked.

"Pipes are OK," Cooper said. "I checked those over the winter. Meant to get to that window, just haven't yet. I have a new sheet of glass in the back to replace it."

"Thanks."

The steps in front were in three sections. The middle section had fallen off its rock and tipped to the side. Cooper pointed at it and swore. "That's new."

They jumped that section of steps and got up on the deck. The old enameled white fridge was still sitting next to the front door on a concrete pad with a padlock on the doors. Claw marks from frustrated raccoons reached up the front of the door. Chew marks showed on the cord too, but it was covered in a metal sheath.

"Fridge's off but the power's still on," Cooper said.

Conrad opened the screen and unlocked the front door.

The place smelled musty and was ten degrees warmer than outside. He glanced through the rooms quickly: comfortable but ugly furniture, wood floors, and rugs that were cut from old pieces of remnant carpet. Thank God there was no water damage on the popcorn walls or ceiling. That stuff was a pain to deal with.

The toilets flushed, the sinks ran, the lights turned on, and the windows were all good except for the one in the living room. Upstairs, the beds were unmade but there were sheets in the cupboards. In the basement, the deep freeze was standing open and was unplugged. The cellar was still locked and hadn't been disturbed.

He practically skipped back up the stairs. Cooper was in the utility room, bending over the washing machine to look at the pipes behind it. A quick glance at the shelves showed all kinds of tools neatly stacked.

It wouldn't take too much effort to get the place ready to sell, or to rent out over the summer.

"Looks good, Cooper."

Cooper straightened up, his scowling face breaking into a smile. For a while, Conrad had wondered whether his brother had helped those bastards who had so slyly got him sealed up behind bars, waiting for death. Their alibis for him had been too good. And Cooper had repeated every one of them, almost word for word, like he'd rehearsed it.

In prison, you think about a lot of things. You spend so much time thinking, you forget what things are like in reality.

His brother hadn't help set him up. Not Cooper! Who had told so many lies to help Conrad keep his affairs secret from his wife, who had helped Conrad get rid of some unaccounted for evidence from a few murder investigations that had fortuitously led Conrad into some extra cash and goods. Cooper was solid—solid as an oak.

"Still there," Cooper said, pulling out a thick silver bank bag, the top still locked with a combination lock. Inside were some records and photographs, not especially flattering, of some people neither one of them especially liked—blackmail material, to put it bluntly.

"Wouldn't want a couple of tourists to find *that*."

They both chuckled. No, Cooper hadn't been in on the betrayal. He'd just been covering up for his brother, as always, to the best of his ability. You couldn't ask for more than that.

"Are you going to use the stuff against Penny?" Cooper asked.

Conrad shook his head. "Nah. Let her keep what she has. I put her through enough hell."

Cooper shrugged—no skin off his nose. "So what do you think? Put it up for sale, or rent it out?"

"I still haven't decided," Conrad said honestly. "Regardless of what I do, I'll split the profits with you, you know that. Mom leaving me the place, that wasn't fair."

Cooper shrugged. "I got the house in Manchester, Conrad, and we're moved in now. If you think that I'm going to give you half the value of that place, you're out of your mind."

"But this place is worth more, once you count the land."

Cooper set the bank bag on top of the washing machine and put his heavy, meaty hands on Conrad's shoulders. Conrad had never noticed, but Cooper was almost an inch taller than he was—and probably had another fifty pounds of muscle on him, under the beer gut. "Conrad. You're my brother. I mean, I *am* one mean, money-grubbing son of a bitch. I'll admit that. But Jesus, give me a little credit for having your back. This place is *yours*. If you don't want to sell it or rent it out or whatever, I'll still drive up here and check up on it for you. Just because it's yours." There were tears beading up in Cooper's eyes. "You've been out of it for ten years. I've got the time to help you get on your feet. You don't need to feel like you owe me anything for it. Don't insult me like that."

Conrad's chest tightened—his brother was innocent. "All right."

Cooper gave him a little shake that made his head rattle on his neck. "If you split the money on this place with me, Mom would come back from the dead and take a ruler to your bottom. You know that, right?"

"She would, wouldn't she?"

They both chuckled.

"The first thing to do is get the front tidied up and the window fixed," Cooper said. "Even with all the house hunting that people do on the internet these days, you shouldn't underestimate the power of curb appeal."

"That old carpet has to go," Conrad added.

"I want to sand and refinish the floors, too," Cooper said. "Doesn't cost hardly anything when you already own a floor sander."

"The fridge," Conrad said.

Cooper sighed. "We could move it down to the basement. I hate to give up a second fridge, especially on a summer rental place. This cabin, it isn't the lap of luxury, but it does have access to some pretty good fishing back in the woods. You could do a lot of business with a second fridge to keep your fish and beer in."

"Too bad this place doesn't have a garage."

They went on like that, smearing the dust off the pine walls, cleaning spider webs out of the gas grill, checking closet doors to make sure they still opened smoothly, discussing who they should hire to bring in cordwood for the wood stove. Better to get it sooner rather than later and let it dry out. The old smokehouse in the back, looking like nothing more than a garden shed with a few extra vents, was still in good condition, was made completely out of wood, but was still sound along the walls and the cinderblock base. A few mice, squirrels, and spiders had climbed in, but were easy enough to chase away.

"Eat the last of the venison?" Conrad asked. "And the smoked trout?"

"You bet," Cooper said. "Wouldn't mind going on a fishing trip or two before you sell the place, if that's how you're going to do it. Get stocked up."

"We should do that anyway," Conrad said. Seeing the empty freezer downstairs had made him even more nostalgic than seeing the cabin had already. "Just like old times."

"Poach a deer or two before the season opens," Cooper said casually.

They both chuckled. Just like old times, all right.

Almost.

Chapter 31 - The other case

Three box lunches from the cafe upstairs sat on the white plastic table along with three legal pads, three pens, and three manila folders marked *Craig Moreau*.

It was kind of awkward with four people sitting around the cheap plastic table in Alex's quiet room: Jake, Regan, Alex, and, against Jake's better judgment but only by a percentage or two, say 53% against and 47% for, Gary.

Gary stared at the egg carton foam walls and ceiling and cement floor like he was in Batman's secret cave or something, with eyes just a little too wide.

Jake forced himself not to crack a smile. He cleared his throat. "All right. Here we are, the four of us, after a successful exoneration. I know everyone's flying high at the moment, but there's no reason to get cocky. We *could* have freed the guy without the real killer's confession, probably. But we're not here for the glory. We're here to plan our next case."

Regan snorted through her nose. That was fair. He was being kind of a goof today. It was as much of a struggle for him to get himself back under control as it was to get everyone else motivated.

But what did they want to do for the rest of their lives—pat each other's backs forever?

He took a breath.

"Craig Moreau. Thirty-four years in prison." He paused to let that sink in for a moment.

The amusement wiped itself off Regan's face. Her eyes narrowed and she stared at the far wall, putting facts in order.

Alex's hands, which had rested in loose fists on the tabletop, started to twitch. The guy was so connected to the Internet that he barely knew he didn't have a keyboard in front of him. Gary's eyebrows popped up, and the look of naive wonder vanished off his face like it had never been there. It was replaced by the cynical gossiper look—the man who could find out more in five minutes of trading favors over the phone than Alex could in weeks—as long as it wasn't on a computer database somewhere.

"The guy's twenty-nine years old at the time," Jake said. "He lives with his parents on a dairy farm. They're brutally murdered while he's at his day job as a bank teller. He drives home, notices they're missing, goes looking for them, and finds them murdered in their own RV. He starts to perform first aid but passes out when it becomes obvious he is far, far too late to do any good. When he comes to, he calls 911 and promptly gets his ass arrested for murder, even before they have the bodies bagged up and back to the hospital.

"Later, they find his DNA all over the murder weapon. A snitch in jail says he heard Moreau talking in his sleep about the crime, details nobody but the cops knew. A couple of his 'friends' show up, claiming he was selling coke on the side. An ex comes out of the woodwork to say he actually planned to murder his parents in their RV and drive it across the border to Canada, which makes no sense whatsoever.

"The guy has no previous record. It doesn't just smell like a setup; it screams of it. Pavo says the Organization wasn't involved—but the file was in with the rest of the dirty files in Marando's apartment. I believe Pavo, for what it's worth. But the more I learn about the Organization, the more I start to wonder if they hide things from each other on purpose."

Gary leaned back and crossed his arms over his chest. "If he trusted my brother—if he allowed my brother access to any information whatsoever—he must be at least a little naive."

"There is that. So who wants to go first? If Craig Moreau didn't kill his parents, who did? Any theories?"

Alex cleared his throat. "The Sherlock Holmes saying seems applicable here."

"Yeah?"

"It is a capital mistake to theorize in advance of the facts," Regan said. "That one?"

"Indeed," Alex said. He pushed his box lunch toward Gary. "I'm going upstairs to get another. My apologies. Does anyone need any coffee?"

"Bring a pot," Regan said. She held her hands about a foot apart. "Like that."

"I'll see what we have."

Alex exited the room, closing the door tightly behind him.

"What was that all about?" Jake asked.

"Just what he said, I'd guess." Gary leaned back in his chair. "He doesn't want to cook up any theories before he has all the facts at his fingertips. Me, I glanced through the files already. I'm going to say it was some kind of serial killer."

"Serial killer." Jake didn't buy it, but he didn't not buy it, either. "Any history of serial killers in the area?"

Regan leaned forward and stuck her fingers in her ears. When Jake looked at her, she shook her head.

Gary ticked off on his fingers. "Albert DeSalvo, the Boston

strangler, 1962 to 1964. The Connecticut River Valley Killer, that was possibly 1978 to 1987. Unsolved. William Devin Howell, the early to mid-2000s. Stephen Hayes in Connecticut, 2007. The New Bedford highway killer in 1988 to 1989. That one's unsolved, too."

"The fact that Moreau was in prison at the time pretty much rules him out on a couple of them."

Gary clucked his tongue and waggled a finger back and forth while still staring at the wall. "You have to watch out for copycats. They like having someone else take the blame. And they *love* to confuse the issue for their heroes."

"Heroes," Jake said.

"There are over three hundred million people in the United States. Some of them are more than a little screwed up. Who else...Arthur Shawcross, 1988 to 1989. A great year for serial killers—same year they caught Craig Price, the Warwick Slasher. Tony Costa from Cape Cod, that was...1969? Or 1970 when they caught him. Carl Panzram, the guy who was angry at Taft for getting him locked up in Leavenworth, that was in the Twenties. Richard Angelo, the so-called 'Angel of Death,' convicted in 1989. The Son of Sam, David Berkowitz, in the 1970s. And let's not forget the ladies. Amy Archer-Gilligan, a nurse who poisoned her patients, 1910 or thereabouts. Kristen Gilbert, another nurse, caught in 1996. Lizzie Halliday, 1894. Waneta Hoyt, killed all five of her children when they were toddlers and told everyone it was SIDS. 1970 or so. Hannah Hanson Kinney, in the early 1800s in Boston."

Jake raised a hand. "Stop. Just stop."

"I could go on all day," Gary said. "The point being if you're trying to pin the murders on a serial killer, it doesn't narrow the possibilities down that much."

"I guess not," Jake said.

"Like I said, three hundred million people. There are a lot more serial killers than we think—and a lot more serial killers than we *know* about. A lot of these people operated for a number of years before they got caught. How many of them are never caught?"

"I don't even want to think about it," Jake said. "And they're just random sickos running around out there, looking for people to murder."

"Sometimes," Gary said.

Regan said, "Done now?"

"I think I've convinced him that 'serial killers' wasn't the easy answer he was looking for, yes."

"And that you're our resident serial killer expert," Jake said.

"Don't forget poisons," Gary said. At Jake's wince, he laughed. "I swear I haven't killed anyone. It's just a hobby."

Jake glanced at Regan.

"Superhero figurines and murder," she said. "Why do you think he works for a judge? He stalks FBI profilers for fun."

Jake took the opportunity of a thump at the door to get up and break off the conversation. He was used to dealing with psychopaths, sure, but they almost always had some kind of political thing going on and were kidnapping people "for the cause"—not murdering for fun or whatever it was that drove these guys.

Alex was at the door, stacked to the gills with a coffee carafe, mugs, a pint of cream, a box of sugar packets, a box lunch, and half a dozen limp breakfast pastries that Krista had pawned off on him, probably to get them out of the display case.

"Safe to come in?" he asked.

Jake opened the door but didn't take anything. No sense unbalancing the guy since he'd clearly made it downstairs without dropping anything.

"I've had the serial killer lecture," Jake said.

"Depressing, isn't it?" Alex said, as Regan unloaded his haul. "The idea that some people will take enormous risks just to kill someone... just for fun. Not only is it evil, the relevant data is hard to sort out of the noise. Just the fact that someone's been murdered can be difficult to determine. You have to wait for a pattern to jump out at you basically."

Jake sighed. So much for skipping to the end of the investigation and working backward to find the evidence. He sat next to Regan.

She clasped his hand. "Jake, he's been in prison for a long time. A little more time probably won't hurt. The way we did it last time worked. We got the information we needed to get Wilson out of prison, even if we didn't end up needing it. Let's just do it that way again."

"You're not creeped out by this guy?" Jake said.

She shook her head. "There are a lot of crimes I can see this guy committing. He was on the road a lot, worked at a bank, drove up to Canada on a regular basis... but not murdering his parents... no."

"Why not?" He half expected her to say something like, *because he looked too sad*. But this was Regan, not some blonde from a TV show—she would have a logical reason.

"Because the dairy farm was making a profit, but not enough to support him, and it still had a mortgage," she said. "He might have been able to sell it, but not before he had to make mortgage payments he couldn't afford. If he'd killed his parents for some kind of financial profit, he would have straightened that out first."

"You think he was involved in the Organization?" Jake asked.

"On the road a lot, worked at a bank, drove up to Canada on a regular basis," she said. "Why not?"

Jake let go of her hand and leaned forward, clutching his head in his hands. "Maybe it was a mistake to start with this one. Maybe we should go in order of obvious solutions."

"Too hard for Jake Westley? I can't believe that." Regan chuckled—a good sound. She grabbed one of the thin white cardboard boxes and opened it. "Let's go at this methodically and make sure our facts are in order and find out what gaps there are in the evidence. It's just another puzzle."

"Yeah, but if we get stuck, we can't just look up the solution on the Internet," Jake lamented.

Regan pointed toward Alex, who had popped the top on one of his disgusting energy drinks and was guzzling it down. "Don't be so sure about that."

Chapter 32 - A puzzle waiting to be solved

It was dark except for the cherries flashing at the top of the hill. Wilson slowed down and turned on his blinker, and moved over into the passing lane. A pair of units bracketed a flaming red sports car with its trunk open and its owner with his hands on his head. One of the officers had his pistol pointed at the man.

An incompetent criminal.

Wilson was driving back to Portsmouth on Highway 101, just under the speed limit in a car he'd purchased for cash a couple of days ago. It was a fifteen-year-old tan Honda, nothing special, with two square haloes in the back seat that meant two toddlers had sat back there for a while, shedding dirt and fabric stains.

An incompetent criminal – say, an incompetent drug dealer – would be a low class character in a flashy expensive car driving over the speed limit. An easy obvious law would be broken, indicating a lack of self-control. The criminal would be apprehended, and anybody who was any kind of cop would start sniffing around to unravel the rest of the situation: drugs in the trunk; driving under the influence; prostitution; driving on a suspended license. The whole thing will fall apart like a house of cards.

A competent criminal would drive the speed limit in a car so nondescript as to be invisible. They would have dealer plates, valid insurance, a new driver's license, and nothing incriminating in the goddamned trunk.

A competent criminal would try to mimic the appearance and behavior of a good citizen as much as possible. A competent criminal wouldn't have impulse control problems. The prison system was full of criminals with impulse control problems.

Because, really, it was the impulse control that was the problem, not the criminal behavior.

He turned on his blinker and pulled back into the slow lane. The cherries faded in his rear view mirror.

Clark Turnbull, Dan Stenberg, and Jay Hatchell. The three cops who screwed me over by trying too hard to cover for me. The three cops whose testimony had been rubbed so thin by the prosecutor that it looked like they were covering for me.

Had I worked with them for a time? Had I gone drinking with them? Yeah, Turnbull and Stenberg especially. Hatchell hadn't been around all that long.

Had they been my buddies? No.

For as charming as everyone seemed to find me, especially women, nobody seemed to find it necessary to become an especially close friend of mine. Penny had married me because she thought I was a bad boy she could turn into a good man.

I cheated on her—repeatedly. But other than that, she had no cause for complaint. And she hadn't known about the cheating until I'd been arrested for murder. What the eyes can't see, the heart can't feel.

Given proof of her "bad boy," she turned tail and ran, taking my bank accounts, house, and cars with her.

Poor impulse control, in my opinion, but ultimately not something I needed to worry about. I'd build up a nest egg again—no doubts.

He grinned.

The road stretched in front of him. It was nice settling into the routine of pushing a tin can around on tarmac. Unfortunately, it wasn't going to last much longer.

He took the Beede Hill exit and doubled back on the access road until he reached the abandoned farmhouse. He parked the car behind the house, dressed in his disposable coverall and gloves, and went inside. Upstairs, past the creaking and half missing stairs, he found the duffel bag he'd left there before, undisturbed. It was nice to see it, but he could have maintained control and tried again another day. He squatted down behind the window frame and looked out.

A good view of the highway. He took out his cell phone and checked the app he'd installed. It allowed him to keep track of GPS signals on cell phones that didn't belong to him. An ally—you couldn't call someone like Cade a buddy, not by any stretch of the imagination—had told him how to get it in exchange for certain favors.

Initially, he'd thought to use a rifle to pick off the two men in the car, Turnbull and Stenberg. But upon further thought, it struck him as too risky. First, because he wasn't an expert marksman—definitely not if the target was moving at seventy miles an hour or more. Second, because transporting a rifle, whether registered or otherwise, would attract attention if he were pulled over or had a traffic accident. It could happen. He'd caught several murderers that way and had learned from their bad examples.

No, instead he'd planted a small explosive device on the fuel line of their car. It was packed with shards of glass and fragments of metal matching the car's undercarriage. One small spark, and all would be well.

He unpacked the rest of the material in the bag and dispersed it around the room: two thirty ought six shell casings; a jar of urine, splashed against the corner; a few hairs at the windowsill; a partial fingerprint on a shard of glass; and a smear of blood on the edge of the glass and another droplet on the floor.

The car approached. He held the smart phone in front of him in one hand, the app active, and the radio transmitter in his other.

The car, a dark blue SUV of aggressively heavy weight, almost old enough to be considered a classic model, approached.

He pressed the preprogrammed button on the device.

At first he was disappointed—despite reminding himself he was prepared for failure. Maybe he'd tagged the wrong car, or the signal had been confused by the distance, speed, and the amount of metal in the car.

The car passed the window, heading back from Portsmouth toward Manchester. He watched the headlights, glancing back and forth from his small screen to the highway. Nothing.

He squinted at the transmitter, shook it, then pressed each of the buttons in turn.

The headlights on the car swerved. Then smoke began pouring out of the rear end of the car. Wilson clucked his tongue. Of all the results, this was the worst—the bomb had gone off, but it hadn't sufficiently damaged the car.

The SUV pulled over to the side of the road. Smoke quickly surrounded the vehicle in a dark haze, obscuring whether or not the doors opened. It was so thick the taillights were no longer visible.

Other vehicles on the road began to slow and stop. It was summer, and the highways were full of people who were, by definition, looking for something interesting.

He really should get going.

Suddenly a gust of wind rattled through the house, making the entire building sway. Wilson clenched his fists and stuck them in his armpits. Wouldn't it be ironic if he cut himself on a piece of glass in the window frame and managed to leave his own DNA behind?

When he looked back, the car had become a bright ball of flame.

From his post inside the house, the fire was almost completely silent, no louder than the sound of the wind moaning through the house.

The flames surrounding the car gusted with the wind for a moment—a candle flame about to go out—then stabilized as the wind died down.

A perfect ball of flame surrounded the car, a delicate flower of destruction.

A scream echoed across the night.

Wilson snapped out of it. He'd almost stood there, hypnotized, until a patrol car arrived. About a dozen cars had stopped already, with more slowing in the distance. A real traffic snarl was forming.

A silhouette approached the SUV with an arm raised in front of their face... then stopped and backed away. The fire was simply too hot to approach, although several other people made the attempt, and failed.

Smiling, he turned back to the stairs and worked his way down, careful not to tear the suit or gloves. He slipped his phone and the radio transmitter inside his shirt so he could feel their comforting weight against his skin and his tucked in shirt.

Then it was out to his car, off with the disposable suit, and down the country road leading into the wilderness. A dirt-track a few miles distant would let him take the car from one back road to another. From there he could drive the back roads all the way to Manchester.

He stopped for a few minutes to turn the disposable suit into a wad of black tar, which he dropped into a ditch.

My actions tonight were only the tip of the iceberg.

Another favor called in had seen certain transactions in the bank accounts of Turnbull and Stenberg—ones that couldn't be accounted for legally. And a convincing amount of blackmail material on Jay Hatchell rested in the safe in Stenberg's guest room closet. He even had a suicide note for Hatchell, should it prove necessary.

But, all things considered, Hatchell hadn't screwed him over so much as he allowed Turnbull and Stenberg to do it.

Magnanimous. He mouthed the word and kept an eye out for deer.

Too far away for his muddy license plate to be spotted—just close enough for a pair of taillights to be seen driving away from an abandoned building, like a pair of arrows in reverse.

A charming puzzle, just waiting to be solved.

Chapter 33 - Damned if you do

The elevator door opened onto the penthouse lobby of Paul's office. There were no guards or obvious security cameras, just a wide wood floored lobby with a curved reception desk and a small water fountain by a discreet toilet.

The male secretary at the desk, balding and clean shaven, glanced up at him, meeting John's eyes for half a second, then pressed a button that made the double doors into Paul's office click.

John shoved through them.

Paul, at the desk, had his fingers steepled in front of him and his desk cleared, as though that's how he spent his time—watching the door to see who would come through.

John marched up to the desk and slapped his palms down on it. "You son of a bitch."

Paul, the look on his face much like that of his secretary, said, "What particular sin have you found me out on, John?"

"One involving my daughter."

Paul's eyebrow lifted. He gestured toward the single chair on the other side of the desk.

John clenched his teeth and forced himself not to act like a fool. What he wanted to do was pound on the top of the desk like a gorilla and demand answers to questions he hadn't even asked yet. This was Paul at his worst, driving him to the irrational, just trying to get the man to admit he was wrong—he'd long since given up on getting him to apologize.

John leaned against the desk on his knuckles, imagining his

hands wrapped around Paul's throat for just a moment. Then he let go of the image and parked himself on the chair.

"Craig Moreau. You said the Organization wasn't involved... that you knew of."

Paul glanced down at his desk—nothing there to see, not even a blotter. The corners of his mouth turned down. He blinked. "Craig Moreau."

"The other case. The one we originally met at my house to talk about. You said the Organization wasn't involved, to the best of your knowledge. You said it like butter wouldn't melt in your mouth even though it was one of the files in that corrupt bastard detective's apartment."

Paul's eyebrows pinched together. "The one who murdered his parents at the dairy farm."

"Yes!"

"He—" Paul's voice tightened. "The Organization wasn't involved in the case."

John lifted his chin. "You know what those kids found out?"

Paul's mouth started to open—then the secretary pushed open one of the doors and stuck his head in.

"Paul," he said in a low cultured voice that carried clearly across the room. "There's news."

Paul stood up, clenching his hands together in front of him. His slacks were creased along the front, a small spot of coffee on them. "What is it? Were they able to trace ballistics on the casing?"

John bit his tongue.

"Bad news," the secretary said. "It's the third officer. He was found dead in his home a short while ago."

"How?"

"Suicide—shotgun shell to the head. A note was found."

The blood had gone out of Paul's face. "Noted. Any further details?"

"I will keep you informed."

Paul gave the man a curt nod, and he withdrew to the lobby. Paul sat, put both hands in front of him on the desk. He looked like he was staring at his fingernails, which were short and chewed, almost bloody.

"Where is Regan now?" Paul asked.

"Brooklyn. At the computer whiz's coffee shop."

"Contact her and tell her to stay there for now."

John pulled out his cell phone and dialed. "What explanation should I give her?"

"Tell her I asked her to do it." His sweaty hands clenched on the desk, leaving a trace of parallel smears across the top when he moved them. "John. I don't know what else to say. Tell her whatever will convince her."

Regan picked up. "Hello, Daddy. No, we haven't found anything else yet. No, I won't be having babies anytime soon. Did I cover it?"

She had such a light, innocent tone to her voice that his throat tightened. "Are you still at the coffee shop with Jake and Alex?"

"Yes. I'd offer to pick something up for you, but it'd be cold by the time I get to you."

He cleared his throat. "Regan... your Uncle Paul asks that you stay where you are for now, at the coffee shop. I take it there's some kind of emergency."

"Is he all right?" Her tone had changed. It had gone tight and strained.

"He's fine."

A pause. He could just about hear the hamster wheels turning.

"Are you..." She broke off. He could tell she wanted to ask him whether he was involved in the Organization again but was forcing herself not to. It was the first thing her mother would have asked. "Never mind, I assume all the questions I want to ask aren't ones you can answer yet, and hang up so you can get answers to them."

"I'll call you and let you know what's going on as soon as I can."

"I'll keep the line clear."

She hung up.

"She says she'll stay put," John said. "What's this about?"

"I'll tell you in a moment. But first, tell me what they found out on the Moreau case."

"Damn you," John said. "Is my daughter in danger?"

Paul's tone was reasonable, but his expression was not. He was a haunted man. "I don't know yet, because you haven't answered my question."

John forced his shoulders to relax and took a breath. "The Moreau case. They found evidence of a possible serial killer in the area—one targeting people smuggling goods back and forth over the Canadian border, mainly in Canada. One who continued their work after Moreau's arrest, all the way into the nineteen-nineties, then stopped abruptly. The M.O. of the killer matches—if you take into account the possibility that the killer might have been interrupted in the process. Apparently what they liked to do was drain all the blood out of the bodies and let them hang on large tripods or teepees or some damn thing in the middle of the woods—some kind of ritual murder.

"Other DNA was found in the RV, but the physical evidence has been lost in a bureaucratic shuffle. Sound familiar?"

He was getting riled up again. He shook his head. If Regan was in danger, he had to keep a clear head, not run around shouting at Paul.

Paul turned his head and lowered it until his cheek was on his shoulder. His jaw worked, chewing on the inside of his other cheek. Gray skin against a gray suit, with dark circles under his eyes, and skin hanging loosely like it would on a seriously ill man.

"Answer me, Paul. Is my daughter in danger?" His voice came out rough and angry.

"I don't know what it means," Paul said. "Nineteen eighty-six. When was Wilson born?"

"I don't know. He couldn't have been more than, say, ten. Is it important?"

Paul shrugged the shoulder he wasn't leaning against. "Two of the police officers who were involved in the Wilson case as witnesses for the defense died in an automobile wreck last night. Apparently the third officer just shot himself."

"You don't think—"

"The victim's friend—name, name, what was her name—Rossier, that was it, has disappeared. Once is happenstance—"

"Twice could be coincidence. Three times is enemy action."

They stared at each other. John had no doubt where Paul's mind had gone. His own had been pulled inevitably in a certain direction that Paul's couldn't help but follow, like iron filings to a magnet.

Toward Linda.

"I'm sorry to have dragged you back into this," Paul said.

John shook his head. Beads of cold sweat had begun to roll down his forehead and covered his upper lip. His hands felt like damp ice—his heart was racing in his chest. It was Paul being paranoid about Wilson—had to be. This was nothing—a false alarm.

But he had to be sure.

"For the best, especially if..." The words got away from him. It wasn't important now. "Wilson. What kind of alibi does he have?"

"The time of Rossier's disappearance was so vague as to be impractical for establishing alibis," Paul said. "He may or may not have an alibi, depending on the time she actually disappeared. During the automobile wreck, he was supposed to have been in Brooklyn with his brother searching for apartments. According to the assistant D.A., Laura Provost, who is one of our higher level agents, he was supposed to be in an orientation session this morning and through the afternoon."

"Orientation?"

"He has accepted a position with Brooklyn P.D. as an officer, with an eye on promotion to the vacant detective position."

"So there's no way he could have done it?" John asked.

Paul lifted his head and squared his shoulders. It was the look of a man at a sentencing hearing. "I don't know," he said. "But say the word, John, and I'll have him killed."

"Do you think he's guilty, then?"

"I don't *know*."

"You can't condemn a man to death for the crime of your own doubt."

"Can't you? If it means saving the life of your goddaughter? The one light remaining to my life in a smog of chaos and doubt?"

John shook his head. Paul had dug himself a hole, all right. It was taking most of his willpower not to tell the man he'd told him so. Regan never would have believed it of him, he knew.

Paul collapsed forward onto his elbows and put his head in his hands. "If I'd killed *him*...Lassiter..."

John raised a hand, palm out. "If you'd had Lassiter killed, Linda would have figured it out eventually."

"But she'd still be alive."

John had spent time, decades in fact, thinking over the same question. What if he'd given Paul the go ahead to kill Lassiter all those years ago? He still stopped every time her birthday came around and asked himself again. Some years, he would argue it would have been better to kill him; other years, he'd swing the other way.

In the end, he'd come to realize asking the question was eating up the memories of his wife. He hadn't been able to stop, not exactly, but he'd tried not to let it get under his skin.

"I was a judge for a lifetime, Paul. All I can say is, there's a reason we have the legal system that we do. And it's not so we can be sure of punishing the guilty and sparing the innocent. It's so there's something bigger than ourselves, called the Law, that keeps individual men from having to hold the power of life and death in their bare hands."

Paul just stared at him as if he'd started barking out loud.

"You're damning yourself to hell every time you send a man to die because of your own pride," John said. "Whether they deserve it or not, just the act of condemning a man without the law behind you destroys your soul."

Once again, he'd said the wrong thing at the wrong time. He could see the armor, hard as steel and cold as ice, sliding across Paul's eyes again. He straightened himself, ran a hand through the last of his thinning, widow-peaked hair, and pulled his sleeves straight.

"I have no soul, no belief in justice or happiness, and no interest in playing fair for the sake of the incompetent, short sighted, and stupid," he said. "I have the Organization. I may, at times, long for a divorce, but I also understand it is, and has always been, until death do us part."

"Paul—"

He shook his head and kept talking. "I live in terror of what the Organization might do to Regan. I live in terror of what it might be doing, in some kind of madness, to the innocent. I fear that if the Organization decided the survival of a monster were, in the long term, in the best interests of humanity itself, it would not only allow it, but encourage the monster's actions. *Survival of the fittest.* I have tried to protect those I oversee as best I can...but the Organization is a cruel beast, and the weakest must be thinned out of the herd, if any are to survive.

"I will continue to investigate Wilson. Say nothing to Regan, if you please, and try to keep her attention directed away from him. What little pride I have left is tied up more in her opinion of me than in anything else."

"You can't—"

"No," Paul said. "*You* can't. There's a difference."

Chapter 34 -Spider webs

Wilson took the stairs of the third floor walkup two at a time, yanking himself upward along the rail. He wasn't that experienced in the matter of what did or did not constitute a good apartment in Bed-Stuy. In fact, he kept catching himself being almost horrified by the way everyone lived—literally—on top of each other.

No matter how cramped it felt compared to his now sold home in Manchester or to the cabin, it was a luxury suite compared to his cell or the plain white video screening room he'd been trapped in all day.

It had been a long day catching up on training videos and paperwork. Some of it he'd just stared at blankly, it was so surreal. Either a lot had changed while he was in the slammer, or the Manchester P.D. had been behind the times. A bit of both, probably.

The hallway smelled like strange cooking spices and cigarettes. There were dark stains on the worn red carpet underfoot. The lights were dim or flickered or both. It was a murder scene in a horror movie, just waiting to happen.

He unlocked the three locks on the door, keeping an eye out for scratches in the metal and the wood. He'd had new ones put in but had given a set to the super. A tiny silent alarm on the other side of the door would tell him whether it had been opened during the day. It hadn't.

The apartment hadn't come cheap. Wilson had to bribe the previous tenant to leave, then the building super to keep him from raising a fuss about his new sub-lettor. The previous tenant left behind some furniture: a pair of comfortable armchairs, a TV stand with an old television on it, a bed, the insignificant kitchen table, a dresser, one of those rattan hutch things that sat over the toilet, and curtains.

More than likely, they'd belonged to the tenant that had lived in the apartment before—a guy named Peter Marando who'd been a Brooklyn P.D. detective before he'd killed himself—the person Wilson was hoping to replace.

A good detective sits at the center of his web like a spider, always keeping one foot on the strands to see if any vibrate. It might seem like he just shows up at the scene of a crime, boom, like some kind of superhero, but really he's always there, lurking around, keeping on top of things.

It had seemed like a good idea at the time, taking over this place. It had swallowed up a lot of the last of his ready cash sitting in the most obvious bank accounts, but so be it.

He locked the door behind him. He didn't want to have to deal with salesmen, nosy neighbors, or crackheads at the moment. Sitting around all day had worn out his patience.

He tossed himself together a quick meal from the fridge and ate it in front of the TV, watching the news. Local news took precedent, of course. New York might think of itself as cosmopolitan, but its TV news stations were still mostly wrapped up in local politics, construction, weather, and cultural crap. The two cops' deaths up in New Hampshire were featured eventually, but not the disappearance of the Rossier woman.

Annoyingly, the fate of the third cop wasn't mentioned as being implicated in the deaths of the other two. Did that mean that nothing had been found yet, that too much had been found, or that the department was covering the whole thing up? *Manchester P.D.—I wouldn't put much past those guys. I would just have to assume it was a cover-up until I heard something different.*

He clicked the television off and leaned back in the armchair. It was comfortable, all right, even if it did smell a bit like old cigarette butts. Too bad he wasn't in the mood to just lean back and relax. Tonight he was keyed up for action. Too bad he didn't have anything lined up, but if he stayed in the room all night, he was going to go crazy.

He grabbed his keys and wallet but left his cell phone behind—the GPS app had been deleted, the phone encrypted, wiped, and reloaded—and went out to explore the building.

The place had four apartments. One of them was accessed from a hallway in the entryway that went down a half flight of steps. One of them, the cooking spices place, was on the first floor. A chain smoker lived upstairs.

Another flight of stairs led up to the roof.

He climbed out of a small shed at the top of the building and kicked a handy rock in the doorjamb to keep the door from locking behind him.

The setting sun left streaks of gold and orange cloud across the sky. The sky had a haze to it, but not as bad as he would have guessed—if he'd stopped to think about it. The rooftops here weren't skyscrapers or anything; the tops of the trees sometimes came up higher than the roofs. A lot of red brick and heavy greenery, lit up by streetlights. A church steeple nearby had a white cupola at the top. A bunch of TV aerials and satellite dishes were bolted to big air ducts. A couple of cheap aluminum deck chairs had been set out, with a coffee can full of beer tops beside one of them—a bottle opener built right into the arm of the chair.

Not a bad idea.

He could walk from his end of the block all the way to the other end, stepping over the low brick walls that separated the rooftops, if he'd wanted to. The back of the building led to a narrow alley and a fire escape that didn't go all the way up to the roof. It looked like it was attached to his kitchen.

Big green dumpsters lurked in the alley. It clearly wasn't a place to park a car. The car he'd borrowed from his brother was parked along the street, not in front of his building, but a couple of blocks further down at the first open parking spot he'd spotted.

He wondered how much the guy in the apartment below could hear of his footsteps or whether anybody ran around up here at night. Looking across at the rooftops he could see from here, it didn't look like many people left anything valuable up here to steal: green flowerboxes, a few aluminum picnic shelters with Christmas lights on them, lawn chairs—that was about it. If he squinted, he thought he could make out some kind of grill on the other side of the street.

He turned back toward the brick shed covering the stairs, then stopped.

One of the bricks had a different color mortar around it than the others. It jutted out a little from the rest, too.

He walked over to it and gave it a jiggle. It was pasted in but just a little loose.

Wilson dug out a pocketknife and scratched it along the mortar. It was rubbery—tub sealant, not mortar at all.

He ran the blade of his pocketknife around the outside of the brick, loosening it, then gave it another jiggle.

With a little encouragement, it slid free. He set it on the roof and peered into the hole.

Spider webs, dust, and a sandwich sized freezer bag with a thumb drive in it.

He pulled it out and brushed it off. Who knew how long it had been sitting there. Wouldn't that be funny if he plugged it into his computer and it gave him a ten-year-old computer virus, or had some kind of password he couldn't figure out?

He never could pass up that kind of puzzle. He put the brick back and skipped down the stairs back to his apartment.

***

Later that evening, he found the bad tile patch job behind the toilet tank, but the dossiers the files on the thumb drive had insisted would be there were missing.

Peter Marando had been a spider sitting in the middle of a web, all right. Apparently, a bird had swooped down and plucked the spider away. But before it had been eaten, it had left some eggs behind.

Chapter 35 - The private investigator or the detective?

One look at the driveway told him that the dairy farm belonging to Craig Moreau and his parents in upstate New York had been swallowed by a big corporate farm. The white farmhouse and red dairy barn that had been sitting behind the blocky RV in the crime scene photos were gone, replaced by long tin buildings that looked like they belonged on the site of a prison or a manufacturing plant. The green fields had become oceans of brown muck. A guy in gray coveralls hosed off a filthy yellow plow with a pressure washer.

The stench was bad, so repugnant he was tempted to pull his shirt up over his nose, and he hadn't even stepped out of the car yet.

He pulled up next to a spanking clean gray sedan on the grass in front of the closest building and put the car in park.

Jake had assigned himself the least appealing of the assignments necessary, if they were going to approach the case in a methodical fashion. It wasn't the kind of case where you could go in with guns blazing. For one thing, he wouldn't know who to threaten yet. For another thing, the last thing he wanted to do was stir up a serial killer, possibly working for the Organization.

He was here to check out the scene of the crime and get a sense of whether the new owners of the farm had been involved in the case or had just taken advantage of the opportunity to buy the farm.

Meanwhile, Gary was using a microfiche machine to go through a local newspaper looking for patterns in the deaths in the area over the last forty years. Graham was up in Canada to look at one of the sites where bodies had been found—the ritual sacrifices.

The Moreau case was going to be a tough nut to crack. He needed to be digging where the dirt was deepest.

He closed the car door and started picking his way across the grass in front of the barns, which was muddy from a rainstorm a few days ago. He didn't think it was possible, but it smelled even worse out here in the open. Maybe he'd get lucky and his nose would go senseless in a few minutes.

The air was getting warmer; it was going to be a warm, beautiful, sewage filled, spring day.

The guy in the overalls looked up, then turned off the water on the pressure washer. His face was spattered with brown and white muck—even a few drops of what looked like milky blood.

"Can I help you?"

Jake held out a hand for a shake, but the guy shook his head and put his hands behind his back—too wet and dirty.

"Jake Westley," he said. "I'm here to ask a few questions about Craig Moreau and his parents, the couple who was murdered here thirty years ago."

The guy seemed to shrink inside himself a little. In another life, in Brooklyn, he probably would have been a hipster, with his black framed glasses, pasty skin, and trimmed black goatee. "You're not some animal rights activist, are you?"

Jake laughed. "You want me to go back to the car and pull out my leather jacket for you?"

"No, that's cool, that's cool." He started walking to a glass door set in front of one of the barns—a row of fluorescent lights was lit up inside, and a table and double door refrigerator stood inside the room. "Let me wash up and go on break. Are you a reporter?"

"Nah, don't worry. Just a private investigator, hunting down some legal stuff."

The guy's eyes glazed over and he turned away. "That's cool," he said and waved Jake through the glass door and into the combination break room and office. "I'll be back in a sec."

Jake scraped his feet on the dirty mat by the door and wandered into the break room, which smelled better, but only a little. Here, the dominant stench was that of spoiled milk, an odor he had never experienced before—but identified immediately.

It was cooler inside, too. The air conditioner had kicked on, even though it was only seventy degrees outside.

Jake sat at the picnic bench table by the front window and waited. A cup of coffee sat at the table, swirling with cream. A few drops of coffee lay on the table. They wobbled as Jake sat down at the attached bench. He glanced at the counter and sink next to the fridge. The coffeepot was empty.

One more glance at the coffee in front of him—he wasn't that desperate.

He pulled out his cell phone and checked it: no updates from Gary or Graham, nothing from Alex or Regan. He put the phone back.

Legwork. It had to be done.

He scratched the back of his neck. The hairs back there were standing up straight; the ones on his arms were rising up in goosebumps. He rubbed his hand across the back of his arm and looked around. It wasn't that cold in here.

The attendant came through a door in the back of the room,

the side that butted up against the rest of the big barn. "Sorry about the wait." He was wearing blue jeans and an old gray high school lacrosse t-shirt, and his face and arms were still wet, all the way to the neck and elbows. There were drops of water on his glasses.

He, too, was covered with goosebumps.

"I'm Will Vrooman," the guy said. Now they shook hands. Vrooman's hand was cold, damp, and just slightly shivering.

Jake's grip might have been a hair stronger, but his hands weren't nearly as calloused. It was like gripping a toenail.

"The Moreaus," Vrooman said, with a nervous edge to his voice. "What did you want to know about them?"

"Don't worry, it doesn't have anything to do with the ownership of the farm," Jake assured him. "We're trying to track down some papers they had related to possible part ownership of a lakefront property in New Hampshire."

Jake almost smiled as he made it up on the spot; it sounded plausible.

Vrooman squinted, not suspiciously, but like he was doing a search in his mental database. "New Hampshire. I'd have to see if Mr. Leete knows anything. I've never heard of them owning any property over there."

"It would be north of Manchester. I can provide more details if you need them."

He shrugged. "Leave me a card and I'll pass it on to Mr. Leete. You can tell him."

"Okay." Jake pulled out a card and slid it over.

"Anything else you wanted to know?"

"My client? No, that should cover it."

Vrooman swallowed. "But..."

"But you know I'm curious about the murders." Jake grinned. "I saw it on the Internet the other day. What a mess. But I get the impression there is more to it than what I saw on the website. Do you know what really happened?"

Vrooman twisted around and looked at a white dial clock on the wall above the back door. "I've heard some rumors, sure," he said. "Everyone around here does."

"Yeah?"

Another nervous swallow. Maybe the break room was under surveillance from a hidden camera—a boss concerned about employees slacking off on the job. "A lot of people around here don't think that Craig Moreau, the son, did it."

Jake grinned. "Yeah, that was exactly what went through my mind when I read that article on the website. Did you know them?"

"Dude, I'm like twenty-three years old. Craig Moreau's been in jail for longer than I've been alive."

"He's been in jail for almost as long as I've been alive," Jake said. "I was three. I guess it was a dumb question."

"My parents knew him, though," Vrooman said. "They went to high school with him. Everybody was surprised when he didn't drop out to become a mechanic, and he got a job at a bank and started putting himself through school at Empire State studying chemistry."

"Interesting," Jake said.

"Yeah, one of those tough guys that have more going on upstairs than you realize," Vrooman said. "Anyway, the story goes he was working at the bank and selling drugs on the side. Kind of like *Breaking Bad*, if you know that show."

"I do."

"Yeah well, apparently one night, he made a mistake and sold some to a guy he shouldn't have."

"A cop?"

"Nah. Worse than a cop. Someone from the Mafia. The guy from the Mafia sent some thugs down to the farm to investigate the situation, see if the parents were involved. The Mafia doesn't like it when people nose in on their turf, right?" Vrooman was staring over Jake's shoulder at the wall. He was visualizing it as he talked. "But the thing was, there was *also* a serial killer running loose at the time. When the Mafia men arrived to question the parents, the serial killer was already there, busy killing them."

As Vrooman told the story, he seemed to relax; it was as if he'd told the same tale a hundred times.

"The dad, he was killed quickly; that's what they say. But the killer was interrupted in the middle of doing the mom, and things got messy. The Mafia men tried to shoot the killer, but he had a gun too, and was hiding in the back bedroom of the RV with the mom and the dad's body. The mom was screaming her head off and bleeding all over the place.

"The lights were out inside the RV. The Mafia men tried to sneak in and find out what was going on...but the killer killed both of them, one at a time, with a forty-five, right through the head." Vrooman touched his forehead with a fingertip, then looked down at the table. "That's what they say, anyway."

"And then what?"

"And then the killer finished his dirty work with the mom and left."

"Leaving four bodies for Craig to find."

"Yeah."

"But two of the bodies disappeared and Craig's framed for the murders, because the Mafia doesn't want to be involved."

"Yeah. The Mafia, they had connections with the police department. The cops made it look like only two bodies were found, and the next year the police department gets an anonymous donation and buys themselves a bunch of equipment—pretty suspicious, in my opinion."

Jake shook his head. "I don't know if I can buy all that. From what I found on the Internet, there was no hint of there being two extra bodies or anything like that, or bullet holes in the RV."

"Yeah, I don't know either," Vrooman said. "It's just a rumor—an urban legend, I guess. A farm legend, if you want to get technical about it."

"I wonder what happened to the RV," Jake said. "Now, that would be something to look at."

"There's a haunted corn maze outside of West Lowville that's supposed to have it," Vrooman said. "But it has to be a fake. The last thing the cops would want was for anyone to look at the RV. But, you know, Halloween. Things get crazy up here."

Jake nodded, as if he did know. Vrooman looked over his shoulder at the clock and the door again, then seemed to sink back into himself again. "I guess I better get back to work."

Jake stood and shook the guy's hand again. "Thanks," he said.

"For what?"

"For giving your boss Leete my card so I can ask him about the New Hampshire property."

The guy mimed slapping himself on the head. "That, yeah." He slid the card off the tabletop toward him and put it in his pocket.

Jake was pondering whether to offer Vrooman a five or not for delivering the card. He decided not to. If the boss called, it would just mean making some crap up about the missing property. He wasn't likely to learn much more from the boss than he'd just found out from the assistant anyway.

Jake nodded to Vrooman and let himself out of the break area. The smell of sour milk had faded pretty quickly from his memory. The smell of warm manure, on the other hand, hit him like a brick. He was going to have to get the inside of his car cleaned after this. Just the smell hanging in the air was enough to make his sinuses run.

He pulled the door closed behind him. The kid went into the barn through the back door, still holding Jake's card in his hand. The fluorescent lights went out. It was broad daylight—the kid had probably just missed them from this morning.

The next step would be the nearest junk yard to ask about the rumor the RV might be around. He needed to come up with a plausible reason to be asking around about it.

He *needed* to stop for some coffee.

A few minutes later when Jake was on the highway, he remembered Vrooman's car—a late model, almost clean and new enough to be a rental. *They must pay dairy farmers pretty well.*

Something about the license plate had been unusual. He wished he'd paid a little more attention.

He drove to the next town and had just ordered a coffee at a Dunkin' Donuts when it hit him. The plates had been green, not the blue and white of New York plates.

Green was for New Hampshire.

A quick drive back to the dairy farm showed Vrooman out front again, hosing down the yellow plow, dressed in his coveralls.

The car was gone.

Jake pulled to a stop but didn't get out. He rolled down the window. "Hey, Will," he said.

The guy looked up and turned off the water. "Uh, yeah?"

"What happened to the car that was here?"

For a moment, Jake thought he was going to say, "What car?" But there were two pairs of tire marks in the mud. He blinked a few times, then said, "My girlfriend came to pick it up."

"Your girlfriend's from New Hampshire?"

Vrooman's mouth opened. Jake could see him giving himself a mental *Aha* as he remembered the cover story about trying to track down ownership of the fictitious New Hampshire property. "Her parents are. They pay for some of her stuff. You know how it is."

"Had my hopes up," Jake admitted.

"Sorry."

"Sorry to bother you." He rolled up the window. Vrooman turned on the pressure washer again and aimed it at the front of the plow. Chunks of mud came off in clumps and fell into the grass.

***

Will Vrooman watched the private investigator's car disappear down the gravel road, stop at the stop sign, then turn onto the highway. It accelerated, then disappeared behind some trees. He tried to finish power washing the Caterpillar but his hands wouldn't stop shaking.

Which one of them would come back first, the private investigator or the detective?

He turned off the water and watched the highway for a few minutes, flinching every time a car, truck, or semi slowed as it approached the driveway to the farm.

Finally, he walked to the other side of the barn, where his old Ford 150 was parked, and smoked a joint with shaking hands, then sent a text to his girlfriend telling her he loved her and was looking forward to seeing her later that night.

The whole time, he felt like he was still being watched by that crazy-ass detective, with his too wide eyes and his too wide grin.

When he was done with the joint, he went back out front, finished cleaning the Cat, and glanced one more time at the road. A light flashed at him from the trees. It put him in mind of a pair of binoculars.

Or a rifle scope.

He went back to work—an itchy feeling between his shoulder blades.

Chapter 36 -Kill two birds with one stone

Saturday and Sunday had been productive, more productive than Wilson had expected. Saturday, he'd expected to be a waste of time, a necessary but boring loose end that needed to be wrapped up. But the visit to the farm had produced far better results than he'd expected. Someone else had been nosing around the Craig Moreau case—someone interested in local rumors of a serial killer.

Someone who'd driven around the area, stopping at several junk yards and classic car dealerships before managing to spot and promptly evade his tail.

Someone who'd been tracking down information about a property in New Hampshire.

It could have been coincidence. It didn't really matter if it was or not; it was *interesting*, and he'd learned a long time ago that if something was *interesting*, it was almost always useful to know everything sooner or later.

It was his last weekend off before he had to go on duty, and he didn't have anything better to do.

Sunday, he'd spent some time on his computer, getting up to date, putting information in order, trying to remember passwords over a decade old. Most of them had expired, of course, and had to be reset.

He'd tracked down a few old friends and a couple of old enemies, and he'd spent some quality time with Peter Marando's thumb drive.

Peter Marando.

Along with multiple other customers, he'd been known to accept payments from a mysterious, unnamed organization, not the Mafia or another organized crime syndicate—although he had dealings with those too—that sounded a lot like T.H.E.M.

T.H.E.M was a made-up group created, or rather pulled, out of the fertile imaginations of a group of kids who had been in the habit of writing him letters while he was in prison. They believed this group controlled most of the legal system in the U.S., many major politicians, and had spies everywhere. You could, they believed, be a spy for T.H.E.M. and not even know it.

They were a bunch of computer hackers, which meant their brains were used to seeing patterns where none existed. They'd decided T.H.E.M. was responsible for the frame job that had been done on him and had vowed to help him fight back.

Their letters had always been the brightest part of his day.

But now, looking at Marando's files, he had to wonder. The group would reach out to Marando, give him some of the weirdest instructions Wilson had ever seen, and then pay for favors rendered—not by cash under the table, but by coincidence.

Marando would suppress a certain piece of evidence as directed, usually via an anonymous envelope that showed up in his mailbox. The accused might still be convicted, but that wasn't the important part, apparently. Then he'd go into a newsstand and buy a scratch ticket. Bam! A couple of hundred bucks.

Horse races, lottery tickets, restaurants that offered him free meals, cash on the sidewalk, refund checks, overpaid tax refunds, pawn shops that gave him ten times the dollar value... whichever way it happened, from time to time extra money showed up in Marando's pocket.

And he kept notes about it.

He'd suppressed evidence, manufactured evidence, looked the other way at evidence, pushed harder than he should have to question a suspect, went easier on them, questioned someone who wasn't even involved, framed people, fake framed them so it looked like they were being framed when they'd done it, switched DNA samples, destroyed DNA samples, changed numbers on DNA samples, made records and dossiers disappear...

Looking at the amount of illegal activity Marando had gotten up to, it was almost easy to believe in a group like T.H.E.M. Only a conspiracy would have been able to keep the guy from getting busted.

The last record in the files was of an unknown person nosing around in the Andrew Gibbons case, one that Marando had been involved in earlier, setting up a black guy to take a fall for a murder he didn't commit.

A quick Internet search showed that Andrew Gibbons had been exonerated soon after Marando's death.

The majority of the credit for the exoneration had gone to Assistant D.A. Laura Provost—blonde, tall, slender, forty-five or so, somewhat hawk beaked and beady eyed, but clearly intelligent, ruthless, and aggressive.

He printed out her picture and tacked it to the wall. He needed to stop and pick up a corkboard, but right now, he was feeling a financial crunch, and all he could think of was the damage deposit on the apartment.

Ridiculous, but sometimes he just had to go with it. His subconscious had bailed him out of trouble so often he didn't like to screw with it. He was in tune with himself and wanted to keep it that way.

Monday—another boring day full of paperwork and training videos, but the end was in sight. He had already identified the crucial administrative personnel he needed to befriend and had casually found out their favorite bribes: bagels, cupcakes, brownies. Food, it wasn't just fuel in an office, it was the social grease that made mistakes disappear and brought vital information to his feet. One of the admins liked cutesy earrings, too. On Friday, she'd been wearing a pair of kites. Today she had on a pair of turtles. They looked cheap, so she probably didn't have sensitive skin. He'd keep an eye out for something she might like.

It was the little things, always the little things. Big plans rested on the little things.

After work, he decided to drive out to the house where those three nutty T.H.E.M. believers were living. It wasn't too far from his place, and—like a sign from above—there was an open parking spot nearby.

At the address, he found a blue clapboard house with a skeleton doorknocker and a keypad. Clearly, he was at the right place.

He pressed the bell and heard it *ding dong* inside the house. After half a minute, he tried it again. When that didn't work, he used both his fist and the doorknocker to make a noise.

He eyeballed the area around the door again and spotted a small camera at the corner. He looked straight at it and said, "Hey, guys, it's me. Conrad Wilson. I thought I'd come look you up now that I'm out of prison." He inserted his most charming grin. "But I guess you're out, or wanking off to some piece of Japanese porn, something like that." He grinned. "When you get a chance, look me up. My new cell phone number is..." He rattled it off. "Catch you later. Ta-ta."

He waved at the camera and walked off, his hands in his pockets.

On the way home, he picked up a sandwich at a deli and brought it upstairs to eat while he read up on the private investigator who'd been nosing around the old Moreau farm.

Jake Westley. His old contact information was for a tiny office in Brooklyn. Then, he'd moved to White Plains and set up a new office there.

It almost looked like he'd been fleeing the same situation that had dragged Marando under. It might prove useful to give the guy a visit—or Andrew Gibbons, he had to know *something*.

The funny thing was, he and his family were living in White Plains now too. If he was lucky, he could kill two birds with one stone, which was good because his first check wouldn't be coming in for another three weeks.

He wiped his hands with a napkin and drank the last of his Coke.

He kept having to remind himself not to get too wound up and overstretch himself. *As long as you have a good policy to keep yourself out of trouble, there is always plenty of time.*

Chapter 37 -Either would do

The man waiting for Andrew Gibbons in front of the Power Authority building wanted something. It was in the way he smiled, more than anything else. He wore blue jeans and a light medium shade of blue jacket, stood about five foot eight, and had broad shoulders like a bull, with short cropped blond hair and fair skin that looked as if it would take about five minutes of sunlight before it turned red.

But his grin. It was like looking at a living jack-o-lantern. Andy half expected his eyes to be glowing with live coals.

"Hey," the guy said. "You're Andrew Gibbons, right?"

"Sure. Who's asking?"

The man extended his hand and Andrew shook it. For a moment he thought it was going to be a real tussle. Then the guy yielded and let his hand go limp.

"Conrad Wilson," he said.

Andy grunted. It was the guy who'd just been exonerated off of death row up in New Hampshire. Regan and Jake had been involved somehow. It was just too much of a coincidence.

And now the guy was nosing around, trying to find out who his benefactors were.

The fact that Wilson was here, rather than in Laura Provost's office where he should have been, put Andy's hackles up.

Or maybe it was just that unholy grin.

"Hello," he said. "How's life treating you, now that you're out of prison?"

The grin widened. It looked like his jaw was about to fall off.

"It's treating me fine," Wilson said. "Mighty fine."

"Yeah, me too," Andy said. He had a job as an apprentice electrician now that got him out of the office most days. It didn't pay as well as the warehouse supervisor job he had in New York—but then again housing wasn't as bad up here, either. And the boys had a better school.

He did sometimes feel like he was in a witness protection program, though. This place was so vanilla it was like being caught in the time warp of a classic movie.

"I wanted to ask you about something," Wilson said. "Laura Provost. She has a righteousness bug up her rear end or what?"

Andy shrugged. "I don't know, man. I'm just grateful she got me out."

Wilson looked around at the boring cement and glass buildings that spread across downtown. "She put you here to get rid of you or what?"

Andy shook his head. "I got kids, you know. It was time to get out of the City—too much temptation for them to get in trouble there. There's about as much temptation in White Plains as there is in your grandma's underwear."

"But White Plains?"

He shrugged again. The sooner this guy got himself gone, the better. "I'm happy here. Now, if you'll excuse me, I gotta get home. The wife, you know."

He started walking down the sidewalk toward the parking garage. Wilson started walking with him, side by side, as if they were old buddies. "Provost, she doesn't strike me as an idealist—ambitious more than anything else."

Andy made a noncommittal noise in the back of his throat and shrugged.

"I think it's a cover-up for an anonymous benefactor who doesn't want to take credit." They walked along together, passing under the branches of trees planted in holes in the sidewalk. "Or perhaps some kind of organization."

The normal thing to do would have been to speculate along with the guy, *oh yeah, yeah, wouldn't that be interesting*. But Andy couldn't force himself to do it—his throat had tightened up into a knot.

"Uh-huh," he said.

"Which? The benefactor or the organization?"

Andy shrugged. "No idea, I'm just grateful." Damn it, he sounded like a robot.

That grin flashed at him again out of the corner of his eye. It was disturbing. "Know a man named Jake Westley?"

He stumbled on a crack in the sidewalk. Wilson grabbed his arm to steady him. "Steady there," he said, the same tone of voice you might use on a horse. "You all right?"

"I'm fine."

"Jake Westley," he repeated. "Know him?"

The man, Andy reminded himself, had been a detective before he'd been framed for murder. An outright lie would only make the man circle like a vulture.

He turned to look Wilson full in the face and frowned. "Jake? Of course, I know Jake. He's the boyfriend of a friend of my wife's. But what's that got to do with anything?"

Friend of my wife's. Wilson mouthed the words.

"His name came up, that's all," Wilson said.

Andy raised an eyebrow and refrained from asking in what context Jake's name had come up. "He's a good guy. Wouldn't want to get on his bad side, though. Runs a detective agency up here now."

"He used to operate out of Brooklyn, from what I understand."

"Sure."

"He on the run from someone?"

These weren't the kind of questions someone he'd just met should be asking him. He was being pumped all right—but why?

Too bad he wasn't a master of conversational tactics. He might be able to pry something out of the guy. He would have given a twenty-dollar bill to have Jamie here right now. *She'd* get something out of him, all right.

"No, why?"

"He moved up here in a hurry."

Andy shrugged again. "Well, that's the effect a beautiful woman has on a man."

They had come up to the entrance to the parking garage, a driveway disappearing downward into the shadows under the Power Authority building. Andy hesitated. He had no desire whatsoever to have this guy following him down into the dark.

Hell with it. He stopped in the middle of the sidewalk; he wasn't going to go another step further with this guy. He was just going to stand here in broad daylight until he was safe. If that didn't work, he would go back into the building and ask Harry, the security guard, for help.

"Ah, romance," Wilson said. "You're lucky your wife waited for you. Mine divorced me as soon as she could. Got the house, the cars, everything."

"Ah," Andy said.

"Well, I can see you're in a hurry to get to the missus. I'll let you go and head back to my car now. Nice chatting with you." He gave a half-flicked wave and headed toward the parking garage elevator. He stopped suddenly and looked back. "Unless you're parked down here, too? We could walk down together."

Andy shook his head—no way, no how. In prison he'd developed an instinct for violence, when to use it, when to run like hell. Now was time to run like hell.

"No? All right then." Wilson turned around, stuck his hands in his pockets, and started whistling as he strode away.

Andy stood and watched until the man had gone into the elevator and the doors had closed on him.

Then he walked stiff-legged back to the lobby and called home to Jamie on his cell phone. "We're good on milk," she said.

"I'm going to be late," he said.

"What is it?" She had picked up on the tension in his voice immediately and grew suspicious.

"It's about Jake and Regan," he said. "Somebody's come asking around about them."

"Who?"

"Conrad Wilson."

He could hear her drawing breath. "What did you tell him?"

"Nothing, I think. But he's a slick talker."

She made him go back over the conversation, word for word, while Harry watched him over the side of the security desk. He wasn't close enough to hear Andy's side of the conversation, but Andy could see him starting to hone in on his face, trying to decide whether to come over and find out what was going on.

When he was done repeating what had been said, Jamie said, "Hm."

"Yeah? What do you think?"

"I'll call Regan. I take it you're waiting for him to leave, right?"

"Right."

"You call Jake, give him the head's up. Don't try to follow the man. Whatever else he is, he's still a cop."

"Whatever else he is?" Andy asked. "They just proved he wasn't a murderer."

"They just proved that he didn't murder *that* girl," Jamie said. "Who knows what else he's been up to? I just wish Regan had told me earlier they were looking to get involved with that case. I would have told them."

"Told them what?"

"The same thing your gut's telling you, Andrew. The same thing your gut's been telling you."

***

Wilson had parked next to Andrew Gibbons's car, a light blue Honda Accord from sometime back in the Nineties. It had hail damage on the roof and one of the taillights was busted. The registration sticker was for March—the same month he'd been let out of prison.

He paused at the back of the car, then took a finger drew a smiley face on the back of the trunk and wrote '*Be seeing you Gibbons'* in the dust. Then he pulled down his sleeve to erase the words.

He stopped with his arm in the air. Why not? Gibbons didn't strike him as a guy to take stupid chances. Maybe before prison, sure. But not now. This would just reinforce the fear that had been pouring out of him. *What a crackup.*

He unlocked his car door with the fob, backed carefully out of the spot, and drove out to the street. He drove past the front door of the building. The glass of the revolving doors reflected his car back at him; he couldn't see inside.

He still had the impression of a shadow watching the car drive past from within.

He waved.

Dollars to donuts, as his mother would have said, if Jake Westley was involved with the case, his girlfriend was too.

He'd already found out who that was by asking around at Jake's office. The big burly man sitting at the front desk like some kind of administrative assistant had challenged him when he'd come in the door, but melted like a puppy when Wilson had brought in the big stuffed bear and asked where he could leave it out of sight, so Mr.

Westley's girlfriend couldn't see it.

The bear had been locked up in Jake Westley's office with a chuckle and the assurance that he, Chuck, wouldn't dream of letting Regan see it if she stopped by after work.

The photograph on the desk in the bare little office was of a confident, intelligent looking blonde woman with an arrogant lift to her chin, a lioness to Laura Provost's eagle.

Two attractive women to choose from—in his fantasies, if nothing else.

He preferred Regan—Regan St. Claire, a judge, he later learned—but really, either would do.

Chapter 38 -Damned if you don't

"You're in trouble," Jamie said. "The deep kind of stuff."

Regan rubbed the back of her neck. She had stopped when she got into the car to check her phone and had seen the message from Jamie. It was six o'clock and she was starving and trying to decide whether she wanted to go out to eat, pick something up, or call Jake to throw herself on his mercy—if he was back in town, that was. But the voicemail said it was something important.

Mondays had never really been Regan's friend. This Monday was worse than most—she and Jake had spent most of the weekend, either together or separately, gathering information on the Craig Moreau case, but hadn't made much progress.

Then at work, it had been a day full of backfilling for another judge—a series of minor cases she hadn't been familiar with but was expected to be able to handle competently, as well as about twice as fast as she was comfortable with.

Then she'd come out to the car and seen that some jerk had drawn a smiley face in the dirt on the trunk.

Look. Just because she'd been too distracted to have the car washed was no reason to single her out. She kept looking around outside at the other cars, as if she could spot the joker who'd done it, as if he or she were still hanging around.

It was to be expected not everything would come together as easily or wildly unpredictably as Andy's case—or Conrad Wilson's for that matter—but this one seemed like it was full of nothing but dead ends and late night searches on the Internet, and it was getting on her nerves, making her irritable for no reason at all.

And now this—Jamie was angry at her again. Regan could hear

the tension in her voice.

She sighed and let go of her day as well as she could. Her troubles were nothing compared to what the world had put Jamie through. "How so?"

"Conrad Wilson is after the two of you. At the very least, he has Jake's name and place of business, and he is going to get yours in about two seconds."

Regan blinked. Of all the things she'd expected Jamie to say, that wasn't even on the list. "Conrad Wilson?"

"He stopped by the Power Authority to talk to Andy. Had some extremely impertinent questions to ask, but the general gist of it was to try to find out whether Jake was connected with either Andy's or his release in some way."

"Maybe he's just being grateful...or curious. He's a detective, you know."

"I might have noticed. Regan, are you listening to me?"

She sighed again. "Jamie, everything to do with that case is just... off. Just looking at his picture made my hackles stand up."

"And you didn't listen to your instincts?"

"Just because he gives me the creeps doesn't mean he wasn't innocent."

"Oh, Regan. You have to listen to your instincts. That man is no good. Promise me you and Jake won't have anything to do with him."

It wasn't like they were likely to ever meet the man. And if they did, Regan would have made her excuses to get the hell out of the room anyway, fair or not. An easy promise. "I promise," she said.

"Like I said, the man gives me the creeps."

A pair of admins walked out of the building and over to their cars. The early evening light made them look like they were in a movie, some kind of heartwarming film about the power of friendship. A single guy walked out of the building after them, looking like he was stalking them. A heartwarming film about the power of locking your doors at night.

"What was he like when you met him?" Jamie said.

"What do you mean?"

"What was he *like* when you *met* him?" Jamie repeated, as if not quite able to believe that Regan didn't understand the question.

"I haven't met him in person at all," Regan said. "We decided it would be safer for everyone involved if there was no way to connect us with the people we're trying to help."

Jamie made an *I-can't-believe-this* noise. "You never met him. How did you even figure out he wasn't guilty in the first place if you didn't meet him?"

Ah. She was talking about intuition. "I try not to go off on that kind of thing," Regan said. "I trust facts, not impressions."

"You met with Andy more than once," Jamie said.

"I thought it was important that he understood what we were doing. He was charming, of course. But I tried not to take my emotions into account when I was trying to determine whether he was innocent or not. I hate being blinded like that. Also, it was our first case, and we didn't realize what harm it would bring if we met with him."

"It's not blind to listen to your gut," Jamie said. "You have to—

you're damned if you don't."

Regan closed her eyes. Her hands were shaking. She needed help with her blood sugar *now*. "Jamie, I'm starving and I can't think straight, let alone try to argue with you, or even really take in what you're trying to say. I promise I'll stay away from Wilson and that I'll call you back tomorrow."

"Tomorrow?" Jamie asked sharply.

"I have a bunch of phone calls to make for this other case that we're on."

"Have you met *him*?"

"No. But..." She took a breath. "But I will, before we go any further. I'll meet with Provost and see if she can get me in to see him anonymously or under another name or something."

"Thank you," Jamie said. "That would make me feel a lot better. It should make you feel a lot better too."

Regan smiled. "It will...after I've eaten."

"Go eat then, and not a bunch of junk."

"All right, all right."

"Take care, Regan. You're in our prayers."

"Thank you. Tell the boys to stay out of trouble."

Jamie snorted. "A fine statement, coming from you."

They hung up. Regan leaned back in her seat. She should call Jake... Laura Provost. She obviously needed to call Provost. Would it help to call Alex and have him look at Wilson's case yet again? Probably not. Ugh, she couldn't think. She closed her eyes and tried to get it together enough to decide what she wanted to eat. The rest could come later.

La Ruche, she decided. The wait would be longer than at a fast food restaurant, but the little basket of slices of hot French bread and fresh butter would go a long way to helping her get her head on straight.

She put her foot on the brake and shifted into reverse, then turned around to check the parking lot behind her as she started to take her foot off the brake.

A thump came from the back of the car and she slammed on the brake again. She drew in a quick breath.

Then she had finally turned around enough to see what she'd just hit.

A man was standing directly behind the car, earbuds in his ears, a paper bag in one arm, and a monster cup of coffee in the other.

The top of the coffee cup had gone flying, the paper cup crushed in the guy's hand. Coffee sparkled on her back window. The guy was wide eyed, staring at her.

She put the car in park and jumped out. "Oh my God, I am so sorry."

The man stared at her. The back bumper was up against his thigh.

"Are you hurt?" she asked.

He wore blue jeans, work boots, t-shirt, plaid button-up shirt, and a baseball cap. The front of his shirt was soaked with coffee. Grease looked like it was soaking through the paper bag at the bottom.

"I'm so sorry," she repeated.

He put the smashed paper cup on the back of the trunk, wiped his hand on his jeans, and held it out. "Don't worry about it. I'm just...well, damn. I'm pleased to meet you."

He had a strong grip but kept it restrained—a lady was present. She was half tempted to push her luck and shake it more firmly than he was leading, but didn't. She *had* almost just run over the guy.

"Finally," the guy added.

She frowned. She hadn't been listening, really—just worrying whether she'd hurt him. She did a mental rewind.

"Who...?" she said. The sun was behind him. She had a sense of the astonishment on his face, but couldn't really get a good look at the guy otherwise.

He laughed, almost giddily. "It really is different meeting someone in real life, isn't it? You think you'd recognize someone from their pictures. But that's not how it works. You get an image in your head from the picture, and then when they show up with a different hairstyle or even just a different shirt..."

He shook his head. "Meeting you in person... it's like meeting a stranger. Ms. St. Claire, Conrad Wilson at your service."

Chapter 39 -Lady Luck

The Honorable Regan St. Claire was taller and even more beautiful than he'd anticipated. The pictures of her online didn't do her justice. It was like the difference between looking at a statue and standing in the presence of a goddess.

Luck. Luck was what had brought him here. He'd only driven over to the Westchester County Judicial Building to get a sense of where she worked and see how hard it would be to pick her up there.

He'd gone across the street from the parking lot to pick up some of the lifeblood of any investigation: thick, burnt black coffee. Also to take a leak. No matter how much he'd thought prison had toughened him up, it had also let his bladder atrophy to the point where he couldn't spend eight or ten hours in the car without a break anymore—not to mention his back. He'd almost been limping on his way over to the coffee shop. Then the credit card machine wouldn't take either of his cards, and he'd been forced to walk down the street to an ATM... a list of irritations he'd been mentally cursing for the last twenty minutes.

He should have known better. Lady Luck would eventually be on his side—sometimes she just took a little while to carry herself out. Ten years in prison was pushing it, but she always arrived, just in the nick of time.

The blonde goddess smiled at him. She looked sick with adrenaline—not one of those women who got jazzed up by danger, apparently.

Good.

"Are you all right?" she repeated.

He looked down. Soaked with coffee, yes, but otherwise on top of the world. "I'm not hurt, if that's what you mean."

The tight line between her eyebrows relaxed a little. "I'm sorry about your coffee."

He laughed again. An image opened up in front of him—the blonde goddess being worshipped on his altar in the basement of the cabin.

The opening lyrics of "Bad Moon Rising" started playing in his head—one of his favorite hunting songs. He took it as a sign his subconscious had a plan.

Even if he didn't know it yet.

Go for it, the lyrics told him.

"Not to be a complete stalker or anything," he said, "but I could absolutely use a favor from you."

One eyebrow lifted. *Surprise me*, it seemed to say.

Oh, he thought, *I will.*

"What's that?" she asked.

"Let me take you to dinner," he said. "I found out what you and your, ah… crew tried to do for me, and it was impressive. It was really only random chance that Byron Parker came forward and admitted his guilt, but the evidence you picked up would have freed me even if he hadn't."

Her face went through several expressions, none of them obviously pleased or distressed. She was careful, he noticed, to keep the corner of the trunk between the two of them.

She didn't trust him. Time to throw out some more bait.

"I've found…" He broke off with another laugh. "Listen, you're never going to believe this. While I was apartment hunting in Brooklyn, I found this great little apartment. A guy had killed himself there a couple of months ago, and the next guy renting the apartment claimed it was haunted and moved out before his lease was up.

"I couldn't resist; I put down a deposit and moved in."

"Any ghosts?" she asked politely

"Yeah, but not in the way you might think. I was cleaning out some junk in the closet and found a... a set of files. Tell me, Ms. St. Claire, do you know anything about Andrew Gibbons? Or Craig Moreau?"

Her eyes widened prettily. "You're living in Peter Marando's old apartment."

"Yes, ma'am. And I've found some pretty incredible stuff...stuff about an org—"

She put her hand up and shook her head. "Not out here, all right?"

He grinned. "So there's something to that, is there?"

Her eyes narrowed. She gave him a look of cold, clear, and logical assessment.

It was a look he'd seen a hundred times before, from all kinds of women—and some men. As a detective, Wilson had been practicing for years to bypass that look. When questioning witnesses and suspects, a flash of that look almost always led to the subject shutting down and going quiet. It meant he had lost control.

He let his face fall. "You're talking yourself out of it, aren't you?" He puffed out his cheeks and blew a sigh toward his feet, then reached for his wallet. He didn't have business cards printed up yet, but he had a couple of slips of scrap paper inside—shopping lists for apartment supplies.

He pulled one out and turned it over, found a dry spot on the trunk and wrote down his cell phone number and email address.

"Here, take this," he said, holding it out to her. "I'm dying of curiosity over here. But if you don't feel comfortable, we can email."

She shook her head again. "Not over email, we can't."

He saw her balance curiosity against caution. The scales balanced evenly for a moment.

When she stepped forward to take the note, his right arm shot out around her neck and his left hand clasped tight over her mouth.

Chapter 40 -Rather stayed on death row

It was almost eleven in the evening. The dew was already thick on the grass and tree leaves sparkled in the street lights. Jake braced his cell phone against his shoulder and followed traffic down the boulevard.

Once again, the call went to voice mail.

He tossed the phone in the seat beside him and turned into the parking lot of the Judicial Building, then circled through the mostly empty lot to the general area where Regan often parked her car. He'd already checked La Ruche—but there was no sign of her there.

Regan's navy Lexus glittered under the orange and green streetlights, orange for the street and green for the parking lot. The back of the car jutted out from between the lines of the parking space. It hadn't been pulled all the way forward, and something had dulled the shine on the back of her trunk.

He pulled up behind it. Brown slurry had run all over the back window.

He got out.

It looked like someone had pitched a cup of coffee at the back window. Jake touched the trunk with the back of a knuckle. It was tacky from sugar, and therefore, not Regan's coffee.

The stuff had run all over the taillights and license plate, over the bumper and onto the ground—at least a quart of the stuff. He crouched down. The puddle on the ground was just barely wet where it had puddled on the tarmac.

He got out and checked the driver side door, careful to use the tail end of his shirt and only touch the edges of the handle, just in case.

The door wasn't locked.

And, her soft sided black briefcase was still tucked down on the floor in the passenger seat.

He straightened up and looked around, then jogged up to the revolving doors at the front of the building. The doors were locked. He tried the door for the handicapped—locked as well—then knocked on the glass. The security desk was just on the other side.

The security guard, an ancient woman who looked like she was about a hundred years old and weighed no more than a hundred and ten pounds soaking wet, looked up at him with lucid eyes.

"Help," he said. "Help me."

A speaker next to the handicapped door came to life. "Yes?"

"Hello. There may be an emergency. I've been trying to reach Judge St. Claire, but I can't get her. Her car is still in the parking lot with the door unlocked and her briefcase on the floor, and there's some kind of fluid all over the back of the car."

The woman's white eyebrows pinched together in the middle.

"I'll call her office."

"Thank you."

The woman looked down, then lifted a receiver to her ear. After a few seconds, it was clear nobody was picking up. Jake cursed himself, then dialed Gary's number.

"Hello, handsome detective. Is something the matter?"

"Regan. Where is she? She's not answering her phone and her car's been abandoned in the parking lot."

Gary cursed. "She left at six." In the background, Jake could hear the sound of movement—a television going dead, footsteps across the carpet. "Have you checked her house? I'll check the police band and call the hospitals."

"I'm at the Judicial Building. I'll be there in a few minutes."

"She just spoke with Jamie Gibbons today before she left. I didn't hear the whole conversation, but she was promising to do something just before she hung up. I don't know if it's important...from what Regan was saying, it sounded like Jamie was upset."

The security guard was looking up from her desk at him, frowning. She hung up the phone and started walking toward him.

"I gotta go," Jake said. "Drop Jamie a line and see if she knows anything."

"Sure, boss," Gary said. The line went dead.

Jake put the phone in his pocket and stepped closer to the door. It opened a crack, and the guard said, "I called the guard from the last shift, Thomas. He said that she and a man had an altercation in the parking lot at about six pm, but that it was resolved amicably, and she got in a car with him."

"An altercation?"

"Thomas said that she almost backed into a pedestrian carrying a paper bag from the coffee shop across the street."

"And she got into the car with him."

There was no reason for the security guard to be telling him this; Jake could have been anyone. They both realized it at the same time. The guard shook her head.

Jake said, "Thanks. I'm going to go back and lock the car door and see if she's at home. If she calls, let her know that Jake's looking for her."

"I certainly will," the guard said, then pulled the door closed until the lock snapped in place.

She stood at the door and watched him until he was out of sight.

She wasn't at home. He did a quick sweep through the house to make sure she hadn't fallen or the house been burglarized. But it was empty. In the fridge was a slice of pecan pie and a note from Regan's maid, Ellen—definitive proof in Jake's mind that she'd never been here.

He called Gary.

"Boss, Jamie says she was hounding Regan to stay away from Wilson. He came to talk to Andy at work today..." Gary summed up the situation, including the message drawn in the dust on the back of Andy's car.

Jake cursed. He didn't know what game Wilson was playing, but Jamie had been right. They should have met him, at least once, or at least gone with Regan's instincts.

Hindsight and foresight—it was too late.

He got off the phone with Gary and dialed Alex. As Jake explained to him the situation, the background was full of the sound of a keyboard buzzing.

"Jake," Alex interrupted him, "Regan's cell phones. I have GPS software on both of them. They're both not functioning."

"Not functioning."

Jake's lips tingled. His fingers were going numb. He paced across the kitchen floor.

"The phones had to have been destroyed, Jake."

He shook his head. "Can you give me any information about them? Anything at all?"

A pause, more typing. "The furthest I can track them is to Newton, Connecticut."

"He isn't headed back to Brooklyn then," Jake said. "Somewhere else. Probably New Hampshire. Does he still own any property out there? Find out. If not, start tracking down the stuff that belongs to his brother."

"Will do."

"And call her father. I'm going to get on the road and see if I can catch up to them."

Jake could hear the wince in Alex's voice. "I'll call Pavo. Her father's just going to shout at me."

"Let Pavo take the heat," Jake agreed. "Check in with Gary, and call me if you come up with something."

"I will."

Jake hung up.

If he so much as lay a finger on Regan, Wilson was gonna wish he'd stayed on death row.

Chapter 41 -I'm ready

John's phone rang, pulling him up from the darkness. He sat up and swung his legs over the side of the bed in one movement, putting his feet into his slippers and grabbing the phone.

"Hello?"

"John," Paul's voice said.

A quick glance at the clock said it must be an emergency call. "Paul. What happened."

"A car will pull up to your front door in a few minutes. Get dressed and get into it."

His nostrils flared and he almost kicked the dresser in the dark. He stopped himself and reached around for the lights, flipped them on.

He was already pulling a pair of pants out of a drawer.

"Damn you, Paul. None of your cloak and dagger stuff. What's going on."

"Are you getting dressed?"

He cursed and tossed the cell phone onto the top of the dresser, stripped off his pajamas, and put on an undershirt, then a polo shirt. He picked up the phone again, trapped it against his shoulder, and sat on the bed to pull on his pants.

"I am almost dressed." He zipped up his fly. "I'm dressed, all right?"

"Socks and shoes...your wallet and keys."

His arms and the back of his neck were covered with goosebumps. He grabbed a pair of socks, his wallet, his keys, a pocketknife, and keyed in the combination for the gun safe in his bedside table. He lay it on the bed beside him, then put on his socks.

The background noise on the phone went from a low murmur to some kind of loud hum, which rose in volume until John was fairly sure Paul wouldn't be able to hear him. He tracked down his shoulder holster, pulled off his polo shirt, put the holster on, then replaced the polo and added a light windbreaker.

John pulled the envelope full of cash out of the safe and tucked it into his inside jacket pocket and zipped it in, then used the toilet and washed his hands.

It was like being back in the Organization and going out to fulfill mysterious tasks with Paul all over again. *Sleep when you can, eat when you can, piss when you can.*

The background noise cut off with a thump—then the sound of radio chatter.

"I'm ready," John said, walking toward the front door.

"The cab will take you to the Westchester County Airport," Paul said. "My plane will stop for you a few moments after you arrive, I think. The driver's name is Maxwell and you don't need to pay him. It is a privately owned car, so please don't damage it. I have instructed him to bring sandwiches and coffee."

"Paul!"

"Regan has been abducted by Wilson," Paul said. "I have found a property that his family has owned and now belongs to him in New Hampshire. I strongly suspect he is on his way there—their last known location was Newport, Connecticut. We are on our way to reacquire my goddaughter and remove that son of a bitch off the face of the earth."

John opened the door. A car was just pulling up, lights turned off.

"Good," John said. "The car is here. See you soon."

Chapter 42 -What it's like to pass out

The streetlight turned his shadow into a giant monster approaching the front door of the blue clapboard house.

It grew smaller as Alex climbed the steps, cleverly disguising as a geek in sweatpants, sandals, and a Miskatonic University t-shirt. It had seemed wrong to change clothes before he left his apartment at the top of the coffee shop.

Alex pressed the bell, then knocked on the door at The T.H.E.M. Three's house. At one in the morning the sound was loud and almost threatening. He half expected lights to come on and alarms to go off. There was no answer. He looked up at the door camera, then punched in the key code for the door and opened it.

"Hello? Anyone home?"

The sound echoed through the house. He was about to announce himself, then stopped. For some reason, he didn't want whoever was in the house to hear him identify himself—an odd thought. Nevertheless, he followed it.

He walked through the front rooms to the kitchen, then stopped at the basement door and knocked again. "Guys? Anyone home?"

The basement was silent. Before he went downstairs, he stopped and listened at the door to the upper floor. That too was silent.

After biting his lip for a moment, he went downstairs.

At the bottom of the stairs, the room was dark, quiet and looked like it had been ransacked—which was about standard. Pizza boxes and soda cans were everywhere, with cushions piled up on the floor and tossed against the walls. A blue LED game logo sign glowed on the far wall, serving as a nightlight.

A mess, but nothing really out of place.

He edged between the cushions on the floor to the laundry room. The laundry room was shallow and held a matched pair of shiny metallic appliances, along with massive piles of sorted whites and colors.

In the back of the room was a line of pipes. Placed awkwardly behind it was a storage room under the stairs. If you didn't know to look for it, you wouldn't have known it was there.

He ducked under the stairs and tapped on the door handle. On the other side of the door was a quiet room. If you knocked on the door itself, nobody inside would be able to hear you.

A second later the handle jerked and the door opened.

All three guys were there, along with Mary, Bosco's girlfriend. TDB, dressed in cartoon character pajamas, had answered the door; the others were packed around a small table that took up most of the space. The room reeked of sour sweat and energy drinks. They all had paper notebooks laid out around them, along with piles of printouts.

They stared at him. Their expressions were unreadable, and they were all in their brightly colored pajamas—even Mary.

Alex stepped inside and closed the door behind him.

"Where's Wilson?" TDB said.

Alex blinked. "You know about Wilson?"

"*You* know about Wilson?" TDB said.

Alex cleared his throat. "He's abducted a friend of mine."

"Then what are you doing *here*?" TDB said.

"We used to be the Conrad Wilson fan club," Bosco said, "if you don't remember."

"Oh, yeah." TDB sat at the table to Alex's left. "Long story short, he was here earlier today looking for us."

"And?"

"And we didn't answer the doorbell."

"Why?"

The three guys all looked at Mary, sitting to Alex's right at the end of the table, next to Bosco.

"Because I told them he was dangerous," she said. "I have information."

Alex hesitated, licked his lips, and reached across the table for one of the unopened energy drinks. It was cold, but not refrigerator cold. They'd been in here for a while. "I, uh, have a personal question to ask—no offense intended."

Mary drew herself up. Alex had the impression she was preparing herself for some kind of backstabbing racist or sexist comment from him. Hopefully what he was about to say wouldn't be worse.

"Are you part of the Organization?"

Her mouth, which was open to rebut whatever offensive thing he had to say, clicked shut.

Alex cleared his throat again, then started twirling the ends of his mustache. "I only ask because the person who's been abducted is Pavo's goddaughter, and he would probably appreciate whatever help he can get."

The four of them looked at each other. Then Mary said, "Would you step outside for a moment?"

Alex nodded, then opened the door.

Outside the room, someone's phone was ringing.

The rule was—and Alex had tried to drill this home over and over to all the contractors who worked with him—no electronic equipment could go inside the quiet room. No wires, no gaps, no vents, no heaters. The lights had to be battery operated. If the room got stuffy, you stepped outside.

If the door was open, you didn't talk. No exceptions.

Mary got up and pushed past him, grabbing a purse from the floor behind one of the cushions. She answered the phone.

"Hello?"

Alex left the door open and stood in the laundry room, watching her. She nodded, then started pacing. He could hear the murmur of someone talking on the other end of the call.

Finally, she said, "We have a guest here at the moment, named Alex. Yes, that one. He says that..."

She cut herself off and started pacing again.

"Yes," she said, then, "No, I'm pretty sure he's worked it out. No, I don't think so, but he could be useful. Yes, of course. All right, I'll call back from there."

She turned toward Alex, a silhouette against a blue background. She moved smoothly, like a ninja, and slipped the phone back into her purse on the floor.

"Close the door," she said.

Alex leaned over and pulled the door closed, shutting his three friends off from the conversation and himself off from the light coming from the room. He hoped she wasn't about to knife him. They probably wouldn't be able to hear him if he started screaming.

"How much do you know?" she asked.

He shrugged. "About the Organization?"

"About Wilson."

"Just that he was set up as the murderer of Kristin Walker, and that he gives Regan the creeps."

Her shadow moved slightly. She might have been nodding her head.

"He was set up for a murder he didn't commit, because there wasn't any proof for the murders he did commit—not by the Organization, but by a group of his coworkers, other detectives. The Organization has been watching him... they've convinced themselves that he's a superior human being.

"Smart, aggressive, adaptable—a real alpha male," Mary said bitterly. "The boys don't know much about the Organization at this point..."

"Even though you've been pushing them to join," Alex said.

"Even though I'm trying to recruit them," Mary said. "And even though eventually I would have tried to recruit you."

Alex made a face.

"Not in bed," she said. "I don't do that. My relationship with Bosco has nothing to do with this. If he says no, he says no. I can live with that. But the important part here is you don't talk crap about us. You and I, we can have a discussion after this is over. But don't screw this up for me now."

Alex said, "Otherwise, you'll lose recruits."

Her voice was tight. "Otherwise, I'll lose Bosco. These are good guys. Even Paddy is starting to take me as more than just another pretty face, if you know what I mean, and that's saying something. Don't screw this up for *me*, is what I'm saying. I need all the friends I can get."

She might have been playing him, but his heart went out to her anyway. He was a geek, and had known more isolation over the years than he'd ever admit.

"Okay," he said. "I mean, obviously I'm keeping an eye on you, and we'll talk about this later."

"That's good enough for now," she said. With nothing more than a breath of air, she slipped past him and into the quiet room. "We need to hurry," she said. "A friend of mine isn't answering her phone, and it might be an emergency. Come with me now if you want to go."

***

TDB drove the van, the rest of them sitting in back in what was probably an illegal but extremely handy conversion: no seatbelts, just a table and a pair of benches running along the sides in the back.

In a few minutes they were at a gray townhouse in Crown Heights with a basement of a two story apartment. The windows were covered with wrought-iron grills and the masonry was decorated with molded cement vines.

Mary let them into the first floor apartment with a key she picked from a rather large keyring while Bosco held a flashlight for her.

No one asked how she had a key to the apartment of the assistant D.A. In fact, no one said much of anything.

They would *all* have to have a talk at some point or they would never be able to trust each other again.

It was a typical Crown Heights sort of townhouse, all decorative molding around the doorways and parquet floors. Mary stepped inside, then let the rest of them in while watching the street behind them. It was as silent as the city ever got—a few sirens in the distance, a baby crying nearby, a few lighted windows.

If anyone was watching them, they were playing it cool.

When they were all inside, Mary said, "Laura? Are you all right?"

It was a formality. The house was silent.

"Check the rooms, but don't leave fingerprints," Mary said.

If the qualification bothered any of the others, they didn't say so, but spread out into the main rooms and down the hallway. Alex headed for the kitchen.

Mary put a hand on his shoulder. "The refrigerator," she said.

A hot stream of bile rose in the back of his throat. He turned away from her and walked forward, trying to keep his sandals from making too much noise on the parquet floors. The soles snapped against his heels.

A fine outfit to be sneaking around in.

The closer he came to the kitchen, the more impossible it was not to notice the scent of air freshener, a heavy sweet scent of flowers and fruit that very quickly made him sick to his stomach.

The combination kitchen/dining room had a marble fireplace on one wall and hideous boxy cabinetry out of the Seventies on the other. Some dishes had been left out on the counter, and one of the lights under the cupboards was on. Three spindly, antique dining chairs sat at a cheap Ikea table. The overhead lamp looked like a cheap Japanese lantern.

He walked past the dining room table and up to the refrigerator. The oven was silver and had a nice range hood, but the fridge was an ancient, sickly green color. Mary's "friend" Laura, was probably replacing the contents of her condo as fast as she could afford.

The fridge kicked in and started to rattle.

Alex reached for the handle, then stopped. *Don't leave any fingerprints.*

As the saying went, 'he'd lose his head if it wasn't attached.' He looked around and found a folded towel between the two halves of the sink. He picked it up; it was cold and damp.

He used it to pull the refrigerator door open, then closed it

He turned around and found Mary in the bathroom, looking through the medicine cabinet. She closed it, using a washcloth. Her face reflected back at him, looking sick and tense, her eyebrows pinched together.

She wanted to know, but she didn't want to know.

"Confirm," he said. "Laura is Laura Provost, correct?"

"Oh, God," she said. "The bathtub, too."

He looked down at the wet towel in his hand; it was stained a dingy brown.

There would be knives in the pile of dishes by the side of the sink and a sharpening steel.

Maybe a cleaver.

He walked over to the bathtub. It was one of those old claw foot ones, a brass hoop overhead to hold the shower curtain, which was a mint green color.

He found the opening at the back end of the tub and looked inside.

He looked up.

Yes, there were her feet, just visible over the top of the shower rod.

"Excuse me," he said, and stepped into the hallway where he allowed himself to slide down the wall and onto the floor. His ears rang and the edges of his vision went gray.

His last thought before passing out was, "So this is what it's like to pass out."

Thump.

Chapter 43 -What good does that do us?

Provost's apartment was locked up, and they drove away at a swift but legal speed with Paddy at the wheel while Alex, still shaking, ogled the surrounding windows to see if anyone was watching. They were quiet—too nauseated to talk.

Clearly, the five of them would have to be dragged back into this at some point. A large, windowless white van parked illegally along the street, even just after one in the morning, wouldn't have gone completely unnoticed, and someone would jump to a conclusion.

No doubt, they *would* be pulled in for questioning.

An average detective or officer on the street—even the average FBI agent—didn't have to be more brilliant than a hacker running a dictionary attack to crack someone's password.

Eventually, the officer or agent would ask the right question.

Bosco had taken video and photos of everything in the house. The kitchen and the bathroom, especially, had been extensively recorded. It was obvious the job had been done hours earlier. Speckles of blood all over the shower curtain showed that the killer had run the shower over the body to wash most of the blood down the drain, yet the plastic curtain was completely dry.

The hamper was full of well rinsed but still stained washcloths and hand towels. The bed was mussed, but not bloody. A hunting magazine lay next to the bed, folded back along the spine. Some stains on the rugs on the parquet floor had been sprinkled with a pink powder and left to set.

Tidy. It was all very tidy, except for the mess in the bathroom and the fridge. Her body had been strung upside down in the tub and left to bleed out. Her head—in the fridge—was carefully wrapped in plastic wrap.

Alex was very close to tossing his cookies.

Mary had given Paddy Marando's address in Bed-Stuy; she wanted to search the place before the cops arrived.

But in Alex's opinion, the potential benefits couldn't possibly be worth the risk.

For example, what if Wilson was still there?

He wasn't. He couldn't be. He'd kidnapped Regan...

Oh, God. He'd kidnapped Regan.

***

Gary had always liked to pretend his office was a kind of information hub. He had six screens and could view a different news program on each of them, or research on one while being surrounded by the various shows in progress.

Someone else could play superhero.

He just wanted to be the super competent assistant back in the underground lair, on call for any emergency.

In reality, it sucked—big time.

He had thrown his headset across the room a dozen times, knocked over a cup of coffee, and snapped a second rate figurine in half, twisting its legs off and tossing them full force at the wall.

It's all fun and games until someone you care about is in danger. And then you're stuck in one location with nothing to do to relieve the stress but pace—nothing to do but worry and wait.

Gary had reached the point where he'd begun by calling Laura

Provost's home number and hanging up on the machine when she didn't answer. He'd made a list of—God forbid—media in New Hampshire to call in order to drum up support for a missing person's investigation. He'd called all of Jake's SEAL buddies to tell them what was going on and to send them out into the night. He had the cops on speed dial...

But Alex told him Jake wanted him to wait.

Why? The police could surround the house before he ever got there...

But the two police officers who had "defended" him in court, saying he'd never left the party when clearly he had, were dead.

The third, who had been accused of blackmailing them, had blown his brains out with a shotgun.

Nancy Rossier, the friend of the original victim, was missing.

And so was Shasta Leighton, the woman who had collected the semen sample from Wilson's tryst with his mistress.

If Wilson thought for one second he was being followed...he'd kill Regan...in a heartbeat.

And so Gary decided *not* to ignore Jake's orders.

The phone rang—Alex.

"It's me," Gary said.

"We went to Provost's apartment," Alex said. "She's been butchered."

The world gave an awful lurch. Gary grabbed the side of his glass topped oak desk. "Murdered?"

"Butchered...reduced down to chunks of meat. Blood down the drain and her intestines and gall bladder double wrapped in the garbage."

Gary blinked. The screens in front of him had gone to sleep; he shook the mouse to wake them up. "A hunter," he whispered. Cold shivers were running down his spine.

"He has a cabin in New Hampshire—belonged to his family."

A hunter... a hunter. Where had he heard of a serial killer hunter lately? He should remember these things, have some way to access them during times of stress. It felt like his head was stuffed with foam cushions. "Are you all right?"

"We're headed to his apartment. It's Marando's old apartment."

"Good thing Jake removed those files," Gary said. He was doing a quick search on serial killers. *Hunters...*

"The person we're with is worried Marando might have left more than one copy."

Gary clucked his tongue. "We should have searched the place ourselves. *I* should have searched it."

"You?"

"Nosey bastard, at your service."

"I have to go now... we're just about to go in."

"Be careful."

"He's not here."

"That, unfortunately, is true," Gary murmured, not really listening. "Good luck."

Alex grunted; the call cut off.

Gary pointed at the screen on the upper left. The information he wanted had been on *that* screen just a few minutes ago, he knew it.

A hunter...

Blood down the drain and her intestines...

Blood down the drain and...

The killer up in Canada—the one that had looked like some sort of ritual killing. The bodies had been hung on a tripod and left to drain out in the snow...

His fingers flew.

No... that had been in the Eighties.

Right around the time of the Moreau killings.

***

The two of them had accepted the use of a Mercedes-Benz delivered to the airport. Paul had insisted upon driving, as he always had when the two of them had gone out on a job for the Organization.

John had the explosive nerves, the ones built for action.

Paul's were colder, able to keep the car on the road for the thirty dark, twisting miles between the airport and the cabin, which left John with the phone.

John said, "All right. You be careful, too," and hung up.

Pavo said, "Yes?"

"That was Gary, Regan's secretary."

"The one from the hospital room?"

"That's right, Fiducioso's brother."

Paul had stayed calm throughout the flight and the drive. Now his jaw clenched. "What, pray tell, did *he* have to say?"

"Gary said Alex called. Provost is dead. She was butchered, he says, as if Wilson were a deer hunter."

"What good does that do us?"

***

Jake sped through the darkness, praying he hadn't made a mistake in telling the others not to call for police backup. What he really wanted was his buddies Chuck, Doug, Graham, and four ski masks—they could take care of this whole situation faster than your ma could call you in for dinner.

John and Pavo were ahead of him on the road. And Gary had called to report—among other things—that the SEALs were behind him in case things ran long.

Just when a guy needed access to a private helicopter.

Chapter 44 -Not an easy task

Johnny Cash played on the radio, and the miles rolled by.

Wilson stroked the top of Regan's head. She was seat-belted in place, her head supported with a workout towel. Unfortunately, he didn't have a neck pillow. The angle of her neck looked uncomfortable. She was going to wake up with a cramp; he knew it. *Poor thing.*

He smiled tenderly at her. It was like riding in the car with his wife—if he had actually loved his wife, that was.

He'd left a trail behind him, he knew. If any of the "missing" bodies turned up, it was practically a stepping stone path through a well-tended garden. And in fact, he was practically guaranteeing he'd be followed by the same crew that got Andrew Gibbons out of jail, which at the bare minimum included the woman's boyfriend, a former Delta Force operator.

Too bad for him. I'm stealing your girlfriend, and I'm pretty sure I'm going to get away with it.

Some men are just jealous. Why can't they share?

She was such an angel—so well spoken, so intelligent. Charming. The bruise on her temple was already turning into a darker shadow. He could see it in the dashboard lights—what a pity. Since then, of course, he'd had more time and had injected her with tranquilizers from the stash he'd bought in Portsmouth. It would be a shame to have to hit her again. He would hate to ruin such a pretty face with another blow.

Some people had to be killed because there was no other way for justice to catch up to them.

Some people had to be killed because… it was hard to put into words, really. But it always made him feel that all was right in the world, that order had been restored when he did it.

Regan was going to be perfect.

She was going to be one of those who kept on fighting until they passed out.

He knew it, and he was looking forward to it. Restoring order was not an easy task.

***

She was in a car, almost fast asleep. The road hummed underneath the wheels, hypnotizing her.

It was dark. The heater was on, aimed at her feet, but the window was also open, pulling cold air over her face. It smelled like her parents' old station wagon, the first car smell she could ever remember—a smell a little bit like bread.

The green dashboard lights winked at her. Her head nodded forward.

She wanted to pull it back upright, but she couldn't. She wasn't really awake, just dreaming.

She wasn't a little girl anymore, and yet it felt as though her legs were too short for the seat, and her feet couldn't touch the ground.

Behind the wheel, her father was driving. Her mother wasn't here. It must have been chess night, and her father was driving her home from meeting with Uncle Paul.

Home. They were on the way home.

Her mother was dead, wasn't she? The man, Lassiter, had hit her with his car. No, she would have been older if her mother was dead. Her feet would have reached the ground.

It didn't matter.

Her dad would carry her inside if she was asleep—she loved it when he did that. She kept her eyes closed so her dad would think she was sleeping.

Chapter 45 - The family album

The first one at the door of Marando's old apartment was Mary. Again her keyring produced a miraculous result on the door locks, and they entered via the slowly creaking door.

She scanned the front room and hesitated.

Alex couldn't blame her. What if Wilson was there? Unlikely, but not impossible. His heart thudded in his chest forcefully, drowning out the sounds of his friends' breathing and moving, the sounds of the building, and the sounds coming from the street.

Bosco said, "Mary. Let me go in first. If there's someone in here, I'll take care of it."

Mary's mouth tightened. She looked up at Bosco, then back at the rest of them. "No, I'll do it."

Alex leaned forward and touched her on the arm. It was covered in gooseflesh.

He shook his head and pointed back toward Paddy.

She hesitated with one foot in the air. Paddy stood back from the rest of them, with his arms crossed over his chest. He raised an eye toward Alex, then nodded and took up a karate stance, just like the heroes in his computer games.

Mary hesitated again. Bosco took her by the shoulder and gently pulled her back with him. If he could resist the urge to charge in and protect everyone, then she could too.

Paddy slipped off his shoes. Alex couldn't decide whether that was a good idea or not. There could be glass, but when Paddy walked into the room, he didn't make a sound on the red rug or the bare wood just inside the door.

The rest of them leaned in to watch.

Paddy stopped inside to take a look around—his ears practically pricked up like a dog's. When he turned his head to the side, Alex could see his nostrils were flared, taking in the scents of the room, again like a dog's.

Paddy moved out of sight of those watching from the doorway. The loudest sound was that of his flannel pajama bottoms brushing his skin.

A door creaked.

It was one they could see at the far end of the room—the kitchen, maybe, or the bathroom.

"Shit!" Bosco whispered.

The door creaked again, then stopped.

The tip of a black shoe lingered in the opening at the bottom of the door. A set of fingertips at the edge of the white painted door became visible.

"Come out where we can see you with your hands up," Mary said aloud. She used the voice of authority. It was something you only had if you were a parent, cop, or agent.

The voice of a parent almost always had a flavor of fear or exasperation. The voice of a cop shouting through a doorway was, in Alex's experience, just a little more panicked.

"Ah, my dear," a voice said. "But you don't have a gun."

Bosco shifted his weight, as if getting ready to push past Mary and take any bullets coming her way.

She put her hand on his arm. She had a purse slung over one shoulder and could have had a small pistol tucked into her waistband or in a shoulder holster for all Alex knew. But if so, she didn't go for it.

"This doesn't have to get violent," Mary said.

"Agreed," the voice said. "All you have to do is close the door, turn around, and walk back down the stairs."

One look at Mary's posture told him that was not how this scenario was going to play out. Besides, he couldn't imagine someone talking Paddy out of beating the shit out of the guy at this point.

And... what's more, the voice sounded familiar.

The room was mostly bare—nothing on the walls, no shelving units, no end tables stacked with knickknacks—only a battered leather chair that faced the door, presumably a television, an end table with a coaster, and a lamp.

A stack of newspapers.

A few doors along the wall.

Among the newspapers was a manila folder—the kind that Regan was so obsessed with, and the kind that Marando had used.

"I can't do that," Mary said. "I have orders."

"As do I."

"From whom?"

"It needn't concern you."

"I'm making it my concern."

This situation was going to deteriorate in a moment. Someone would get twitchy. He could almost smell the one upsmanship in the air.

Alex wasn't normally the kind of guy to take action in a physical conflict. In fact, he had a tendency to freeze up in the first few moments after an emergency struck.

But now he had had time to assess the situation and rub two brain cells together.

Alex stuck his hands in his pockets, finding two cell phones, his wallet and a set of keys.

He pulled out the normal phone and dialed Regan's father.

"Last warning," the voice said. "Get out of here now or I'll shoot."

***

The cabin might be isolated and miles away from its nearest neighbors, but Wilson still pulled the car around to the far end of the drive, then turned up onto the dirt path that led behind the house to the RV parking. If you were careful, you could completely conceal the whole thing. A canvas tarp and a few branches, and the night shadows would do the rest.

The car would be much easier to conceal.

He pulled to a stop, got out, and checked the dirt trail behind him. He tossed a few broken branches into the woods, and dragged out a couple of others.

He kicked around in the layer of dead leaves and branches behind the house until he found the brown canvas tarp. It had rotted through in places but had held together well enough, if he turned the good side toward the dirt path, to conceal the car—for now.

He folded up the passenger's side of the tarp and pulled Regan out.

She was still unconscious, at least a couple of hours away from waking. *Plenty of time.* He hefted her over his shoulder in a fireman's carry. She was heavier than she looked—not a frail woman.

He carried her to the back door and unlocked it awkwardly, one foot holding open the screen door and trying to dig his keys out of his pocket without dropping her. Then, when he had the door open, he had to scoot sideways through the door to keep from banging her head against the door frame. *Don't want to hurt this beautiful face.*

The screen creaked and slammed shut after him.

He closed the back door, locked it, and turned on the lights.

The back of the house was next to the stairs to the basement, which was lucky. He sidled down the stairs, turning carefully at the landing, and cursing as Regan's blonde hair got caught against the rough wood of the basement wall. It was supposed to give the place "character," but really it was a pain to clean.

The cellar door was still locked; so was the deep freeze.

He put Regan down on the tattered old white couch with big orange flowers, perfectly hideous and ragged from use.

He got the door open and took her downstairs. This was harder—the ceiling was so low and the cement stairs so sharp edged and narrow. But they made it down without accident.

The second door was jammed, and he struggled with it for a moment. Here he had to drag her for a short while into the final room.

He'd cleaned and prepared it already, of course. You never knew.

***

John answered the phone. It was Alex.

"Sir," the kid said. His voice was shaking.

They were almost at the cabin, according to the GPS. "Make it quick."

"We have a situation at the Marando apartment. Fiducioso is here, searching the place. A shot has been fired, using a silencer. Nobody's hurt yet... can you have Pavo call him off?"

"Can't you handle it?"

"Honestly? No, sir."

John held the phone close to Paul's mouth and said, "Situation. Alex and his friends are at Marando's apartment. Fiducioso is there. He shot at them. Tell Fiducioso to calm the hell down."

The GPS voice on the phone said, *"Turn right in five hundred feet."*

Paul said, "Fiducioso. I am in the middle of an operation. There may be information in that apartment which may determine my success or failure. If all parties involved do not call a truce and work together to produce what I need, I will personally ensure the reassignment of any operatives involved to the sewers. I do not jest."

Paul turned onto a gravel road, the car lurched and bumped uphill. They were headed into the hills.

John turned the phone back toward his ear. "That work?"

"I hope so." Alex replied.

"Call back if you get anything. I'll answer if I can."

"Yes, sir."

The call ended. The trees loomed over the road, cutting off the moonlight. The headlights seemed to vanish in the tangles of leaves.

"Turn left in five hundred feet," the phone said.

Paul turned off the headlights. By the dim glow of the running lights, they turned onto another gravel road, this one a single lane. A tiny sign reflected the street number.

Something moved in the shadows in front of them.

"Paul!"

The car ran into something. Branches shattered.

The seat belt was a brick wall across his chest. Then the airbag in front of him exploded—right in his face.

Thirty miles an hour still made for a hell of a stop.

He gagged and pushed himself backward. That was almost worse. The belt tightened even further, pinning him to his seat. The breath had been knocked out of him.

Suddenly his seatbelt loosened with a zipping noise.

"Get down," Paul said.

John slid forward and the tail end of the belt came loose—Paul had slit it. He crouched down below the dashboard. He was sore from the plane trip and the drive and the crash.

John unsnapped the holster for his Colt .45 and drew it. "Rifle, you think?" he whispered.

"I have no doubt whatsoever."

The engine had cut out; one of the back windows was

shattered.

He strained to hear movement over the night noises. An owl hooted.

Too many variables. Wilson could be sitting in a blind spot with his sights on them. He could be in the cabin, just now starting to respond to the noise outside.

"Your call," John whispered.

"On the count of three, open your door."

They were sitting ducks, and they both knew it. But he nodded.

Paul leaned forward, looking into the woods. "One...two..."

He took a breath.

"Three."

The doors flew open and they jumped out.

***

Paul had seen movement next to the house on his side of the automobile.

Very well. Perhaps Wilson would miss.

Paul crouched nearly in half and made for the nearest piece of cover—a large rock sitting between the house and the driveway.

Just before he reached it, a blow from a sledgehammer hit him in the chest—a heart attack? It knocked him backward, forcing him onto his side on the gravel drive. A gush of black blood flowed out of him in the darkness.

Not simply a heart attack, then.

Everything went dark.

***

The phone call ended.

Alex lowered his shaking arm and stuffed the phone back in his pocket.

"Fiducioso?" he said. "Can we have a truce? Is that copacetic?"

Fiducioso sighed. Alex heard the sound of what he fervently hoped was a safety being put back on and a gun being holstered. "I'm coming out. Anyone attacking me will be shot. Is *that* copacetic?"

Mary glared over to the shadows where Paddy had disappeared. "We are *backing off*. Paddy, is that understood?"

A grunt from that side of the room. Paddy wasn't going to like it... but he wasn't going to attack. Probably. Not for a few minutes at least—Alex hoped.

"What are you doing here?" Fiducioso asked.

"Wilson has Regan," Alex said. "Pavo and her father—"

Fiducioso snorted. "Are going to try to save her. Someone should have told him it was time to let the next generation start to handle things."

Alex cleared his throat. "Shouldn't that person have been you? Also, I assume they told Jake and the rest of the guys from the detective agency, so they—"

"Ha, ha," Fiducioso interrupted him. "Well, at least you brought some help. If Wilson has anything hidden in this apartment, it's not going to be easy to find. We might have to take the walls apart."

Mary glanced back at Alex and rolled her eyes. It was true that if anyone was technically in charge here, it was her—although Fiducioso seemed to be perfectly happy pretending she didn't exist.

He raised his eyebrows in a question: *What next?*

"You take whatever room the computers are in. I'll take the kitchen, Paddy can take the toilet, TDB gets the bedroom."

"And me?" Bosco asked.

"The living room—books, television and audio equipment, everything. Pretend you're at my apartment, looking for pictures of my exes."

Bosco chuckled.

"And me?" Fiducioso called from the bedroom.

"You can supervise."

A few minutes later, Bosco found it sitting on the mantle: a family photo album. Bosco noticed that most of the "cousins" shown in the photographs didn't look a lot like Wilson. He pulled a couple of the photographs (mostly polaroids) and found newspaper obituaries tucked behind them.

A short trip down Internet lane on his smartphone brought the collection to light. Every single one of them had been murdered—even the ones going back to the 1920s.

The obituaries were all marked with a single word in pencil on the back.

Sinner.

Sinner.

Sinner.

Sinner.

Sinner.

Sinner.

Just for fun.

The ones marked "just for fun," approximately one-seventh of the victims, were all intelligent looking, attractive blonde women. The Wilson family definitely had a type.

Alex swallowed as he leaned back from the photo album, looking over Bosco's shoulder in the big armchair. Paddy and TDB had their phones out, still searching the names of the people in the album. Fiducioso was texting someone. Bosco turned page after page, the old plastic protectors covering the pages crinkling as they turned.

Mary had gone to the back of the apartment to the kitchen window overlooking the alley.

"Erm, you okay?" he asked her.

"Just needed a glass of water."

She didn't have one in her hand, and there wasn't one on the counter. He nodded, then backed away.

The important thing was to get the information to Pavo and John St. Clair in time. He pulled out his phone.

Chapter 46 -Touché!

The gravel road off the highway was a black cave under the thick cover of the trees. Wilson's cabin was supposed to be a couple of miles up the road, according to Jake's GPS. He was out of time, and John was no longer answering his phone.

He drove half a mile up the road and found a place to hide his car amongst the trees and bushes.

He popped the trunk of the car, and in the glare of a tiny penlight went to work. He pulled out his revolver, changed into black clothes, put black face paint around his eyes and mouth, and pulled his ski mask over his head. Finally, he retrieved the Savage 10FP sniper tactical rifle from its bag and loaded the magazine with .308 rounds. The Savage 10FP was the official rifle for the New York State Police Rapid Response Team, popular amongst rifle shooting sports enthusiast and vermin hunters.

Jake was out vermin hunting tonight.

He checked his pockets to make sure they were closed tightly and jumped up and down twice to make sure nothing was rattling. He put the revolver in his waist holster, checked his GPS one last time, and started making his way up the gravel road with the rifle pressing against his back—a bullet in the breech.

The moon was bright but it was impossible to see anything under the shadow of the trees.

Good.

He followed the gravel road until it made a turn to the left, snaking its way up the hill. The cabin would be a left turn off this road about a mile ahead.

Half a mile before the house, he left the road and carefully worked his way up the hill, cutting across the woods. Evergreens mixed with deciduous trees, and the ground underfoot was padded and damp with leaves and twigs.

Jake had to balance his need to get to the house as quickly as possible with the need to get there unnoticed. The owls and night birds had gone quiet, watching him.

Regan...

This was the second time some psychopath had come after her.

The cold hearted bastard, the Delta Force operative, had taken him over completely. The private detective, an inconvenient illusion of civilization draped over the hunter inside him, was gone.

He sat in the crook of a maple and pulled a pair of binoculars out of a side pocket.

The car, a Mercedes, had come to a stop no more than fifty feet past the end of the driveway. The rear end had slewed to the right, and the front end looked crumpled.

He searched the front of the car and caught the dull wink of metal. A chain hung across the road in front of the bar. A little more searching showed raw, splintered wood and bent trunks where the chain had bit in.

Both doors of the car were open.

No bodies were to be seen, but the shadows might have been mocking him. Hard to say.

Silently, he dropped out of the tree and started working his way to the road. He crossed a hundred yards to get to a spot overlooking the house, then started working his way down.

A glimpse of moonlight through the trees revealed the shine of glass. He stopped.

A second car was parked behind the house under a ragged tarp—Wilson's car.

No lights showed from inside the house. The moon glinted on the back door and the windows.

The moon was over his shoulder. Jake cut around the back of the house noiselessly, threading quickly through the birch trees.

A scent lingered on the east side of the house. Not wood smoke... some kind of furnace.

He didn't want to know what it meant. He circled to the front of the house.

A stand of scrub oak concealed him from view. He crawled through the undergrowth, careful not to disturb it, and pulled out the binoculars again.

A refrigerator sat near the front door on a cement foundation. *Why put a refrigerator at the front door?*

He searched the windows. They were covered with light blocking curtains lined with white plastic and stapled—or taped—down to the frames.

He spotted no cameras, but that didn't mean there weren't any.

Neither John nor Pavo were in sight, either.

The shadow of the house covered the rest of the driveway.

*T*he guy had been in prison for ten years. How could he have planned this so quickly? He couldn't have set everything up perfectly. There must be a hole somewhere. He had to find it.

He put the binoculars back in his thigh pocket, drew his legs up underneath him, and got ready to make a run for the house.

Tch. Thwack.

The echo of the bullet hitting wood echoed through the woods.

Jake lowered himself back down. Above him and about three yards to the right, one of the leaves fluttered. It had been punctured with a perfect bullet hole.

He heard a chuckle coming out of the woods.

"I thought it was a cowardly move for you to send two old men to do your dirty work for you," said a happy, pleasant voice.

Jake pulled his binoculars out and searched the front of the house, the roof, and then the woods.

A shape moved.

Slowly, from his stomach, he unclipped the rifle strap and pulled the rifle off his back. His elbows dug down into the damp leaves. He thumbed off the safety.

He uncovered the scope, checked to make sure he wasn't putting it into the moonlight, and sighted through it.

He saw a thousand silhouettes that could have been Wilson, or they could have been leaves. He stayed patient.

There.

He watched the shape for a few seconds. Leaves fluttered. He didn't breathe.

Jake relaxed. His trigger finger tightened gently—squeezing.

Tch. Puh.

A stifled grunt. Then Wilson was up and running for the back of the house, shouting, "Touché!"

Jake fired again—he saw the silhouette falter—then he heard

the sound of the bullet hitting the fiberglass chassis of the car under the tarp.

A graze.

Wilson was gone.

A light came on in the house.

Jake started to move.

Chapter 47 -A dead end

Wilson made it to the back door, threw it open, then slammed it behind him. He leaned against it, breathing hard. His hands and feet were tingling.

The house was dark and quiet. He sucked in his breath and tried to listen. He could feel the air from the vent by the back door stirring his hair. The furnace downstairs was filling the house with warm comfortable air.

He smiled. Sadly, he was probably going to miss the after-kill ritual: sitting in the house, wrapped up in that ancient quilt, with his hands around a mug of hot coffee with cream and cocoa, sugar, and just a dash of salt.

This is bad, very bad.

At least, that's what he told himself. Actually he'd never had so much fun in his life. It was literally criminal to have so much fun—and stupid. Was he going to get out of this one? Probably not.

He chuckled. It wasn't a pretty sound.

One too many blondes. They are like bacon. Too much and they'd give you a heart attack.

The second shot had caught him in the back of his left arm; it was bleeding but probably nothing to worry about at the moment. It would be a pain to try to sew it up himself. Should he try to get Regan St. Clair to do it for him?

He imagined forcing her to sew him up. A sexy scene, full of trembling and tears.

No, there were always consequences. She'd take one look at the wound and realize that someone was here to "save" her. And then she'd try to stab me in the eye with the needle.

He imagined wrestling with her, bashing her hand against the wall until the needle dropped. Then biting her on the cheek, hard enough to draw blood.

But not enough to tear—not yet.

He shook his head. The adrenaline in his system was messing with his head.

Hell, he'd been warned not to let himself get too excited until everything was one hundred percent perfectly *safe*. But everybody had a time to die, and he'd rather go out like this than by a heart attack like both of his parents.

Disgusting. A lawman, one of those who are destined to restore order, goes out like this—not by heart attack or lethal injection.

He leaned the rifle against the wall and put his right hand against the place in his shoulder where Westley's first shot had hit him between the collarbone and the neck into the lung and out between his small ribs.

The lung had collapsed. Frothy pink blood was bubbling out of the hole in his shirt and jacket, and the surrounding area was soaking wet.

Time to make some decisions.

Do I want to make it alive out of this? No. The answer might have been different if he were still married, or if he and his ex had ever managed to have children. He might have someone to pass this on to. Cooper would inherit the house—and the mess. He'd never wanted to be involved with their parents' work, not even when it was just their mother, carrying on alone the work or restoring order.

Wilson closed his eyes for a second and sent out a little *goodbye* to his brother. Hopefully his business wouldn't suffer too much.

Now, it was time to focus on the here and now.

He was going to go out. It was a done deal. No sense worrying about it anymore.

The question was...how did he want it to go?

Fighting it out with some special forces predator...or down in his super-secret hideout with his new best friend?

That was an easy question, all right.

The harder one was...did he want Westley to follow him to try to rescue Regan St. Clair—or not?

***

Jake had just reached the shadow at the front of the house when he heard the unmistakable buzz of a cell phone.

Nnn nnn.

The sound was coming from the driveway, just a few yards away from him.

"*Shit,*" a voice whispered.

Jake pressed himself against the siding under the window, then called, "It's Westley. Wilson just went in the house. Status."

"Paul's been shot. I'm applying pressure."

"Did you call for help?"

"Couldn't. Wilson was looking for us."

"Do it now. I'm going in after him.

Jake could hear John muttering in the darkness. He probably wasn't liking being told what to do. *Too bad.*

Part of the front porch was a cement pad in front of the doorway. A locked up white refrigerator sat on the far side of the pad. The other part was a wood deck. A set of stairs in front of the deck was missing some of the planks—some rotten wood had been stacked beside the cement.

Jake crouched out of sight of the front window and climbed down under the wooden part of the deck.

A half-window casement had been set into the basement. It was strange, a place in the hills having a basement that dug down into the rock. Usually if a place had a basement, it was a walkout, bracing the house against an angled slope.

It was a piece of acrylic, cut to fit around a vent pipe, of some kind. Jake put his face up to the grille at the end of the pipe. He smelled heating oil... and something else.

He swallowed.

Out of his pants came a knife. Swiftly, he cut the acrylic out of the frame, trying not to disturb the pipe.

The pane came out. Behind it was a layer of plastic—a light blocking curtain stapled into the frame. Jake slipped his knife out its thigh sheath and used it to lift the curtain away from the frame.

A dull light shone through the window.

He didn't hear any sounds of movement or breathing...

Then, muffled, from very far away he heard the sound of a woman's shout.

He cut the curtain out of the window frame with four quick

slashes. No time to wait for the police, his friends, or anyone else.

An ugly couch sat against the far wall, with a stained coffee table in front of it. The walls were lined with tin shelves covered with hunting and fishing equipment.

He dropped into the basement room onto some ugly tile and a ragged patch of orange-brown carpet. The place smelled rancid with fish.

Beside the couch was a freezer. Locked.

Jake ignored it. Washer, dryer. Furnace, vents. Pipes, sink. Narrow stairs upward. A door with a padlock hanging open on the latch.

It was quiet, until the freezer kicked in.

Jake went to the light switch by the stairs and shut off the overhead light. The only light came from the window—and the window was on the shadowed side of the house. It was as good as being blind.

He stayed low against the wall, crept past the ancient TV set under the window, and past the shelves, careful not to touch anything.

He reached the door. The handle was cool.

He turned it and pulled, but the door was stuck in its frame.

He drew his revolver and pulled harder.

The door groaned as it opened, scraping on the floor tiles.

Inside—nothing. A set of cement stairs leading downward.

"Regan," he whispered hoarsely.

No answer. He felt around for a light switch. Found it, but didn't flip it. Instead, he moved around until he was behind the wall, then reached around with his left hand and flicked the switch.

No lights came on.

He crept down the narrow cement stairs. The walls were bare cement down here, with no drywall, studs, or insulation. The ceiling felt low overhead, lower than the level of the basement ceiling.

He reached the bottom. His ears drank in the sound and started feeding him the sound of his own breath and heartbeat.

He moved forward. His feet felt the depression of a floor drain, the cord of a pump, and then the back wall.

"Regan?"

Still no answer.

He flicked on his flashlight.

On the wall opposite him were wooden shelves stacked with ancient, dusty glass jars filled with rotting shapes: peaches; apples; tomato sauce.

He made a quick check along the walls. An air vent led upward, showing a dim glow—the vent outside.

Jake cursed himself and climbed back up the stairs.

A dead end.

Chapter 48 -It was time to begin

Regan was having one of those nightmares, the bad ones that never seem to end, where she was asleep and couldn't wake up. She couldn't move her arms or legs, and a terrible pressure held her chest to the bed which kept her from breathing deeply. The room swam around her, very dark except for her nightlight against the wall.

She'd been having a nightmare a few minutes ago. A man was chasing her through city streets full of quaint shops and flowerboxes. Wrought iron railings decorated the fronts of buildings and marked the edge between a cafe's tables and the street.

Red umbrellas gusted in the wind.

She ran as fast as she could, which was in slow motion. The man chasing her was whistling and moving at a walk, stopping to look into windows, to pick up cups of tea from the cafe tables and drink from them, to pick up dogs who tried to bark and bite him in slow motion, to drag his fingernails against the cheek of a woman who was holding her big floppy hat and smiling to keep it from blowing away in the wind.

Time had gone all wrong. It was going too slow for Regan and for everyone else around her.

It was going perfectly quickly for the man chasing her.

He had finally become bored with teasing the other people along the street and was walking toward her. The hell of it was, she couldn't turn her head to look, but she could see everything happening around her, even directly behind her, as if it were a movie being played before her eyes at her pursuer's will so she could feel even more dread than she would otherwise.

She forced herself out of the nightmare and into something worse—being trapped inside her own sleeping body, unable to awake.

Her room echoed with the sound of her shout, the one she made when she forced herself out of the dream. She waited for her mother or father to come into the room and turn on the light... They would look at her, apparently sleeping soundly in her bed, smile, turn off the light, and close the door, leaving her still trapped... It had happened before.

She struggled to call out, but her throat would release no sound other than her easy, calm breathing.

She tried to turn her head.

It was as if someone else were moving it. Honestly, it didn't feel as though she had any control—her head turned slowly to the side.

Ah. She hadn't woken at all. She was still dreaming.

It wasn't her bedroom. It was a... prison cell of some kind.

The walls were made of cement and painted blue gray. The light overhead was covered with a heavy plastic cover that was caulked to the ceiling. A metal ring in the ceiling looked like it was some kind of torture device. On one wall was fastened a steel electrical box with a plastic cover, as if to keep babies from sticking their fingers in.

A small box sat under a tube that went into the ceiling and through the wall. A larger square... vent (heating vent?) came out from the top...

A folding steel cart sat beside the box. A heavy grate was in the floor, probably a drain.

Near the floor was a short door; it looked like it must be heavy. It was bolted to the wall with thick hinges and painted the same color as the walls and floor. It reminded her of a coal cellar door.

She watched the door for a while, trying to see where the dream was taking her.

Rats, she decided. Soon, the mysterious door in the floor would open, and then the room would be flooded with rats.

The handle on the door began to turn. Nice trick, rats with opposable thumbs.

The door began to move open—a black slit at the far side that widened slowly at first, then more quickly.

She waited for the first little rat noses to emerge, but no, it was fingers.

Then a pleasant male face appeared, grinning at her. He must be here to rescue her.

She chuckled to herself. What had she eaten for supper? She couldn't remember. It must have been a doozy.

Rats. A prison room flooded with rats. What was her subconscious thinking?

It was fine. Everything was fine.

Her eyes closed and she drifted into the darkness of true sleep.

***

Regan was still strapped to the cot, fully dressed. Her head had turned to the side and her eyes were open, watching him vacantly as he crawled through the crawlspace door. He grinned at her.

With his shoulders just pushing through the doorway, she started chuckling.

He frowned at her.

"Rats," she said, or something like that.

Then her eyes closed.

She chuckled a few more times under her breath, then stopped.

He slid the rest of the way through the crawlspace, reversed direction, then crawled back out and pulled the box of moonshine bottles back in after him.

Then he sealed the door shut, bolting it from inside.

He watched Regan for a few more moments. She had started to snore—it was adorable.

But then he shook himself. He had limited time available.

And it was time to begin.

***

Jake searched the rest of the house, upstairs and downstairs—a quick search of a cabin that hadn't been touched since the Seventies.

The place was a warren of cardboard boxes. But he couldn't see anywhere that didn't match up. There were no secret rooms.

The bloodstains by the back door showed tiny bubbles coagulated in a few of the blood puddles. He'd hit a lung.

Wilson's rifle lay against the wall by the back door.

A few splatters of blood led him into the kitchen.

A wadded piece of shirt lay in the sink, soaked with blood. A pair of pants and a jacket rested on the floor, also soaked.

A pile of wet towels and an open first aid kit...

The trail ended.

Nothing to follow.

He cracked his neck and walked slowly down the stairs.

If secrets—big ones, as in a place to hide at least two people—were hidden in this house, it had to be downstairs in the basement, underground.

He eyed the basement, taking it in. The piles of crap would make for a terrible secret door; that stuff would go everywhere.

He closed his eyes and breathed in.

The room smelled like fish. The warm air blowing from the furnace...

The furnace wasn't running—not the one at the bottom of the stairs, next to the washer and dryer.

He glanced toward the window. The vent that led through the window was still there. It led down the wall, behind the TV set.

He jerked the ancient cabinet forward, ripping the cords from the wall. The cabinet hit a snag and the set did a face plant onto the carpet with a muffled explosion of glass as the vacuum tube burst.

The vent went down into the floor.

The cellar he'd been in was nowhere near it.

The cement pad by the front door with the refrigerator on it. What was that for— a solid block of cement that jutted in front of the house?

He shoved the busted TV out of the way, pulled up the carpet. Nothing.

He wasn't surprised. Wilson, who had been shot, had gone down his bolt hole. He hadn't pulled a carpet and coffee table over the top of him on the way down.

Jake paced the walls. Shelves full of crap wasn't the same as a rich man's swinging bookshelf.

He tossed everything off the shelves where the cement slab would have stood at the front of the house, to the right of the window. The shelves had been screwed into the concrete.

He jerked on them, trying to push—or pull—them off the wall. They were solid.

He paced the room. Where...?

The rug in front of the couch. It showed an arc in the pile.

He yanked on the couch. It swung outward easily, following the arc in the rug. Behind it was a plywood panel in the concrete, the same color of gray as the walls.

Jake studied it for a second, then pushed in on the panel. It was on a magnetic latch. It clicked and came outward half an inch. He pulled it open with his fingernails.

Behind it was darkness, a low tunnel.

No, stairs running parallel to the back of the house.

A long blonde hair hung off the magnetic latch.

He turned on his flashlight, lay on the floor and looked through the hole. The stairs led downward and disappeared in a blank wall.

The cement ceiling was low, but a little higher than the doorway.

He ducked inside.

***

The blood loss had slowed from Paul's chest. Whether that was a good thing or not remained to be seen—it had been a lot of blood.

John leaned against his folded jacket. The phone lay on the ground next to him. An ambulance was on the way.

It could have been either of them. But as it happened Paul's side of the car was facing the house.

"Go," Paul said. "Help Jake to save your daughter."

"He's got it covered."

"John. Tell her I honor her, as well as the memory of her mother."

"You can tell her yourself."

The phone rang. Alex again. He reached over and tapped the screen to answer it. It left a smudge of blood on the screen.

"Sir?" Alex asked. "You said to call if..."

John cut him off. "Get to the point. We're busy over here."

"Information on the Wilson family." Alex paused. "You're not going to believe this."

"Son, you don't know what I can or can't believe."

He took a deep breath. "Wilson's parents may have been serial killers who taught their son how to kill. We've found records in the apartment that seem to show... he's basically killed two different groups of people, criminals and... women."

"Women are criminals?"

"I think one group is out of duty, the other one out of, uh, fun. The case we're working on, the Moreau case, that may have been his mother."

John blinked.

Red and blue lights started flashing through the trees. "Son, the ambulance is here. Save it... Pavo's not looking too good."

"Sorry, sir. One more thing."

"Can't it wait?"

"I... I can't remember your wife's name, sir. Was it Linda?"

John shuddered. No. It couldn't have been. "Son, I appreciate it, but no. Tell me later. And make sure those idiots from the Organization don't make any trouble. Don't tell them. Don't tell them anything."

John looked down at the dark shape in front of him, pale skin illuminated by the light of the phone.

"See how they like it."

Chapter 49 -It was a hook

The room wasn't a prison cell—it was a miniature abattoir.

This time when Regan woke up, she knew.

Wilson squatted next to her, stroking the side of her face, holding something in front of her face that stung her eyes. The room reeked of ammonia—smelling salts.

Her heart raced.

She was strapped down to a camping cot, wearing all her clothes but only one of her shoes.

Wilson smiled at her. "Good. You're awake."

His face was pale, covered with droplets of sweat. He'd taken off all his clothes, as far as she could tell. His right shoulder was covered with a sloppy bandage, soaked with blood. And his left arm had been wound with gauze.

Good. He'd been shot. Jake is here.

She glanced over the room, sorting out what had been a dream and what hadn't.

Except for the rats, her dream had been spot on—but Wilson was blocking part of the room. She couldn't see the odd little door she remembered.

Ironic, how just his photograph had creeped her out...but that she'd still been sucked into the field of his charm in person. *I am so stupid.*

Thinking I could handle him.

Thinking... he was just another guy pushing me a little too hard to get something he wanted.

Something harmless.

She looked in his eyes. They were tender...yet ruthless.

The charisma was still being piled on. *Interesting. He wants something from me.*

Something he couldn't just hurt me into giving him.

She wanted to fight back—she tensed against the straps. But she wasn't Superman.

They both knew that. His grin broadened.

On the metal folding table by the miniature furnace were weapons. Knives. Tools. *If I have a chance to get to them, I will.*

What do I have in my pockets? What else could I use?

Car keys, wallet, a pair of phones, if they hadn't fallen out.

She liked to travel light—*Not even a pocket knife.*

Spit in his eyes, claw at his bandages, kick him in the groin.

All of these things were impractical fantasies at the moment.

Time.

All she had left was playing for time.

She kept her face blank. No happiness...no sadness...no anger.

Make him work for whatever he wants out of me.

"I suppose you're wondering why I brought you here," Wilson said.

As if it wasn't perfectly obvious. He'd brought her here to kill her. But of course he would have to explain it. In great, laborious, self-aggrandizing detail.

His kind always do.

"No," she said. "You're going to murder me. I think you made that clear."

"You and I are going to have a dance together."

If his purpose was to make her panic before he killed her, he was succeeding. She evened her breathing and put on her judicial face, the ice shield of everyone sitting on the bench.

He was just another perp, after all.

"A dance that will take us into eternity together." He smiled. "You know, I was brought up to fight injustice and restore order, just like you, but in a different manner. But still, I fought injustice. Criminals... most of the people I killed were criminals. Some of my biggest cases were broken in this way, by breaking the men responsible for them."

He waited for her to respond.

Instead of rolling her eyes, she said, "It was the poisoned fruit of a tainted tree."

"Let's not argue legalities," he said. "In order to accomplish what you did on the Gibbons case in so short a time, you would have had to step across the line yourself. Past that... you're a vigilante, just like me."

If he wanted her to swoon, he shouldn't have strapped her to a cot.

"I see that you fail to follow the logic. You see—"

"No, I follow it. I've been pondering it for months, in fact— trying to determine my boundaries." This was the last thing she wanted to talk about with him. But if it gave Jake another five minutes, she would keep on talking. "On the one hand, walking outside the law from time to time allows me a lot of freedom. If something needs to be done, I can do it. But there's a problem—my judgment."

His one eyebrow lifted. "Are you afraid your judgment will become skewed by the power? 'Absolute power corrupts absolutely,' and that bullshit?"

"I would think it was obvious from my current position that my judgment is flawed. If it had been accurate..."

"I would still be out of prison."

"But you would not have come to Brooklyn if I hadn't pushed Provost to give you a job."

He grimaced and put his hand to his side. Another bandage there. "Provost," he said disgustedly. "Nothing but a screamer. Not like you. I had to do her quickly. I think I knew, even then, what would have to happen."

So Laura Provost was dead, all her ambitions and negotiations collapsed into whatever he had done to her.

Blondes. Of course.

"You were never after Kristin Walker," Regan said. "It was her friend, Nancy... what was her name?"

His face lit up. Oh, he was delighted with her. "Excellent! Nancy Rossier. Yes, my lovely blonde legal secretary. She was on the road to become a full law partner at her firm. I was so proud of her."

"Yet you killed her."

"I," he said grandly, "killed a lot of people. She died well." He glanced at the drain in the floor. "Not perfectly, but well. I'm sure you'll do much better."

She swallowed back a sarcastic response.

Cold. Think like Uncle Paul. Everything was strategy. Everything was policy.

He coughed lightly in the back of his throat, an ugly sound. He turned and spat toward the grate in the floor. Blood.

"It's too bad we won't have more time together," he said. "I looked forward to finding excuses to visit you, get to know you better, and let you get to know me."

He stood, not straightening fully but keeping his hand pressed to his side, and shuffled over to the metal table. He *was* fully nude—blood had seeped through the bandage on his arm and the one on his side, and begun to run down his skin in rivulets.

Time.

In a sense, all she needed was more time.

Well, that and some way to get unstrapped from this damned cot. Wouldn't it be ironic if he collapsed and she was unable to escape and died here... wherever here was?

Wilson touched something on the table, then moved his hand and selected something else.

He lifted up an old Swiss Army knife and pulled out a short, two-and-a-half-inch blade. He turned to her, grimacing.

"It's so difficult knowing what to choose. Something sharp? Something long and ugly? Something smooth? Something serrated? I've been using this tomato knife lately..."

He shrugged. His breath was coming faster and more hoarsely.

"I'm talking shop, aren't I? But this was the first knife I ever had. Lots of animals and beautiful blonde women dead because of this knife."

He chuckled.

"You're such a good listener. I could talk all night... but I'm afraid we don't have the time."

He reached overhead and pulled the silver ring out of the ceiling. It was attached to a chain, but it wasn't a ring at all.

It was a hook.

***

At the bottom of the secret stairs was a hole, smaller than the doorway, set in the concrete. A case of capped beer bottles sat inside it about six feet back.

Jake crawled inside the hole on his elbows and pulled the case back out with him. The bottles weren't as heavy as they should have been. He pulled one out—it was full of white powder.

Something illegal.

A distraction.

He crawled deeper into the tunnel.

At the end of the tunnel was a cement slab. He aimed his flashlight around the area. A crack ran around the edges of the slab.

Fake.

He looked for a way in and saw nothing—no variation in the plain gray concrete.

He pressed on the door. Unfortunately, it wasn't on a magnetic lock. It didn't budge—not an inch.

He crawled out, reversed, and scooted back in. The tunnel was inches over his head. There wasn't room to curl up his knees and get a good kick.

He shoved at the door with both feet. *Did it budge?*

He slithered out, then crawled back in. The gap around the door hadn't widened.

He put his hand on the concrete panel. It was cold. *Bring a sledgehammer down here? Wait until the SEALs, or at least the cops, arrived? Cover the exhaust pipe of the furnace hidden down here and hope that it made Wilson open the door and come out...without killing Regan first or smothering her?*

He leaned his head on the floor.

Find a way to flood the room? Have the electricity shut off to the house?

Call the guy on his cell phone and beg him not to hurt her?

His hand was shaking.

He'd lose her. He'd already lost her. There was no part of him that could answer this. Attacking the door with brute force would just make Wilson kill her faster.

Above him, he could hear sounds in the house. Breaking sounds—glass shattering, wood breaking. The SEALs. The cops would have been more cautious. The SEALs, not so much.

The only hope he had left was Wilson didn't have security cameras. If he could see what was going on outside...

No. It didn't matter. The guy was as good as dead. There was no way he could think he was going to make it anywhere other than prison or the grave.

Wilson was going to go down killing Regan.

"Regan," he said. "God. Please help me, God."

Chapter 50 -Why don't you find out?

In order to undress her and tie her hands together, he was going to have to unstrap her.

If he was going to hang her from that hook, cut her throat, and let her drain out over the grate in the floor, he was going to have to take her off the cot.

And therefore, he was going to have to loosen the straps.

He could drug her, which would take care of his problems nicely—but he wouldn't.

He still wanted something from her.

Wilson took the Swiss Army Knife and laid it against her cheek. She kept the icy judicial visage intact, thank God. She had no doubt if she had begged for her life, he would cut her.

She would have failed his crazy test.

What does he want from me? To praise him for being so clever? To fall in love with him? To carry his child?

Too bad. Even if he raped me, I'm already on birth control.

The knife blade, initially cold, quickly warmed up from the heat of her own skin. He had to know that the second he untied her, she would move. He certainly wasn't trying too hard to terrify her into submission.

The blade disappeared from her cheek.

Sssst.

The first strap loosened. Part of the weight on her chest disappeared.

She raised one shoulder, then the other. Her hands were still pinned...but she could probably rip them out from under the strap.

Wilson tensed—not his body. His left hand stayed poised with the knife, ready to stab...slash... The blade must be sharp if it had cut through the nylon strap with one slash. Who knew, he might have replaced it with a similarly shaped razor.

Does he want me to kill him?

Or just to try?

He began lowering the knife toward her stomach. It probably wouldn't do much good to stab such a blade through the tough fabric. She'd get hurt, but she wouldn't let it distract her.

She sent a prayer up. *Please let Jake be on the other side of the door.*

Then she kicked off her other shoe.

Wilson froze, his hand in midair. "Planning something?" he asked coyly, like a guy who was wondering whether his girlfriend was thinking about a surprise party for his birthday—like he was flirting.

"Why don't you find out?" she asked, as blandly as she could.

His hand lowered. Her hands clenched on the aluminum sides of the cot.

Ssst.

The next strap came loose.

***

Something was happening on the other side of the door.

Jake couldn't hear it through the thick cement...

But he could feel it—through his fingertips.

He crawled forward until he was leaning against the door with his shoulder, cramped up almost into a ball. He shoved against the cement panel with the soles of his boots. He braced one elbow against the cement panel, the other against his ribs.

The revolver was aimed upward.

If Regan can give me an inch, I'm going to take a mile.

***

She jerked her legs free from the last two straps and rolled them upward, kicking at Wilson's face.

She missed.

She would have missed anyway, but it made him jerk back for a second.

She kept her hands on the sides of the cot and rolled to the side, pulling it with her.

Steel bit down into the aluminum. Hissed.

It made a tearing sound in the canvas.

She kept rolling but let go of the cot. The edge of it caught her side. He'd jumped on top of it, trying to pin her.

Instead he got her coat...and one arm.

She didn't waste time trying to reach for the door. She knew she wasn't close enough yet.

Instead she jerked her arm out from under the cot, leaving the empty sleeve behind.

Wilson was already taking his next move. He was rolling off the other side of the cot, knife up.

If only he'd stabbed himself, rolling around like that.

She jerked the coat out from under the cot. The fabric slapped against her legs.

She backed toward the corner, holding the coat in front of her against the charging of the bull.

He was up on his feet and kicked the cot toward her.

It skidded across the floor and became another barrier between them. He realized this and picked it up to throw it out of the way.

It bounced against the wall and into the table full of shining, awful bits of metal.

She hooked her foot against the handle of the squat, heavy door and flung the handle upward.

Chapter 51 -Stay with me

The door opened, throwing Jake backward and to the side as he slid across the concrete floor into the room.

The shape in front of him was a naked beast, covered in streams of blood—male, golden blond hair.

The concrete room was a friendly fire bullet ricochet trap in the making.

So he took his time and waited until he'd stopped sliding, no more than a half second delay. He squeezed the trigger three times.

Red blossoms opened up in the middle of the naked man's chest. Blood splattered the gray walls.

Three tightly clustered, perfect shots.

The tightness of Jake's vision loosened a little, watching the man fall. He kept his finger on the trigger—ready to fire again.

Wilson's face was naked with shock...surprise...something, as if he hadn't seen it coming. Although obviously, he'd known Jake was closing in on him.

Jake looked for something evil in the man's eyes, but he couldn't find any—there was only surprise.

He planted another slug in his chest, thumbed on the safety, then rolled to the side—in case the brother was here in the room, too.

When he got a look at the opposite side of the room, the gun fell out of his hands.

Regan was crushed against the wall, limp. Her head was tilted to the side, blood pouring out of her forehead.

One hand lay next to a knife.

The world tightened up again.

Every heartbeat became a measure of time wasted.

He crawled toward her.

The concrete door was in the way.

He pushed it aside.

Her coat lay on top of her.

He pulled it away.

Her clothes were soaked with blood.

He put his fingers against her carotid artery.

A pulse.

He pushed her hair away from her face. The blood was matting up and tried to cling to her skin.

The skin above her eye had split open—a sharp slash that ran from her temple along her brow and almost touched the opposite eye.

The knife blade was bloody, but not completely covered with gore.

Jake almost grabbed it to cut off a strip of her shirt, then kicked it out of the way. He needed the fingerprints.

Instead he grabbed a scalpel off the floor underneath the aluminum cot that had been kicked into the corner. It looked like it had upended a metal cart full of autopsy instruments. As he moved the cot to reach the scalpel, he spotted a few packets of gauze and some rolls of tape.

Jake had a flash. The gauze wasn't there to help close up

wounds or stop the bleeding. It was there to sop up extra blood, so Wilson would be able to see what was underneath.

He almost threw the damned gauze across the room.

No.

He would use the bastard's tools against him.

He bound up Regan's forehead, making sure the tape was tight enough to put pressure on the wound. He used the extra gauze to mop up her face.

Unconscious. Wilson's knife had cut her, knocked her backward against the cement, and knocked her unconscious.

When that was done, he stood up. He had a minute or two.

Wilson was still breathing.

And there was a room full of saws, knives, and probes just waiting to be used.

Jake wanted him to hurt—or not so much hurt as see the results of hurt. He wanted to see the bastard beg for mercy. He wanted to hear him confess what he'd done, confess to all the damage he'd done to the world and to women like Regan.

He wanted to hurt the guy until he had the information they needed to be able to put those women to rest.

Proof.

Jake bent over and picked up the scalpel from the floor. It was cold in his hand and felt right. If he'd picked up a different heavier blade, then he wouldn't have been able to stop himself from killing the guy right away.

What he wanted to do was to torture him – to death – not put him out of his misery.

Wilson's mouth opened and closed like a fish. His abdomen jerked, trying to get oxygen into the body in short, starving gasps. But the holes in Wilson's chest gaped open with every breath. Blood poured out of his body and down into the drain in the floor.

What should he do, tie the guy's ankles together, hoist him up on the hook and let him drain out over the hole in the floor?

Do unto Wilson what he'd planned to do to Regan?

It was tempting.

He squatted next to him. From this angle he could almost see the shuddering of Wilson's heart in his chest.

"I want information. If I can get a diary from you, a record of your kills so that we can put some of these bodies to rest, then I'll cut your throat. This could all be over in a second."

Wilson grinned, teeth pink with blood. He couldn't speak out loud, even if he wanted to.

His lips moved.

Do it, his lips seemed to say.

You know you want to.

And Jake did. He really, really wanted to. All the times he'd beaten the shit out of someone to get information... It was tempting, just to make sure the guy was *done*, if nothing else.

A whisper came from the other side of the room.

"Jake?"

It was hoarse, without a real voice behind it. It still pulled him to his feet and made him throw down the scalpel in a heartbeat.

Regan's eyes were open, confused. Her face was still a smeared mask of blood.

"Jake? Is that you?"

He sat down beside her and wiped her face again. Now she looked like she'd been smearing red greasepaint on her face before going into the jungle.

"It's me, Regan. It's Jake."

"Did you kill that bastard?"

"He's dying—you don't have to be scared anymore. I'm here."

"Good." Her eyes closed again. He could see the pupils jerking behind the lids. Her throat swallowed several times. She probably had a concussion.

"Regan," he said. "You have to stay awake for me, please. Okay? We have to get the paramedics here so they can check your neck and monitor you. You have a concussion."

Her eyes struggled to open again. They wandered over the room, seeing but not seeing.

"What did you do to him?" she whispered.

"I shot him—in the chest."

"Is he suffering?"

Jake glanced over at Wilson. He was still grinning... still trying to breathe. But the grin was fixed and forced now, not the merry little smile of superiority and amusement that it had been a minute ago.

"Yes," Jake lied.

"Good. I want him to suffer," she whispered. "He killed Laura Provost, did you know that? And Nancy Ross...."

"I want him to suffer, too." Jake said. "But that's not what's important right now."

She grunted, annoyed. Her eyes closed again. "So dizzy."

She took a breath, then tried to lean forward. He put a hand on her chest to keep her still. Noise was coming from the tunnel.

"We're in here!" he shouted. "Wilson's down... we need paramedics!"

The sound rang in his ears for a second, drowning out something that Regan was saying.

"What did you say, love?" he asked.

She swallowed. Lights were shining down the tunnel now.

This way! Down here!

"Stay with me," she said. "That's what's important. Forget about Wilson. Just stay with me... stay with me..."

"I'm here," he said. He clasped her hand tight. She squeezed back until it was painful.

She kept muttering the words until the paramedics had her on top of a stretcher and were dragging her out through the tunnel.

Chuck, Doug, and Graham had crawled in after the paramedics had left, and the four of them looked down at Wilson, arms crossed over their chests.

Wilson was still alive—still trying to breathe. Jake flashed back to Afghanistan. The room was filled with stench now—the intestines had finally burst. That just made it harder to stop remembering.

"What do you want us to do with him?" Chuck said.

Just one kick in the groin. It would be so satisfying.

"Leave him," Jake said. "He's not gonna talk. I already tried. We have better things to do. Let forensics have their fun."

He squatted down and crawled out of the tunnel on his elbows, trying not to hit his head.

He may or may not have heard the sound of a boot hitting flesh and a groan.

It didn't matter.

Regan was headed out to the ambulance, and if he didn't hurry up, the ambulance was going to leave without him.

Chapter 52 -Epilogue

The sky was big and blue, with the shadows of tree branches stretching overhead. Leaves rustled. Birds chirped at each other, tree-to-tree gossip. The wind tossed the leaves, drowning out most of the sounds of civilization around the cemetery and replacing it with a soft meaningless moan.

Somewhere on the other side of the cemetery, someone had hired a bagpipe player for another funeral. It echoed across the green hills, bounced around the big marble slabs, dodged between the trees and the big old stone funeral home, and made the statues hold their hands toward the heaven and look upward, as if begging for mercy.

It was, Jake had to admit, the end of an era.

Pavo had been shipped back in the first of several ambulances that had arrived at the Wilson cabin. John St. Clair accompanied his friend, saying he trusted Jake to take care of his daughter.

Remembering he'd said that, always made Jake have to blink back a couple of tears. With any luck, John would never know how close Jake had come to losing his daughter.

It was a small group standing at the graveside. Jake, Regan, and John stood together. That was the extent of "family" as far as Pavo was concerned. Not a single living relative appeared at the cemetery—not a brother or sister, no distant cousins. Pavo's secretary, sure, but that was about it from his work at the sewers, too. Jake suspected Pavo's secretary hadn't passed the information around.

It was what Pavo would have wanted.

Behind them stood Chuck, Doug and Graham, looking like Mafia thugs in their black suits. Andy and Jamie Gibbons had come and brought their boys with them. They came in support of Regan and Jake—not to honor Pavo. Jake was pretty sure Jamie had lectured the boys on the way over, telling them to be respectful and keep their questions to themselves. He was also pretty sure she'd told them, maybe not outright, but at least hinting, Pavo had gotten what he deserved. He was a bad man who had justified bad actions and thought that made him good. She just had that look on her face. Stiff—with her nose lifted just a hair too high for Christian humility.

But it had been her husband Pavo had sent to jail for a decade for a murder he hadn't committed.

All in all, Jake couldn't blame her.

Alex had come, bringing a small gang of friends with him—the ones who'd been helping with the Wilson case. Slightly apart from the others stood an attractive black woman with a look on her face that said she knew more than she was letting on somehow. Jake made a mental note to check in with Alex about her. Alex had been acting a little strange over the last few days—disorganized, unable to focus, distressed. He was constantly twirling his mustache and scowling—toward the black woman.

He'd somehow resolved a situation at one of Wilson's victim's homes, a conflict with Fiducioso, Gary's brother...

He couldn't keep track of it all.

Regan and John had been too shattered for him to be able to do anything other than cope with funeral arrangements, lawyers, and calls from the cops. If it wasn't one thing, it was another. The SEALs had been running his detective agency since the day Wilson died. He was too busy trying to coordinate things.

Fortunately, Pavo only had one real request: to be buried next to Linda St. Clair.

The plot had already been set up that way, with a single marble headstone set up for Linda and John—Linda's dates already filled in—and a second one set up a couple of feet away, waiting for Paul.

The date hadn't been cut in, yet.

The hole in the ground was covered with green fabric, then a border of heavy, brown rubber-backed rugs, in case of rain. The mound of dirt was ready and waiting, and so was the vault, painted gray. The lid of the vault stood back from the gravesite, along the road on a specialized wheeled trailer that could be hooked up to a motor so it could be lowered safely.

Jake had glossed over the selection of the vault—the model he'd picked was only available in a couple of colors, and he didn't think either black or bronze would have been appropriate.

But now he wished he'd picked any color other than gray.

It was the same damned color as the walls inside the hidden cellar.

The coffin was steel colored and had been closed after the memorial service at the funeral home. Pavo, as the saying went, had cleaned up well.

As always, Jake had the sensation the body was going to move, and the longer he looked at it, the worse it got. He kept expecting the frown lines between Pavo's eyebrows to deepen, and his hands to lift off his chest, fingertips steepled together...

Regan held on to the lapels of John's suit jacket and lay her head on his chest. She was panting for breath, not sobbing. She'd only just been released from the hospital that morning, and she wasn't doing well. She needed to get off her feet.

She needed to cry.

The minister—a Unitarian who had been cautioned the person being mourned was a vehement atheist—clearly had the same thought Jake did, and started the service quickly.

Jake didn't hear half the words said; the rest didn't make sense. He chalked it up to how tired he was.

And how alone he felt.

Regan had spent a lot of time in the hospital in and out of consciousness. And when she was awake, she was distant. John had told her about Pavo, about her beloved—and difficult—uncle.

And since then she had been looking straight through both of them as if they didn't exist.

Jake had this sickening feeling it was over between them. Not because of anything he had done or omitted—although he was eating himself up inside over some of it—but because of something he had no control over.

He wanted her to at least blame him for Pavo's death, as unreasonable as it would have been.

Anger he could deal with. Hate. Weeping.

But not this blankness.

The minister droned on, not trying to fill the cemetery with divine love—just making noise. Giving them time to stand there, stunned.

Giving them somewhere to look that wasn't at each other.

It was strange. He couldn't remember whether he'd liked or

hadn't liked Pavo anymore. He could remember the guy's face, sure. But how he'd felt about him, it just didn't seem important.

Now, if John St. Clair had been the one who'd been shot...

His throat tensed up.

According to John, it had been close. If he'd been driving, it would have been him in the steel coffin on top of the braces.

And then what?

Regan straightened up. Her face was waxy and had a sheen of sweat on it. John gave Jake a helpless look.

Jake went jogging off toward a large tent spread over the grass, rows of folding chairs set up underneath. Whoever's funeral it was, they could just suck it up for a few minutes while Regan caught her breath.

***

Regan forced herself to turn around and look at the casket... and at the hole in the ground underneath the vault.

Soon, it was going to swallow up Uncle Paul.

She had stared at him lying in the coffin all throughout the memorial service. Perversely, it felt like he'd abandoned her, on purpose.

Everywhere she looked, she saw them—people from the Organization, come to force her into Uncle Paul's old role.

She realized (of course she realized) that part of her paranoia was just that, anxiety mixed with a knock on the head. The concussion had taken more out of her, psychologically speaking, than she could believe.

When she'd lost her mother, she'd been inconsolable. Now, it was like she was fighting a war not to have her true emotions overwhelmed by dizziness and nausea. She didn't grieve for Uncle Paul, she felt disgust for him—revulsion.

Confusion.

Jake stole a folding chair from a nearby funeral—the grievers hadn't arrived yet—and put it on the grass for her. Jake and her father lowered her to the chair; her father gave her a *look* telling her to stay put.

Oh, she wasn't going to fight them. It was all she could do, suddenly, to keep from passing out.

Uncle Paul was gone. The Organization was going to force her to take his place.

How could he do this to her?

How could he?

How could he die like that?

Trying to save her?

Her eyes misted up. She fought to keep them clear, blinking and rubbing them, trying to swallow back the tears in her throat.

Suddenly Jake was beside her, holding her in his arms. And she couldn't hold it back anymore.

A lump rose out of her throat, burst in her mouth. She shouted:

"I hate you, I hate you! Don't leave me here, Uncle Paul! Don't make me take care of all of this without you!"

For a moment she thought the sound echoed back to her across the cemetery. But her head was tucked into Jake's shoulder. She was beating her fists against his arms.

It was all coming out. She was weeping now, smearing his shoulder with all the ugliness inside her. Everyone was watching her, seeing how weak she was. She hated it.

"I love you," he said, over and over again. "I'm here. I love you."

It didn't seem like the tears would ever end. She held on to Jake's arms and tried to silence her grief. But she couldn't.

"Stay with me," she begged him. Just like she'd begged him before, in that horrible coffin of a room. "Don't let them use me like they used him. Stay with me."

"I will," he said. "You don't have to do anything you don't want to."

But she also knew it was going to be more a lot complicated than that.

~ The End~

Thank You

Thank you for taking the time to read my book. Please keep in touch with me at www.jcryanbooks.com and also sign up for special offers and pre-release notifications of upcoming books.

Please Review

If you enjoyed this story, please let others know by leaving an honest review on Amazon. Your review will help to inform others about this book and the series.
Thank you so much for your support, I appreciate it very much.

JC Ryan

Other books by JC Ryan

The Exonerated Series

https://www.amazon.com/gp/product/B01MQJEQ5R

Book 1 - Judgment Call
Amazon USA - http://amzn.com/B01EQ1P0UI
Amazon UK - http://amzn.co.uk/dp/B01EQ1P0UI

Book 2 - Damned if you do, Damned if you don't
Amazon USA - http://amzn.com/B01GGIJMA8
Amazon UK - http://amzn.co.uk/dp/B01GGIJMA8

Book 3 - The End Justifies the Means
Amazon USA - http://amzn.com/B01MRIS56Q
Amazon UK - http://amzn.co.uk/dp/B01MRIS56Q

Please visit my website and my Amazon author page to see my other books.
http://jcryanbooks.com

https://www.amazon.com/author/jcryan

The Rossler Foundation Mysteries Series
http://www.amazon.com/gp/product/B016PWGAKA/

The Tenth Cycle - http://amzn.com/B00JMV358M
Ninth Cycle Antarctica - http://amzn.com/B00K8LRTLE
Genetic Bullets - http://amzn.com/B00M0DQGXU
The Sword Of Cyrus - http://amzn.com/B00N3K2LMO
The Skywalkers - http://amzn.com/B00VSIFBJ8
The Phoenix Agenda - http://amzn.com/B016A8MALC

Click the link below to see more details about each of the books.

http://www.amazon.com/gp/product/B016PWGAKA/

The Carter Devereux Series

http://www.amazon.com/gp/product/B01DPUGKH8/

Click the link below to see more details.

http://www.amazon.com/gp/product/B01DPUGKH8/

Made in the USA
Middletown, DE
05 February 2021